I0774604

The FORTUNE & SORROW of Rachel Anne Praline

Tessa Van Wade

ISBN: 978-1-964440-00-2 (hardcover)
ISBN: 978-1-964440-01-9 (paperback)
ISBN: 978-1-964440-02-6 (ebook)

Printed in the United States of America
1st Edition 2025

To my daughters.

Surround yourself with strong and intuitive women. They will raise you up when life has torn you down...and remember you when you think you've been forgotten.

Chapter One

1998

"Bobby!"

I hear the panic in Ma's voice through the phone, forcing me to sit up from a dead sleep. It's not until then that I realize my sheet has come off the corner of my mattress from an anxious night, following several weeks of anxious nights, and my smooth dark skin is glistening with sweat despite the light chill in the air. "What's wrong, Ma?"

"... your daddy ... he's in the ... the hospital." Through the loud and soft of her deep guttural sobs, she manages, "... a stroke."

Finally, the words ring clearer while my dream-fog dissipates, leaving me just a racing heart to deal with. I rub my bare chest as I turn on the bedside lamp, while the rest of my blankets end up in a pile on the floor. "When?"

"Last night. Just before we went to bed!" She's pacing, I can tell.

"Have you talked to anyone else?"

She either ignores my question or doesn't hear it over her crying, "I just don't know what to do with myself, Bobby. Oh my God!" She wails.

"Just breathe, Ma."

"How . . . can . . . can," she stutters, her breathing getting shallower with each second.

"Ma." I drop my voice to be stern, just like she does with my siblings and me. "I can get there soon, but you have to settle down. I'll be there soon."

"You'll come?" Her surprise tells me everything.

I've been away for nearly five years. In fact, my thirty-ninth birthday was the last time I was home, and I can't even say my age now. All this number means is that I'm old and drowning in disappointments. I still haven't been in love, made a million dollars, or walked on water—everything that I once believed I could achieve.

It was my father who always said, "I've given my life so you could have good things. Don't let me down. Don't come home unless you have news to share. I got our family where we are, now show me that you have what it takes." I suppose that's why I haven't been home in five years.

He's not wrong. He is a master of the hustle, with tenacity—beyond words—to not just surpass, but leap over the highest obstacle; never letting his rough childhood stop him from achieving his dreams. His expectations were clear and I—at one time—was confident enough to accept the challenge.

I was valedictorian of my high school. I graduated at the top of my class at Yale in Journalism. Every woman made eyes at me, and every man wanted to be me—or at least that's what I told myself.

Yet, in my first few years as a professional, my articles and cover stories didn't save the world, and that once profound passion turned from a wild storm to a cold breeze.

My father's dissatisfaction only grew. He wasn't the kind of man to hide it. Especially when Stacey, my college girlfriend, broke my heart, or Val, my coworker and girlfriend at NBC, left me for an intern. "You're not giving them what they need, Bobby," my father said. "They need a man who earns their respect. Take your mother and I for example." Naturally, he is the standard to follow. I avoided telling him that Stacey became a leading broadcaster, outshining me by one Pulitzer and two degrees, and Val ended up marrying that intern while rising to a prominent position at NBC, from which I was let go last year.

My momma sniffles, which forces me to my feet and brings my thoughts back to the predicament at hand. I walk to my closet.

"Is dad talking?"

"No! He just looked at me and then fell to the floor. Bobby, I've never seen him like this! I had to wait for the ambulance to come. They don't know when he'll wake up. Oh my God, Oh Lord Jesus, what if he doesn't wake up? What'll I do? How long until you can be here?"

Once I pull my bag down and throw it on the bed, I walk to the window and look out at the new dawn over Washington D.C., as the city begins to rise: from bakers, to clerks, to two people running through the park. I've tried to conquer this place for ten years, only to wake up each morning a little older and a bit more behind due to the flood of fresh Ivy Leaguers still green with hope and excitement.

"I have to drop my notes by the office at eight, so I can get there about lunchtime."

Her sigh of relief calms even me and I can just picture her chubby face, with the shine of tears down her skin.

A few hours later, my boss, who looks a bit like David Hassel-hoff, is glowering at me with irritation. "This sounds like a personal problem. Should I have to pay the price for your personal problem?"

"My father's in the hospital."

"My father's dead."

"Uh," I stutter. Then I widen my eyes and click my jaw with tension. "Yeah, okay."

"If you don't need this job, I can find someone who eagerly does."

My shoulders are tense as I try to hold back a response that I'll regret and grind my teeth until they hurt. "Listen, I get it. But my work is done. I turned in something good, if you'll read it this weekend . . . I can be back here on Monday morning, ready to give it my all."

His annoyance stays plastered to his face. However, saying no to my momma is not an option either, and I make this clear by wrapping my arms around my chest for protection. It's a standoff and he speaks just as I'm about to surrender, so I'm grateful when he says, "Fine, be ready to go early Monday morning."

By nine a.m. I am on the road to Atlantic City. The drive seems longer than usual. A gust of wind suddenly blows through my car sending papers in every direction. One covers my eyes, causing me to swerve, forcing a car beside me to honk. "Ahh hell," I yell as I grapple for them with one free hand. "Sorry, sorry!" I call out to the angry driver even though they can't hear me. Trying to steer with my knee, I hit the buttons to roll up my windows with my left hand and scrape the air for the papers with my right. My eyes catch a bit of writing and I try to read the last couple of lines while on the highway.

I am meant to write. People's lives and stories captivate me. If I am to believe that my life has no higher purpose, then why continue?

Journalism isn't what it used to be. Just last year in 1997, BBC news online was launched. I swear to you, our understanding of the world will never be the same. "We have to grow with the times," my boss told us last week. The competition is on and yet somehow, I feel like a fish out of water. Magazines, newspapers, and books are meant to be held in our hands, not looked at on a screen, or at least that is how I see it.

As I drive through my old neighborhood the barbeque aroma hits me harder than my old boss when I dropped a plate of wings. Every tree is huge compared to my memory of them and even though the children playing on the street aren't the same, the games are.

Before my tires even touch the driveway, Momma races out of the house with her stubby hands in the air. "Honey, you're here! Lord, bless you for gettin' here so fast."

"Is anyone else here yet?" I ask, as I pull my bags from my trunk.

"You're the only one that could make it so quick."

"What world problem are they solving now?" Even though I whisper this, my momma has ears like an owl.

"Bobby, don't start already. They'll be here soon." She stops me, places her hands on my cheeks and smiles. "I'm so glad you're here."

"Thanks, Momma."

We enter the large foyer of our 1940s colonial house and the first thing I see in the reflection of an antique mirror is a forty-four-year-old man who is tired. I am the blend of my father's deep charcoal skin, and the beautiful coppery-brown of my mother's. I stare so long that I wonder, was it this mirror I was trying so hard to avoid?

Mrs. Patterson, one of my gramma's dearest and oldest friends from church, reads a cookbook in the living room as we pass.

"Hello, Mrs. Patterson." I call out.

My momma brushes up against me. "She can't hear or see anymore."

"She's reading a book?"

"Yeah, I don't know."

I stare at Mrs. Patterson wondering when she became an old woman, but when my back spasms as I pick up my bags, it reminds me that time is brutal.

"What's she doin' here?" We pass through the hallway, then Ma pushes open the swinging door into the kitchen where the aroma of buttermilk biscuits sends me into a trance as I lay my bags in the corner.

"We're taking care of her."

"Mrs. Patterson lives here?"

"No, she's just staying while her family is out of town. I keep tryin' to tell them how great the place where Gramma Johnson is, but it's too expensive. You hungry? You always get that look when you are hungry."

"I always get this look when you make your biscuits. It doesn't matter if I'm hungry."

"Well, are you?"

"I am now."

She smiles and pulls the basket from the cupboard.

"Here," she says with a grin, "the jelly is in the refrigerator."

"Nobody needs jelly."

"Speaking of Gramma Johnson, I told her you would see her tomorrow," she says nonchalantly as though this is as normal as going to the grocery store, but it is not.

"Ahhh, Momma. This isn't fair. Filling my mouth with biscuits so I can't refuse."

She stops what she is doing, makes the serious Eddy—her birth name is Edwina—face, and places a hand upon her wide hip. "I should not have to bribe you to see your gramma. You should want to go and it should be a treat."

"A treat? She can't remember a damn thing. She won't even know why I am there or who I am."

"She'll remember you."

"She hasn't for the last ten years."

"You're goin' to see her, Bobby. There isn't any arguing about it. She's nearly 94 . . . you don't know how long she'll be around."

"You've been sayin' that for the last fifteen years." My momma scowls at me until I can't chew anymore, and I wonder if freezing my jaw is part of a mother's powers, because I've never known a time that she couldn't make it happen. "Fine, I'll go."

"Thank you."

"You haven't said one word about Dad. Where is he?"

"He's at Cape Regional and they're going to be doing surgery on him tomorrow." Her chin wobbles. "I was just waitin' for you to get here so I can go back." She turns back to the sink and fiddles with the dirty pans.

I walk to her side and throw my arm around her shoulders. "I'll take care of the dishes. You go back."

"Thank you, honey."

When she walks in the door at eleven that evening, it is obvious from her swollen eyes that she is exhausted and my father must not be doing well, so I hand her a cup of tea which makes her smile. "Mrs. Patterson did fine. She ate dinner and is asleep now."

"Thank you, honey." She pats my arm with a smile.

"How's dad?"

"We'll see. God only knows. I'm goin' to bed." Her voice drops like a flat note as she wanders to her room. Her walking alone makes me picture my parents heading to bed together for as many years as I can remember.

As I trudge through the house turning off the lights and locking doors, I pay attention to the walls of memories. Nearly every man and woman in the Johnson family line for five generations is represented by at least one photo. Family history is a source of pride for my parents. And the next morning I will see Gramma Johnson—the matriarch. I squeeze my temples and sigh, "Tomorrow's going to be a long day."

Chapter Two

1998

The home where Gramma Johnson lives used to be The Darling Hotel. A combination of Art Deco and old glamour, it helps the patients to feel that they are at a resort rather than an "old folks' home". Even I see the benefits of a place where you're surrounded by friends and people who are paid to take care of you. It worries me that the thought of living here sounds better than my life right now.

I've been sitting across from Gramma Johnson, who wears her familiar argyle sweater, for three hours and she hasn't recognized me for two hours and fifty-eight minutes. She whips her knitting needles back and forth so fast that, I figure, she'll make a blanket in one day, while keeping her suspicious eyes on me from above the yarn. This isn't awkward at all.

Her Truetone plays a scratchy record and I've been changing it over every few minutes since I got here, because she refuses to listen to anything but the rustic sound of old-timey singers. Every so often, her apprehensive eyes turn to irritation, then back again, so I lift a record, "This one next?" to calm her down.

When a nurse enters with pills and water, she notices the showdown we are having like an old western, so she smiles. "Try and talk to her."

"Yeah, okay."

"Gramma Johnson," the nurse says, "Your grandson, Bobby, is here."

"Huh?" Gramma says.

"Your grandson, Bobby, is here."

"My Bobby goes to Yale," she says with a shake of her head.

"Yep, that's me, Gramma."

Instead of diving into conversation, she eyes me shadily, whispers something in the nurse's ear and goes back to knitting.

Just before the nurse leaves, she smiles and whispers, "Every once in a while, she comes back to us. Keep trying. Once she remembers, she'll be so grateful that you're here."

"Yeah, okay, thanks."

Another long hour passes. I promised Ma that I would stay until one o'clock at least, but the hands of the clock are moving so slowly that I get up to check the battery. As I do, a song comes on her Truetone that seems to get her attention.

"I knew this woman who's singin' now," she says.

The woman's voice is so rich and sexy that I smile. "I wish I did."

For a moment, I lose myself in the love affair that she sings about and I lean against the wall with the clock in my hands. The clock isn't broken: I am.

"Who is this, Gramma?" Stupid me. I roll my eyes. What's the use? Really.

She looks up and a smile spreads along her face. "Oh Bobby, when did you get here?"

"Just now," I say. No need to embarrass the lady.

"Oh baby, it's so good to see you! Where you been? You taking a break from college just to see me?"

I walk to her recliner and kiss her forehead. It's been over twenty years since college, but my momma always says, "You got to live in her world, not try and bring her into ours."

So, I reply, "Yeah, Gramma. How you been? They treatin' you good in here?"

"I'm good, honey! They treat me just fine."

"That's good, that's good. Who is this singer, Gramma?"

"Oh…" she looks thoughtful for a moment, "This is Rachel Anne Praline." Her smile makes her eyes squinty due to her fat cheeks.

"You knew her, Gramma?"

"Better than most. Stunnin' girl . . . lived quite a life. Honey?" she asks me as if all of the fog has suddenly dissipated.

"Yes, Gramma?"

"Her CD is over there. Put it in for me."

I glance at her with wonderment. For years everyone has been listening to her dusty old Truetone while all along she knew about compact discs? I walk to the table under the small window. A handful of CD cases are stacked and I pick them up.

"It says Rachel Anne Praline in big letters."

The plastic cover, with an obviously vintage photograph of Rachel's silhouette sits on the top of the stack. "Huh." I pull the silver disc out and a player that I never noticed before squeals as it eats it. Within moments, the woman's voice begins, but without the familiar scratch.

"She's amazing."

"Always was from the time she was a little girl. She could stand her own against the best. All who ever knew her," she gives me a wide grin, "knew she was somethin' special. Speaking of special, who you datin' these days?"

Suddenly, I'm transported back to her sun-kissed kitchen when I was fifteen and she would ask me questions about my love life. "I used to be the hot ticket, huh, Gramma?"

"Used to be? What's wrong with you? That's not the Bobby I know. You gotta have someone."

"Nobody, Gramma . . . can't find someone as sweet as you."

"Oh sugar, it will take you a lifetime for that!" she says with a pleased laugh.

The disc plays through several songs. A mixture of blues, big band, ragtime, choral, and even hymns. Her voice is aching, almost pleading. I am mesmerized and, as crazy as it seems, I want to help her. Which obviously is ridiculous, but the more she sings, the more I fall. Her voice is young and smooth, but there's something about her that I believe. If she says, "He ain't never comin' back," she means it. "So, Gramma…" I pull a chair closer to hers and grab the ball of yarn that is starting to tangle in the basket at her feet, "Tell me about her."

"Who, honey?"

Damn. I lost her. "Rachel Praline."

"You interested? I'm not surprised. Men were always interested. Her beauty and talent took her around the world, yet it also stole so much." It was nearly impossible to tell by Gramma's eyes how much time I had left with her. I'd seen it many times when her dementia would eat up every memory within a second—like the last flicker of a bulb just before it goes out. "The facts are a bit off. You know how it is. Everyone adds their own bit of the story and suddenly the particulars become clouded by over-embellished rumors."

With each song, I want to know more about this mysterious and strangely irresistible Rachel. "That's okay. Tell me what you know." I lift my Gramma's cup of water and help her sip from the straw. She smiles.

"Well . . . she was born here in New Jersey, and even on that day somehow her life was tragic."

"Tragic?" Rachel's voice wasn't just smooth and rich, but there was also thirst that only comes from someone who has experienced true sorrow.

"She was special, Bobby. It all began in that small hospital on the outskirts of town. You know the one. They tore it down years ago."

I hang on to every miraculous word, with the fear that at any moment the clock will strike twelve.

Chapter Three

July 7th, 1908

"Well, she looks healthy to me, Mrs. Praline," the doctor says. He looks past the weary mother's legs and notices the tears running down her cheeks, wetting her messy blonde hair; but there is no joy—only deep despair. "Would you like to see her?"

It is the seventh day of July in the year 1908 and after three hours of arduous pushing, the doctor finally holds the petite baby in his arms and cuts the cord from her mother—that just minutes before was her only source of life. The infant lets out a soft cry that brings a smile to every face in the white-tiled room, except for her mother.

When Mrs. Praline tries to bring her hand to her temple, the clang of metal handcuffs hits the tin bars of her hospital bed, reminding everyone that this isn't a grand occasion. There will be no banners hung and no cigars passed.

"No," the exhausted woman says, "no," then turns her head away from the child.

March 1907 Mrs. Praline and Mabel

Elizabeth Praline smiles at her husband, Mike, as he drives them into Atlantic City for a new job and a new life—one they've hoped for, for many years. The small home isn't what either of them expects, but there is hope of what is to come, and Elizabeth immediately gets to work turning every aged corner into the perfect vision of all their dreams. However, after several months, things begin to change. Mike comes home later and later, dragging himself into bed, no longer eating with her, speaking much to her, or touching her.

"It's just not what I thought it would be." Elizabeth says, as she pours his coffee one morning.

"And I'm just having the time of my life!" He jumps to his feet, slamming his fist on the table, as his napkin falls to the floor, scaring her so much that she drops his plate and it shatters into a thousand pieces. "Pick that up!" He stomps off, grabbing his keys, and leaving before she can say another word.

Days turn into weeks and weeks into months, in which his harsh words become more common and his affection less.

"What aren't you doing?" one of the ladies from church says as she peers over her teacup on a rainy afternoon.

"His house is clean, his food is made, his clothes are pressed." Elizabeth assures them.

"There's always something," they tell her.

Every night when the lights are off, the moon casts light across his empty pillow. She thinks about the times he would smile, roll over, and kiss her, but tonight—and nearly every night—his side of the bed is empty. When was the last time he looked at her? Or the last time he touched her?

Once he drags himself to bed, she rolls over and says, "Kiss me." Only to have him ignore it, pull the covers over himself and turn away. Within the year, he becomes just a ghost of the man she used to love.

Then one day, as if the evils of the world know how desperate Elizabeth is for something powerful and alive, a charismatic man with nice features knocks on her door. He is a traveling salesman of cleaners, brushes, and mops, and he smiles as she opens the door. "Hello."

"Hello," she says, bowing her head slightly as she blushes.

"Can I interest you in this magic cleaning solution?" He lifts the blue liquid up to her, but she pays very little attention to it.

"It's magic?" Elizabeth asks. "I don't believe that."

"Don't you believe in magic? That's too bad. Would you let me inside and I'll show you?"

"Okay."

He steps inside and nearly four hours later he finally retreats, but not before his shirt is unbuttoned and his hair is messed from her roaming hands.

Just a few weeks later she wakes up one morning sick as a dog and realizes that she hasn't had her cycle for some time. Soon, she nervously taps her high heels on the floor of the doctor's waiting room in a small clinic on the opposite side of town, while she desperately hopes her sickness isn't what she suspects.

But, in fact, it is.

"Doctor, I cannot . . . I cannot have a baby."

The doctor looks at the beautiful, fair-skinned woman with question. "I'm sorry, Mrs. Praline. I'd expect this to be something important for a married woman, something worth celebrating."

"Oh God," she cries, as she bends over in the yellow chair, "Oh God, doctor, we have to do somethin'. What can we do?"

"I'm sorry . . . there is nothing." He hesitantly smiles. "Mrs. Praline, it is very normal for women to have fear about havin' a baby. But don't worry, you will be a---"

"---No . . . I won't. No. I cannot have this baby."

The doctor sends her away, nonetheless.

She could easily lie and tell everyone that she is with her husband's child, but the only person who matters knows they haven't made love in over a year. Running away isn't an option considering Mrs. Praline has nothing without him.

Two months pass, but her belly is beginning to show, so she takes Mr. Praline out to dinner hoping that the crowd will keep her safe. It isn't until dessert that she finally conjures up the courage to tell him of her infidelity. Before she is able to finish her story, she is chasing him down the sidewalk just outside the row of restaurants as he curses her name.

"Killing myself . . . for what!" He yells as people stare from every direction.

Elizabeth trips when her toe catches a lifted brick. Mike hesitates for a moment but stops himself from helping her, then continues on as she struggles to get to her feet. "Mike . . . I . . ." she cries. Just as he reaches the middle of the street, she stops, tightens her tummy and yells from the deepest recesses of her lonely soul. "You left me!"

Despite the car that has been forced to stop for Mr. Praline, he turns around to look at her with his fists clenched. "Every day I've worked to provide for you!"

"What does that mean?" She asks, as her hair falls in front of her face, but she does nothing to bat it away. "For us! What does provision even mean when I've forgotten what you feel like?"

The car honks as it sneaks around him, but soon, he walks away leaving her on the sidewalk. At ten o'clock at night, pregnant and hopeless, she trudges home finding him asleep in their bed by the time she arrives.

In the following days and weeks, the wedge grows deeper, as he leaves before the sun rises and comes home when the moon is high. He refuses to look at her, even though everything he asks, she gives, and everything she wants, he ignores.

Then one day, the salesman knocks on her door once more, only Mrs. Praline doesn't answer. It isn't quite understood how Mr.

Praline knows, but he grabs the salesman by the shoulders and pulls him inside.

"I'm sorry!" the man yells as Mr. Praline throws him from one side of the room, to the next.

"Mike!" Elizabeth yells, protectively clutching her belly.

He winds back, sending punch after punch, until the salesman crawls toward the back door through the kitchen. Mr. Praline grabs a knife from the counter and Elizabeth sees that there's nothing but rage behind his eyes. She runs into the room, throws the box open where Mr. Praline keeps his gun, and runs back into the kitchen. By the time, she calls out his name, blood drips from the knife as he pulls back to swipe again. "Michael Praline!"

No one knows exactly what happened, but it is said that Mrs. Praline knew he wasn't going to stop. Others believe that he turned on her and she feared for the baby, but whatever it was, the police found Mr. Praline face down on the floor with a gunshot wound in his back. The salesman is treated and released the same day, while incessantly blaming Mrs. Praline and then, testifying against her in court.

In a marriage, secrets are kept deep within the walls of the home and when Mrs. Praline tries to explain those secrets to the police, it isn't enough. All they see is a woman, with another man's baby in her belly, holding the gun that killed her own husband. The judge, who is typically lenient, has a bad day on his way to court the morning they are to sentence her, and he slams his gavel faster than a lumberjack with an axe. "Mrs. Elizabeth Marie Praline is sentenced to life in prison," he grumbles.

Mrs. Praline's belly continues to grow, day by day, until they give her special suits to wear. Despite what she's done, the guards come to love her since she gives no trouble and helps care for the grounds, so they let her visit the library nearly every day.

"What do you do here?" one of the guards asks her.

"I'm learning how to find my baby a better life." The guard grins, but only for a second when Mrs. Praline's chains remind her of the truth. "The last thing I want to do is give my baby over to the state."

"How are you going to make sure that doesn't happen?"

"I have an uncle that has say in this town, and I'm waiting for his return letter. I've done my research and he can have her."

A few weeks before she gives birth, that same guard hands Elizabeth a letter from William Harr—her maiden name. Together they open it and Mrs. Praline cries out with joy. "He'll take her!" She laughs.

So, when the doctor asks if she wants to see the baby in the quiet hospital room, she knows that she can't. The baby belongs to her uncle now. If she stares into her blue eyes or touches the small tuft of golden hair, she might never let go.

"Mrs. Praline, are you sure?" he asks one more time.

"Yes, please go," Mrs. Praline says as she buries her head in the sheets. "Just make sure, please, that she has her papers. The ones I've set aside for her."

"Where are they?" The doctor asks.

"In a folder, with the state, that my uncle will pick up when he takes her."

"Okay," the doctor replies solemnly as he reluctantly hands the baby over to one of the nurses named Mabel. Mabel takes the miniature person in her arms with a smile and talks to her as she rubs her clean, all the while, the newborn lets out song-like coos. Two more nurses and one security guard come to her side to make happy faces at the precious baby. Her blue eyes are bright with innocence, seeming, also, to look around the room with curiosity and the nurses shake their heads.

"You sure are perfect," Nurse Mabel says. Then, she looks at the devastated mother. "You have a name for her?"

Mrs. Praline is silent as though she hasn't thought about it until her small voice whispers, "Rachel Anne Praline."

"Rachel. That's a beautiful name, Mrs. Praline." Mabel starts singing to the child.

"Please take her away," Mrs. Praline begs. The doctor nods at the nurse.

As Mabel walks through the hallway, her heart connects with the wide-eyed newborn, and she runs her finger along her cheek. "It'll be okay. You'll see."

"Is that the baby everyone is talkin' about?" Henry, a tough-looking, older man with an inquiring spirit asks as Mabel passes him in the hall. She lowers the blanket and presents the new addition. "Well, well, well," he chuckles. "I've been standin' at these doors for twelve years and I ain't never seen a baby so . . ." he hesitates, ". . . so sweet."

Mabel walks past him with a grin. "All babies are sweet, Henry. That isn't the word you're lookin' for. It's special. This baby is special."

"You're right, Miss Mabel . . . you are right. Special. That's what it is."

"She's goin' to do some big things, Henry . . . some big things."

"Well, you watch out for that little one, you hear?"

Mabel smiles as she turns the corner, "Oh, I will." She looks down at Rachel, "I will, sweetheart."

For three days Mabel doesn't go home. It doesn't matter when her shift ends or that her mother calls every few minutes, Rachel has become her main focus. Their skin doesn't match, but their hearts do. Bottles, blankets, cuddles, and cries, Mabel finds herself in a world she's never known. But while she waits for the New Jersey State Department, the worry for this baby brews within her body. She rocks back and forth, humming quietly.

"Excuse me?" A man's voice echoes in the sterilized room.

Mabel glances over her shoulder. A good-looking man dressed in a brown suit, his hair plastered heavily against his head with thick pomade, stands stiffly. Attractive in a studious sort of way, his strong brow bones are lifted with confusion, behind dark glasses.

"Excuse me, my name is Dick Jenner. I am here for..." he stops suddenly as though his mind has gone blank. Mabel smiles when he cusses at himself and hastily jams his hands in his pockets to search, then finds a folded piece of paper. "Uhhh...yes, yes, yes, Rachel Anne Praline. I am here for Rachel Anne Praline."

Mabel turns suspicious and clears her throat. "You're here for Rachel? Why would they send you?"

"Uhhh, I . . . uh . . ." he stammers, but can't come up with the answer.

Mabel stops him with a hand up, "Honey, you seem as lost as a blind kitten. I'm not sendin' Rachel with you."

"Well . . . I . . . uhhh . . . that's my job, ma'am. I'm just doing what I was told."

"Oh? And who told you?"

"Well, I work for the State, ma'am. The State told me." He smiles with pride that he has an answer to give her.

"Don't give me more reason to dislike you. You are here to take Rachel from my care without giving any hint as to why you are qualified?"

"No, ma'am. You see, I'm just a transport. I'm only taking Rachel from here to there." He pulls out his official identification to show her.

"So, she's goin' to the uncle that her mother petitioned for?"

"Well, honestly, ma'am, I don't know what family is goin' to take her. I am just the deliveryman, but she will be fine. There are plenty of capable hands."

"Dick, I will never forgive myself should anything ever happen to her. You," she points accusingly, "have no idea how close I am to kicking you out the door."

"May I see her? I can do this," he says unconvincingly.

Mabel steps forward and waits for him to look at the fresh baby wrapped in blankets, but he only stands with his briefcase to his chest, drumming his fingertips.

"I thought you wanted to see Rachel."

"Yes ma'am, you can take me to her at any time."

"You don't even know who you are lookin' for?" She howls, "This is Rachel!"

His eyes grow wide, and he takes a step back. "A baby? No . . . she can't be but a few days old."

"Three . . . she is three days old!" Mabel's anger boils to the surface.

"They didn't tell me she was a newborn."

"It seems they didn't tell you much of anything now, did they? Why else do you think you'd come to the hospital to pick up a child?"

"I guess I really hadn't thought about it . . . please. I am only taking her a few miles into Atlantic City."

"And she'll see her uncle there?"

"Yes, I believe so," he says carefully.

"Now you listen to me, Dick. If I hear that anything has happened to this child, I will come and find you. She is special, you hear me . . . special . . . and I want you takin' care of her as though she's your own."

"Yes, ma'am."

Moments later, as Mabel looks over the baby secured in the seat of the state-owned Cadillac, she runs her finger along Rachel's chin. The sleeping bundle doesn't move except to purse her lips just a smidge. "You're a special girl, Rachel Anne. You be safe, you hear me? Get plenty of sleep and grow up happy." Mabel must force herself away from the car, but when she does, she gives Dick a stern mother's stare.

"She is now in your hands. You make sure to take her straight to her family, ya hear?"

"Yes, ma'am. I'll make sure."

Mabel stands so long over Rachel with no movement, that she finally whispers, "I can't walk away."

Dick leans over, "Ma'am?" She doesn't reply, so he presses again, "Ma'am, I know you don't know me, but I'm a good man. I promise you that I will get her into the hands of people who will care for her." Her eyes turn to his. "I promise."

For the first time Mabel recognizes that he seems genuine. She breathes in, then sighs, "Have a good life, baby girl." Then, she nods at Dick, still sternly. As he drives away, the tears fall down her cheeks suddenly becoming desperately aware of how tired she is. Several families walk into the hospital with their sick children in their arms, as Mabel thinks about how unfair life can be.

Henry, the guard, comes to her side and sets a hand on her shoulder. "You okay?"

"I am. Just wondering what will come of her. There are too many children to care for in this world and not enough hands."

"You're a good woman, Mabel," he says. "You care a lot about anyone and everyone, so I say . . . you need to venture out and do more with that."

Less than a year later, the guard gets a letter from Mabel. "Dear Henry, I did it. I followed Miss Mary Eliza Mahoney and have become one of the first members of the National Association of Colored Nurses. I'm proud of it and what we are doing. We deserve equality . . . we deserve more. I hope you're doing well. Sincerely, Mabel Coleman"

Chapter Four

1908

A couple of miles before Dick reaches the government office, Rachel begins to cry.

"Uhhh . . . shhh . . . no baby . . . uhhh . . . it's okay Rachel . . ." His efforts are futile, as her cries escalate, and her arms fly about. "Come on, Rachel, I know you're upset, but we have just a small drive. Won't you stop crying?"

She screams louder.

"Are you cold? Don't know how you would be cold with the thirty blankets already covering you in July." He pulls another blanket over her, but it only makes her crying worse.

When he reaches a four-way stop, he places his hands on his head as a dark circle now stains his collared shirt at his armpits. He notices a small bag on the floorboard that Mabel sent. Quickly, he raids the sack. A horn blares from the vehicle behind him so he motions with his hand for the car to pass. "Aha!" He says as he finds a bottle. "Do you want this?" His hands move in an awkward dance around her mouth searching for the best entrance. It takes longer than he expects, so several cars honk at him, forcing him to yell, "Go around!" Finally, Rachel takes the nipple in her mouth and begins to sip at it. Dick drops his head back in relief.

"Thank you," Dick says looking up at the sky, but it isn't long before Rachel spits out the milk and begins to cry even harder. Now, a vehicle sits at each section of the four-way stop and all passengers have become irritated. More horns and more yells come from every direction. "Oh, to hell with it." Dick presses on the gas as her screams cause his headache.

When he parks in front of the office, he jumps out of the car and races to the other side—his compassion wearing thin. With gentle hands, he raises the tiny baby to his chest. He's never held something seemingly so fragile.

Something amazing happens—something one would compare to the sun falling behind a sea of diamonds, or flowers that bloom in a brisk spring. It is magical. Rachel stops crying. Her blue eyes look up at him as though she knows him. Something within Dick melts, along with any worry in his world.

"Is that what you wanted?" he asks.

Her mouth opens and she makes a funny face that causes him to laugh. His arms turn from stiff limbs, like that of a tree, to a round, soft cradle.

"Okay, Rachel…" he says grabbing her bag, "okay . . . maybe I can get you to your new family, safe and sound."

He walks into the office filled with the sound of clicking typewriters and the cloud of cigarette smoke that hangs just below the ceiling—his focus never leaving the child.

"Dick!" a woman's voice calls.

There is only one thing that could pull his attention from his new friend, and that is Sylvia Pearson. Dick looks up. A plain-looking woman is walking his way, and his heart pounds like thunder. Now,

Dick is a good-looking man, even though his clothes are outdated and his hands sweat when he's nervous, which is quite often, but many women have thought him handsome, whether he knew it or not. Many would wonder why Sylvia caught his eye, but after years of working beside her, he became mesmerized by her heart that gathers up the gray and makes sunshine.

Only now he has Rachel and strangely, the baby provides a comfortable barrier between him and the love of his life.

"Dick…" Sylvia comes to his side.

She smells like lavender soap, and he breathes in heavily while watching her every move. Her mousy brown hair touches his arm as she squeezes in close to him and looks over his shoulder at Rachel. "Look at her, Dick; she's so content in your arms. Is this her bag? Let me take it…" Soon, it is over her shoulder. "Come into my office until Ralph gets back."

"Okay." Dick has spent plenty of hours in Sylvia's closet-sized office. It isn't often that women received offices of their own, but Sylvia's uncle got her this job.

As soon as she closes the door she rushes to his side. "Let me see her again."

"You should have seen it, Sylvia. She was crying and crying and the moment that I picked her up, it was instantaneous . . . she stopped." Dick smiles.

"You're a natural."

"Maybe so . . . but it's more like . . . well, I think it's her."

"Who?"

"Rachel. Mabel went on and on telling me how special she was."

"Mabel?" For a second Dick detects a bit of jealousy in her voice.

"Yes. Mabel. She was the nurse taking care of Rachel. We got along really well . . . I think she really liked me." Dick watches Sylvia carefully, as he twists the truth.

Sylvia walks to her desk and sits on the edge. "Did you hear about Rachel's uncle's fire?"

"What fire?"

"Some secretary started a fire in his business processing office and he lost everything . . . burnt to ash. His secretary dropped her cigarette directly into her trashcan. Now he won't take Rachel."

Dick is immediately concerned. "He can't just do that, right?"

"Ralph says yes. They're saying that there are too many kids already on the list. You know what that means, don't you? She doesn't have a home to go to."

"What are they gonna do with her?"

"I don't know. I think Uncle Ralph is trying to figure out something right now . . ." Sylvia looks out her office window and her eyes change from soft to nervous, "Oh, there's Ralph now."

Dick notices that Rachel's eyes are closed. "Do you see this? She's perfectly happy." Suddenly his mind begins to wander. He wishes to be perfectly happy, too. He wishes to be contentedly held in someone's arms and that's when his eyes follow Sylvia across the room.

Ralph comes straight to Sylvia's office and lets himself in. He is a large, bald, and blithering man with no care for his own personal hygiene. His shirt is untucked under a hard and round belly, his neck hair sneaks up to his chin and down to his back, and he always seems to smell of cheese. Although, suddenly Dick sniffs his own shirt after sweating so much and second guesses his judgment. "Well, you finally came back with her," Ralph says.

"Yes, sir. Is there something I should do?"

"Joe's comin' to pick her up tomorrow."

"Joe?" Dick's eyes grow wide.

Joe is the caretaker of the orphanage and most kids cry at the sight of him. For years Dick has watched this happen and yet he has never thought one way or another about it . . . until now.

"Didn't Rachel have some home to go to?"

"Not anymore, Dick," Ralph answers, annoyed.

"Sir, I don't think that Joe should be the one to take in such a newborn."

"He's done it before."

Just the answer alone makes Dick's cheeks burn with fire. "Sir…"

"Don't want to hear any more about it, Dick…" Ralph exits indifferently.

"But, sir…"

"Why do you care so much?" Ralph keeps walking.

"I don't know, sir, but are you sure there is no one else?"

"Son," Ralph turns to Dick in the middle of the main office. There subtly seems to be less typing all around as the secretaries strain to listen. "Do you know how many children are out there without homes? We don't have room for every child. If you wanna figure out something, figure out how to keep women from getting knocked up, or parents from getting the fever. That's a better use of your time. Besides, Joe has connections with the Orphan Train."

Panic rises in Dick's chest. "The Orphan Train? I heard they're just shipping them out West. Some of those kids, sir, are sent just to become workers in the fields---"

"--It'll teach them some life skills if that's the case." Ralph says as he throws his jacket at one of the women.

"They're housing those children in asylums, I heard."

"It's a roof over their head." Ralph grunts.

"She'll be placed with strangers," Dick erupts more than usual.

Sylvia has been following quietly, knowing her uncle is a stubborn man that just needs the right persuasion. "Uncle Ralph, what if I find someone?"

Now, Ralph is irritated, so he stops with his hands up. "Are you two serious?"

"We'll take care of her tonight and then we'll have someone to pick her up by tomorrow," Sylvia says.

Ralph surrenders, "Just make sure whatever you do is processed with the county."

"Thank you, Uncle!" Sylvia says with a smile.

"Yes, sir!" Dick nods.

When Ralph slams the door in their faces, Dick and Sylvia turn to each other with glee. By evening, Dick is still holding Rachel in his arms as he sits on Sylvia's couch in the basement of the home that she shares with her parents. Although she is nearly twenty-four, Dick had to sneak in through the cellar door. He keeps his coat and shoes on, even forgetting his hat until Sylvia suggests he take it off.

Into the wee night hours, the pair searches through the list of possible foster parents in a leather-bound book with handwritten details, but comes up empty-handed.

As Rachel sleeps on the love seat, Dick can't help but confide in Sylvia. "She's made me think."

"Okay?"

"I'm quitting, Sylvia. I can't do this job anymore. I'm going to go out there and find a job that suits me. One that brings me joy."

Sylvia is startled. "Are you sure?"

"Yes . . ."

After several moments of hesitation, she faintly responds. "Okay . . . I think it's a good idea."

When he sees the sadness in her eyes, the words unexpectedly explode from him, "I think you should do it with me!"

"What?" Sylvia is startled, but laughs. "I have bills!"

"I know, but I'll help you with them. We can make it work."

As if to distract herself, Sylvia hurriedly sorts through the files again with nervous fingers. Her knee bounces anxiously as she shakes her head, so he scooches closer. He's almost about to lay his hand on hers when her eyes change. She shakily lifts a paper in her hands. "I think I've found someone!"

Dick reads the name Bernadette Brown—a woman he knows well. Suddenly, his heart calms. "I think you have."

Sylvia gives him a hug that lingers ever so slightly.

The next day, they walk into Ralph's office together. Joe, a squirmy old man, with yellow fingernails and wiry lips, is already there to take Rachel.

"Good morning, Joe. This one won't be coming with you today." Dick tells him.

"What do ya mean?" Ralph bellows.

"She's going to a good foster home," Sylvia answers.

"What the hell's goin' on here?" Joe jumps to his feet angrily. "You bring me out here for this? My orphanage is just fine."

"You won't get paid for this one, Joe." Dick says, knowing that kids are Joe's business, not his charity.

Ralph shrugs. "Don't know what to tell you, Joe. I left it up to these kids to find someone to take the baby. They must've done it."

Chapter Five

1908

Bernadette Brown, (or Bernie as most people call her) has an unhealthy obsession with hats. No matter the day, her mood is either helped or hindered based on what adorns her head. On the morning she is to meet Rachel, she wears the hat with the green and blue peacock feathers since, obviously, the day will be adventurous. She sings to herself all the way to pick up Rachel and continues along the walkway to the government building. People quickly notice her.

"Mornin', Bernie!" an Italian man named Frankie, who works on a construction crew nearby, says while he takes his break under the nearest oak tree. His bare feet are resting on top of one another in the newly mowed grass.

"Oh, good mornin', Frankie!"

"Sure is a nice automobile," he says of the car she just parked.

"Borrowed it from Mrs. Ashton. I woulda preferred to walk, but I thought in the heat with the baby, I might find another way to bring 'em home."

"You've come to get another one, huh?"

"Sure have . . . 'nother baby's comin' home! Seems they don't care how old I am!"

"As they shouldn't!" Frankie says with a smile.

"Seems they also forgot how fat I am!"

"Fat? You ain't fat!"

Bernie stops and gives him a stern look. "Come on now, Frankie. Don't make me come over there and sit on you!"

He laughs a loud hyena-type laugh. "Well, congratulations, Miss Brown!"

"Thank you, Frankie!"

Although she is getting older and is terribly aware of it, from her eyesight to the strange ache in her hands, she never cares about her weight. Women in her family were built with large everything and taught to enjoy food. And she does, every day, all day long. People often stare at her because of her size, but she smiles and says, "The Lord has blessed me richly." Only she knows that the "richly" she speaks of is popping in a frying pan or poured heavily over biscuits.

When she reaches the front doors of the government building, she checks her hat in the reflection of the nearest window. Then, with one push, she makes her way into the familiar office.

"Bernie! So good to have you back." Sylvia runs to Bernie's side.

"Thanks for gettin' a hold of me! Where's my baby?!"

"She's over here." Sylvia leads her with a gentle hand on the shoulder.

"Oh, it's a girl! Does she have a name?"

"Rachel Anne Praline."

"Oh, you know, I'm not usually fond of the names they choose but that's a good one. Rachel . . . I love that name . . . I had a grand-mother named Rachel."

Sylvia opens the door to her office. "Here she is."

In the nearest chair Dick is holding Rachel as though she is his own. Without a moment's hesitation Bernie walks to Dick and holds her arms out for the baby. "Oh, hand that beautiful baby over!"

It isn't that Dick doesn't recognize all the good that Bernadette Brown has done as a foster parent over the years; but letting go of Rachel means saying goodbye to her beautiful blue eyes. In two days, a man who had never wanted children of his own was completely changed. A baby can do a lot for a man, whether he wants to admit the reality of his soft mushy insides or not.

Intuitively, Bernie sits down in the chair beside him. "Let me see her face."

Dick moves the blanket.

"Oh, she's white," Bernie says with surprise.

Both Dick and Sylvia's faces flush as their hearts beat faster.

"Mrs. Brown, you are the only thing that saved this little girl from being sent on the Orphan Train. Her mother is in jail, her uncle won't take her, and nobody's goin' to want her. You're the best with babies, and we just need--"

"Hush now!" Bernie says as she watches her sleep. "I didn't say I wouldn't take her. Just surprised me, is all." Rachel's eyes open and she stares at Bernadette. "Oh, she is special, isn't she?" Bernie smiles.

"She sure is."

Bernadette lays a compassionate hand on Dick's arm. "I'm goin' to take good care of her."

Dick nods and then, ever so delicately, hands her the baby.

Sylvia comes to Bernie's side with a stack of papers in her hands. "Here are Rachel's papers. And there are papers on the desk that you will need to sign."

"Of course." Before she moves, she stares at the baby just a bit more. They don't have the same shade of skin, but all she sees is a child's potential.

When all the papers are signed, Bernadette shakes their hands.

"Let us walk you out," Dick says gently.

Bernadette is curious as she watches Dick and Sylvia grab boxes filled with personal items.

Their boss quickly notices. "Where are you two going?"

"Our letters of resignation are on your desk. We're off to discover the world," Dick says with a smile.

"What?" Ralph says angrily.

"Sorry, Uncle," Sylvia says quietly.

Ralph yells at them, "Get back here!" Yet both know he would never follow them outside due to the heat. When they reach the open air, Dick and Sylvia breathe in as though it is the first time.

"You sure had a lot to do today," Bernie says.

"Because of that baby," Dick explains. "She's changed my life."

"My, my . . . in just two days, huh? Well, goodness."

Once Bernadette is behind the wheel, she looks at the couple with big eyes, as Dick leans beside the door.

"Miss Brown, I want you to take this." He hands her a small piece of paper. "This is my folks. I don't know where I may be, but if anything happens . . . anything at all . . . please contact me. I need to know that Rachel's going to be okay."

"Of course, honey. I'll put it with her papers, and I will never move it," Bernie smiles.

"Thank you. I hope she's happy," he whispers. "In just a short time she's opened my eyes to so much."

"Children often do." Bernie pats his hand.

"I hope I see her again."

"If it's God's will."

"Right."

Then together, Sylvia and Dick wave as Bernadette drives away with the child.

Chapter Six

1908

Bernadette understands that adding a mouth to feed would be difficult in a time when the average family's annual income is two hundred to four hundred dollars. However, when entertainment is limited to radios, books, theaters, and saloons, a baby to pay attention to is a way to pass the time. Rachel will bring life and a sense of purpose back to Bernadette.

Bernadette's family moved to Atlantic City in 1843, when she was only five, after being granted their freedom. Having autonomy meant no longer answering to the white man, nevertheless, it also gave her parents the difficult task of finding work. While technically they were no longer slaves, this didn't mean that the white community needed to like it or make it fair to find jobs. One day, after months of searching, her mother and father received word that they had been offered positions working for a wealthy black man named Joseph Ashton. Joseph worked for the politician Blanche

Bruce, United States Senator in Mississippi from 1875 to 1881, until Blanche Bruce's death in 1898.

Before this offer, Bernadette's parents struggled selling flowers on the roadside, bringing in far less money than they needed to survive. So, when they received the letter from Joseph, they eagerly accepted. Bernadette's mother was to care for the Ashton children and her father was tasked with the grounds-keeping. It was going to be a new life. Her father was sure of it—and he was right.

Now, at the beginning of the twentieth century, years after Bernadette's parents had died and Joseph Ashton had passed, Bernadette was still living on the Ashton Estate taking care of poor old Mrs. Ashton. She was a terribly heartbroken woman since her children never came to see her anymore. Her memory had deteriorated, but Bernie was devoted to the old woman.

On the day that Bernie brings Rachel home, Mrs. Ashton seems to be in an even deeper fog than usual. When Bernie walks in with the baby in her arms, Mrs. Ashton looks at the "intruder" fearfully.

"What are you doin' in here?" Mrs. Ashton, the always proper, always pristine woman asks as she pastes herself against the wall as though she thinks Bernie will hurt her.

"Now what's got into you, Mrs. Ashton? It's me, Bernie."

"Bernie, I don't know no Bernie."

"Oh, yes you do. We're not doing this today. It's a good day and I won't let you forget yourself. And you never say improper grammar like that, Mrs. Ashton. Shame on you." Bernie laughs as she casually proceeds through the house opening some windows and letting the bright sunshine across the expensive furniture.

"You shouldn't be in my house."

"I'm in your house 'cause I've been in your house every day since I was five years old, Mrs. Ashton. Come on now…" Bernadette passes the skittish woman and enters the bright kitchen. "You'll remember. Just gotta give you a second. Now, I'm goin' to make food for you, 'cause I'm sure you haven't eaten today."

Rachel sleeps snuggly swaddled against Bernie's chest with a wrap that she had used for all of her children. Even with the clang of the pots and pans Rachel doesn't stir from her deep sleep.

"Who are you again?" the tiny voice asks from the hall. Then Mrs. Ashton sticks her head around the wall, showing her white hair first and then her timid brown eyes.

Bernie laughs. "Bernadette . . . you like to call me Bernie. Have you eaten today, Mrs. Ashton?"

"Eaten? Of course. I had eggs and bacon and biscuits."

Bernie studies the clean stove. "Your brain is goin' to starve you. If I wasn't here..." She doesn't finish her thought as she pulls food from the icebox.

Then a shining glimmer comes to Mrs. Ashton's eyes. She takes a few more steps in the kitchen and tries to see the front of Bernie.

"Bernie..." she says as though she clearly remembers her. "What have you got there?"

Bernie tenderly brushes Rachel's cheek with her finger.

"This is Rachel. I'm takin' care of her for a while."

Mrs. Ashton comes close with tears in her eyes. "She reminds me of my babies." The old woman reaches out and touches the soft head of the newborn. "My Shelby. Where's her momma?"

"Doesn't have one. I'm gonna be her momma for a while. Would you like to hold her, Mrs. Ashton?" Bernie isn't prepared for the wide-eyed reaction from her friend.

"Oh, may I?"

"Of course. You hold the baby while I make you some lunch. Then Rachel's gotta eat."

Little did Bernadette know that Rachel would be a light for Mrs. Ashton. Days, weeks, and months go by without a single miserable day where Mrs. Ashton can't remember. It is as though having something to take care of is enough to bring a little youth back to her.

Every day Bernie takes the baby with her wherever she goes. To the store, to church, and back to Mrs. Ashton's house—the baby is happy as long as Bernadette is there. She grows fast and the two elderly women watch with fascination. Everything the child does brings them joy. When she crawls for the first time, Mrs. Ashton claps her hands from her rocking chair as Bernie looks in from the kitchen with a proud grin. Walking is a triumph and a bit of irony at the same time—as Mrs. Ashton loses her ability to be mobile, Rachel dives into the skill headfirst. The child learns to sing before she can even speak and claps her hands in rhythm with Bernadette as they sit on the wide porch while the sun collapses—taking its own night of sleep during the hot summer.

Before anyone knows it, it is Christmastime in 1911. This year Harriett Quimby becomes the first woman to earn her pilot's certificate, Omar Bradley enters Westpoint, the Mona Lisa is stolen from the Louvre, and Bernadette is chasing after Rachel. People are doing everything in their power to survive. "It isn't a horrible time to live, but it isn't that wonderful either," Bernadette says to Rachel as they brush her hair.

Some of Bernie's friends grow tired of Atlantic City and its evil ways so they move westward, but Bernadette is comfortable in her place. It is Mrs. Ashton, the baby, and her. At this point in time Bernie ignores the strange looks she gets when out and about with Rachel. Rachel is her daughter, plain and simple.

Motherhood comes naturally to Bernie. She disciplines Rachel when needed and kisses her bruises when she falls. Every week they go to church where Rachel loves dancing in the aisles. At first people stare, wondering why Bernadette has agreed to take care of the white baby, but before long, all of that changes. No one whispers or judges—Rachel Anne Praline becomes part of the family. If she doesn't know she is different, they don't need to tell her.

In most ways she is the picture of a normal child. Her straw-colored hair falls to the middle of her back and her eyes are as blue as the ocean on a clear day. Every day she is reprimanded for going after things that she shouldn't and every day she is praised for all the beautiful and wonderfully sweet things that little girls say. She eats very little and runs a lot. Her best friend in the entire world is a little girl with smooth black skin and thick black hair named Simone. Together they entertain the worshipers before the music begins with their sweet smiles as they walk through the old school building that has been converted into a church.

One day, as Bernie dusts the tables and windowsills of her house, she hears a rich voice filling her halls. It doesn't sound like a child. On her toes, she sneaks closer to Rachel's bedroom and presses her ear to the door. Bernie's eyes widen with surprise at the perfect pitch and rich tone. Somehow deep inside she knows to keep this a secret, so Bernie doesn't tell a soul. Nonetheless, when they are home, she introduces Rachel to the piano. Something comes alive in the child as she sings. If not for dinner and Bernie's urging to play with the other kids outside, Rachel would stay at the piano all day.

At church during Christmastime, when the aisles are adorned with red and green plaid bows, poinsettias hang from rafter to rafter, and a small Christmas tree sits in all four corners—Rachel happily skips from Sunday school into the sanctuary where Bernie is talking to several women from the congregation.

"What are you smilin' about, honey?" Bernadette asks.

"I'm goin' to sing," Rachel answers with pride.

"To sing?"

"Yeah."

Just then the Sunday school teacher appears at Bernadette's side. "It's the Christmas show. We gave all the kids a small solo."

"I got one, too," Simone exclaims as she pulls at Rachel's hand.

It isn't that Bernadette doesn't want Rachel to shine, in fact, she expects her to—someday. She just knows that it isn't time yet.

When Pastor Affie and his wife, Clarine, come over for lunch, they sit at the table for quite some time in discussion. "What problem do you have with her singin' in front of the church, Bernie?" Clarine asks.

"I don't know. Call it the Lord or something . . . I just don't want that little girl changing and I don't want anybody tryin' to change her."

"They gave solos to everyone. Bentley told me that he got one of the solos and I had to hold myself from laughin'. That boy can't sing and has no business trying to croak out a song in front of the congregation."

Bernie looks at the woman, horrified. "Clarine, that is your son. You should encourage him in all things. Even if he sounds like a frog."

"Now why don't you say the same for Rachel?"

"It isn't the same."

"Why? Cause she can sing? What is it that you're afraid of?"

A few moments later, while she dries the dishes, Bernadette stops and places her hands on the edge of the water basin. She watches Rachel playing with her friends on the two acres of land just outside her window. Bernadette Brown is known to feel things from her soul. There is no need for facts or tangible pieces, rather she stays in constant conversation with her Higher Power.

"I don't know, Clarine…" Her words fall to just above a whisper, which is so very different from her normal volume. "There's just something. There's something that I worry about . . . about this gift. Just don't want anyone to steal it, is all."

"Oh, you're just sayin' that because of her beginnin's."

"I'm not so sure. This age is delicate and this world's a scary place."

Clarine comes to Bernadette's side. "She's gonna be fine. Look at her, she's a strong child."

"Something's tellin' me to hold her back."

"Well…" Clarine looks at Bernie's profile. "You've always been good at readin' your intuition. Don't stop now. But you'd better be careful, Bentley's gonna get all of the attention." Just as she says this, a large croak comes from the hall. Bentley, the pastor and his wife's only son, walks past the door trying to sing, but failing miserably.

"Son, don't do that. It's awful, just pure awful!" Clarine yells as she leaves the room.

When Christmas arrives, everyone sits snugly in their seats bundled up in the drafty building. Proud parents wait as they hear the excitement of the kids behind the curtains.

During the show, the children sing from their hearts—good and bad. Bernie fidgets as she waits for Rachel to take the stage. Finally, Rachel, looking neither nervous nor scared, taps the wooden stage with her secondhand shoes. The piano begins followed by the prettiest version of Silent Night that Bernie has ever heard.

Many have heard stories from others who were in the audience this night. It's said that up until this moment the room had been full of chatter, but when Rachel began, the room was silent.

Bernadette Brown notices.

The smooth sound floats to the sky as though the roof has no barrier. Standing close to the back, Pastor Affie and Clarine watch the little girl with wide eyes. They have never heard anything like it. The candles that keep the church lit aren't as bright as this child's future and Pastor Affie is sure of it.

When she finishes, she doesn't receive applause, only open-mouthed stares. Finally, Pastor Affie claps, pulling people from their shock. In seconds, there is thunderous applause while people hoot and holler, but Bernadette is glued to her seat. She shakes her head, unsure about what she has just done to the poor child.

Chapter Seven

1913

In the year that Woodrow Wilson is sworn in, the sixteenth amendment is ratified, allowing the federal government to impose and collect taxes, the Woolworth building opens in New York City, the Ford Motor Company starts production of the Model T, and Louis Armstrong plays in the band of the New Orleans Home for Colored Waifs, Pastor Affie adjusts his tie and presses his hair down as he picks up his case and walks stealthily along the dry grass toward Bernadette's home. As he rounds the corner of the patio, the afternoon sun hits his face. Simone and Rachel play with their dolls on the porch swing.

"Hi, Pastor Baker," Rachel says shyly, her voice in a singsong tune.

"Whatchya doin' here, Pastor Affie?" Simone asks as she dances around the man's feet.

"I've come to talk with your…" he isn't sure what Bernadette is to Rachel, "Bernadette. Is she here?"

"Yes, sir. She's takin' care of Mrs. Ashton." Rachel walks to the screen door and opens it for him. He steps inside thinking that the child might follow him in, but instead, she stays with Simone to take care of their rag babies.

Affie sets his briefcase down and rubs where the sweat is trapped in the creases of his hot palms. Before long, Bernie descends the stairs. Affie hopes that she will give him a look of joy; instead, her head instantly twists from side to side. "Not today, Pastor Affie. I haven't got the time to talk with you. My answer's the same as it's been for the last two years. No."

She heads to the kitchen, where in just moments he meets her at the stove. "Bernadette, I know you're sick of me comin' to you. I know what your answer has been in the past, but ya got to know that I have her best interest in mind."

With a loud laugh Bernadette slaps a pan against the large stove scaring even her with the loud clang. "You just don't stop, Affie. I said no . . . I mean no."

"If I remember correctly, you said that you may at some point feel as though she could do somethin' with her voice."

"Yes, when she is old enough to make her own decisions and she isn't there yet. She's only five and you've religiously been askin' me for two years."

Affie steps away and places his back against the wall. "Well, I've not been known as a quitter, that's for sure."

"I'm not lettin' anyone get their hands on her. Not just yet."

"I understand. But I also give my word, Bernadette, that I will make sure no one takes advantage of Rachel. She'll be singing for herself and when she wants to stop, she can."

"The answer is no, Affie. The answer is no."

Affie has learned there is not a whole lot of arguing to do with this strong-headed woman. He's a good pastor, but his ambition has been known to come before logic.

One time, someone offered to buy the land where their church meets, and he accepted before asking the congregation, when it wasn't his to sell. Old Lady Gertie owned it and had denied buyers for fifty years. When Gertie told him that she would never sell it, Affie had to climb out of the hole he had created—both with buyer and congregation.

"There is money to be made from her kind of talent, money that could help the church—yet Bernie watches over her like a shepherd does their flock," he explains to Clarine on a regular basis.

Down in Tin Pan Alley, Affie spoke to his friend about Rachel more than a year before. Tin Pan Alley is a place in New York City on West 28th between Fifth and Sixth Avenue. Simply put, it is a dense population of musical folks, from publishers to music stores. It will eventually become Manhattan's Flatiron District with a plaque dedicated to the once lively sounds of punching piano keys, but when Affie speaks to his friend it is a place for the organic magic of music—any kind, at any time.

About every six months, Affie's friend from Tin Pan Alley calls to put a fire under Affie to try once again, but so far, his efforts have been futile. Bernie once locked the door as he was climbing the porch steps, another time she chased him out with a spatula, and she even stood in front of the congregation reprimanding him several months prior. However, as stubborn as Bernie can be, Affie is worse. He calls it optimism.

"Okay, Bernie," Affie tries to adjust his face so that it isn't stern, or harsh, but rather hopeful and inspiring. He turns, but Bernie stops him with a hand up.

"I have been praying to God, asking why you are pushing so hard. After all, there has to be a reason." As Bernie is speaking, he feels a bit of enthusiasm. "Affie can't be a bad man, I have said, but you know what I keep hearing God say?"

"What?"

"He's just an idiot." Bernie crosses her arms in front of her.

Her answer surprises him, and his throat catches before he can say anything. "God tells you I'm an idiot?"

"In so many words."

"Well, Bernie, I don't think God---" he begins, but she interrupts.

"Oh, I do. God is very clear to me when people aren't thinking with their spirit, but rather their greed and I don't think Jesus was ever afraid of telling men when they were idiots."

"Bernie, but isn't it God that gave her this voice?"

"Absolutely. And God will make it clear to her when it's time to use it. I'm not sure why you're pushin' so hard. You must think that it's best for Rachel…" she looks at him with questions in her eyes. "But I know what's best for her. She is special. I believe it . . . you believe it. But I'm not gonna warp it until it looks nothin' like the beautiful gift it started as."

"I just want to make sure she gets what she deserves, Bernadette."

"She deserves a peaceful childhood surrounded by people that love her."

"You're right, Bernie. You're right. I know it." Affie looks up the stairs when he hears Mrs. Ashton call out weakly. "She doin' alright?"

"She refuses to take her medication and she can't remember how to do much of anything. I'm not expectin' her to stay around for much longer."

"Well, if you need any help, Bernadette, you know where to find me."

"I sure do."

"Sure." Affie walks out, passing Rachel and Simone who are now sitting on the steps with small flowers in their hair. "Y'all be good now."

Simone

Within the schoolhouse, there are kids from the age of four to eighteen with only one teacher, Miss Gaffrey. Miss Gaffrey is a tiny little thing with curly hair and light eyes, but her hand is harsh in dealing with the children, or else they would run her ragged. When the weather is cold they keep the windows and doors shut, and the older kids chop wood outside, while others stoke the fire on the inside. This often makes their eyes burn, but it is better than fighting with the icy weather. When it is warm, they open the windows and doors, hoping to catch some cool breeze and possibly the sweet scent from the nearby flower field that Rachel and Simone love to roam. The spring and summer when the windows are open is the time that the orange flowers bloom and Rachel can't help but stare for hours. Rachel and Simone both take their schooling seriously, but no matter how hard Rachel tries, she can never keep up with Simone. In fact, no one can.

Miss Gaffrey, as it's getting closer to the summer and the kids are restless, finds that engaging them in a spelling bee, of sorts, keeps their attention. The competition teaches the young ones and challenges the older ones, but it is within the last couple of years that the winner has no longer been dominated by the older students. Simone's face lights up when Miss Gaffrey mentions a spelling bee, or a math competition.

The teeny tiny teacher picks up the yard stick and points to Simone's next word on the board with a smile. One side of the room is piled high with excited students, while the other side of the room has three students left. One seventeen-year-old, one eighteen-year-old, and seven-year-old Simone, stand carefully, waiting for their turn, and the only one who has a smile on her face is Simone. Rachel gets nervous every time it's Simone's turn, but shouts with joy every time Simone seems to have no trouble knowing the answer.

"Okay Simone, can you spell acquiesce?" Miss Gaffrey asks while she fans herself near the window.

Without hesitation, Simone grins only lifting her right cheek, and spells, "A . . . C Q U I E S C E."

Her competitors roll their eyes, while every child in the schoolhouse excitedly yells.

"For extra credit can you tell me what it means?"

"It means to agree without protest or question. Something my brother never does." Simone raises her eyebrow to the other kids as they chuckle.

Miss Gaffrey gives the eighteen-year-old his word, "Arthur, can you spell fuchsia?"

Arthur is irritated when he gets it wrong and must cross to the other side of the schoolhouse. The seventeen-year-old girl, Martha, gets it right, so she is able to stay in the competition.

"Alright you two . . . just a couple more and we find our winner. Simone, I would like you to spell both Nanticoke and Lenni-Lenape," a tribe known to have been ushered out of New Jersey. Miss Gaffrey often feels it important to teach from actual history, rather than the text books—because of the large amount of this tribe still in New Jersey, despite their ancestors being among the first to be forced on reservations.

Simone and Rachel's closest friend, besides each other, is Chepi from this indigenous tribe. Simone smiles at her friend and says, "N A N T I C O K E and L E N N I – L E N A P E." When the room begins to cheer, Simone points at Rachel and Chepi with confidence and a nod.

Miss Gaffrey looks at Martha who seems more than nervous to lose to a seven-year-old and says, "Pharaoh."

Martha breathes out, grateful that the word isn't too difficult. "P H A R O A H."

It isn't until Miss Gaffrey hesitates that Martha realizes she must have gotten it wrong and her eyes widen in disbelief. The students, especially the younger ones, are all on pins and needles waiting for Miss Gaffrey to make it clear whether Martha is correct. "I'm sorry Martha, that is incorrect. Simone, can you spell it for me?"

"Of course, I can. P H A R A O H."

The schoolhouse and everything in it, is frozen despite the heat, just waiting. Finally, Miss Gaffrey nods. "That's correct."

Screaming and jumping fills the classroom while the kids gather around Simone with praise. At seven years old, she is the queen of everyone her age and younger.

The next week, the excitement gets even bigger when Miss Gaffrey uses algebraic equations for the competition. Simone wins again.

Rachel and Simone walk hand in hand across the field of orange flowers, still smiling after Simone beats all of her competition. "How do you know it?" Rachel asks.

"What?"

"Everything. Everything you know."

"Don't know. Just do."

1914

1914 is remembered for many things but for all the wrong reasons. Archduke Franz Ferdinand is assassinated which allows Austria-Hungary to declare war on Serbia, stoking the fire of World War I; then Germany invades Luxembourg and Belgium, and, on a somewhat pleasant note, the Panama Canal officially opens after a decade of construction. So, it's no wonder in such a turbulent year that Bernie is forced to say goodbye to sweet Mrs. Ashton. After several weeks of Mrs. Ashton's decline Rachel waits outside the bedroom door while Bernie and the doctor stay with the old woman. "It's okay, Mrs. Ashton," Bernie says as she leans over her with a hand tenderly stroking her hair. It has been so long since Mrs. Ashton spoke that when she whispers, Bernie swiftly gets closer. "What did you say?"

"I see him." With that, she takes her last breath.

"You're with him now." Bernie thinks about the husband and wife reuniting and she smiles through tears.

Rachel notices the change on Bernie's face when she finally exits into the hall. "What's happened, Momma?"

"Well, my girl, Mrs. Ashton has gone to be with our Lord."

"Is she standin' at the pearly gates, dancing for joy, finding peace in God's presence?"

Bernadette can't help but laugh. "She is all of those things."

The doctor exits the room, having expected this for quite some time. "I'll have someone come and get Mrs. Ashton soon."

"Okay. They'll make her look nice for her funeral?"

"Yes, ma'am. They'll put makeup on her and everythin'."

"Okay. In good taste, of course?"

"Of course." Doctor Avery had been the doctor in the Ashton house since he was newly graduated fifty years prior. So, he knows Bernie like family. He looks at her curiously, "Have you been talked to, Bernie?"

"What do you mean?"

"Well, I was contacted by a lawyer. You and I are the only ones figuring things out for Mrs. Ashton."

"That's the way I figured it. She hasn't got children around no more and you and I were her family. What'd the lawyer say?"

"He says there should be paperwork or else all is goin' to the state."

Bernadette nods. Not once has Bernadette wondered how she might get Mrs. Ashton's property. She was a friend and loyal employee, not an opportunist. The way she saw it, their families had merged and become one in the eyes of God. "Let it all go to the state."

Dr. Avery looks at her with concern. "But where will you go? You have a child you're takin' care of, Bernie."

"This girl and I will be fine. We're on the path meant for us. Aren't we, baby?"

Rachel had heard it time and again. Why would she ever question it? Bernadette had shown her all she needed to live a happy childhood and things were good. It was a time to believe. "Yeah," Rachel smiles as she pushes some blonde hair away from her face.

"Okay, Bernadette," the doctor continues, "Well, you never know. Maybe Mrs. Ashton took care of it. But if you need anythin', please get ahold of me."

"I will, Doctor Avery."

"Okay . . . like I said, I'll send someone to care for Mrs. Ashton's body."

"You do that."

Dr. Avery walks away with his medicine bag. Bernadette peers down at Rachel. "Well, it's just you and me. That enough for you?"

"Yeah," Rachel says as she puts her arm around Bernie's legs.

Turns out, Mrs. Ashton had a will. Even though she had left the large home to her children, she gladly gave the small home to Bernadette. When Bernie receives the letter, she laughs and shows it to Rachel even though the small child couldn't read it.

Time moves on and in 1915, at the age of seven, Bernadette finally allows Rachel to sing in church. So, every couple of weeks, only when Rachel says that she wants to, Bernadette helps her learn spirituals. It is something of a hope revival to hear Rachel sing the notes as if they are coming from an angel.

She sings Some Sweet Day, By and By, Amazing Grace, and The Old Rugged Cross. While people fan themselves with paper in the summer heat, they nod their heads in agreement as they listen to the child. No matter what is going on in the tough world outside, the smooth voice is wiping the pains away for just a moment. Affie stands in the back, dreaming.

Although it is never right to talk about a pastor as though their title takes away their human desires, most would agree that they have just as hard of a time distinguishing between what they want and what they need. Pastor Affie is a good man—he just loses sight of how things should be. Rachel began singing so often that gradually his ambition got the best of him when he simply couldn't allow this talent to go to waste.

"Bernadette just doesn't see how this is gonna help her," Affie tells Clarine as they lay in bed.

One day when Rachel is closing the service with one of his

favorite hymns, he smiles when the church doors open behind him. His close friend, Freddy Conroy, from Tin Pan Alley, walks in. He has played a big part in the boom of Blues and Slap-Your-Leg-Jazz that is happening all around. He had been, in some capacity, responsible for men like W.C. Handy (sometimes referred to as Father of the Blues) and Buddy Bolden (known as King Bolden, a bandleader in New Orleans—or so he had told Affie). No one was quite sure whether he had truly met either man.

"Thought you weren't goin' to make it," Affie whispers out of the side of his mouth.

"Just busy, that's all. This the girl?"

The piano is playing, but Rachel has yet to sing. Finally, after her pick-up note, she begins to lead the congregation in What A Friend We Have In Jesus. Affie felt as much pride as a father. When the song ends Affie instantly knows Freddy has seen the child's gift.

"I have to get her out to see some people," Freddy agrees.

"I thought you might. Now look," Affie says as the people depart, "I haven't gotten Bernie to say yes yet."

"Ya need me to talk with her?"

"That isn't gonna be any better. Just give me some time."

"I'm a good salesman, Affie."

"Salesman isn't gonna do it, Freddy. Now just give me some time."

1915 Phillip

In this year, Pluto is photographed for the first time, however, what it is, is still unknown, Charlie Chaplin's "The Tramp" is released, and when Jess Willard defeats Jack Johnson in a boxing match he becomes popular for "bringing back the championship to the white race".

The same field outside their schoolhouse—the one with all of the orange flowers that Rachel and Simone love so much—has a small shop on the other side of it. There is a rope swing and a train track that shakes this little store almost off its foundation.

One morning, Rachel swings back and forth through the air while she waits for Bernadette to pay for their items within the store. Suddenly the heavy chug of a large locomotive fills the air as it passes only feet from where she swings and several of the neighborhood kids gather to watch. Just months before, Pastor Affie and Clarine's little boy, Bentley, was playing on those very tracks and was struck by a passing train. She remembers standing at the grave site as Affie and Clarine wept inconsolably.

A young boy named Phillip interrupts her thoughts as she jumps down from the swing and joins the group of kids, "I don't never get tired of that train."

"You see it a lot?" Rachel asks.

"Every day."

"One of my friends died here."

"You talkin' 'bout Bentley? Bentley was my friend too," Phillip says quickly. "It comes 'bout same time ever'day. I wait for it." Phillip moves on, "Where do you live?"

"Not very far. But my momma wouldn't let me come every day. I got school in the morning, just across that field." She points ahead.

"My momma does my schooling." The boy turns and sticks a hand out to Rachel. "What's your name?"

"Rachel Anne Praline." She takes his hand.

"Name's Phillip Murphy. I live just there." He points to a small rundown home behind the store.

Just then, both of them hear Bernie's call. The children look at the woman as she comes around the corner of the shop with bags in her hands and a perfectly matching hat to her handkerchief around her neck.

"Rachel, I've been callin' you," Bernie calls out.

"Sorry, Momma."

Phillip looks at her with wide eyes. "That's your momma?"

"Yeah." Rachel says, lowering her eyebrows with curiosity.

"Where'd you come from?" He asks.

"What do ya mean?"

"That cain't be yo' momma."

"Why not?"

"She's black. You ain't. You's white." When he sees a strange look in her eye, he continues. "Nah, she cain't be yo' momma. White people don't like black people."

"Why?"

"I don't know. Is jus' the way it is."

"That don't sound right."

"It may not, but it's the way it is."

Another woman comes to Bernie's side, distracting her for a moment as the children discuss the matter further. "In some parts, white folks hang black folks all the time."

"What does that mean?"

"Ahhh, man…you's fresh…it means some white men take a rope like this…" he touches the rope of the swing with his fingertips and brings it to her face, "wrap it 'round they's neck and pull it 'til they's feet don't touch the ground…kill 'em."

Tears come to Rachel's eyes. It isn't true. None of it can be true. She checks for Bernie who is still laughing and smiling with another woman.

"Ya see . . . It's jus' the way it is. Ya cain't have a black momma. One day yo' gonna hate her…and you's have ta find a new momma."

"Stop it, Phillip!" Simone's familiar voice interrupts them.

Both of them look up to find Simone standing with her hands at her waist. Relief fills Rachel as Simone comes to her side since she knows that Simone will tell her it all isn't true. "Don't listen to him. He don't ever know what he's talking about."

"Course I do. I seen it wit' my own eyes."

"Phillip, you're stupid." Simone links arms with Rachel. "Come on, Rachel. Don't listen to him." Simone gives him a dirty look as they walk away.

As Bernie chats with the woman, Simone and Rachel use the bridge to walk over the train tracks to reach the field of beautiful orange chrysanthemums. After they take a few steps along the uneven ground, they circle around chuckling at the sight. It's just them in a sea of orange petals. "I wanted to get away from my brother."

Rachel pulls a flower from the field and twirls it in her little fingers, then she walks to Simone, takes her hand and lays it in her palm. Simone picks one as well and lays it in Rachel's hand. "We'll keep them, okay," Simone says as she throws her arm over Rachel's shoulder.

"Okay."

"And anytime you go to my house and I'm not there. I'm probably here . . . but only if the mums are in bloom." Simone says.

"Mums?" Rachel asks.

"These are chrysanthemums. They started in China."

"How do you know that?"

"Just do." Simone grins.

"Rachel!" Bernie calls out. "Come back you two! Simone, your momma wants me to bring you home."

"Alright!" Simone yells, then the two of them run up the bridge and reach Bernie's side in record time. Rachel looks long and hard at her friend and her momma. More than anything in the world, she loves them.

When she sees her looking, Simone says to Rachel, "It's not that I don't see that our skin looks different . . . I just don't put any weight to it, that's all."

Rachel whispers, "I hope we can always be friends."

"Me too. My momma says you're what we call a friend for life."

Rachel smiles, "What does that mean?"

Simone answers without thinking, "It means . . . forever." From that day on, they never walk without holding hands—their little fingers making a two-colored braid; and in their rooms, the mums wither, but remain protected smashed in their books.

Later that night, Bernie is cooking while Rachel sits at the table waiting. "What are you thinking, Miss Rachel?"

"I'm thinkin' . . . I love you . . ."

Bernie leans forward and rubs the little girl's cheek. Rachel grabs her momma's hand and places hers beside it. They are so different, yet so much the same. They have the same number of fingers and each of those fingers bend at the same place. Hands are used to pick things up and move things around.

Bernadette watches the little girl carefully. "I love you, Rachel Anne. I always have and will forever." Bernie brings her hand to her face and fans it. "You ready for some dinner?"

Rachel stays close to her momma's side all evening.

1998

Hours ago, I pulled my computer out of my bag and started taking notes. It seems that Gramma is as invested in telling me as I am in hearing it, but every once in a while, she takes a break and will stare out the window. If she's quiet for too long, I get worried, but then she'll just take right back up where we left off.

When it's getting to be too long, I clear my throat. "Why was Bernie so worried about Rachel singing?"

"Have you ever felt something in your gut?"

"Like nerves?" I ask.

"A bit, but more like an answer to a question. A feeling. Bernadette Brown just knew, in all her divine wisdom, that Rachel's gift would be . . . misused. When people see a good thing, they want to work it until there isn't anything left of it. This world works hard at ruining good things."

"So that's gonna happen to Rachel?"

Gramma smiles at my curiosity, then winks at me. "Are ya worried?"

In a strange way, I am. I know it is ridiculous, but there is something in me that wants to find Rachel when she's my age. A soft song finishes from Rachel's CD, so I press replay. I want to hear it again. The first words of the song are "I'll love you no matter what" and I wish that line transcended time—that she could love me no matter the fact that I was born in a completely different era. Most importantly that she'd love me no matter the fact that I haven't accomplished anything.

"Rachel struggled to think about anything other than what that boy Phillip said to her. It wasn't unlike Rachel to feel everythin' so intensely, which was the very thing, I believe, that everyone had noticed in her eyes since she was a baby. Rachel wished she could go back to when she didn't know about our differences, but we all know that's not possible or healthy. Simone and Bernie would have to deal with things Rachel would never understand." Gramma swings her fingers and yarn around the metal piece. "But Simone made it clear to Rachel. It was important to know that people could be cruel to each other. Simone's intelligence wasn't just her mind, she was smarter emotionally, more than many."

I bring my hands to my head and think about when I was a child. I'll never forget the first time I realized there was something there, some barrier that I had been completely unaware of. The first time my father got pulled over by the cops for doing nothing wrong. As I cried in the back seat and the men in uniform treated him like trash under their feet, I'll never forget my father's controlled, but angry, voice. My mother drove us home that day since they took my father in. Later that week, my father lost his promotion to the board within his company. He looked at me later that evening, "I hope someday you will be known by your worth, not by the fear and discrimination of men."

Chapter Eight

1915

Pastor Affie sits uncomfortably at his desk. Sweat pours from his skin making the material of his collar and under his armpits a darker shade of blue than the rest of his shirt even though the chilly weather has started to return. He stares at the financial papers in front of him wondering how he can figure out a way to get the congregation to give more. Tithing had gone down in recent months and there was no easy solution. People didn't want to be told to give to the church even though they used the place as their home every Sunday. They wanted to give freely when their hearts said to, but unfortunately, during rough times, this only meant that the church's bills often went unpaid. The week before, they were well below what they needed to make the place run. Affie shakes his head. He hated giving sermons about tithing.

He sits back in his chair and rubs his face. His mind wanders to his little boy. For a moment he swears that he hears the sound of a train and it feels as though it might make his ears bleed. He jumps to his feet and turns on the radio. Instantly, he gains relief.

Clarine sticks her head in the door. "Bernadette Brown is on the wire for you."

He looks up and nods even though he is just partially listening. "Okay."

"I'm goin' to take my lunch now, Pastor Affie." Clarine has always tried to call him by his professional name when she works in the front office. It helps others know that she takes her position seriously.

Again, he doesn't look up as his thoughts are in a whole different world, and he answers her with a lifted hand. He walks out to the hall where the only telephone is hanging heavily on the wall. The receiver is sitting on the top of it and he gently places it to his ear. "This is Pastor Affie."

"Pastor Affie, it's Bernadette Brown."

"Well, good afternoon. How are you?"

Bernadette doesn't take much time and drives straight into business as usual.

"I need your help, Affie."

"Anything, Bernie. I am always here to help."

"Well, I appreciate it. I haven't been feelin' well for the last few weeks and I need someone to take Rachel for a short time."

Suddenly, Affie stops moving. He looks at the phone. Affie believes in signs, and this phone call is no exception. To him it is clear that God is giving him the answer to the church's financial troubles. "Of course, Bernie. Of course. We'd be glad to watch her for a while."

1998

Gramma looks at me with a scowl almost as though I had done something wrong and I sit up straight in my chair. The women in my life have always had the ability to do this to me. I wait to see if I am in trouble, but then after a moment her face softens and my shoulders drop back to their normal place at the bottom of my neck.

"Now, I don't believe in signs," she says more as though she is trying to teach me or sway me in how I believe. "The more you try and find signs, the more confused you will be. For if God intends us to do something, He'll tell us. We are moronic people and if God had led us with signs, we would be going in opposite directions every other day. I've known some people to never move a muscle because they truly believed they couldn't read the signs God was puttin' out there. I'm not gonna believe that God will do anything else but tell us what he wants us to hear, loud and clear."

"Okay, Gramma," I say as though she has just hit me upside the head even though she is across the room.

"I'm just telling you that cause I know you, and if I'm gonna be telling you Rachel's story, I want you to know this first. There are no signs that will lead you to the right woman, Bobby."

I can't believe how, between my mother and my grandma, I (a grown man, nearly six-foot-three, who has been on his own for years) easily cower as though I don't know how to put my left foot in front of my right without them. "Sure, Gramma. Can we just move on?"

"Well, where was I? I've lost it…"

"Bernie's asked Affie to take care of Rachel."

"Oh, yep, that's right. I think Affie and Clarine lost their senses when Bentley was hit by that train. It was like they just wanted their suffering to stop so they were searching for any distraction—which was Rachel. Affie believed the girl was meant for great things and he would be able to make everyone's lives better—includin' Rachel's and Bernie's…"

1915

In only two days' time, Affie and Clarine have Rachel sitting at their table for lunch. They look at her as though at any moment something brilliant will come from her mouth.

"Do you like singin'?" Affie asks.

Rachel takes another bite of her cookie. "Yes."

Clarine reaches her hand out and touches the child's tiny fingers. "And you are a wonderful singer, darlin'."

"Thank you," Rachel responds shyly.

"We have somethin' special for you, Rachel," Affie says with a grin like the child has just won a prize and Clarine's eyes are as big as silver dollars. Rachel just continues to eat her cookie and look back and forth at the couple. "I have a friend that says you can sing for him. And if you want to, you can record somethin' for him."

Still, Rachel says nothing as the two look on. Although delight is what the pastor expects, it is not what he receives.

"This could be a great opportunity for you, sweet pea," Clarine chimes.

"My momma won't like it."

"Your momma won't mind at all. We'll just go to the city for a couple of days and then we'll be back…" he pauses for a moment knowing that everyone at this table knows Bernadette Brown will be against all that he is saying. The woman just doesn't understand that this is a good opportunity. "Rachel . . . Bernie told me before that you are special. She believes that you are goin' to soar in this life. Just think of me as someone who is helpin' you get your wings."

Rachel finishes her cookie and Clarine sets another one right where that one had been. A smile comes to Rachel's face with the easy-to-please nature of a child. Bernadette never let her have more than one cookie.

"How many songs do you know?" Affie asks.

Rachel thinks about it for a moment and then shrugs. "I don't know."

"Well, I guess that doesn't really matter cause we're gonna teach you a few new songs."

"I like learnin' new songs."

"Well, good. After you eat your cookie we're gonna take a drive and I'll teach you along the way." Clarine says as she pulls the sheet music to the table. "These are love songs."

"About God?"

The pastor and his wife laugh. "Well, not exactly, but you can sing them to God if you like. This is real big right now. It's called Ragtime."

"Ragtime?"

"Yeah, you like the sound of that?" Clarine asks.

"Yeah."

"You just finish what you are doin' and don't worry. I'll teach you well."

"Okay."

After a long drive, the city is overwhelming to Rachel compared to the wide-open spaces she's used to. With wide eyes, she holds on to Clarine's hand as they saunter down the sidewalk. She doesn't know whether to be scared or amazed at the amount of people all in one place. Many people stare at them.

When they reach Freddy's hotel, they wait for him in the lobby. In just moments he exits the elevator.

"Affie! So, you've finally come with her," Freddy turns to Rachel who is standing as close to Clarine as possible.

"I have. She's ready," Affie smiles. "She said she wanted to sing for you."

"Is that right?" Freddy asks Rachel with a smile. "Well, let's not waste any time. I have the studio booked for the rest of the day."

"She'll go straight into recordin'?" Affie asks.

"Yes, unless you think it's too soon." The question isn't really a question, in fact it skips by faster than a flat rock on a still lake, "I also have a place booked tonight for a small show. There are some pretty impressive people that will be there. Everyone's very excited to have James Reese Europe and the Tempo Club in town tonight.

So most everyone will be comin' for them, but that's why it's great. Everyone will go crazy over this kid."

Freddy walks to the door of the hotel and waits for them to follow.

"Where we goin'?" Affie asks.

"We can walk to the studio. It's close. I got a couple of people that should see this child."

Together, they walk down the street as Freddy talks. He seems like a respectable man and knows a lot about music. When they reach the studio, he steps aside and lets them enter first. As they pass the waiting room, the secretary smiles.

"Good afternoon, Mr. Conroy," she says sweetly as she stacks papers on the side of her desk.

For 1915, the place is tops. It has all the latest technology that has only been around for a short time. Freddy takes them down a hall where they can peek into open doors. All kinds of music can be heard along the way and for the first time since entering the city, Rachel smiles.

"I never thought there were places like this," Affie says in awe.

Freddy nods with a grin. "You ain't been livin,' Affie. This is the time to make your voice known."

"I guess so."

"Long gone are the days of field hollers and work songs. We got heavy beats and crazy rhythms. You know what I'm saying?" Freddy says with a smile as he stops in front of a closed door and looks at the group he brought. He looks down at the child. "You got some things to sing for me?"

"Yes, sir."

"Yes, sir…" Affie says quickly "we taught her some ragtime…"

"That's good, that's good," Freddy says with a smile, "but I got somethin' even better. Come on in."

Freddy opens the door and instantly the sound of the studio pours out like water rushing over their feet. It is a free-for-all inside.

There are instruments blazing and men talking. The moment Freddy pulls the child in, the conversations stop and the instrumentalists let their hands drop.

"Afternoon, fellas. I think I brought a kid y'all will want to hear," Freddy says as he slaps hands with the nearest man who sits on some equipment.

"What are you talkin' bout, Freddy?" one of them asks from behind a glass window where they have been recording.

"Just wait and see. Just wait and see."

"We ain't got time. Take her back to where she came. She don't look old enough to be out of diapers," Ernie, the owner, says.

"I'm seven. Don't you know seven-year-olds don't wear diapers?" Rachel says with confusion.

The rest of the men laugh and whistle through their teeth.

A nice-looking young man gets to his feet and walks to Freddy's side. With his hands on his hips, he looks down at the little girl.

"You got a voice then?" he asks.

"I like to sing," Rachel says with a shrug.

"Alright, let's hear somethin'."

Freddy looks at Affie who hasn't stopped smiling since they set foot in the studio. "Everybody, this is Eubie Blake. He plays the piano. You'd never believe the sounds this man can play. It ain't the old ragtime. It's better."

No one knew at the time that this man would be in the good graces of the public eye as a musical genius for nearly eight decades. The brilliance that he would offer to the world and culture changed people. Although Rachel didn't know how lucky she was as a little girl to be meeting the man before her, she would remember the day for the rest of her life.

"Thanks, Freddy," Eubie says politely. He looks back at the little girl with a gleam in his eye. "Whatchya know, sweetie?"

It doesn't seem as though Rachel knows how to respond.

"What do ya like to sing best?" Eubie asks again.

"I like Let Me Call You Sweetheart."

"Okay." Eubie says turning to the group of musicians. "Let's play it for her. See what this kid can do." He turns back around to Rachel. "Why don't ya come stand by me? That's my piano right there."

"Okay." Just like every other time in her life, music makes her nerves vanish and she is excited to sing when he asks. Eubie begins playing the sweet tune on the piano and the instruments join in not long after. Then jumping in right on the proper beat, Rachel sings. All of the men smile at each other. Her smooth voice sounds ten years older than it should and none of them can believe it. As they reach the middle of the song, Eubie stops playing and silences his band. Rachel looks at him with confusion.

"I want to change it up a little. Can ya follow this rhythm?" Eubie begins playing the song again, but a little faster. Rachel nods and quickly falls in sync with him. A few seconds later Eubie lifts his hand in the air and tells his band members to quicken their pace. He leans over to the singing child. "Go a little faster and feel that bounce."

He sings a little bit with her to get her to understand what he means, but it isn't long until she catches on. Even her little body starts to bob. Suddenly, there is a party going on in the room. The band members play with a dance in their step as Eubie pounds on the piano in ragtime fashion. As Rachel sings, she looks over at Affie and Clarine who are clapping their hands and loving every moment of it.

This is the genuine beginning of Rachel's love affair with music. It is as though music is as delicate as a lost soul that needs to be cared for. When they are done, the room is quiet. Eubie looks at her and shakes his head. Then he turns to Freddy.

"I never heard anythin' like it. Did you say you were seven?"

Rachel nods, unaware that anything unusual has happened. To her, everyone is able to sing and with that assumption her uniquity is lost on her and she doesn't understand the depths of their surprise.

"Ernie, take a recordin' of this next one."

Ernie, the blue-suited owner, has already taken notice and is preparing the horn. Just a few minutes later Eubie shows Rachel how to stand in front of the phonograph machine and then he kneels down beside her. "Is there somethin' else you want to sing?" Rachel can't believe that they know just what to do. If she wants to sing a certain song, they'll be able to play it as though they have memorized every song ever written. She shrugs her shoulders.

She likes Eubie. He seems eager and almost as obsessed with music as she is. His smile feels genuine and perhaps it's because deep within a music lover's soul, there is no greater gift than to play—whether it be alone or for someone. It's obvious the joy of song runs through his veins.

He encourages her. "You know you can take anythin' and give it a beat. Whatchya say we give Swing Low Sweet Chariot a beat? Do ya know that one?"

Rachel smiles, so Eubie steps back to his piano and looks at Ernie who gives him a sign when he's ready to record.

For well over an hour, the little girl and a bunch of foul-mouthed, passionate musicians make music. When they are done, Eubie comes to Rachel's side and takes her hand. "You got a great future, kid. Don't stop singin'."

"I won't."

Freddy walks to Affie's side with a smile. "She gonna be able to make it tonight?"

Affie nods his head eagerly, "You'd better believe it."

After getting the child lunch and finding a hotel that suits Affie's pocketbook, they make their way down the street. By nightfall, the city has come to life. Couples are strolling down the sidewalks hand in hand, music pours from restaurants and taverns, and everyone seems to have a glow about them. Rachel's excitement settles Affie's apprehension about deceiving Bernadette. The child holds on to their hands as they walk past much of the hoopla. Men and women are selling trinkets as they pass; others are dressed as clowns.

"We should bring momma here!" Rachel says gleefully.

"Maybe someday, Rachel," Affie responds hesitantly.

"This is what we're lookin' for," Clarine says pointing at the sign above a restaurant.

A line nearly a half-mile long snakes out the door from which a man walks past and Affie politely stops him. "Excuse me, sir. Can you tell us why there is a line?"

"James Reese Europe is comin' tonight!" the man hollers as he dances across the street.

Just ahead, with a cigarette in his hand, Freddy is trying to get to them as he pushes through the line of people. "Well, good evenin' everyone! Rachel, how are you?"

"Good! Thank you."

"Are you ready to sing tonight?"

"Is Eubie here?"

"Yes, he is, my girl. Come on. Let's go in and see him." Freddy throws down his cigarette and smiles at a pretty woman waiting in line. Had Rachel not been there, he might have picked her up, but instead he takes Rachel's hand and they hurry inside. "It ain't usually this tight, but everyone's here to see James." He has to yell above the noise of the crowd.

Rachel stares at the flashy jewelry and the fashionable Fall clothes that are meant to impress as she holds tightly to Clarine and Freddy. People watch Rachel, surprised to see a child in such a place. Finally, they reach a gold-rimmed door with an intricate Asian design and Freddy flings it open. On the other side is a room where the crowds stop and the volume drops, but the smoke rises. Three red couches sit along the walls and men lounge while laughing and smoking cigars.

"There she is!" Eubie calls out. Feeling slightly shy, Rachel grins as she looks around. "Come on over." Eubie extends a hand.

Clarine scoots her forward, "Go on now."

Rachel crawls up beside him.

"You know, kid, I was thinkin'. This is awfully late for you, isn't it?"

"I'm alright."

"You see all these men here . . . they got children of their own and those young'uns wouldn't be caught dead in a place like this at this hour."

Rachel nods, but she couldn't feel tired even if she wanted to.

"That there your daddy?" Eubie asks about Affie.

"No. I don't got a daddy. My momma's at home. She's not feelin' right. They're just watchin' me."

"Oh . . . well . . . hmmm . . . she know you're here?" Rachel shakes her head. "Well, we're gonna do our best to stay right on schedule so you can get home." He takes a drink of his coffee. "You know I was doin' stuff like this at fifteen and I thought I was young." Rachel doesn't say much. She just politely folds her hands in her lap. "Someday I'm gonna write somethin' for you."

"For me?"

"Yeah. It's gonna be real sweet and it's gonna have that smooth sound like you got. Would ya' like that?"

"Yeah."

A stocky man with wire-rimmed glasses comes into the room and instantly everyone hollers and cheers. He is the man of the night— the one everyone has come to see—James Europe. The crowd nearby reaches out for him, while those across the room cast their wide eyes on him, since he seemed to be turning ragtime into the past, and jazz into the future. He created the sound of the Tempo Club, and added the rise of the New York social life to his list of achievements.

"Who's that?" Rachel asks Eubie.

"Oh, you're in for a treat. He's the best bandleader in the world. We get front seats to see him. You're even singin' with him."

She turns to him. "I thought I was singin' with you?"

"Not tonight. Don't worry; he'll take care of you."

By ten o'clock, the music begins. James Europe moves and dances with the music in such a way that he oozes cool. They have a loose rhythm that seems to make the most difficult things easy. Rachel watches, falling more and more in love. Whatever name they call it—ragtime, jazz, or blues—it is what she wants to hear; it is what she needs to hear.

When James calls her up, she doesn't feel nervous after having watched them play so lively for so long. She had wanted to join in from the second song. When she starts singing, he looks at her with lifted eyebrows. She knows now what that means. James Reese Europe is impressed. Hoots and hollers burst in the air from the crowd as they clap for the child. She moves with the beat just as Eubie told her to do. It isn't until nearly one in the morning that the party comes to an end.

Eubie walks to Affie as Rachel rests quietly on a nearby sofa.

"She's good," Eubie says with a nod, "but she's too young, Affie. She can't be here this late. She needs to be gettin' kissed good night."

"I know . . . I know," Affie says as he wipes sweat from his face with his handkerchief. "It's only for tonight and only to meet you fellas. She's goin' right back home tomorrow."

"She needs to keep singin' though. There ain't no doubt 'bout it."

"Where's the child?" a heavy voice comes from behind Affie and Eubie.

Affie and Eubie turn to find James Europe with sweat covering his uniform, but a smile across his face, knowing that the night has gone well. Just as Affie is about to point to the sofa, they hear a small voice.

"I'm here." Rachel is sitting up and wiping her eyes.

James walks to her side with his hand out. "You're a prize Rachel, a real prize."

"Thank you," she says quietly.

"I'd love to have you on my stage any time. Grow up just a bit and I'll see that we do more."

1998

Gramma Johnson has finished another left sock. She ties off the end as she continues her story. "Although Rachel wishes and hopes that what he says is true, there wasn't much time left in James Europe's short life. When World War I starts, he signs up and becomes a lieutenant for the 15th regiment under Colonel Hayward and creates a masterpiece of a band. When he comes home from the war, he is considered a hero for all that he has done and quickly follows his fame on tour. Not long into his tour, the poor man is knifed by his drummer before he is to play in Boston and dies an hour later. Rachel never got a chance to play with him again, but the one chance she'd had, she always remembered."

"She got to meet Eubie Blake, record with Eubie Blake, sing on stage with James Reese Europe, all at such a young age." I'm falling in love with her, but a bit jealous as well. My life doesn't measure up to what I thought it would.

"Oh yes, but remember, Rachel's life has beautiful ups and incredible downs. Just as we all do. Can't take someone else's success and let it measure your life. Just wait for your story, Bobby."

"To be in the same room with those greats. Affie and Clarine must have gotten in trouble?"

"As we all do sometimes. Affie was a good-hearted man. Thought he was doing what was best for Rachel and everyone else really."

"But he wasn't?"

"No, my God, he wasn't."

1915

The next day as they are about to make their way home, a tall, older man in a business suit stops Affie, Clarine, and Rachel on the street. His skin is pale, his nose bulbous, with a heavy mustache on his lip.

"Aren't you the young lady from last night? You sang with Jimmy

Europe?"

Affie smiles and looks down at the child who has suddenly backed away seeming nervous about the man in front of her. "She was and she did."

"Well, I thought I would tell you what a great job you done. Where you off to now?"

"Home," Rachel says, still very shy and ready to see Bernadette and Simone.

"I was wonderin' why I hadn't heard of you. Where's home?"

"All the way in Atlantic City," Affie answers with a smile.

"Name's Bill Manchuron." The man places his hand out for Affie. Affie takes it, excited by how much fame this one night in New York City has already gotten them.

"Affie Baker."

"And who are you?" Bill asks politely.

Seeing that she is nervous, Clarine sticks her hand out and takes it instead. "This is Rachel Anne Praline, and I'm Clarine Baker."

Something in the man's eyes changes and he looks at the couple for a moment.

"Where are your parents?" he asks.

"My momma's at home," Rachel finally says, wishing she was there now.

"You live in Atlantic City?"

"On the outskirts. Sir…" Affie says quickly, "I'm sorry, but we really must be goin'. Her momma's comin' to pick her up today."

"Well, I would just love to have her sing for my restaurant, may I have her mother's name?"

Affie doesn't know what to say. They can make some money to have her sing for the man, and Bernadette needs the money. He'll have a chance to talk with her before anything happens.

"Her name is Bernadette Brown."

The man writes the name on a piece of paper. "Are you adopted, child?"

Suddenly it is clear what Affie has been noticing on the man's face. He shakes his head and passes the man while keeping Rachel's hand in his. "We really must be goin'. Thanks," Affie says.

As they walk away, Rachel notices the man standing with his hands on his hips as he watches with a concerned expression. She's never felt this before, but there is something deep down about this stranger that makes her uncomfortable—afraid even. Everything they have done has been fun, but she no longer wants to be in fast-paced New York City.

On the ride home, Affie and Clarine make sure that the child knows not to say anything to Bernadette about what happened this week. Only when any possible singing deal is given will they make it all clear to the old woman—but not now—she needs to know nothing. When they pull onto the large Ashton property, Rachel has never been so happy to be home. Before the car has even stopped, the little girl jumps from it and runs up the stairs of the porch nearly missing that Bernadette is sitting on the porch swing with a blanket over her lap.

"Right here, little lady," Bernie calls with a smile. Her voice alone halts the girl's first step into the house and she swings around with glee.

"Momma!" She runs up to Bernie and throws her arms around her. Bernie is her life. Bernie has given her everything she needs and she wonders why Pastor Affie thinks anything else is better than what they already have. Their small home, where the wood is almost rotted out, with the view of the larger Ashton house, is all that is needed to make a home feel fine. For years and years Rachel would speak of that little house as the time in her life when happiness, comfort, and safety all met in one place.

"I missed you," Rachel says with a smile.

"I missed you, baby. Did you have fun?" Bernie looks at Affie and Clarine who are walking up the steps with the little girl's bags.

"Yeah!"

"Good. Why don't you run inside and make somethin' to eat while I talk with the pastor."

"Okay, momma."

When the child is gone, Affie sets the bag down by the front door with palms that are sweating even though there is no chance that Bernie knows anything. "How are you feelin', Bernie?"

"Not sure. The doctor isn't quite sure what I've got."

"Is there anythin' we can do to help?" Clarine asks as she sits on the chair next to the old woman.

"You've done enough."

"Well, Bernie we are here for you."

"I know you are." Bernie looks contemplative as she stares into the striped evening sky. "Thank you for taking care of her."

A week goes by before they hear a heavy knock on the front door. Bernie throws a damp rag over her shoulder as she answers it with a smile. A large man with a thick mustache stands with his hands behind his back holding a briefcase.

"Can I help you?" Bernie asks.

"Good mornin'. My name is Bill Manchuron." Bernadette immediately picks up on his New York accent through the screen door.

"Yes?"

"Well, ma'am, I believe that you have Rachel Anne Praline here, is that correct?"

Immediately she crosses her arms and furrows her eyebrows. "Why do you want to know?"

"Well, ma'am, I'm afraid I have some bad news."

"What kind of bad news?"

"I met your child in the city just last week---"

She interrupts with a deep breath, "---I'm sorry, did you say the city? Well, there it is. You just got the wrong girl."

"No, I'm afraid I don't. Can I come in?"

"No, sir, you can't. Not until you tell me what you want."

"You see, after meeting her---" Before he can continue, Rachel walks through the foyer with flowers in her hands until she sees Bill and they drop to the ground and scatter. Her small frame seems paralyzed by the presence of the man at the door and Bernie grinds her teeth with anger. "Good morning, Rachel. Your momma doesn't seem to believe that you were in the city just the other day. You want to help me here?"

Bernie looks at Rachel with question.

"Affie and Clarine took me there to sing," Rachel reluctantly explains.

If you know Bernie, you know there is nothing scarier than when she is quiet and at this moment, her silence is terrifying. Fumes are nearly spewing out of her ears and she tries to hold it in as she looks back at the man in front of her. "What do ya want, Mr. Manchuron?"

"Well, I'm afraid Bernie that I was a little concerned about the child. She was singing in clubs and stayin' out till early hours of the mornin'. So, I am sorry to say that I did a little searchin'. It just didn't seem right what was happenin' to this child, and I wanted to make sure that she was getting the best possible care."

"And she is. By me."

"But ma'am, no offense, she wasn't with you…" He shakes his head and pulls his briefcase in front of him. "No mind to that, but I did some searching and found that you have still not adopted this child."

"Rachel is mine. I don't care what the papers say."

"Well, unfortunately, the State does care and when I told them what I saw, they too, decided it seemed unfit for the child to be stay-ing with you."

"Now you look here!" Bernie waves her finger at the man, but stops suddenly as her other hand flies to her chest. "Now, you…" she starts again, but then she winces and catches the door jamb, leaning against it.

"Ma'am, are you okay?" Bill asks with a quick step forward.

Rachel runs to Bernie and looks into the woman's eyes. Bernie sounds as though her breathing is pinched and she struggles to pull the air in and out. The older woman keeps her hand on her chest and squeezes her fingers tight around her thick skin.

"Momma?" Rachel asks as tears come to her eyes.

"Get Doctor Avery," Bernie whispers.

Rachel finds Affie in just minutes, "Come now! There's something wrong. Momma says bring Dr. Avery."

Affie drops the rake in his hands and races off to find the doctor. When Rachel makes it back home, Bill Manchuron is still there with his briefcase and Bernie is now lying completely on her back, looking up.

"Momma," Rachel kneels by her side.

"I'll be fine, Rachel. I'll be fine."

When Affie reaches the porch, his heart drops when he sees Bill Manchuron. "What are you doin' here?" Affie asks.

"Come on!" Bill hollers, pointing to Bernie lying on the ground. "We have to take care of her."

Doctor Avery hurries up the steps with his medicine bag and kneels beside Bernie. She can barely speak and yet he can see that she is aware of his presence. "We have to move her to a better place out of the heat."

They need more help. Two more men are found pulling weeds around the Ashton estate and together they move the old woman to her room. After an hour, Doctor Avery comes out shaking his head. "She's not going to make it through the night, Rachel. You remember how Mrs. Ashton went to be with the Lord? Come with me now." Rachel nods her head and takes the doctor's hand. Together they make the sad walk, but as Clarine begins to follow, the doctor stops her with his hand. "Bernie only wants to speak with Rachel." She seems slightly offended as they walk away.

Soon, the doctor closes the door behind them. Rachel stiffens and holds onto the table when she sees Bernie laying still. Fear grips her insides and her tears seem to be in a race down her cheeks.

The doctor hushes his voice until she can barely hear him. "Rachel, there will be times in your life when you will see death. It's natural. We're all gonna die. I know it's hard and that you might be afraid of seein' your momma like she is, but you have to see her. You'll never feel right about it if you don't."

Rachel only nods. There isn't much that a seven-year-old can say. She takes small steps and finally reaches the side of the bed.

"Momma," Rachel whispers.

Bernie opens her eyes and looks tenderly at the little girl. "Child, you have to listen to me. There is no time to be scared or wonder about death. It is what it is, and there is much to do before it happens. It's your turn now. You are seven years old—practically an adult," Bernie gives the little girl a wink and a smile. "I have been praying that God would protect you. In fact, I believe, long before you were born, he sent someone to protect you. Now that I can't do it, it's your turn." Bernie turns her head to Doctor Avery who is standing near the window with his hands behind his back, resigned to the fact that he will always watch his friends pass away. "Doctor Avery, bring me those papers I had you find."

Her voice is not as smooth as normal, rather it is as though something inside of her is restricting it from coming out. Every so often she presses on her chest with pain and Rachel holds her breath waiting for her momma's pain to pass. The doctor hands Bernie the papers she asked for and Bernie hands them to Rachel. "Here is everything about you, baby. Whatever you do, don't let anybody take this away from you. This is where your life began and you deserve to keep it by your side."

"Momma, is that man gonna take me away?"

"No, he isn't. You can't let him."

Suddenly, as though the strong child can't hold it in anymore, she begins to cry. "I don't want you to go, momma. I don't want you to die."

"I know, baby. I know," she says as large tears stream down her fleshy cheeks.

Bernie grows weaker and weaker as the hours pass. While the doctor and the child watch her fight, it is clear that her heart does not want to go. She loves her child and has done right by her in every way. Now death is there like a thief at her door.

"Rachel…" she says softly, "there is always a reason for everything. Remember that. Wherever God takes you, it is because it was meant to be. There is no way that you can stop it or change it. It will happen as it should. You hear me?"

Rachel nods and then lays her head on Bernie's shoulder. "I'm gonna miss you, Momma," Rachel cries.

"But you're gonna do just fine. I love you, baby." Bernie grows quieter and quieter. "Go on out there and send Affie in."

"I don't want to leave."

"Come on now. I have to talk to him. Send him in here."

Not long after Rachel exits, Affie enters looking eager to talk with Bernie. "Bernie, how you feeling?"

"Don't talk to me so sweetly. You're a damn fool."

Surprised by her words he looks at Doctor Avery who only shakes his head. "What are you saying, Bernie?"

"Did you take my little girl to sing in clubs?"

Affie swallows his embarrassment hard. "Yes, I did, Bernie. But you have to know we met some good people there and they want---"

"Listen to me, it is your fault that man out there wants Rachel. It is your fault that he is going to take her from this place."

"Who? Bill?"

"He doesn't feel as though we are taking care of Rachel as we should and now the State wants to take the child. Honestly, right now I'm not so sure it isn't a good idea. Take her as far away from you."

"Bernie, I--"

"--Don't say anything else. It is your job to make this right. You make sure she gets a good home."

"What about us, Bernadette? Clarine and I would take her in."

"So you can send her to the wolves? Not a chance. No. You will find her a good home. And Affie?" She lifts her finger in the air calling him closer to her. So, he leans forward. "I believe I will be watching and if I find that you have done anything that I don't like, even in the slightest, I'll make sure that you are haunted every day of your life."

"Yes, ma'am."

Hours pass and each person stands around without saying a word. It is as though they are all just waiting to hear her soul leave as if her large personality would be loud as it exits this world. Rachel holds on to her. Then, in the middle of the night, when the house is silent, Rachel wakes up to Bernie's gasps. Instantly, the child calls the doctor from his cot.

"Rachel," the doctor says, "you must say your goodbyes. Would you like to pray for Bernie?" Rachel nods. Doctor Avery, like a dry weathered board, closes his eyes. Together they pray for Bernie and just as they say amen, Bernie's pain stops. Rachel holds her breath as Doctor Avery leans over the bed and closes Bernie's eyes.

"Momma!" Rachel cries out, unable to stop herself. "Momma!"

The doctor doesn't try to quiet her down. Instead, she cries until she has no more energy. The next day many of the men from church come to carry Bernadette to the parlor. As they prepare for the funeral, Clarine and Rachel look through Bernie's closet to see what they might dress her in. When Rachel finds the red hat with blue feathers spraying from one side, she climbs her cupboards to get it.

"What's that honey?" Clarine asks.

"I want her to wear this," Rachel says as she walks from the room.

"But honey, we're putting her in a purple dress." Clarine rushes after the little girl.

"I don't care. I want her to wear this one."

"Okay," Clarine says as Rachel walks away.

Bernie's funeral is the first time that Rachel doesn't want to sing. Many people ask and each time she says no. The morning is clean and crisp. The only person that Rachel wants to see is Simone who is the first person to come to Rachel's side. With fingers intertwined, Simone looks at Rachel.

"You alright?" Simone asks.

Rachel nods, but doesn't say anything, otherwise she would cry. The two friends hold on to each other the entire morning. Only a couple of times does Rachel look across the green grass, over the high flowers piled on the raw pine coffin, to catch a glimpse of Bill Manchuron. Just the sight of him makes her anxious and she cowers into Simone.

Chapter Nine

Before the week is over, Bill Manchuron brings legal papers to back up his case. Affie's hands are tied. The following Saturday afternoon, Rachel walks out of Affie and Clarine's home with a soft teddy bear in hand. Families from the neighboring homes come outside and cry as they watch her. They are losing a part of their family.

She looks from side to side to find Simone. Her heart pulses in her toes as though she is walking in boiling water. Even with her hair piled on top of her head, small trails of sweat glisten on her forehead. Bill throws her things in his car and pressures her to hurry up. She hugs Affie and Clarine. A feeling of panic pours over her when she can't find her friend. Carefully she climbs into the man's automobile until she hears the cry. Simone is running down the street at full speed. Rachel begins to cry and jumps from the vehicle.

"Rachel!" Simone yells, her skinny legs running as fast as she can.

Bill prods Rachel to be quick about it.

"You couldn't leave until I said goodbye," Simone says as she throws her arms around her best friend.

"I don't want to go!" Rachel cries.

"I'm gonna come get you someday," Simone says. "My momma said that we're gonna find you so we can take care of you."

"She said that?"

"Yeah."

Bill comes to Rachel's side and gives her a frustrated glare. "We have to go now, Rachel. Say good bye."

"I don't wanna go!" Rachel cries. She grabs Simone and won't let go. Bill wraps his thick fingers around her arm and pulls. Yet Rachel and Simone's strength is surprising and soon he has to lift her in his arms to try and pull them apart. "Simone!" Rachel cries and screams as Bill finally pulls the best friends from one another and carries her to the car.

"Momma says don't worry!" Simone cries out.

§ § §

Everyone watches Bill's car roll away leaving clouds of dust behind the back wheels, while Rachel peeks out through the window. Simone stands there with her hands on her hips as if she were an old soul in a child's body. Her chest is rising and falling with such intensity, and her jaw is clenching down so tightly, that she can feel the explosion to come. One by one, the people from the neighborhood begin walking away, chatting with each other, and shaking their heads, however Simone stands there for several minutes.

When she turns around, she sees Affie standing there also watching, with Clarine not too far behind. This is the first time in her life that Simone understood exactly where her rage should be directed, but for a moment, makes it clear with just her eyes. As Affie breathes out, he looks down and actually jumps back from the glare.

"You." Simone growls.

"What . . ." Affie stutters. "Simone . . . I . . I . ."

Simone carefully walks up to the grown man and although she's tall at such a young age, he still towers over her in size, but is dwarfed by her confidence. "Don't think I don't know what you did, Pastor Affie. Don't assume my age makes me blind." She moves closer, until Clarine isn't sure whether she should intervene. "You may believe God will forgive you . . . but I will not. And I will make sure that you never forget what you did here."

"Simone, I . . ."

"You what? You gonna get her back? You know where he's taking her?"

Affie is speechless and a bit afraid. Finally, Simone passes by him and Clarine, with tense arms and the sadness beginning to boil over into emotion, which she's desperate not to show to him. Yet after a few steps, she stops and turns, staring both of them down.

"I'll never forgive you. Not ever."

Chapter Ten

1998

Gramma stops talking when the door opens and one of the nurses comes in with a large smile on her face. "Mrs. Johnson, you ready for those tests we're gonna do?"

I hadn't realized it, but the room is growing warm, so I walk to the window air-conditioning unit. I dread the thought that I might never get the rest of the story. So, I keep my eyes on the women while I try to check the knobs of the cooler.

"Tests?" Gramma asks.

"Yes, honey. It should only take an hour or two."

"Oh, alright. Bobby?" She looks around the room as though she can't find me so I step into her line of sight.

"Yes, Gramma?"

"I don't want to take up your afternoon. Go on home."

"Okay, Gramma." I can hear the sound of my voice drop three decibels in disappointment.

The nurse helps Gramma to her feet by pulling her thick arm and when she stands, I think of something. "Can I come back tonight, Gramma?"

"Oh, you don't have to do that just to make an old woman happy."

"Come on, Gramma, you know that isn't the case."

"Bobby, make sure to tell your sister that Alpert called yesterday. She'll be wanting to know that."

I shake my head. Alpert hasn't been a boyfriend of my sister's for over a decade. She is now married to a good man named Sean and has two kids running around.

"Okay, Gramma." I smile even though underneath, I want to kick the chair across the room.

"If you go see your daddy, come back here and I'll tell you more about Rachel."

My hopes are high. I nod and then when they shut the door behind them, I turn to the CD player. Gramma will never know. I pull out the disc and place it in the case. In my car, before I turn on Rachel's music, I call my momma. "Ma?" I say when she picks up the phone.

"Oh Bobby, did you see Gramma?"

"Yeah, I'm just leaving now."

"Just leaving? Honey, I didn't mean for you to have such a miserable afternoon."

"Ahhh, no, it wasn't that miserable. I actually enjoyed it."

"Well, good. Lou, Shandra, and Jimmy are here. I think it might be nice if you came by."

I sigh heavily and lean my head back against the seat. "Okay, Momma. I'm coming."

On the drive over I turn the music up loud and listen to Rachel sing to me. My breathing slows and my body is no longer tense. What a strange relationship this is turning out to be. The closest I've been in ten years to finding the girl of my dreams, and she is just a voice on the radio.

At the hospital, I head to the Medical/Surgical floor and find room 15. I peer through the small crack in the door, but my mother's radar is on fire so she yells at me from the chair beside my father's bed, "Come in, Bobby!"

I nudge my way in and although I had prepared myself for the curiosity and chastising of my brothers and sister, I had not prepared myself for the sight of my father. He appears small and thin suddenly, with the copious amounts of wires surrounding him while he sleeps. For the first time since all of this began, I feel my first bout of emotion that I have to fight to control. The knot in my throat reminds me of how serious this might actually be.

My younger brother, Jimmy, a successful doctor, is the first to come to my side and he wraps his arms around me. "Sorry that you were the first with grandma duty today."

"Oh no, it was alright actually." I nod as I hit his chest with my palm. He has never outgrown me physically for which I am grateful.

My other brother Lou, an accomplished lawyer, grins as he wraps his arms around me. "You're looking really good, Bobby."

"Thanks," I say with a nod.

Shandra, the sibling that I am closest to in age and relationship, is next in my arms, and I can see that she has been crying. When we were kids, she never left our daddy's side. When I cradle her in my arms she begins to sob.

"It'll be okay." I kiss her head.

Her brown eyes are soaked until mascara seeps down her cheeks. "It's good to see you, Bobby."

"You too."

When I look up, Ma is crying just from the sight of us. So, I pull away from Shandra and walk to her side. Then I take my dad's hand by his thick fingers that he passed on to me. The fact that he's not aware enough to throw insults my way is disturbing.

"Has the doctor said much?"

"We won't know anything until Wednesday morning,"

Momma says.

"Three days?"

"Yeah. There's a specialist out of town that hasn't had a chance to look at his tests," Lou explains.

"Come on, Jimmy, you're nearly a full-fledged doctor, can't you tell us anything?" I say with a grin. Everyone else laughs, but Jimmy. He is quiet for a minute, then shakes his head. "I'm not a heart specialist."

"I'm just kidding." In order to keep us from going into battle, I change the subject. "He looks peaceful without his usual hard edge."

All of us are quiet as we stare at the man who usually owns the room. After a while, we talk about how Jimmy ran out on a surgery to be here quickly while his girlfriend Tiffany stayed behind to finish her finals for college. My brother Lou is in the middle of a very high-profile divorce case with two celebrities who are at each other's throats. He has a couple more cases on the side, but he really doesn't need many—one is enough to pay for a year of expenses, and then some. And Shandra just finished an art show in New York where she nearly sold out and one piece sold for more than I make in two years.

"What about you, Booby." Lou has always enjoyed this ridiculous nickname that makes me so angry all I can see is red.

"I don't have much coming up so my boss was fine with letting me go. I have four articles in print this month, but they'll most likely get tagged straight to the back of the magazine." Shandra places a hand on my arm for support which only irritates me.

After a couple of hours when we have stared at dad long enough, I finally pull my keys from my pocket.

"You leavin'?" Lou asks.

"Well, I promised Gramma that I would come back tonight and just spend some time with her before she goes to bed."

"Oh, well isn't that nice of you," Momma says, seeming to not truly believe it.

"The good grandson, huh?" Lou asks with a raised eyebrow. "Is her nurse good looking or something?"

"Nah. She's remembered a lot today so it's nice being able to have a conversation with her."

"Gramma Johnson, has remembered somethin'?" Ma exclaims. She leans over to my dad, "See honey, miracles happen."

I hurry out of the cold hospital and into the warm humidity. Disappointment is what I am headed for and I know it. Rachel, her silky hum filling my car the moment I turn it on, has lost the only mother she's ever known, and I know Bill Manchuron is no good. From the way Gramma describes it—Rachel senses it too.

On my way, I stop and grab a bouquet of flowers. This isn't a typical move of mine to be so kind to my usually boring grandma, but in just one afternoon I have suddenly been reminded of the affable, interesting woman she once was.

I sit for a moment after pulling to the curb wondering if I should give the CD back. "One more day," I whisper and leave it where it is.

When I walk into her room, she is now sitting up in her bed with a pink shirt that looks more like a muumuu than an actual shirt. Her eyes light up when she sees me and I hold the flowers out to her. "I thought you might like to brighten up your room."

"Bobby, Bobby, you are a sweet boy. When did you get into town?"

The flowers drop just a bit in my hand. "Yesterday. But I was here this morning. Don't you remember?" I fill an empty vase with water and set the flowers inside.

"You were?"

"Yeah. We talked for a long time."

"We did?" Her face turns sad. "Oh, well, how are you?"

"Fine," I say as I sit down in the soft chair beside her bed and rest my elbows on her mattress.

"You still dating Sadie?"

"Not for a few years now." Her mind holds on to these questions like a June bug to a screen. I suppose love is big enough to pierce the dementia.

"You datin' anyone?"

You could say I am. When you want to know every detail about the person's life hoping that in the end, in some way we can be together, I'd say that's something. Ridiculous. I am being ridiculous and I know it, but something in me doesn't care. I am along for the ride; just enjoying the sparks of wonder that Rachel's story gives me.

"Hey, Gramma you were telling me about Rachel Anne Praline. Do you remember?"

"Rachel?"

"Yeah."

"No, I don't remember that." She had to. How can I not know what happened to Rachel? Gramma dusts off a crumb from her chest. "What was I telling you?"

"Well, she was born an orphan, but Dick and Sylvia found a home for her with Bernie. Affie and Clarine take her to New York City when they shouldn't. Bernie dies and now she's on her way to live with Bill Manchuron and leaving Simone behind."

"Oh my goodness, I must have been ramblin' on a long time."

"No, I loved it. I came back so you can continue."

"You did, honey? You want to know about Rachel?"

"Yes. Rachel, Simone, Affie, Clarine . . . everyone."

She laughs. "Oh, I'm not surprised. People were always just drawn to Rachel."

"You've mentioned that."

"Well, she and Simone were devastated to leave each other. Neither ate, drank, or slept without thinking about the other . . . for years really. Rachel hadn't a clue of where she was going in the back of Bill Manchuron's car. It seemed her comfortable life with Bernie was gone so quickly."

1915

Rachel silently cries in the backseat as they make the five-hour drive to New York. Horses, cows, small towns, fields, and many other things pass by, but most of the time she can't see past her tears. Since they left New Jersey, Bill has yet to be kind and he speeds down the road until she grips the seat beneath her with her fingernails. She hugs her teddy bear tight in her little arms until its stuffing nearly busts out of its seams. "Momma, come save me," she prays.

Earlier when Bill spoke with Affie, he was clear about what needed to be done. "I'll be taking her to the government building where I have secured a foster family to take her in." Rachel wondered what a new family would be like, and her heart pumped so hard it thumped in her ears.

It isn't until they drive down a residential street that Rachel looks at Bill. Still, even with her blue eyes filled with questions, he makes no effort to tell her where they might be going. Bill circles the cul-de-sac of pretty homes, yet there is one, rough and overgrown, that doesn't fit the well-manicured area. Sure enough, Bill Manchuron pulls into the driveway of this neglected brick home. Her small hands shake uncontrollably, and she closes her eyes to picture Bernie's smile and red hat.

"Well, we're here," Bill grumbles.

"Where?"

"Home. This is where you are gonna stay. I'm gonna take care of you." With that, he swings his car door open and waits for her to step out.

She doesn't move. "I thought you were taking me to the government buildin'."

"I already worked it out with them and I'm your new daddy."

Tears flow from Rachel's eyes and her heart races. She doesn't move a muscle and Bill notices. "Get out!" he hollers. However, she's paralyzed with fear. Even her hands are stiff and rigid around her bear. Finally, Bill reaches in and yanks her small arm until she nearly falls out of the car, leaving red marks.

He mumbles as he grabs his things, which leaves Rachel a moment to look around. The neighborhood is quiet except for just a few voices behind her. When she turns, there are three teenage boys across the street, standing around the bed of a truck while they laugh and carry on. Rachel watches for a while. Her life, in just weeks, has been turned inside out, but these boys show her that there is still laughter somewhere. All life has not ended, just hers.

One of them seems to be the leader since he is tall and handsome with deep hazel eyes and brown hair, but it is mostly his confidence that is impossible to ignore. They are dressed in smart school clothes, but the buttons of their jackets are undone and their hats sit on the hood of the truck. It is quite improper and Rachel likes it. She looks down at her dress, jacket, and feels the hat on top of her head. It is fairly warm outside, and she would still love to take off her hat.

Bill kicks a bucket with anger when he can't seem to find something he needs, but it rolls back into his way and he growls. When two of the boys walk away, the handsome one remains. As he reaches over his truck and grabs his hat, he looks up, noticing Rachel. Instantly, their eyes lock. When he raises his hand to wave, she does the same. Maybe she wishes he will run across the street and help her understand what has just happened to her life or maybe she simply wants him to know that she is there, whatever it is, the thought of him going inside his house without her makes her small lungs constrict.

"Get inside!" Bill yells harshly when he turns around and sees the boy looking at her. She jumps at the sound and quickly does as she is told.

§ § §

The boy across the street is named Levi Price. He watches the little girl with confusion since he's never seen a child with this particular neighbor. In fact, this neighbor has never really said much to anyone; rather he lives like a hermit and yells at anyone who walks on his messy lawn. The blonde little girl is unexpected, for certain.

Levi is a rich kid, which is not common in 1915. His family moved from England to New York after his father's business merger only a year and a half before, against Levi's wishes. Despite making friends and having a girlfriend, nothing makes him miss Surrey more than chilly nights that remind him of home. This is why he finds it strange as his friends leave, that this little girl is wearing a thin coat that is poorly buttoned and has a suitcase. Her eyes are gravely sad, which is why he raises his hand to say hello. Levi doesn't pay attention to much of anything most of the time, but he can't seem to look away.

Since moving, his rebellious streak meant that instead of going to school, he made love to his girlfriend Vanity Carol, and instead of working like most kids his age, he often chose trouble like drinking and gambling at bars. Which is probably why he steps toward the girl when the man in the garage yells at her angrily. Levi's selfish mood is distracted for a moment by his unexpected curiosity. The girl does as she's commanded and hurries inside the cluttered house but takes one last look before she disappears.

One of the next-door neighbors, Kayla, a middle-aged woman with a crush on Levi's father, appears on the front lawn to pick some of her blooming roses.

"What are you doing, honey?" Kayla asks with a flirtatious smile.

She jolts Levi from his thoughts, and he turns back to the house. "Uhh, nothing." Just before he steps inside, he stops, "Excuse me, Kayla?"

"Yes?"

"Do you know much about this neighborhood?"

"I know enough." She smiles.

"Who's the man that lives across the street?"

"I believe his name is Bill."

"You believe?"

"Well, I've only spoken to him once. Why?"

"Is he married?"

"Umm, no. I don't believe so. Never seen a woman there."

"No kids then?"

"No, honey. Why are you interested in all of this stuff?"

"Never mind. There's no reason. Thank you though."

"You're welcome." As Levi walks away she shouts, "Tell your daddy hi for me."

Levi doesn't answer, but instead walks inside where he freezes in thought at the hook where he hangs his hat in the foyer. After a moment, he walks to the living room window and stares at Bill's house.

His mother, Paula, is a beautiful woman with plenty of confidence, except for when it comes to her rebellious son. She hesitantly comes closer. "What are you looking at?"

"There's a little girl at that man's home and I'm just wondering why she's there."

"Maybe she's a niece or something. Why are you interested?"

Levi looks at his mother and is immediately irritated by her presence. "I'm not."

"You look like you are."

Within seconds his wall is built and he walks away. "I'm not."

"Dinner's almost ready," she calls sweetly after him.

"I'm not hungry."

§ § §

Rachel sits on Bill's couch holding her bear in her arms afraid to move. He ignores her if she says nothing and yells at her if she says something, so she remains silent while he goes about his business until she falls asleep. Before long, she wakes to another voice in the room. A new man, who doesn't resemble Bill in the slightest, stands at the coat closet near the front door. He is short and skinny with a wiry mustache on his top lip. He wears a terribly high-top hat and a plaid scarf with a deep red running through it. Just his presence alone makes her rise quickly.

Surprisingly, he turns to her with a smile. "Well, you must be Rachel. Bill's told me so much."

Rachel ignores him as Bill walks into the room. She looks at Bill with pleading eyes. "Mr. Manchuron, are you going to take me to my new home?"

"I already told you, kid; this is your new home. I'm adoptin' you. Don't be rude to Mr. Penny. He's gonna be helpin' you."

"Helpin' me?"

"That's right," Mr. Penny says with a smile. "Bill says that you can sing. Can you show me?"

He is unexpectedly kind.

"What do you want me to sing?" Rachel asks.

"Anything you want," Mr. Penny responds and sits across from her on a large chair with worn out arms that squeaks.

"I really don't want to, Mr. Penny."

Before Rachel can understand what is happening, Bill rushes forward and grabs her arm until she thinks the bone might crack and she lets out a cry of pain when he forces her to her feet.

"You sing for the man," Bill yells.

When his large hand lets go of hers, she can still feel the deep pain beneath her shoulder and tries to rub it out. With a knot in her throat, she doesn't know how she is going to be able to sing. In fact, she is sure that her voice will shake worse than her legs. Bill threatens her again and again, until she quietly does so. Although the life isn't in her voice, she sings a spiritual that is soft and rich. It reminds her of Bernie, which only makes her tears fall faster. When she is done, Mr. Penny claps.

"That was brilliant." He smiles a genuine smile. "You're gonna go far, Rachel. You really are."

"May I go to bed?" she asks even though she hasn't eaten anything since breakfast.

Bill grumbles as he walks her down the hallway and then tosses her bag in a small room with a window facing the street.

"Tomorrow you're goin' to school and then you're gonna start training with Mr. Penny."

"Trainin'?"

"Singing. We're gonna make some money, you and me. That's what we're gonna do…" he looks at her for a moment as though he doesn't know what to say to the small child who is now taking up residence in his home. "Just a warning, kid . . . don't even try to leave or I will find you. I have spies all over the place and you will get the worst beating of your life if you try to leave. You hear me?"

"Yes, sir."

"Sir? Hmm. I like that. Good night then." He is finally gone.

That night Rachel lies in her room, cuddling with her bear, and concentrating on images of Bernadette. The hours seem to last days until finally the light of morning begins to choke out the darkness. She steps tentatively out into the hall. Bill has yet to come from his bedroom so she tiptoes past. When she reaches the kitchen, a thought hits her that she can run. He isn't up yet. There will be no way that he can find her. Yet she has no money and she is starving.

She notices a loaf of bread in the breadbox. Running to it, she quickly grabs a handful and stuffs it in her mouth, then hurries to the icebox and throws open the door. Not much is inside except for beer. Just as she's about to shut the door, she catches sight of a small jar of jelly, from which she takes a bit after finding a butter knife in one of the drawers. The taste is intoxicating and for a moment, she thinks she might eat the entire loaf.

When her tummy is full, she walks around the home. It has been so poorly taken care of compared to every other home around the neighborhood. There are holes along the walls, a couple of the windows are cracked, and the floor is so scuffed that the dirt can never be cleaned out of the grooves.

"What are you doing?" The heavy voice makes her jump. Bill

stands, large and unkempt, at the end of the hallway while still trying to wake.

"Nothin'."

"It had better stay that way. I don't want you touching nothing. You got that?" he threatens.

"Yes, sir."

He walks into the kitchen leaving her alone in the living room and she breathes a sigh of relief. Before the breath can finish, she hears his yell loud enough to shake the walls. "Rachel! Come in here." Her eyes swell with tears. There is no telling what this man will do. Carefully, she follows the wall until it meets the opening of the kitchen. "Rachel!"

"Yes?"

"What is this?" His thick sausage finger roughly points at the bread on the counter.

"Bread," she answers politely.

"That's right and why is there some missing?"

She places her hand on her stomach because instantly she wants to rid herself of the evidence inside. "I was hungry, Mr. Manchuron. I needed something to eat."

"I didn't tell you that you could touch anythin'."

"I know."

She backs against the wall when he comes close. "That's my bread. Don't touch it!"

"Yes, sir. I just-]-"

With a flick, he slaps her with his palm sending her hair in front of her face. Besides the pain, she is filled with shock and horror.

"Now go get dressed. You gotta go to school." Rachel starts walking away. "Rachel," he leans close to her face, "don't you be tellin' nobody at school anything, ya hear me? That little friend you got at home . . . what was her name? Simone? The one you held so tight to . . . I know where she lives. You talk to anyone and I'll be sure to take care of her. You understand me?"

"Yes, sir."

Before long, Rachel walks out the front door with her bag on her arm. She waits for Bill to walk her to school and when he sees her standing there, he pushes her away with his foot. "Get going."

"I don't know where to go."

"Just follow them other kids."

He points to a group of kids across the street, in an open field, that have books and bags and are clearly walking to the school house. Catching up to them will be near impossible, but to appease Bill she heads in that direction.

All she can do is watch the other children disappear and the tears come fast. Unexpectedly, she hears voices and she hastily dries her face with her sleeve. With a quick turn, she sees the boy from across the street. He is driving in his truck very slowly and smiling at an older girl who is walking on the side of the road. "Come on. Get in and let's go."

"Not today, Levi. I'm working. Remember, I graduated and have to be an adult now."

"That's why you can come with me. You're not like those young girls. Come on, Vanity. Come on."

Rachel can't stop staring at the exchange and his unique accent intrigues her.

"Bye, Levi." Vanity waves as she reaches an office. With a sweet smile she bids him goodbye and steps inside. Levi stops his car in the middle of the street and smiles at the closed door, until he catches sight of Rachel walking alone. He steps on the gas and pulls up beside her.

"Where you off to, kid?" Levi yells out the window.

Rachel's heart skips. She ignores him, and stays quiet. Even though she had wiped at the tears, it seems Levi can tell.

"Where are you off to?" he asks a little less playful than before.

"I'm trying to get to school." She works desperately hard, but she just can't say it without a small quiver in her chin.

"Okay. Do you know where it is?"

"No, sir," she says quietly.

He hesitates. "I really don't want to drive by that school. If the teacher sees my car, she'll force me in or tell my parents."

"It's okay. Where is it?" Rachel asks.

He thinks for a moment, then shrugs. "But maybe I can give up one day of gallivanting to help you out." He grins. Rachel doesn't know what to feel. Her life has just been thrown about as if in a twister and set down again in a strange land. He's a stranger, but no worse than Bill. "Well, I can give you a ride if you'd like?"

Rachel looks at him carefully.

"I'm not going to hurt you, I swear. Besides, I guess I'll go to school today, too," he sighs as he raises his arms up along the back of his front seat. After a moment he looks at her again with a raised eyebrow. "What do you think? It's cold today and that jacket doesn't look warm enough."

She is extremely cold and her toes have gone numb, so, she takes his offer. He opens the door for her from the inside and she climbs in without a lot of trouble. This is the first time that Rachel takes in the smell of Levi, something that she later would refer to as the best smell in the world until the day she dies. For whatever reason, it makes her feel comfortable with him right away.

"What's your name?" he asks.

"Rachel Anne Praline," she says nervously.

"I'm Levi Price. It's nice to meet you…" he smiles at her, but she only fidgets. "So how old are you, kid?"

"I'm seven. I'll be eight in a couple of months."

"Eight? That's a good age. I liked it."

"You did?"

"Yeah. My dad always took me fishing that year."

"How old are you now?"

"Almost seventeen…" They are quiet for a moment, but it isn't awkward, it is more like Levi has something to ask and he is trying to figure out how to ask it. "You live in the house across from me now?"

"I guess."

He chuckles. "What does that mean?"

"I didn't know until yesterday that I was going to live there."

Levi glances at her with curiosity, but he doesn't want to pry.

"Why do you sound like that?" she asks.

"Like what?"

"You don't sound like me."

"Oh, well, my family is from Surrey, England. I moved here just a few years ago. This is how we talk in England."

"I like it," Rachel grins.

As they turn a corner, Levi points out the schoolhouse. "This is your school."

"Where do you go?"

He points just a few hundred feet on the other side of the street. Two schoolhouses, mirror images of each other, sit on the opposite sides of the street. "And that's mine."

"You should be almost done with school." Rachel remembers that kids back home never made it even to fourteen. They had to stop school and work. There had been no other choice.

"This year is my last."

"Wow."

Levi pulls the car to a stop and turns it off. "You impressed?"

"I just never met anyone who's done every grade. How'd you do it?"

"Well, I haven't done it yet, but my parents have plenty of money and I didn't have to work."

"Is that how you got this truck?"

Again, he laughs. "Yep, sure is."

"You sure are lucky."

A strange look comes on his face as though he must digest the food she's just given him. "I guess I am, Rachel. Well, come on. Let's go to school." He meets her on the other side of the truck and walks a short way, then Rachel walks to her schoolhouse and he to his. Before either of them can reach their destination, Levi looks back.

"Rachel," he calls out. She stops. "If you wait at my car after school, I'll give you a ride home."

Rachel smiles. "Thank you."

§ § §

Giving Rachel a ride to school every day gives Levi a reason to go. Every morning she waits patiently for him at his car door and every afternoon she waits for him to come out of the schoolhouse. It has been so long since he has gone to school consistently that being caught up on work strangely makes him feel better about himself. Even his teacher questions his sudden reappearance. Although his relationship with his parents is still rough, he likes to party at the clubs, and he likes to gamble all night; at least one thing is figuring itself out.

He feels a connection to the little girl. When he makes her laugh it is contagious, and although she doesn't speak much of her life at home, she asks him about his. One thing he won't explain to a child is his love life, but beyond that, he answers every question.

On the other hand, Rachel has now gone weeks in a school where she hasn't a soul to talk to. It is her choice of course. When she hadn't spoken after the first week, the other children begin to whisper to one another that she is weird. They ignore her or throw things at her when she isn't looking. Every day she thinks of Simone and wonders when her friend will be coming for her. She never tells Levi anything about her life in New Jersey or New York.

When she gets home, Mr. Penny is always there to teach her more songs. For hours she learns what he calls New Orleans Jazz. Even though Rachel likes singing, the number of hours that she spends studying songs is tedious for a seven-year-old. If she shows any sort of laziness, Bill is there to straighten her out. It takes only one slap across the face, or push to the ground, to let her know she must stay on task.

Then the first night comes when Bill pulls her out of bed at ten o'clock. She barely has time to wake up before they are in his car—Bill, Mr. Penny, and herself. Her eyes dip closed as she tries to stay awake in the back seat. They park on the side of the road on a main strip of town. Restaurants and clubs pulsate with people and suddenly Rachel is wide awake.

As Bill pushes his way through the dark club, Mr. Penny holds on to Rachel's hand. A heavyset man comes to Bill with a serious face and although Rachel can't hear anything they are saying, it seems as though they talk about her. Finally, the large owner nods and turns to a stage that is set up not far away. A band is playing, although it doesn't sound or look like the men from Eubie Blake's band. It can't compare, and even at seven years old, Rachel notices the difference. Eubie Blake and James Reese Europe were brilliant and these musicians are only so-so.

Bill turns to her with a stone-like expression. "Get up there and sing. Mr. Penny will tell you what songs."

Rachel looks around the room realizing what he expects of her. Mr. Penny bends over so that she can hear him. "Are you alright?" he asks in his epicene way.

"What am I goin' to sing?"

"Is there anything that you would like to sing?"

"No."

"Okay, well, let's just sing "In the Sweet By and By"."

There isn't much else the child can do. So, she follows the men past the crowd and takes the stairs up to the stage. The owner steps to the microphone and it takes a while for the mass to quiet down. Finally, after his prodding, the mixed company begins to pay attention. "There's quite a hum about the singer we're bringing up tonight. We heard she's good, but I guess we'll see. Rachel Anne Praline."

It isn't much of an intro, but Rachel steps to the microphone anyway. The crowd is confused. The club that has just been hopping with excitement and lust is so quiet they can hear the rats racing in the walls. A flutter of tiny conversations start. It is nearly eleven o'clock at night and the small child should have been home in bed. The band plays and Rachel sings. The curious looks on the people's faces turn to delight, and they begin to call out praises. With a voice unlike any girl her age, she moves to the beat as she has been taught, and entertains the crowd. Even with all that she has gone through, she comes alive.

When the show is over, Rachel is told that she can go to the bar and get anything she wants. People watch her as she passes and a man helps her as she climbs to the top of the barstool. The bartender comes to her with a grin.

"What can I get you, sweet thing?"

"I don't know."

"You don't got an idea of anything you'd like?"

"No, sir."

The confident young man with attractive brown eyes, who has arrived at his shift just in time to see Rachel sing, nods as though he knows what to give her. "Alright, alright . . . just wait a minute. I think I got somethin' for you."

He hands her a bowl of cherries. She watches him pour a small amount of clear liquid in a glass and follow it with something red. As he hands it to her, he gives a wink and then takes care of the next man. She looks at the drink with wide eyes and then slowly takes a sip. It is sweet just like the cherries.

"You like it, huh?" he asks.

"Yes. Thank you." It is all that she can say as she finishes off the glass. From the tall stool she watches the bouncing crowd and is mesmerized by the men's roaming hands and the women who seductively gaze with half-closed eyes. In a strange way, Rachel feels more at home in the bar than with Bill Manchuron. She likes the sea of color. People are happy and enjoying themselves under the dim lights. When the music changes, so does the dancing. Rachel can't help but notice the effect that music has on people. It is magical.

"You like it?" Rachel turns and sees a familiar pretty face. Then she remembers that her name is Vanity—Levi's girl. She is dressed in a waitress uniform with cigarettes in the pocket of her long white apron, liquor on her tray, and a white cap with a dark bow on the front. "…the dancing?"

Rachel nods. In all reality, she loves music more than life itself and she loves dancing, but above it all, the sight of everyone's hands all over each other is spellbinding.

"Most of the people that come here are good. I'm not sure why this place is the hot ticket because if people knew there were rats in the kitchen and the floors are rarely clean, they might not come back." She looks at Rachel as though she has something to say, "Where's your momma and daddy?"

"I've never had a daddy and my momma just died."

Vanity is horrified. "I'm so sorry."

Bill is now receiving money from the owner just beside the stage and they both smile as though they have cut a deal.

Vanity notices. "Then who's he? He your uncle?"

Rachel shakes her head.

"He's not your uncle?"

"No. He's gonna adopt me."

"What's he got you doing here so late?"

"He wanted me to sing, I guess."

"I'm Vanity," the woman says.

"I'm Rachel."

For a moment there is silence between them as Vanity tells the bartender what drinks she needs.

Vanity sits on the barstool next to Rachel. "You've got school tomorrow. You should be home…" she hesitates and decides not to push this subject. "Hey," Vanity grabs some napkins and throws them on her tray, "if you need anything let me know, okay."

Rachel nods and then watches the nice woman pass out drinks. Before long, Bill comes to Rachel's side. "Come on. Let's go." With a hefty push she opens the front door and finds that Mr. Penny is standing outside with a cigarette in his mouth.

"You did good," he says. "Come on. It's time to get you home."

At least five nights a week for the next six months, Rachel sings in the shadiest bars in town until nearly midnight and then every morning she makes her way to school. Most mornings Levi waits for her and gives her a ride in his car, but if he isn't there, she walks. Summer is now at its peak and her birthday passes without a soul realizing she has turned eight. When school lets out, Bill begins taking her to places that are farther away and forces her to do two shows instead of one. She sleeps in the back of his car on their way home.

Not even music can take her out of this horrible situation. It is a regular occurrence for Bill to take his frustrations out on her. Most of the time she has done nothing wrong and the times that something has been her fault are even worse. One night she is so tired that she nearly passes out while rehearsing. For that, Bill locks her in the basement for two days without food. He says, "It's the way my daddy taught me and I learned." Another time when she was late coming home from school, he sliced her bear from head to toe and left it on the doorstep. She cried for hours, never quite making it to sleep.

Chapter Eleven

1998

"You knew Rachel personally?" I ask. The story has me entranced. I haven't thought about a damn thing other than Rachel as I listen. I can picture every scenario like I have been there myself.

"I did. In the end, the whole world did."

"The poor kid."

"I never said everything about this story would be happy—tragedy mixed with some really great moments."

"I would kill him." Just hearing what he did to Rachel sends me into a rage. It feels good to be so attached to something—so protective. I look at the clock and it's nearly nine p.m. and Gramma often went to bed before that. The temptation to hide the time from my grandma is outrageous.

"Until Rachel was an old woman, she was reluctant to talk about those years of her life. I halfway think she hoped that they would disappear from her memory, but they never did. During that time, Levi kept his eyes on her. He was still up to his wild ways, but in some way having someone to care about gave him a small bit of responsibility." Gramma explains.

Levi and I feel the same way. I'm a bit jealous that he can do something about it, but the question is, will he?

1916

In 1916, the war continues and the Summer Olympics are cancelled in Berlin, John D. Rockefeller becomes the first person to a personal fortune of one billion, and Levi graduates. He spends a lot of his time with Vanity when she isn't working her two jobs. On a very hot day when his parents are out of town, Vanity comes over. She walks up in her pink dress looking pristine and perfect with her small handbag at her side. He meets her outside the door grabbing her and wrapping his arms around her waist. He catches her lips, kissing her passionately.

He turns to lead her inside the house, but just as he does, he hears the familiar sound of Rachel's door across the street slam shut. He squints beneath the glare of the sun when he looks, and Rachel, without a smile, heads down the road alone.

"Hey, Rachel!" Levi calls out quickly.

Rachel waves but continues on. Levi watches Rachel for just a moment more. Vanity, from behind, puts her arms around his waist.

"You've become quite good friends with her."

"She's sweet. Something makes me feel like I have to watch out for her."

"That doesn't sound like the rebel I know."

"Maybe my rebellious days are coming to an end." He turns around, wraps his arms around the slightly older woman, and drops his lips onto hers. When he kisses her neck, she pulls him inside and onto the couch.

"When do you have to be at work?" he asks as his breathing grows heavy.

"I've got time."

"Good." He thinks of something that makes him pause and she looks at him with question as she lay back on the couch. "I just remembered I have something to give Rachel. She never seems to be around and I need to give it to her." Again, he stares outside. His lack of concentration aggravates Vanity and she pulls on his hands so that he will be reminded of why she is there. He doesn't budge.

"Just give it to me. I'll give it to her," Vanity says.

"Why? I live across the street from her." Her statement confuses him and he hesitates before lying on top of her.

"Come on, just kiss me."

He smiles as he finally lowers himself the rest of the way and begins kissing her again. He drops his kisses down her chin and onto her chest, but suddenly he stops.

Almost as though she can read his thoughts, she rolls her eyes. "She comes into the bar all of the time."

He pulls away from her. "What do you mean? She's a kid."

"She comes in to sing."

This time he stands to his feet. "They let a child in there?"

"She's not drinking. She's singing. I know. I thought it was weird too at first, but she's good, she's really good."

"You work there at night."

"That's when she comes in."

"Why didn't you tell me?" Levi's concern is growing.

"You give the kid a ride to school. I didn't know you were her guardian."

"Well, it doesn't seem like anyone's watching out for her, now does it?"

He is starting to get angry and yet he isn't sure why. Vanity is right. Rachel isn't his responsibility, but whose responsibility is she? He has seen the way that Bill looks at her—the man doesn't care.

"You've talked to Rachel?" he asks.

"Yeah."

"What'd she say?"

Vanity thinks for a moment. "Just little things. Bill is adopting her."

"He's not related to her?"

"I wondered the same thing, but she said that he's not. She said she doesn't have a father and her mother just died and that's when Bill took her in."

Levi walks to the window distracted. Clearly annoyed by his lack of attention, Vanity stands up and grabs her purse.

"Where are you goin'?" Levi asks.

"I've got stuff to do if we aren't going to do this."

"Wait, I'm sorry. Wait—come on. It's okay. Let's go to my room."

But even as Levi tries to make love to Vanity, he can't stop thinking about his responsibility to check into the situation. He is the only one who cares about the child and somehow, he knows it is up to him. Before he knows it, Vanity leaves without the satisfaction she came for.

By the time Rachel comes back, the heat of the day is so intense that she can feel her scalp burning. Her heavy dress is terribly uncomfortable and she is nervous about getting back to Bill. It had been a long time since he sent her to the store for his things, and it had passed quickly when she couldn't find what he wanted. She searched many aisles for his hair gel and yet the kind that he asked for wasn't there. Just the thought of his impending anger is bringing her close to tears.

"Rachel!"

She hears Levi's call from across the street and sees that he is sitting on his porch. Lifting her hand in the air, she gives him a quick wave, but he shakes his head telling her that isn't enough. "Come here!"

Rachel looks at Bill's house. She knows it will be better for her to go in there, but the thought of being with Bill makes her recoil. She waits for a slow car to pass and then she hurries across the street.

Shyly, she walks up the porch.

"It's a little too hot for that coat. Your cheeks are a dangerous shade of red." Levi stands up and walks to her side.

"Bill wanted me to put it on."

"Why are you out walking on such a hot day?"

"Bill needed some things. So, he sent me to get them."

"Vanity was here earlier." He sits on the nearest rocker and pats the one next to him. "She says that you're getting to know her pretty well."

"She's nice," Rachel says with a hesitant smile.

Every move that the child makes is careful and reserved. She doesn't speak freely as she has done before, and Levi doesn't know what to say to bring her out of her shell.

"She says you're singing." Rachel smiles with embarrassment. "I'm gonna be honest, Rachel. Please sit down."

"I can't. I have to go."

No other adult has taken the time to find out this girl's story, and now he can see the fear in her eyes. She needn't say a word for him to know how she is being treated. For months now, he has been watching, and for months he has heard his inner-voice telling him that something is wrong.

"Do you sing tonight?"

"Yes."

"I'll go to see you sing tonight."

For the first time in a while Rachel's face brightens. Her joy makes him grin. "You will?"

"Yes. Although I still don't think a seven-year-old should be doing what you're doing."

"Eight."

"What?"

"I'm eight now."

"Oh, well, happy birthday, Rachel."

"Thank you. It was a long time ago."

Rachel starts to walk away, but Levi remembers the book that she left in his car weeks before. He jumps up and grabs her wrist. She pulls her arm away in pain. Instantly, Levi's heart drops. He lifts the arm of her coat. Underneath are bruises in the shape of fingers along her forearm. When he pulls the sleeve higher, the bruises crawl all the way up until he can't move the material anymore.

"You can't go back." He shakes his head.

"I have to. He's waiting for me."

"Rachel, I can't let you."

"It will only make it worse," she says quickly.

"But I…"

"I'm his now. He told me last week. If I don't go now he's gonna be mad and he's gonna hurt Simone." She has never said it out loud before and the moment the words are out, she wishes she'd not said anything.

"Okay, listen. I'll figure something out. You go over there. I'll see you tonight. My parents are coming home tomorrow and we'll figure something out. I promise." He reaches around and gives her the book by placing it in the grocery bag.

"Can you keep it?" Rachel asks.

"The book?"

"He doesn't know that I have it."

"Okay." Levi takes it back and then Rachel starts her long walk across the short street.

§ § §

Levi steps into the bar—a place where he has lost plenty of money at the gambling tables. The usual men are there and they come to his side, but he quickly shakes his head. "Not tonight, fellas."

"Ahh, come on, Levi."

"Nope. I'm only here for one thing tonight."

He walks through the crowd. People say hello and women flirt with him as usual—including a dancer named Judy. She grabs his face and plants a kiss on his lips. In times past, he'd done much more with the woman. Her deep brown hair is swept up high and her makeup is thick.

"What are ya doing here?"

"Not what you think," he answers with an apologetic look.

"Got better things than me?"

"Tonight, yes…" His eyes are caught when Rachel walks on stage with a skinny man by her side. Quietly, she stands with her hands clasped as she listens to him submissively.

The band starts and Rachel begins. Until that moment, Levi hadn't understood how one girl could captivate an audience. Only now, when the bar turns so quiet he can hear a pin drop, Levi listens and things immediately become clearer. Her voice is phenomenal. Moments after she begins, he finds that he has been holding his breath, desiring to hear every note.

Levi looks around. In the back of the restaurant, leaning against the wall, is Bill Manchuron. He isn't paying attention to Rachel; rather he is reading a newspaper.

For an hour, Rachel entertains the crowd while people dance. Loud applause meets her when she says goodnight into the microphone, and it is still loud as she leaves the stage. For a child, many of the men and women reach out to shake her hand or holler their praise as she walks past. Levi loses sight of her as she walks through the crowd because she is so small, so he glances in Bill's direction. The bar owner and Bill are having a heated discussion and it isn't until Rachel reaches them that it erupts into an all-out yelling match. Bill forcefully takes Rachel's hand and yells something in her face as her eyes widen in terror.

Levi's heart races as he runs to Rachel's side. "Hey, let her go!"

"What the hell?" Bill looks at the young man confused.

"Don't handle her like that. Let her go," Levi says coming within inches of Bill's face.

At this point Levi is still a kid. His body hasn't filled out, even though he is more built than the other kids in high school, but standing next to Bill, his age is apparent. He has been in many fights before. In fact, he has been suspended four times from school—but this is different. Bill even laughs. "Leave it alone, kid. Do I know you?"

"I'm not letting you leave with her tonight."

"Oh yeah? Are you going to stop me?"

"Yes, I am."

Paying no attention to Levi, Bill looks down at Rachel since he's still holding her arm. "Get back up there and sing the song that Leo wants. He's paying, so you sing."

"But my throat hurts," Rachel says quietly.

"Don't do it, Rachel," Levi says with a shake of his head.

With a fast jerk Bill throws a fist, sending Levi to the floor. The crowd gasps. Soon Levi is surrounded by his gambling buddies, and he has never been more grateful as they help him up. Blood drips from his nose, but he doesn't care. Inside he roars, and with the men surrounding him he flies forward, wrapping his arms around the tall man. Like a cascade of falling soldiers, men throw punches at anyone around. The fight is on and it doesn't matter who is a part of what. No one really knows the reason, but when alcohol and partying mix, it doesn't matter.

It isn't much safer for a child to be in the middle of this chaos than being forced to sing another song, but for the first time Levi feels he has good reason. This isn't just male bravado like his fighting days at school, there is something bigger at stake.

As grunts and moans fill the bar, bottles are thrown and explode against the walls, so the bar owner calls the police. Meanwhile, Levi wrestles with the older man—their backs against the end of the stage. Mr. Penny runs over and takes Rachel in his arms. The moment people hear sirens, everyone flees the building. Bill clocks Levi, knocking him into the piano; which gives him just enough time to grab Rachel with Mr. Penny and run. By the time Levi has recovered and raced outside to catch them, they are already in their vehicle speeding off. Rachel's wide eyes peer out the back window.

"Shit!" Levi yells angrily as he rips his keys from his back pocket.

"Are you leaving?" the soft voice asks.

Vanity stands calmly, even in the middle of men and women racing away.

"Yeah. Do you want to come with me?"

"No. I work here. I'll be fine. But you should go," she smiles. "The police know you too well. Besides, I have a date."

Levi tucks his hat over his hair. "You do?"

"Like you said. You're going to college."

"Yeah." Levi doesn't move as Vanity is so clearly bidding him goodbye. Police cars fly down the street and screech to a halt just outside the bar.

"Go!" Vanity warns him.

Levi hurries to his car and dives in.

"Help her," Vanity says.

"What?" Levi asks as the engine roars, making it hard for him to hear.

"Help Rachel. She needs it."

"I'm gonna try. Hey Vanity?"

She turns back around, "Yeah?"

"We had a lot of fun."

"We did. Now go!"

Levi pulls his car away just in time. Vanity watches him drive down the road, then walks calmly through the disarray.

Years later, Levi receives a letter from Vanity. She was doing well for herself in getting married and having three children, and had even sold some books. One of them was about a rebellious young man. He picked it up once and read the inscription— 'This book is dedicated to a boy. A boy I once loved but couldn't wait for.'

1998

Gramma doesn't continue. With surprise, I look up and she is staring at me.

"What's wrong, Gramma?"

"I was just watching you, honey. You seem to be concerned."

"Well, I am. I would have done more to Bill than Levi did."

Gramma laughs. "Darling, I knew you just before college and you weren't this strapping man that you are now."

I chuckle. "It's true. I was pretty skinny."

Gramma notices the clock beside her bed.

"Oh my goodness, it's eleven o'clock. No wonder I am so tired. It's past my bedtime."

I know that it's time to go, but I'm anxious about tomorrow. "Thank you for the story, Gramma."

"You're welcome, honey. Come back and I'll tell you more."

"I will." I kiss her forehead.

I quickly make my way to my lonely car sitting in the empty visitors' lot and upon turning the ignition, the methodical brush of the drum, the ting of the guitar, and Rachel's voice meets my ears. I breathe in as if to fill my body with it.

The house is quiet when I get home. I pass the empty living room and climb the stairs, but, before reaching my door, I hear murmurs from Shandra's room. With my knuckle I tap and her door creaks open. Inside, she is sitting on her bed and Jimmy is lying across the foot of it with his hands under his head.

"You're back," Shandra says.

"It was late and Gramma had to sleep."

"You talking Gramma into giving you money or something?" Jimmy jokes.

"No, I'm doing fine on my own, thank you."

Jimmy raises his hands in surrender, "I was just kidding."

In all truth I make a good living, it just isn't great. My brothers and sister are surrounded by greatness—everything is great for them. I turn to walk away, but hear my sister's voice. "Where are you going?"

"I'm tired. I'm going to sleep."

"Well, we'll see you tomorrow morning then." Shandra winks.

Out in the hall, I hear a strange crash in my ma's bedroom and I rush inside. "Ma?" The large room seems empty without my dad's hefty presence. She's not in sight but I can hear her crying in her bathroom.

"Ma?"

"Bobby?"

"Can I come in?"

"Yes."

The door swings lightly on its hinges and as it does white dust-like puffs fill the air. The air is so thick of white powder I can hardly see anything in front of me. It's on the towels, the counters, the floor and the bathtub. It lays so thick on the tile that my shoes slip just a bit beneath me. Then there's Ma, sitting on the floor in her nightgown and she's covered from head to toe in bath powder with tears running down her cheeks. The pink bowl and lid rock back and forth on the ground in front of her. "You okay?" I ask and just this makes her start bawling like a baby. I take a seat beside her no matter how covered my jeans and t-shirt become. "What happened?"

"I was trying to get things ready to take to the hospital," she sobs, "I reached over for my towel and tripped. Next thing I know powder is flying everywhere."

"Okay, well, we'll get it all cleaned up." She looks at me and I try to wipe her face with the nearest towel, but as I do, powder covers her even more. I can't help but laugh until she scowls at me, but then she bubbles over with a combination of sobbing and laughter. A great howl comes from deep within her and echoes in the tiled room.

Before long, Jimmy, Shandra, and Lou stand in the doorway.

"What in the world is going on here?" Lou asks with concern.

Shandra and Jimmy can't help but laugh. My sister comes in

quickly and sits on the other side of Ma and wraps her arms around her. They giggle together and when they are done, I take some powder and sprinkle it over Shandra. Like a child she presses her hand on the ground and then brings it up to her face covering herself with the white substance. "This makes me hungry for powdered sugar."

"Is there anything that doesn't make you hungry?" Lou asks.

Shandra picks up two handfuls and tosses powder all over Lou and Jimmy. Suddenly, it's an all-out war. This goes on for several minutes until Ma yells, "Stop! Someone's going to get hurt."

If my father were around, he would have been appalled. I feel the bitterness rush through my body, wetting my mouth with a bad taste. I think of all the laughter we missed as a family because of him.

Jimmy and I help Ma up and then try to brush off the powder, but it isn't going to be removed without a shower. Later, I revisit her room to see that she is okay. She reads a book with just the night light on. "Come here, Bobby," she says when she sees me. I sit down on the side of the bed. "How are you doin'?"

"Fine. Why do you ask?"

"You've just seemed preoccupied since you came."

"Just worried about Dad, I guess."

She presses her palm against my cheek. I tell her what she needs to hear, but the truth is that my heart and soul are wrapped around Rachel Anne Praline. I want to tell my mom about her, yet what do I say? I try to convince myself that boredom is the reason I have latched onto Rachel's story. If I don't have a valid reason for my infatuation with her, then the only conclusion is that I am just plain pathetic, and I can't bear the thought. So, instead, I stay quiet and kiss my mom goodnight.

Chapter Twelve

1916

Slamming on his brakes, Rachel flies forward and hits her lip on the seat in front of her. The car screeches into the driveway and Bill is angrier than she's ever seen him before. When he grabs for her she can't help but cry out, which only enrages him. "What did you tell him?" Bill yells as he yanks her inside the house.

"Nothing," Rachel cries.

"Come on now, we both know that ain't the truth." He drags her down the hall never letting her feet plant. The closer they get to her room, the more she can feel her skin pulse beneath his tight fat fingers and her skin feels like it might stretch till it breaks. The hall table topples over when she tries to grab it, hoping that it might save her, but he just rips at her harder. Finally, they reach her room, but he stops as though he is thinking. "Not good enough," he whispers to himself.

Instantly, she knows what he is thinking. She holds on to the doorjamb, but he is too strong and her fingers burn as they can't hold on. He drags her body until they are standing outside the basement door and he searches for the key in his pocket. As he does, she begs, "Please! It's okay, I promise. I didn't say anything. I can sleep in my room, I'll be good. Please!"

"Shut up!" Finally, he finds the key and the small door swings open with a squeal.

"Let's go!" he yells and she cries out in pain from his hand twisting around her arm. His heavy hand rears back and she closes her eyes, before feeling two slaps, one after the other, that immediately sting and bruise her cheek. She nearly falls down the steep stairs, but is able to grab the railing just in time. She takes each step very slowly so she can feel for the next one. The darkness frightens her like nothing she has ever experienced and she sobs as she makes her way into the darkness. Instantly, she is cold and the smell of mold and oil fill her nostrils.

Across the street Levi comes home to an empty house. His parents are not expected until the next morning so he sits on the couch fully clothed waiting for them to walk through the door. He doesn't know when he actually fell asleep while staring at the house across the street, but he wakes to the twist of the front door handle and wipes his face, slightly disoriented. His mother and father talk quietly to each other as they enter and hang their things.

It's his mother who notices him first on the couch fully clothed and his eye slightly darkened from the punch to the face. "Levi? Are you all right? What happened to you?" She rushes toward him.

"I need your help." For the first time, he cries, feeling that what he did last night was the wrong thing to do.

His father, David, drops the bags in his hands and takes a few steps forward—always calm and collected, as any lawyer should be. "Help with what? Are you in trouble?"

"No." He regretfully chuckles as he wipes his face. "For the first time it's not me. It's Rachel."

"Who's Rachel?" Paula asks tenderly, touching her son's hand.

Levi is trying desperately to give order to his thoughts, but it is hard considering he has just had a nearly sleepless night. "Rachel is the little girl across the street." He explains the entire story starting from the very beginning. His parents look at each other with surprise that he had been so helpful to this little girl.

"What do you want to do, Levi?" Paula asks.

"What can we do?"

David stares at the house across the way as he thinks carefully. "If anyone can make things happen, you can," Levi says.

This is one of the first noble things Levi has done in quite some time and both parents seem eager to help. "Legal matters are tough, but we can go to my office, son, and try and find something."

Levi stands with bags under his eyes and his hair awry, but he is ready.

"Now?" his father asks.

"Who knows what's happening over there. We need to figure something out."

"Okay…" his father's English accent thickens under the intensity. "Give me just a moment and I'll be ready."

Together they drive to David's office and spend all day trying to find out information on the girl. Time flies by, but, with limited resources, they don't come across anything. Paula keeps her eyes glued to Bill Manchuron's home. Finally, the next night after watching Bill and Rachel drive away, Levi looks at his mother.

"I'm going."

"Okay. Be careful," Paula says patting him on the shoulder.

Through the bare country roads, Levi follows Bill's old 1905 Rambler Surrey. It chugs along in the dark at a steady pace finally pulling in front of a small bar on the other side of the city. Levi waits just a bit before following them inside. When he steps out of his car, he pulls his hat low over his eyes and hurries inside. Just as before, even though Rachel appears tired, her voice is more calming than a bird's song on a sunny day. The crowd adjusts their dancing to every change of the beat. It's strange to Levi that no one seems to wonder or worry about the little girl on the stage.

Bill pulls off his guardianship well—somehow convincing everyone that she is rightfully his, but Levi doesn't believe it for a second. A bowl is passed around the crowd and everyone gives a bit of money to the little girl. Levi glares as every so often Bill empties the bowl and stuffs the money into his pockets. Hustling through the dense crowd, Levi makes it to the stairs at the back of the stage and not a soul pays attention, so he waits quietly behind the curtains. When the set is over, she leaves the stage quietly. Levi catches her hand. When she sees him, tears immediately fill her blue eyes.

"Are you okay?" he asks calmly.

She nods.

"I'm trying to help you, but I have to know some things. Can you help me?" Levi kneels and wipes her tears from her pink cheeks. Again, she nods as though she doesn't want to use her voice. "Do you have anything that can help me know about you?" When they hear Bill's loud voice laughing, they peek around the curtain to find that Bill is still passing the bowl.

"I don't know," Rachel whispers.

"I just need to know something." Her silence worries him and so he presses further, "Rachel, I need you to help me. I'm going to find some way to get you away from him."

It is clear she doesn't know whether to believe him.

"I have papers that my momma gave me before she died…"

Levi's eyes widen. "What kind of papers?"

"I don't know. My momma said they were important."

"Okay, can we get those?"

"He won't let me out."

"Out of the house?" She nods. "Then where are they? I'll get in. I'll find them."

"They're in my pillow."

"Okay. Which room is yours?"

Suddenly, they hear footsteps and Levi ducks behind the curtain. "What the hell are you doin' back here?" Bill's loud voice echoes in the small space.

"Nothing," Rachel says quietly.

"Get your ass out there. I ain't gonna wait on you forever."

At nearly four o'clock in the morning, Levi hurries across the street with a dim lantern. He finds that the back door is unlocked and he hurries to the hall. In each room he searches, but he comes up with nothing. Then, finally, at the last door, he finds remnants of Rachel. His hand brushes something furry and after further investigation he recognizes it to be a nearly shredded teddy bear.

With his hands he searches for the bed. "Rachel," he whispers, but there is nothing but an empty bed. Instantly, his imagination runs wild as to where she might be. He reaches the pillow and presses his hands against it. It is paper-thin and just underneath is a harder surface. At the edge of the pillow, he feels an opening where Rachel has cut it at the seam, and there, sticking out just slightly, is a pile of papers. He pulls them quickly and holds them close to his chest. Then he moves to the hall again. Why hasn't he seen Rachel?

Leaving without knowing will drive him insane, so he searches for any other doors. On the other side of the kitchen is a small door, too small to be a room and he walks to it. A heavy lock secures it from the outside. He plays with the lock, wondering if he might be able to pry it open. His breathing deepens and he stops when he hears something. Footsteps are coming down the hall. With shaking hands, he twists the knob on the lantern and extinguishes the light. He presses himself against a far wall and waits. Bill comes in groggily. Levi closes his eyes and holds his breath. The very large man finds a glass and fills it with bourbon. For a moment while he drinks, Bill looks around even staring in Levi's direction. Levi's stomach muscles scream, wanting to release a loud rush of air. Then, Bill turns and walks back down the hall.

Within moments, Levi is back in his own house with the doors closed. Every thought running through his mind is heavy and morbid and terrifying, so when his father comes and taps him on his shoulder, it nearly sends him through the roof.

"Dad!" Levi grabs his chest feeling his heart squeeze tight.

"Are you alright, son?"

"Yes…" Levi takes a look outside, "No, I'm not."

"Why are you up? Did something happen?"

"I talked to Rachel tonight. She told me where to find her papers."

"What kind of papers?"

"I don't know, but I got them."

Levi lifts them in the air with every intention of skipping another night's sleep. He walks to the couch and turns on the nearest lamp. His father, head to toe in tan pajamas, wipes his eyes and sits beside Levi. They began reading, suddenly privy to information that the child has yet to learn. "Her mother gave her up for adoption before being sent to prison. Then the state issued a temporary custody to Bernadette Brown. But that's where it stops," David says. "At least it gives us some names."

"It never says anything about Bill Manchuron."

"Yes, but these are probably not updated. I'll make some calls today."

"Right now," Levi says standing.

David looks at his son apologetically. "Son, I can't do that right now, it's only four o'clock in the morning."

Levi walks to the window and rubs his skin so hard it makes the blood beneath come to the surface and turns his cheeks bright red. "There's something wrong and we can't let any more time go by."

For years this family has struggled. David and Paula have given their son everything and yet in the end, they were disappointed by Levi's selfishness and his affinity for trouble. Now that he is burdened with someone else's suffering instead of his own pleasures, his father finds a great need to do as he asks. Lines of communication that have been closed for so long are suddenly opened and neither parent wants time to pass.

"You really feel strongly about this?" David lays a hand on his son's shoulder.

"I just broke into someone's home."

"Tonight?" His father steps forward with concern. "You went into Bill's home?"

"Yes, that's how I got these papers."

"Son…"

"She wasn't there." Levi says in a way that he knows his father will understand what he is implying. "I couldn't find her." His father takes a moment, breathes in and out, and then with a quick nod begins walking to his room.

"Where are you going?" Levi calls out.

"I'm getting dressed. I think we're starting our day."

By noon they have spoken with Affie who tells them the story about Bill coming in and claiming he's from the State. For hours they try to get a good connection with the New Jersey State office that took care of orphans and finally one woman answers the phone.

"Good afternoon, this is Moyra, how may I help you?"

Levi clears his throat. "Yes, Moyra, I need to know about a Bill Manchuron that works for your department."

"Please hold."

A few minutes later she returns with a calm voice. "I'm sorry, sir. Whom did you say?"

"Bill Manchuron."

"I have no record of anyone working here by that name."

Levi looks at his father with a raised eyebrow.

"Are you sure of that?"

"Yes, sir."

"Then would you please tell me where a child named Rachel Anne Praline is?"

"Please hold, sir."

Again she is gone for a few minutes. "We have records of her staying with a Bernadette Brown. That is the last of our files, sir."

"Thank you. Thank you very much." Levi hangs up the phone and shakes his head. "Bill doesn't work for them."

"What?"

"They have no one that works there named Bill Manchuron. And they haven't a clue Bernadette has died. The State still thinks that Rachel is with her."

Levi's father immediately grabs the receiver. He speaks with the operator and before long is connected to an old friend from the police department. After a long conversation he says, "Thank you, Lockly, I greatly appreciate it."

When he gets off the telephone, he looks at his son with concern. "There is a prisoner who was released nearly eighteen months ago," his father hesitates, "he goes by the name of William Manchuron. He was supposed to take a job as a condition of his parole, but disappeared nine months ago. The State's watch over orphans isn't much better than their watch over released criminals apparently. In fact, there is no guarantee that the child won't fall into yet another set of incapable hands once they take her out of Bill Manchuron's charge. What can you find in the rest of her things?"

They claw through her papers three more times. A small note card drops on the table.

"What's that say?" Levi asks, leaning against his father.

"Dick Jenner. He's written a note to Bernadette with his parent's information requesting to contact him if something should happen."

Levi takes the note from his father's hands and reads it carefully. "Maybe he can tell us something. His signature is on the papers given to Bernadette."

"We should find out."

After a few calls they finally get an answer. A woman named Pearl Jenner answers the phone with an elderly shaky voice. While

David speaks with her, Levi watches out the window of the office to the main street below. The summer is starting to show signs of changing to fall and yet it is still hot and muggy. Levi has to pull at his collar to keep the material from sticking to his sweaty skin. He doesn't know what is getting at him more—the weather or his nerves. His father is smiling as he finishes his conversation with the person on the phone. "Well, thank you very much. Yes ma'am . . . I'll give him a call. Thank you, ma'am." He hangs up the phone.

"That was Dick Jenner's mother, Pearl. She says that her son is still in Atlantic City. I guess we'll have to contact him. She gave me his number."

"Let's get Rachel first."

It only takes them twenty minutes to drive to the police station. Once the commander hears their story and finds Bill Manchuron's name in some of his records, he is committed to helping release the child. Levi is impressed at how much clout his father has and the outstanding lawyer he's known to be.

It all seems surreal to Levi as they pull up in front of his home in clunky police cars. Nearly ten men in uniform jump out of the squad cars along with Levi and his father. They hurry to the man's door and the Commander knocks. In the bright sun, they stand with beads of sweat forming on their foreheads as they wait. No response. Levi's hands throb as he squeezes them so tight they turn white. Again, the Commander knocks. Another few minutes pass.

"I'm not sure anyone's inside," the Commander shakes his head.

"He's inside. He's never left the house earlier than this." The other men can see the tension in Levi's stance.

Levi pounds on the door relentlessly, nearly shaking it off its hinges. Before long, Bill opens the door already angered over the interruption. It isn't until he sees all of the men in uniform that he steps back in surprise.

"Bill Manchuron?" the Commander asks.

"Who's asking?"

"My name is Pete Valasco and I'm the New York City Police Commander."

"Good morning officer, what do ya need?" Bill asks, intending to appear innocent, but he stares at Levi with a sour expression.

"This man here---" The chief points to Levi who is standing confidently at his left shoulder. "---he says that you have a little girl that isn't yours staying here."

"Ain't no one here but me."

"That's a lie," Levi cries out with his emotions running high. He wanted nothing more than to run inside and find Rachel. His worst fear is that there will be nothing to find. But the Commander stops him with a powerful forearm on his chest.

"Well, then you won't mind if we take a look inside," Pete says calmly.

"This is my home. Nobody's gonna come inside."

"I'm going to come inside, Bill. Whether you let us or not," Pete warns.

He doesn't budge. With two men on either side of the door and the commander standing directly in front of him, there isn't much he can do, but he tries to close the door. The moment he does, every man rushes forward like soldiers on a battlefield. In only seconds Bill is lying face down on the floor and Levi runs past, immediately in search of Rachel.

Again, the voice inside—the one that Levi hasn't listened to until Rachel came along— speaks up and he knows without a doubt where to go. He runs to the door in the kitchen, but there is no key. So instead, he grabs a heavy chair from the table and lifts it over his head. His strong arms throw the solid piece against the metal and with three hits the lock falls to the floor. A narrow and steep flight of stairs into the darkness stares back at him.

"Rachel!" He races to the bottom. There is no light except for the small bit coming from upstairs. When he steps off the last step, he can't see much, just the outlines of things in front of him. "Rachel?"

Just next to Levi there is a small lantern. Carefully, Levi lights it and searches the room. Beneath the stairs there is a crawl space which he investigates. Scared eyes stare back at him. On the hard dirt floor, she sits with a blanket over her entire body and the only thing that can be seen are her eyes. She squints from the lantern's dim light.

"Rachel," he whispers. Setting down the lantern, he walks to her side and kneels sweetly in front of her. "Come with me, Rachel."

For a moment she says nothing and just stares at him as though she can't believe he is there. Then her voice, cracking from fatigue, comes out softly. "Where is he?"

"You don't have to worry about him anymore." Yet, she clearly doesn't believe him. "Trust me. You don't have to live with him anymore. We'll find you a new home."

Levi is uncertain how much he can touch her, so he reaches out a hand giving her the choice to take it. At first, just her fingertips touch his, and then her palm until she's close enough that he can reach out and pick her up. For just a time, he stays there and lets her wrap her arms around his neck. She holds tight. As more men in uniform come down into the basement, Rachel shakes more.

"Don't worry," Levi whispers in her ear. "He can't hurt you anymore." He climbs the stairs. With his hand, he covers her face as they walk past Bill who sits on the floor. Bill's hands are cuffed behind his back—a good sign.

Just ahead, his father stands with his hands on his hips. His face shows a variety of emotions, but the most resonant is pride. For many reasons, Levi will remember this day as one of the best and worst in his life. A point where choices came easy. His father pats him on the back as he walks by.

"I'm taking her to our house," Levi says.

"Okay, son. I'll talk to the Commander about what we can do."

Levi walks across the street and finds his mother shading her eyes with her hands. She touches his neck as he passes.

"You did well, son," he hears her say.

§ § §

For the next few days, Levi never takes his eyes off of Rachel. She sleeps a lot, but he makes sure that she has everything she needs. All the while he and his father contact Dick Jenner—the man who hasn't seen the child since she was five days old.

At lunch one day, waiting at a café halfway between New York and New Jersey, Dick Jenner walks in and is instantly recognized by Levi and his father. He is good-looking with a pleasant smile and just behind him is a woman as plain as the tan-tiled floor with pale skin and mousy brown hair.

Levi takes Dick's hand first. "You are Dick Jenner?"

"Yes…yes, I am. This is my wife, Sylvia."

Levi takes her hand as well and his father follows suit.

"Good afternoon, gentlemen. It's nice to meet you," Sylvia says.

"Won't you sit?" Levi asks them, pointing to the table already adorned with four water glasses.

"Absolutely. I must be honest that I don't know much about what this is regarding. You've said something about Rachel Praline?" Dick asks as he pulls his hat off and waits for his wife to sit down before he does.

"Yes, do you remember her?"

The couple look at each other, smiling from ear to ear. "Of course," Sylvia says, "We owe that baby a lot. My goodness, I suppose she's not a baby anymore."

"No," Levi admits. "She's eight."

"Eight." Sylvia puts her hand to her mouth and shares a moment with Dick.

Dick leans forward. "Is something wrong? Is there a reason that you came to us?"

"Well, to be honest," Levi's father pauses, "We're not sure what you can or will do for us, but we found your note to Bernadette Brown in Rachel's papers, and we thought we would call you first."

"Okay."

They don't know where to begin or how much detail to include.

"Where is Rachel?" Dick asks with concern.

"She's at my house with my mother," Levi answers. "We just took her from her most recent home."

"Oh, she wasn't with Bernie?" Sylvia asks quickly.

"No. Bernadette Brown died well over a year ago."

Sylvia and Dick are obviously distressed about the news and they take each other's hand. Levi begins, "Rachel's been living with a man named Bill Manchuron—"

Unable to stop himself from interrupting, Dick rubs his head, "Levi, is Rachel okay?"

"I think she will be if we can find her a good home. But right now she's a bit bruised."

"What happened?" Dick nearly begs.

Levi explains. As the story continues Dick's eyes glaze over with sadness and Sylvia allows tears to fall down her face. "Rachel changed our lives. I know it seems crazy, but she did…"

"It doesn't seem crazy." Levi knows just what she's feeling.

Sylvia continues, "When we were taking care of her, just having her there, opened our eyes to what we really wanted in life. Dick and I quit our jobs at the State office and we've been making a wonderful living doing what we love—all because of Rachel."

"What is it that you need from us? I'm sorry, but we don't work for the State anymore." Dick asks, a little confused.

"Well, I guess we're not really sure. We knew you were the ones to place Rachel with Bernadette. We just need to know what to do now." Levi's father explains. "My son has just saved this child from a horrible life and what she needs is a good home."

"We'll take her," Sylvia says without wavering. There is disbelief on Dick's face.

"Can I ask you why you would be so eager to change your life like that?" Levi asks.

"We've been trying to have children for years." A tear falls down Sylvia's cheek. "But you see I just recently found that I am unable. Just the other day we asked God to answer our request. And although this isn't the way we thought of it…" she looks at Dick with a smile, "It certainly never is, is it?"

Finally, Dick turns to the men with resolve, "What the beautiful lady wants, the beautiful lady gets."

"We, of course, would be very grateful to have you take her, but we have to make sure that she is getting the best," Levi's father says.

Dick laughs. "Of course. of course."

"What do you do?" Levi asks.

Sylvia and Dick chuckle, and he rubs her hand as he speaks. "I… speak to animals."

The father and son immediately look as if they've made a mistake, to which Dick nods. "I can see it in your eyes . . . I know what you are thinking. I have one of the best acts on the boardwalk in Atlantic City . . . of course, besides the magicians. They always get a good crowd." Dick notices that Levi and his father are still greatly concerned and he grins. "I've always had this gift to understand animals and when we left our jobs, I decided to pursue what I loved the most—performing. In the last eight years we've created a large following and grown bigger every year. I give a great show where animals do tasks; some simple and some hard . . . but, you would be surprised what I can get these animals to do."

"I get what you do, but I have to say I'm a little worried. Rachel has been used to the point that, well, I just . . . she has a true gift, but . . . she's barely talking as it is. It makes me a little concerned that you are a performer. How do we know you aren't going---"

Dick interrupts Levi. "I have no doubt that she's gifted, but a child would have nothing to do with our show. Look Levi…" Dick gives him a strong stare with his tender nature just behind it, "I love this little girl. She changed our lives. It is because of her that Sylvia and I are together and doing what we love. She won't have to do a thing. We will love her like our own child and the only thing I require is that she goes to school and gets a good education. At this time in our lives, we have enough money to give her what she needs. She may actually find that she likes it with us and the animals."

Levi and his father see the truth behind the couple's eyes. They are good people and their connection with Rachel is undeniable.

1998

"Do you remember Dick Jenner?" my Grandma asks.

We have found a bench that sits in front of a small lake outside the retirement home and have taken some time to rest there as she finishes her story. For two days, I had to wait to hear more. Dad is still the same, but the doctors were hopeful that his blood work is looking better. So, in the meantime, I continued to check back on Gramma. It wasn't until this morning that she suddenly remembered where we had left off.

"Yes, of course. He and Sylvia are the couple that found Bernie."

"That's right." Gramma nods and peers out over the water. Then she closes her eyes as the moving sun drops onto her face and breathes in as though she can smell the warmth. "Oh, he was a sweet man."

"Why didn't Levi and his parents take her? They seemed to love her."

Gramma opened her eyes and cocks her head as though she doesn't necessarily know the answer to my question. "Well, some things just aren't meant to be. Levi's father and mother were older and Levi was leaving for college the next month. I suppose they felt she might be lonely. No . . . Sylvia and Dick were the best choice. They were slightly younger and had learned that they couldn't have children. I just know God meant for Rachel to be with them."

Chapter Thirteen

1916

Levi sits on the porch swing with a glass of tea in his hand, just thinking about Rachel. He doesn't want her to go. She has brought out so much in him—so many things that he is proud of. After months of having her around, he can't imagine letting her drive away with Sylvia and Dick. But something tells him that it is simply his time to let her go.

When he hears the screen door open, it is Rachel coming out with a blanket in her one hand and her bear, which his mother has sewn back together, in the other. Without a word she crawls up on the swing and snuggles up next to him. They both know it is their last bit of time together and neither has anything to say. Almost an hour later they are still sitting in the same spot when Dick and Sylvia's car pulls up the driveway. Her blue eyes, twinkling in the sun, seem to have light back within them, but Levi knows, time will be the only thing to heal her broken pieces. Her voice has been lost over the last two weeks, falling into the abyss of pain as she tries to take control back in a child's way. However, Levi hasn't pushed anything, nor have David and Paula, but they hope she will return someday. It would be tragic if the world couldn't hear her voice.

Then, without tears, she walks hand in hand with Levi toward Dick and Sylvia who are cautiously waiting beside their automobile. Dick must have been honest about doing well, as Levi notices his brand-new white with green details, Paige Ardmore Roadster.

"Hello." Dick says with a kind smile. Rachel says nothing back. Neither of them get closer to each other. "Rachel, you probably don't remember us, because you weren't but that size," Dick points to the bear in her arms. The couple stare at the beautiful little girl. Sylvia's eyes fill with tears as she rests her hand on her stomach.

"We're letting Rachel find her own voice, in her own time," Levi explains.

"Of course!" Sylvia exclaims. "Rachel, you don't have to do or say anything that you don't want to when you live with us. You have my promise. Do you accept that?" Sylvia's sweetness is contagious and genuine, and Levi notices that Rachel's hand relaxes in his.

"We do things your way, Rachel," Dick says with a wink.

David brings out Rachel's bags and Dick takes them to the car. Then, when it is time to go, Levi's mother and father hug the little girl. Sylvia and Dick step aside to give them a moment alone.

Levi kneels in front of Rachel, and she lays a hand on his shoulder. For a while, under the setting sun, they hold hands. "Rachel, you're a strong girl. You're going to do great things. But listen," he starts to whisper, "I'm here, if ever you need me." Still, she says nothing. Finally, Levi wraps his arms around her. Tears flow down her cheeks and when Levi lets go, he says, "I'll see you again."

Rachel nods.

"Be good and as soon as I can, I will come see you. I'll be going away for a while, but I promise I will visit."

In Rachel's mind, her mother left her, Bernie left her, Simone has never come to find her, so surely Levi won't come.

After a few minutes, Dick comes to Rachel's side. "May I walk you to the car?"

She nods and, surprisingly, takes his hand. In some strange way, there seems to be something familiar about Dick and Sylvia. Whatever it is, she feels safe with them. She climbs into the back seat, as Levi stands on the front lawn with his parents not far behind and watches them as they drive away.

Neither Rachel or Levi is aware at that moment of the impact they will have on each other's lives.

§ § §

When the car pulls into the driveway of their Atlantic City Farmhouse, Dick turns the key to shut off the engine, but no one moves. After a moment, Dick turns around in his chair and looks at Rachel who has yet to say anything.

"Rachel, I want you to know that this is your home now. You are welcome to anything and everything. Most importantly, we are here to take care of you. Take as much time as you need to get comfortable. We do not request anything of you except for you to be yourself." Rachel nods and Dick grins. "Okay, well let's go. May I show you your room and then after that, I'll show you around the place?"

She nods again.

"Great." Dick jumps out of the car with a skip in his step and Sylvia follows. Rachel turns until she is sitting on her knees with her arms crossed over the back of the seat. She watches Sylvia rub Dick's back and lays her chin on her arms while she does. Dick gives Sylvia a kiss on the lips, and then he reaches in and pulls Rachel's bags out. After a moment, he comes around the side of the car and with gentle eyes, he leans in through the window. "Do you want to stay in here for a while?"

For a moment Rachel thinks about it, but, in the end, she doesn't want to continue sitting on the leather seats since her bottom is getting sore. She carefully touches her feet to the stone-covered ground.

Ahead, Dick and Sylvia's good fortune is apparent—a large home, bigger than anything she has ever lived in. It is well groomed, and in perfect form at the end of summer. The white brick walls start from the ground and rise to the high peaks of the second story. Flowers upon flowers, space beyond measure, and perfectly chiseled details are all around. Even David, Paula, and Levi's home wasn't this grand. It takes her small eyes quite a bit to take it all in, so Dick stands quietly beside her with his arms crossed in front of him as they both study the mansion as though, he too, is looking at it for the first time.

"We looked at a lot of homes when we finally decided to buy, and this is the one we loved. Sylvia had her own reasons for loving it, but if you'll allow me, I'll show you the reason that I love it."

Swiftly, an old man dressed in a black suit with flyaway gray hairs comes from the side of the house with large yellow flowers in his hand. He shuffles to the new family with an enormous smile. "Well, Rachel, it is so nice to have you here. These are for you."

"Rachel, this is Sandy. He manages the place for us," Dick explains.

Rachel can't help but smile as she takes hold of the flimsy green stems. She likes the old man's funny accent—she had never heard the Scottish dialect. "Now there's plenty more where those came from. Just let me know if these wilt." Sandy smiles, revealing his teeth— just a little chipped and darkened with age.

Rachel gives a nod.

"Well, may we show you the place?" Dick asks kindly.

They are soon strolling through the home. The rooms are large enough, but not too large to spoil the quaintness of it. It has been updated to the latest style even though it was built in 1859.

"I eventually want to grow the show and unfortunately that won't be here. Maybe a home in the country would be nice," he says.

"We have too many neighbors here." They show her a room at the top of the stairs. It is much more beautiful than she expects.

Dick walks to her window and opens it. "I'd like to show you something. Would you come here?" His voice is always more than compassionate, giving her no choice but to trust him. So, she walks to him as he points to a large building in the back that looks somewhat like a barn.

"Do you see that? That is my favorite place here." After a moment, they hear the sound of animals. Rachel looks at him with a little tinge of excitement. "Can I take you to see it?"

Rachel nods. He raises his hand in front of her so that she might take it. Deep inside, Rachel knows that Dick isn't the same as Bill. His eyes are different and kind, but the cracks in her bones from Bill's heavy hand seem to be ripping at her heart, reminding her that men can be mean. She is hesitant to takes Dick's hand, but when she does, he smiles, and her heart begins to calm. It isn't long before they are standing in front of a large barn painted a limey shade of green. It has heavy doors with large locks. Dick fidgets with them for just a moment and then he looks down at her. All the while Sylvia stays back letting Rachel get to know Dick. "Are you ready?" An exuberant smile shows Rachel's teeth. "Okay then." With a hefty shove Dick pushes the doors open.

She stands in silence and her eyes widen. Along both sides of the barn, equal in size to an airplane hangar, are beautiful animals fenced with sturdy but wonderfully-crafted fences. The first in line is a large lion. With one big roar, Rachel jumps as he shakes his mane and his loose skin tosses back and forth. As Dick walks into the barn, every single animal leaves their comfy spot to greet him.

"Come in closer. I promise they won't hurt you." Dick's face beams with pride.

Her small feet, covered in little brown sandals, tap the dirt floor as she walks slowly. Dick stands in front of the fenced-in lion and pets the animal as it vies for his attention. Rachel watches in fascination.

His gigantic, but velvety padded paws hold onto Dick's hands as though he is worried Dick will let go. Just behind the gorgeous cat is plenty of room for him to roam as he can come inside and outside as he pleases through a side door. The lion's purring is louder than the rumble of a car and it makes Rachel laugh.

"Good afternoon, Mr. Jenner." A worker enters from a doorway in the back. He waves his hand above his head.

"Good afternoon, Gregory." Dick looks at Rachel. "That's Gregory. He's worked with me for about five years now. And this…" he says pointing to the cat, "…is Oliver."

As his hand rubs the cat's wiry fur, the lion opens his mouth wide and makes a sound like he is speaking to Dick. "Good afternoon to you, too," Dick says to the lion, "He's a bit attached to me." Then he turns to the cat. "I'll come play with you in a while." With that, the cat walks away. Rachel is in awe as Oliver knows how to reach out his paw to open his side door so that he may lay in the sun. "I know," Dick says. "He's smart."

Rachel is confused, but Dick expects this since everyone always is. "I have a gift, Rachel. I've always had it, even before I was your age. In some peculiar way, animals understand me, and I understand them." A loud sound comes from the next enclosure—like the holler of something near human. This grabs Rachel's attention and as she wanders over, there, sitting against a wooden wall with arms crossed like she is lounging in the sunlight (the barn has large windows along the wall and open skylights) is a black gorilla. The animal cocks her head to the side as though she is telling Dick that she has been waiting too long for his presence. Dick reaches over and pets the animal's head. As gentle as a baby, the gorilla takes Dick's hand and makes him continue patting her head for a while. Finally, she gets to her feet, turns around to face Dick, and lays her head in his arms like a child.

"Betty, this is Rachel. Rachel, this is Betty." He looks back at the gorilla. "She's here to play with you, Betty. She's going to be another friend."

Very subtly, the gorilla seems to grin at Rachel and she drops her jaw. Then unexpectedly, the gorilla begins to jump around throwing her arms in the air. Laughter edges to the surface in Rachel, but before it breaks out, something stifles it. Dick is grateful that she even came that close.

"Betty…" Dick begins, but Betty is still too excited. "Betty . . . Bet--" The gorilla finally comes to his side and crosses her arms in front of her. "Betty, I'm going to introduce Rachel to the rest of the gang and then I'm sure that we'll come back to see you." Betty ever so gently reaches out and rubs Rachel's small head.

They start walking. "It all started, Rachel, when Sylvia and I traveled on our very first vacation. We had no money to our name since we had just quit our jobs…this is just after meeting you… anyway, we scrounged enough money from our parents and our plan was to drive all the way across three states. But on our third stop we ran into a man that let us stay with him for a day. In the back of his home was a barn and inside he had a wounded horse. Sylvia and I fell in love with this horse. The man called him Trooper. Unfortunately, because there was something wrong with the horse, he was going to put the animal down." Dick looks at Rachel wondering whether he should have said that, so he continues without embellishing.

"Sylvia and I couldn't bear it, so we took all the money we had and bought Trooper." A glisten comes to Dick's eye when resurrecting this memory. "Instead of a road trip, we had now just begun our greatest quest. Not only to earn our money back but to figure out what exactly this meant." He looks down at her with compassion. "I worked with Trooper and got him healthy, although he still seemed . . . depressed even. You know, animals can get depressed. Did you know that? So, I began experimenting with the gift that I always knew I had. Wouldn't you know it, Trooper happily learned tricks . . . and life came back into his eyes." Dick kneels in front of Rachel and smiles. "For the first time, I would go down to the boardwalk early in the morning and come home at night with a decent day's wage," he explains with pride. "And it never felt like work."

"Then someone got wind that I had helped heal Trooper and this man came to me with an idea. He said, 'I have a lion that has a bad leg. Would ya want him? I'll give him to you for fifty cents.' I couldn't help but say yes and that is how I obtained Oliver. Sylvia and I then nursed Oliver back to health and before long he was also able to perform and enjoyed it as much as I did. With two large animals we hadn't much room in our small place, but before long we were earning enough money to rent a bigger place with a nice barn in the back to take care of Trooper and Oliver." They reach another gate and soon a horse with a brown harness greets them and nudges Dick's arm. He gently pats the horse's nose.

"In only a few years, I've adopted seven animals, and my small performance has become big enough that I've rented out my own space on the boardwalk and sold out every show for months in advance. Last year, we finally left that home with the barn that we rented and bought this house. Sometimes I feel it's always been luck or fortune, but it was you, Rachel, that put a fire in us to do what we love to do. You helped us realize we didn't want to live just trying to earn money, we needed to earn love and joy and peace. What I didn't realize is that when I stopped trying to earn money, happiness came rightfully. And strangely enough, the money started flowing in." He runs his hands down the tall horse, "This is Trooper." When Dick finally gives his undying attention to the horse, it's as though they speak to each other with their touch and eyes.

Now if Rachel had been any older, she would have wondered about Dick Jenner's sanity. Instead, standing there as a young child before him, she is mesmerized.

"Rachel?" The calm and gentle voice behind Dick and Rachel turns both of their heads. Sylvia is standing at the door with her hands on her hips and a smile on her face. "Dinner is ready. Are you hungry?" Sylvia raises her arm out in front of her to beckon

Rachel over. Rachel looks at Dick and then the animals, just before she walks to Sylvia and takes her hand.

As any new father would, Dick worries about her. The thought that maybe they have jumped in over their heads plagues him. They don't know anything about children and especially ones who have been through what Rachel has.

One night as they lay in bed, he turns to his wife. "Are you worried?"

Sylvia grins. "I'm happy."

"No…I know…but what I mean…"

"I know what you mean."

"She hasn't said a word."

"She will," she assures him.

"What do we do with her until then?"

Sylvia laughs at his obvious fear. "Dee," As she calls him when she wants to be tender, "She's a child. She doesn't have to speak for us to know what she wants, and I love having her here. Whether she wants to be with us or not, it's our job to give her what she needs…" She can still see the concern in his eyes. "She seems to love the animals."

"Yeah, I think so."

"I'm just better at reading her heart. I'm a woman and I can tell you that she is happy."

Dick reaches over and guides his hand down her face. There are so many reasons why he loves his wife.

"Just relax. We'll figure things out." Sylvia smiles as he kisses her.

§ § §

Dick stands in front of Rachel's door but he can't bring himself to wake her. It is getting later and later with no sign of the little girl. Sylvia is at the store and it is his job to take care of the child. He rubs his hand along his chin and rocks on his heels until finally, with a soft hand, he knocks. There isn't a sound. He presses his hand against the knob and turns it ever so carefully. When the door is open, his worst fears are realized. There is no sign of her. Not even the bed's quilt has been touched.

"Rachel?" he calls out.

He opens the closet doors and opens the drawers, forgetting that even a child can't fit in them.

"She's run away," he convinces himself. With rabbit-like feet, he moves down the stairs and hurries into the kitchen where Sandy is fixing the leg of the table.

"Now don't panic, Mr. Jenner," Sandy tells him. "We'll find her."

"Where could she have gone?"

"I don't know. Let's search the grounds."

"Please!" Dick can't focus on anything else. "And do it quickly. Before my wife comes home. I'll take the yards."

"Okay…I'll finish looking in the house."

"Yes, yes, that's good." Beads of sweat now sit on his upper lip. He grabs his two animal handlers and sends them searching as well. Minutes pass. No sign of Rachel. He checks behind every bush and every tree, but there is nothing. Finally, Sandy pokes his head out of an upstairs window and calls out for Dick calmly.

"If you can come up here, please, Mr. Jenner?"

"Yes…yes…of course…is she up there?"

But before Sandy can respond Dick has reached the back door and stepped into the mudroom. He runs three steps at a time up the stairs and meets Sandy at the top just inside Rachel's room.

"Did you find her?" Dick asks.

Sandy points down. Just under the long blanket that hangs all the way down to the floor is a furry brown arm of a small teddy bear sticking out. Quietly, but swiftly, Dick drops to his knees and lifts the corner of the bed skirt. Two blue eyes peer out at him.

"Good morning, Rachel. I've been looking for you. Are you okay?"

A small nod is all she gives.

"Do you sleep under there every night?" She nods while holding her teddy bear to her chest. Still on his knees, Dick gives her a sensitive smile. "Rachel," he reaches over and brushes her long golden hair from her shoulder, "I know that you went through quite a lot before you came to live with us, and I want to tell you that you are safe. Maybe someday you'll believe it yourself."

§ § §

It isn't long before Rachel, in a beautiful new dress, is sitting in the backseat of their car watching the trees pass. The morning is still warm and full of fragrance from the wildflowers growing in the fields. When they drive through neighborhoods, Rachel watches closely wondering if they might pass her old one. It makes her wonder about Simone. Where is her best friend?

"We're almost there," Sylvia says quietly, "I think you'll enjoy today. Oh, I have a letter for you. Levi dropped it by."

Rachel looks up with surprise. He had been to the house and not said anything to her?

Sylvia must have noticed the concern. "He didn't have time to come in and it was very early in the morning."

Rachel snatches the letter like a child at a candy store. She quickly opens it and reads his sloppy writing as best as she can.

> *Dear Rachel,*
>
> *Please forgive me that I didn't stop long enough to see you. Although I am confident that you are loving your new home with Sylvia and Dick, please remember that you must send me a letter if, by chance, you do not. It turns out that I have decided to enlist in the army instead of enrolling in college. I guess I feel that I have the capability to make a difference in this world and that is where I am needed. Can*

you imagine me in one of those uniforms? Uptight with a collar? Listen Rachel, I'll always be watching out for you. I'll miss you. Be a good kid. That's what you're supposed to do, even though I never was.

> *With love,*
> *Levi*

When Rachel looks up, she notices that Sylvia is observing her. Rachel closes the letter and tucks it in her arms as she sits back against her seat, feeling a bit shy.

"He's a good friend," Sylvia winks.

When Rachel looks out at the city with the accordion-like progression of people along a wooden-slatted path facing the ocean, the smell of all types of food, and the excitement of kids' voices on the beautiful Saturday morning, she feels joy in her stomach that she hasn't had in a while. Together in their best outfits, the three of them join the large crowd meandering around the boardwalk and gawking at the sights. Before long, Rachel has a pickle in one hand and her teddy bear in the other. Both Dick and Sylvia keep a watchful eye on her at all times, showing her that she is safe.

Along one pier are gardens that are undoubtedly the most beautiful she's ever seen. Large grand hotels, where the people seem to have all the finest accessories, are scattered about. Showboats are filled to the brim with people on the ocean side and it seems that just about everybody has decided today is the day to visit.

"You see, Rachel," Dick begins as they move slowly together. "Each pier has its own unique character. Just like us." He points just ahead of him. "Look at that!" he says as if he too were a child, "It's the Ferris wheel."

The three of them stare at the outlandishly large wheel. Dick kneels next to her as passersby zigzag around them. Rachel finishes the pickle and starts on some taffy that they bought only moments before.

"Do you want to go?" Dick asks her. Although the sight is spectacular, it is also intimidating. She doesn't mind staring at it, but getting on would be an entirely different experience, so she shakes her head. She wonders if she is letting them down, but instead, Dick chuckles and leans closer to her ear. "Don't tell anyone, but I've never been on it before. But it won't keep us from looking at it, right?"

Rachel smiles. It is rare to see her broad gorgeous smile and Dick's heart melts just as it did on the day he met her.

"Well Rachel, the day is yours, what would you like to do?" Dick asks. "Would you like to see a magic show?"

Rachel nods.

"Okay then!" He pops up and eagerly takes her hand, then Sylvia's. "Let's go."

Just a short walk later they come to the "Million Dollar Pier". On a large sign, just above the entrance is a painting of Harry Houdini looking proud with a bird in one hand and handcuffs in the other. Dick hurries through, knowing just where to take them. He passes a long line where Rachel notices a couple of kids laughing, blowing wind wheels, and eating popcorn, but what really catches her eye are the soldiers in uniform. Most of the line is full of young men proudly wearing deep Army-green uniforms with shiny black boots and snug fitting hats.

Dick meets the man at the ticket table with a smile. "Good mornin', Mack!"

"Dicky, whatchya doin'? You gonna watch the show again?"

"Hey, Mack…the way I figure it is that I need to take advantage of the time that Harry's here."

"Sure do…" The short Cuban man with a barrel mustache and thick arms notices Rachel. "Who's this?"

"This is Rachel . . . she's someone that will be around now," Dick states proudly as Rachel shrinks into him.

"Well, enjoy the show."

"Thanks, Mack." And that was that. Dick is able to walk right in without waiting in line or even paying. Rachel's eyes grow wide. He has shown her so many incredible things in such a short time.

Harry Houdini is a true magician. She doesn't even mind when she has to stand on her chair to see above the woman's head in front of her. When he is done, he gives a deep bow and she claps her hands with vigor.

Just before they reach the entrance, Dick shakes the hand of a woman standing by. "Bess. It was a great show as usual."

Sylvia leans into Rachel's ear. "She is Mr. Houdini's wife."

Bess Houdini is a proud woman. She seems to greatly love her husband's wild career and stood by him through the danger. It isn't until years later in 1936, when Rachel is much older, that she reads an article in a newspaper telling the sad story of Harry Houdini's death. Some young man dared Harry to let him punch him in the stomach as hard as possible. Unfortunately, the young man did not wait for Harry's preparation and punched him without warning. The damage caused by the blow was irreversible and Harry died shortly after. At the end of the article, Rachel thought of the day when she met Bess Houdini.

It has been a good day. It is then that Rachel realizes her home is going to be safe once again and maybe just a little exciting as well. On the pier, the smell of food wafts through the air—cotton candy, hotdogs, and popcorn. As the sun cascades above the ocean, Rachel grabs hold of Sylvia and Dick's hands. The screams and laughter of children still brighten the air making it the very best place. It seems that no one had chosen the normal dull colors of everyday clothes to wear; rather, everyone is adorned in their finest outfits. The combination of stripes and solids is dazzling.

Suddenly, the sound of music fills the air. Just ahead she sees the large sign of a restaurant. Quickly, she hurries over to look in the windows. It isn't too crowded, but that would change once the sun went down. A woman stands at the microphone and sings. She is moving seductively, raising her hand in the air as she sings, and immediately Rachel loses track of everything else. With all that has happened to her, she still misses it. It isn't the actual stage that she yearns for—but rather, the music.

The doorman looks at the little girl with a sideways glance as she rushes past him, yet he doesn't say anything. If he hadn't had seven beers and two shots of whiskey before his shift, he might have stopped Rachel to question her. His eyes are heavy, his hands are numb, and the most he can think about at the time is the fact that his belt feels too tight. So instead of questioning the girl, he simply watches her.

Rachel pushes her way through the crowd and stops at the stage. It all seems so glamorous when it isn't her up on the stage. The tall woman moves along with the jazz number. Rachel smiles and finds herself a seat on the first step of the stairs. Her eyes are fixed like cement even as Sylvia and Dick come to stand behind her.

Later, Dick leads Rachel out of the crowded restaurant. "I think it's been a beautiful day," Dick says.

"Beautiful enough to have some ice cream," Sylvia encourages.

"What a wonderful idea, Sylvia. Don't you think, Rachel?"

On their way home, Rachel sits contentedly in the back of the car staring out the window as a train passes and she eats the creamy treat. The chug of the engine makes her wonder if Levi has to take a train wherever he is. Later that night as she lay on the floor under her bed, she reads Levi's letter again and again; hoping that this time, it won't be like Simone, and that she will actually be able to see him again.

Chapter Fourteen

1918

In 1917, the first American troops land on European shores and the United States declares war on Germany on April 6th. By June, nearly 10 million brave U.S. men have begun registering for the draft. Meanwhile, 41 suffragists are arrested in front of the White House, the first jazz record is recorded, and the Red Sox trade Smokey Joe Wood, claiming that his arm is dead at the old age of 26. 1918 is the year of Babe Ruth's 29 home runs, the year of a devastating outbreak of influenza that kills nearly twenty million people, and the year that the Armistice is signed, ending World War I, and it comes quickly without anyone realizing what great things lie ahead.

On the seventh of July in 1918, Rachel wakes to the sweet smell of cake. As any child would do, she tears the covers off and shoots out the door nearly taking Sandy down as she runs into him in the hallway.

"It's a special day, isn't it?" Sandy says with a smile.

Rachel doesn't know what he is talking about, but she smiles anyway. She loves cake and wants to see it and smell it even if she will have to wait until later in the day to have it. Like a bounding lion she takes the stairs so fast that she nearly falls on the very last one. Finally, racing around the banister and into the kitchen, she finds Dick standing next to Sylvia sticking candles into the tallest, pinkest, most beautiful cake she has ever seen. She runs to it with a sideways smile and Dick lays a hand on her blonde head.

"You're up early. I guess that's a good thing. Do you love your cake?"

Rachel looks up at him with question.

"Don't you know what today is?" he asks as she climbs onto the stool near the counter to get closer to the cake. "It's your birthday."

The year before, when Dick and Sylvia tried to celebrate her birthday with her, it meant nothing. She hadn't wanted to join in much of the celebration, but it is different now. "As soon as we sing to you, you can eat your breakfast," Dick explains.

Before long, the entire kitchen is filled with all of the house staff. Gregory and Sandy, the men whom she knows the best, stand close to her and clap their hands as the entire place is filled with singing. Afterwards, she sits at the table waiting for her breakfast. Sylvia takes a knife, cutting from the cake a large piece and setting it carefully on a plate, then Dick offers it to her. He can see her surprise so he lets her in on the secret. "My mom started a tradition when I turned ten. On my birthday every year, I could always eat my cake for breakfast. I woke up to the smell of my favorite kind…" he looks at the cake then at her, "…we didn't know your favorite kind so you're eating mine. Lemon cake with cream filling."

Rachel waits a moment just staring at the cake, then with a large fork and an even larger piece of cake on the end of it, she stuffs it into her mouth. The taste is amazing. Before she takes another bite, she looks up at Dick and Sylvia. It runs across the child's mind for the first time that maybe they are going to be around for a while. Maybe she will actually be able to stay and live her life in this house with them?

"Thank you," she says. Everyone in the room is silent until Dick and Sylvia look at each other with shock and tear-filled emotion, while Rachel looks back at the cake. "I love this cake. I think it's my favorite kind too." Sandy, who stands beside Dick, squeezes his shoulder with controlled glee. From this day on, the house is filled with a little girl's voice.

One day, Dick and Sylvia drive to the outskirts of Atlantic City with Rachel riding happily in the backseat. They follow the straight and dusty road that is straddled on each side by vast open fields. There isn't much but clumps of trees overgrowing into each other. Finally, Dick pulls onto a narrow road that ends at a large, yellow-slatted, brick house. "Don't be scared." He winks when he sees Rachel's concern and then he places a hand on her head. "Sylvia and I feel like we need some more space especially since the show is doing so well. And for you . . . you need a place to run . . . so we found this house and wanted to bring you first. It's up to you, Rachel. We will gladly stay where we are, if you prefer."

They wander through the expansive property and Rachel looks around in awe. It is just like a life-sized dollhouse, perfect in every corner. It doesn't take long before Rachel gives the Jenners the okay to move. So, they leave their house in the city in order to move to the country with all the animals in tow. Just running along the plush land, wild and free, makes Rachel think about Bernie. She started her life in the country and now she is back—this place feels more like home.

The first few weeks are all about discovering every corner of the interior, but it's the rolling hills of the exterior that are her favorite. She tucks herself in a ball and rolls down, landing in a fit of laughter. Nothing has changed with the animals' schedule, they still must be fed and brushed at the same times, but now, there is space to roam. No more cages, no more confinement. Strangely, Rachel understands. Sylvia fills vases with her own homegrown flowers and sticks them in every room nearly every day. It's almost as though everyone has forgotten what happened to Rachel, but Rachel. Her nightmares have remained, and every so often, her wounds come out to play.

One day while Sylvia is out tending her garden, Dick is at the large dining table figuring out their bills. He laughs as Rachel runs by playing with their latest addition to the animal sanctuary—a dog named Ohno. He found them two days after they moved in, and Dick didn't have the heart to tell him to leave even though he loved to irritate the camels.

Rachel tosses the ball here and there, as Ohno chases it happily. Again and again, it hit corners and took cockeyed leaps over the furniture. Then suddenly, bouncing at just the right angle, the ball flies down the hall, so that Ohno doesn't see it. Rachel fetches the toy. It bounces right, then left, then directly into an open doorway and down some stairs. Happily, Rachel races ahead, running down the stairs until she can't see the steps in front of her because it's so dark. It's too late when she realizes she is in the basement. With a rush of wind, the door swings on its hinges and shuts with a heavy thud. Instantly, she is in pitch black as the ball clangs and knocks things over beneath the steps. Panic floods her. She can feel the scream rise from her belly, into her chest, until it breaks free.

"Daddy!" she cries. She can't see anything. The cold, damp, mildew smell is no different than at Bill's house. All has been a dream—a wonderful dream—and now she's realizing that her nightmare never ended. Instantly she starts listening for Bill's footsteps and his deep breathing. "Daddy, help!"

"Rachel!" Dick yells as he jumps to his feet and his strong legs carry him quickly through the hallways. "Rachel!"

Finally, he hears her voice from behind the door to the basement. "Damn!" He throws it open. Rachel is frozen in the middle of the stairs, paralyzed by fear. Taking two steps at a time Dick reaches her fast and grabs her in his arms. "Shhh, I got you. I got you," Dick says as he hurries up the stairs and locks the door behind him.

Her shaking arms wrap tightly around his neck as he leans back against the wall out of breath. "I'm so sorry, Rachel. I'm so sorry," he whispers.

That night as he puts her to bed, he looks in her eyes and brushes her hair back. "Do you want to talk?" But Rachel shakes her head. "You know that you are safe with us?"

"He didn't like me," Rachel says quietly.

"Who?"

"Bill."

"Did he hurt you?"

"I was supposed to sing and sometimes I didn't want to."

"He didn't like that?"

Rachel looks away. "One time I didn't feel good and I said that I couldn't sing." Rachel lifts her shirt and shows Dick many round scars on the side of her stomach. She whispers, "His cigarettes were hot."

Dick tries to keep the emotion out of his eyes, but his chest tightens. "Levi said something about the basement."

She nods. "I could only come out to sing."

"Rachel, we are going to take care of you. You are safe here and I will make sure you stay that way. I promise. Do you know that?" To which she nods.

The next morning, Dick peeks his head into her room, and finds that once again, she's under the bed, not on it.

1998

I never liked basements and I'm pretty sure that every kid I knew wasn't crazy about them either. Once, Lou and I locked Jimmy in our basement for five minutes and in just that time he got so angry with us that he didn't speak to us for three days. In a child's world, three days is forever.

"What are ya thinkin' about, Bobby?" Gramma asks as she sniffs a flower I have just picked for her.

"Just your story, Gramma."

It is strange the things that she remembers. In three minutes, she isn't going to remember how she got the flower in her hand, and she probably won't remember how to get back to the old folks' home, even though it is just behind us about fifty yards. However, she can remember that in 1917 Babe Ruth hit 29 home runs, anything about women's suffrage, and a flu that killed nearly 20 million people just after the war ended.

"It seems like she's happy," I say, grabbing another flower when Gramma accidentally drops hers.

"She was. Dick and Sylvia were in love with that little girl. They wanted her to have everything and they worked hard at bringing her back to life." She pauses for a moment and looks at me. "You gone to see your daddy?"

"Yes, Gramma. I saw him last night."

"How's he doin?" she asks as though she doesn't know he's had a stroke. "He hasn't come to see me in a while."

I stop talking. Momma sometimes chooses to keep things from Gramma because, "she won't remember them anyway, so why worry her". But for some reason, this feels wrong to not tell a woman about her son. "Well, Gramma he hasn't been feeling good."

"Is he sick?"

"Yeah, Gramma, he is."

"Oh, I just knew it. He always comes to see me. You'd tell me if something was wrong wouldn't you, Bobby? I'm no child and yet people treat me like one."

"Okay . . . well then, Gramma, he's had a stroke."

My fears of sharing this information are realized when, in the middle of our walk, surrounded by the serene country, my grandma drops to the ground. Just like a child, she lets all her wailing out, free and without care.

"Gramma," I say dropping to my knees beside her. How can I get her to be quiet? People are starting to look. "You okay?"

"My boy, my boy," she cries over and over almost as though I'm not there. Large tears run down her smooth cheeks racing each other to jump off her chin before she wipes them away.

"Excuse me." I hear the voice behind me. It is calm and collected. "Can I help?"

I turn to see a woman, with tanned skin, chestnut-colored hair, and hazel eyes. She looks at me with concern and I connect the dots of her situation. Just down the sidewalk is an old woman bent at the waist over a walker, looking frail and wrinkled with white hair curled high and flying in the breeze waiting for the woman beside me. She is clearly here to visit—most likely her grandmother.

"Mrs. Johnson," the woman says coming to my grandma's side and laying a hand on her shoulder.

"Oh, you know each other?" I ask.

"Sure, she's friends with my grandma." Gramma is still loud and wailing. The stranger looks at me with soft eyes. "What happened?"

"I just told her about my father. He's had a stroke."

"Oh. You must be her grandson?"

"Yep."

She kneels beside Gramma and points to the lake. "Mrs. Johnson, did you see that they filled the lake nearly to the brim. You remember my grandma and I talking about that last week."

Gramma, as though she was never upset, looks at the water. "Is that why they had those men here last week?"

"Yes," the woman says with a smile, "You remember us talking about that?"

"Of course," Gramma replies. She raises an eyebrow of confusion. "Why in the world am I on the ground?"

"You decided to sit, but do you wanna keep walking?" I ask.

"Yes, of course." Gramma takes my hand as the woman and I help her climb carefully to her feet.

"Thank you." I say to the stranger. "It's kind of you."

"No problem. I think they've tried to tell her about your father a couple of times. But she just forgets too fast," she whispers so that my grandma can't hear.

"It might have been nice if my Ma told me." I laugh.

She chuckles and I instantly like her smile. "It's hard to know what to do. Well, I should go. She's waiting."

"Thank you, really. I would have had no clue what to do."

"Don't worry, I was the same way at first."

"I'm Bobby," I say, sending my hand out to her. She takes it and I feel the warmth from her touch.

"My name is Mandy."

"Mandy." I nod and then reluctantly let go of her hand. "Well, I hope to see you around."

"I come a couple times a week."

"Okay, looking forward to it."

With that, she walks away, but she gives me just a little bit of hope when she peers over her shoulder one more time. Now that Gramma is on her feet, I begin to walk her back home.

"So, Gramma, let's not stray too far in our conversation. Where was Levi through all of this?"

"Through all of what, honey?"

"The years that Rachel lived with Dick and Sylvia."

"He was in that god-awful war . . . left the year before it started and didn't come home until it was over. College had to wait because well, that's how Levi always was after meeting Rachel—full of duty. And he really was a great soldier. He worked hard and earned enough praise that he quickly climbed the ranks." She grins, "He also grew into a man and filled out from head to toe."

1918

At the end of July, Rachel receives her first letter from Levi in over a year. She reads it word for word as she sits on a hilltop just outside the back door of the new yellow house.

Dear Rachel,

I have been unable to write to anyone for quite some time, as we have been very pursuant of the German troops that are trying desperately to push their way into France. You know, I never thought I would see the world under these conditions, but here I am…

As he speaks in the letter, she pictures him in his uniform, surrounded by flashing lights and heavy artillery. Just the thought scares her.

FRANCE

He had been in his uniform writing letters to his family and to Rachel. With sweat on his brow and his face covered in filth, he sits on a brick wall that stands just above a street as tanks amble by. Men shout, "Watch the walls!" and "Get out of the way!" His dusty boots dangle just above the heads of his army buddies.

One of his friends, Carter, reaches up as he walks by and hits the heel of his black leather sole. "Writing to your girl?"

"Haven't got time for a girl, Carter."

"Then family?"

"I figure I should remind them that I'm still here and not in a shallow ditch somewhere."

"Good idea." Carter hurries on passing a large group of French soldiers who laugh and chuckle—most likely the reaction to some dirty joke. In the middle of Europe, knee deep in muddy trenches, this is the first opportunity Levi has had to write home. His first letter is to Rachel. After only one paragraph, his captain comes up behind him and says, "Need you for a moment, Price."

Levi turns around, squinting from the glare of the sun, and smiles. His captain is a good man with dark hair and a deep scar over his left brow. He is someone who cares about the soldiers more than just giving orders and Levi is one of his favorites. His name is Albert Kennel, but everyone calls him Captain Nel.

"Captain Nel!" Levi salutes, then he stuffs the letter into his jacket pocket.

Captain Nel takes out his canteen for a sip of water before he speaks. "I need you to find a way around the church. It seems we've had a few imposing on us from somewhere around it. Take Feederman and one other man and scour that church from top to bottom. If we are going to make a counteroffensive to take back this river, we have to have that church squared away. Don't want any more Krauts breaking through our ranks."

"Yes, sir."

"Watch your backs and be careful." He looks at Levi with a grin, "Maybe when you get back, you'll be able to finish those letters."

"Yes, sir."

"Alright, come back safe, Price."

"Yes, sir."

Instantly, Levi is on a mission. He finds Feederman, a tall and lanky kid, playing cards with a group of soldiers. Feederman is the kind of guy willing to go to battle at any place and time.

Just at that moment, Carter passes by and Levi grabs his arm.

"You wanna come?" Levi asks after he explains the task.

"Not really. Do I have a choice," Carter says confidently.

"Nope." Levi pops his lips together.

A quarter mile down the road toward the front lines sits the church, broken and battered by the constant battle around it. Somehow the bell atop still remains even though most of its roof is caved in. The soldiers plaster themselves to the wall like oil on a rig. It's a ghost town with abandoned still-burning tanks and six-foot high rubble.

"Captain Nel thinks the enemy is somehow getting in through the church." Levi attempts to wipe the dirt from his face, but leaves more instead as he looks up at the sky in thought. Although he isn't higher ranking than either of the men in front of him, Captain Nel declared him leader over several hot spots along the Marne River since they arrived. "Let's take the back door and, Feederman, you just stand at the front." Feedermen agrees and runs out of sight.

Trying not to stumble on the debris, Carter and Levi take the last few paces to the back door. Levi sticks a hand out and carefully unlatches the heavy bolt trying his best to keep it quiet, yet due to the shrapnel and dust it squeals just slightly. Carter and Levi hold their breath until it stops. They enter with their rifles high and ready.

What awaits them is a long, dark hall lined with many doorways where the only light comes from quarter-sized holes made by gunfire from fighter planes. Levi steps in with the butt of his gun tucked into his shoulder and his heart thumping heavily in his chest. His hand shakes as he reaches out to open the first door on his left. Levi had never prayed a moment in his life until he joined the war and at this moment, his prayers are in a continuous cycle under his breath. Luckily, the room is empty. There is a desk with papers strewn about and books line shelves along the walls, but not a soul.

"Check those doors on that side." Levi directs Carter. Signs of the enemy fill every room—books, maps, and even ammunition as though they had to leave in a hurry. Levi searches every nook and cranny, tearing down irrelevant notes in shorthand scratch so he can see the walls, then he runs his hand along the floor under rugs and desks.

By the time he and Carter are done, sweat has darkened their uniforms. Their black boots are heavy so it's a task to keep them quiet as they enter the main sanctuary. Again, they find nothing but ornate detail and gothic-style furnishings. The beauty of the temple where so many have visited to lay their sins before priests is still there despite the broken ceiling, crumbling walls, and shattered glass. As usual, an assembly of American planes fly overhead and Levi looks up to watch them pass by. He'd often wished he'd learned to fly so that he would be in the sky instead of where he was—and if he gets home, that's what he's going to do.

Feederman lets out a whistle before he shows himself.

"Carter, follow along this wall and Feederman this one." Levi points to the two sides of the rectangular room, "Finish at the back. I'll check the pews."

Levi walks every square inch of the floor. The cement is chipped and scratched, but there is nothing out of the ordinary that concerns him. On his hands and knees, he keeps his gun strapped to his back never losing the realization of where he is. From his sight just below one of the benches his eyes fall upon some black boots in the corner of the room. For a moment they are still, and then Levi's hands tense when the boots take one step forward. With utmost precision so as not to disturb any of the rubble around him, Levi creeps just high enough to peek at the owner of the leather soles. The brownish, green suit with the gold encrusted hat gives the German soldier away immediately. Levi drops down, suddenly hoping that Feederman and Carter are just as aware of their company.

Slowly, the soldier crouches as he inches forward with his hands securely around his weapon. Where are Carter and Feederman? They are still hidden by the large confession booths at the end of the room, but Levi knows that it's only a matter of time until they are done searching and come back into view. With flushed cheeks and panic in his chest, he desperately tries to figure out what to do. Just behind a large cross, the enemy soldier lingers—awaiting any possible danger.

Levi holds his breath.

He could easily shoot the soldier, but where did he come from and how do we know there aren't many more? Just as the man, who seems to be only a few years older than Levi, begins to step out of hiding, Carter comes into a clearing and is now in plain view. Levi's ears pulse like a heavy drum, as he checks his gun anxiously. Instantly, the Wehrmacht steps back in the shadows seeming just as scared as he pulls his gun to his chest. His shaky arms lift the weapon to his chin causing Levi to roll over onto his stomach and take aim. Carter will be dead if he doesn't do something. There is no choice.

Before the soldier can pull the trigger, Levi pulls his. The church erupts with the pop of gunfire—the sound feeding off of the high ceilings made for perfect acoustics. Carter and Feederman duck with surprise as Levi jumps to his feet and heads for the soldier who is now lying on the ground—blood seeping from his chest.

"Where'd he come from?" Feederman asks as he reaches Levi's side.

"I don't know. We checked everything." Levi can't pull his eyes away from the man he just killed.

Finally, they turn their eyes back to the hallway. It is eerily quiet. In war, this only exacerbates the dread, knowing that the dark shadows are the perfect place to hide. Levi runs into the hall as Carter and Feederman follow. All three men enter each room together, searching once again. One of the rooms that Carter searched feels a bit different to Levi's gut. It is a classroom. They check every inch. It seems fine. More books are stacked against one of the walls and toys are piled in a corner. The window has been shot out, but the street outside is empty except for debris. Just as they are about to leave, Levi hears something, so he places his hand in the air, telling the others to hold.

Levi points to a large basket in the corner full of trash. Carter makes his way to it and feels the stiff straw under his fingers as he moves it away. Underneath is a circular hole just big enough for a grown man to fit through with a latch holding a circular door in place. They immediately prepare their guns. The hole doesn't seem new. In fact, it seems that it has been there, built as part of the church many years before. As if the French engineers had known that their country would face many wars, they had prepared, building tunnels from one place to another.

Levi signs, telling them that he is going to open it. Silently, he lifts the latch, then the door. There is a small bit of light revealing a dirt floor. Carter and Feederman's nerves show by the glistening of their skin. Captain Nel had known something like this was here. Many men had died from the enemy making their way across the Marne River and sneaking behind the lines only to disappear again.

Levi, using his steady and strong arms, lowers himself to the hard earth. Carter tosses his gun down just before he also shimmies his way through the small hole, then Feederman. Together they stand in a round room the size of a large closet. The walls and floor are carved dirt, but the ceiling is heavy timber. There are wires running along the ceiling, light bulbs burning, and just ahead of them is a door.

"This is---" Levi's voice trails off when he doesn't finish his concerned thought.

"There's something beyond that door," Carter nods.

"Let's go," Feederman says.

"There could be fifteen men behind that door," Levi disagrees.

"Blow it so they can't get through," Feederman suggests.

Just as Carter takes a step, the door ahead shakes as though someone is emerging. Immediately, the men bring their guns to ready position. With not an inch to hide, Levi, Carter, and Feederman feel the strain in their shoulders as they press themselves against the wall of dirt.

The door opens and several German accents fill the space. These voices are calm as though they have nothing to fear. Levi holds his breath. Then, the Germans see the Americans with weapons pointed which causes immediate chaos.

"Kommen Sie jetzt!" one of the soldiers yells.

"Put down your weapons!" Levi shouts with his English accent twisting every word. He knows just a few words in German. "Lassen Sie Ihre Waffen Fallen!" Before long, three more Germans appear. No one shoots, but everyone yells. No one understands each other. One of the short soldiers is sweating so heavily that it is dripping onto the dusty ground. Levi can see the horror in the man's face as his fingertip strokes the trigger. "Don't do it," Levi whispers.

The soldier takes a shot throwing Feederman back against the wall. Feederman drops to the ground and instantly shots ring out from everyone. It doesn't take long for several men to drop. Somehow Levi's body is missed, but he hasn't the time to think about it. He keeps shooting.

Carter takes down two more that rush in. When all of the Germans are down, Levi and Carter look at each other with shock. "You hit?"

"No," Carter says, eyeing his untouched uniform. "You?"

"No." Levi sounds as though he has run a marathon.

They walk into the next underground room, never letting their weapons drop. Four more Germans are prepared and waiting. Carter yells out when a bullet finds his shoulder. Levi pulls the trigger and suddenly it only clicks. He is out of ammo. Taking no time, he pulls his knife and throws himself on the last man standing. Levi stabs the man until his body gives up. "Run and get Captain Nel, Carter," Levi says between breaths. "Tell him that we need to blow this or send men to the other side. I'll wait here and make sure none of them get through."

Levi gathers ammunition from the fallen soldiers and then sits against the wall with the gun in his hand just staring at the door. While Carter goes after the captain, the guilt sets in for Levi. This is his first time taking someone's life. Their dead faces stare at him and he tries not to look as they lay motionless. Levi checks Feederman. He is gone. Moments seem like hours before Captain Nel finally looks down on Levi from above.

"Is Feederman dead?" Captain Nel asks.

Levi nods. "We have to block this tunnel, Captain. They're traveling under."

"Okay. Come on. Let's get Feederman out and then we'll blow it."

"Why don't we use it, Captain?" Levi hears one of the men behind Nel say.

"Won't do us any good . . . it will only bring us trouble."

Levi hoists Feederman's body to the soldiers above and then the captain comes down. He looks over the room beyond the door, grabs a map that the Germans left, then he tells Levi to leave.

"I'll do it, Captain," Levi says noticing the grenade in the captain's hand.

"You've done enough. I'm gonna throw it down and then we'll make sure it did its job."

Levi nods, then jumps up grabbing the arms of a soldier overhead that pulls him through. Moments later, the captain comes running and Levi pulls him up and out of harm's way. Only seconds later, they feel an explosion and dust billows from below.

On their way out of the church the captain looks at Levi. "I wonder how many more of those we'll have to worry about around this place. Good job, kid."

Later, they find that the two grenades did their job. The debris and rubble block any ability to cross the Marne River. That night, the captain lets Levi and a few of the men out for some rest and relaxation. They visit a bar and find some local women who seem all too eager for the Americans' attention. Uninterested, Levi pulls his letters out and continues writing. Suddenly, he doesn't know what to say.

Levi stays for several more months fighting off the Germans, all the while wondering whether he will ever feel the same as when he left New York. Finally, at five o'clock, on the morning of November eleventh, inside a railroad car surrounded by a French forest near the front lines, an armistice is signed. The agreement calls plainly for the cessation of fighting along the entire Western Front to begin at precisely eleven that morning. After more than four years of bloody conflict, the Great War is at an end.

§ § §

One day Dick shares the news with Rachel about the war. He reads the article from the newspaper. This is enough for Rachel to spend the rest of the day singing, whether it be in her room, outside with the animals, or all throughout the house. Dick and Sylvia, until that moment, had never been privy to Rachel's voice. She had barely spoken until recently, but as her sweet voice rises to the ceiling in joy, Dick and Sylvia can't help but look at each other. Rachel speaks incessantly of Levi returning home for many months, but unfortunately, the Levi who comes home isn't the same Levi who left. He doesn't come by to see her. In fact, he doesn't try and see anyone at all. Every time the bright sun hits his eyes, he is reminded of the nighttime flashes in the trenches.

Chapter Fifteen

1923

Time passes quickly. Women's suffrage is ratified in August of 1920 all because a twenty-four-year-old Assemblyman named Harry Burn casts the deciding vote in Tennessee. His mother wrote him a note saying, "Don't forget to be a good boy . . . vote for suffrage." The ladies at Sylvia's Thursday morning tea group laugh and clink their glasses to Harry Burn; meanwhile prohibition begins, Pancho Villa retires after deciding he is done with the Mexican government and these years after the war, people are still adapting to peacetime. In 1921, countries are restructuring their borders and Communist parties are on the rise. But it is the Lincoln Memorial, discovering insulin for diabetics, Benito Mussolini becoming the youngest Prime Minister of Italy, and hyperinflation of the German dollar that all characterize 1922.

It isn't until 1923 that Dick begins to wonder whether he is doing his best for Rachel. Although she sings around the house, she doesn't use her gift anywhere else.

"It's sad really," Dick says to Sylvia as they lay in bed.

"But what are you going to do, Dee? You can't push her."

"Why not? I mean, I know why we didn't at first, but she's fourteen now. Sometimes I wonder if it's time."

"Time for what?"

"I don't know. I just don't know. It's not like I want her to be performing . . . plenty of people never do that, but we've heard the ragtime she sings. It's not about ragtime anymore. Maybe she would want to learn something new. I know people. They could come and introduce her to new music. She clearly loves it. The child never stops singing."

"I just think we have to be careful. Pushing her into anything like that can really affect Rachel after what happened."

"You remember when she was a baby and we looked at her, knowing, just knowing, that she would do something special?" Sylvia looks at him lovingly, but doesn't say anything, so he continues. "We're letting her hide here. For a while that was okay, but what I'm saying is how do we take that gift that she's been given and do what we're supposed to do as loving parents? Train it, give her reason to have confidence, and then let it loose."

"What was in your food tonight?" Sylvia chuckles.

Dick stands and walks to his closet where a mirror hangs on the wall. For just a moment he notices the wrinkles lining his eyes and the gray that speckles his hair, then he turns to Sylvia and grins. "I'm getting older but you know why I don't care? I don't care because I took chances. I met you and I've done what I love for years. I've failed miserably at things as well as succeeded. I'm ready to get old."

"So…"

"So, she needs to do the same."

"She's fourteen."

"Yes, but we started late. Think what she could do. I don't know, Sylvia, I don't really know what to do, but that's why I'm saying something. I simply want to try and bring the true Rachel out so that the abused Rachel is left behind."

"Well, let's talk to her about it."

"No, I don't think we should. I think we should just figure it out on our own."

"Be careful, Dick…"

"Of course." With his dark good looks, he walks across the room and lays on Sylvia. "You two are my life. I want her to be everything that she can be."

"Me too," Sylvia says placing a hand along his cheek.

The next week, Dick sits with Rachel on the edge of a dock as they hold tightly to the end of their fishing poles. Fishing is something they enjoy doing together, soaking up the peace and quiet. When the sun lowers just a bit, a car pulls up behind them and a few men step out. Dick peers behind him.

"Didn't know if y'all would make it," Dick says as he raises his hand to shake that of the first, tall man with dark drown skin, a bit darker than Bernadette's.

"Of course. Fishing is one of our favorite things," the man says.

"Well, it's good to see you." Dick turns to Rachel. "Rachel, meet my friends: P.B. Nelson, Jake Smith, and Carl Fitts. Boys, this is my daughter, Rachel."

The men are surprised to see such a beautiful teenager, as they always considered Sylvia to be absolutely lovely, but nothing to look at. Dick never mentioned her adoption or her unfortunate time with Bill Manchuron.

"It's great to meet you. We've heard quite a bit about you."

It is common for Rachel to meet friends of her father, however, this time one of them grabs her attention immediately. He introduces himself to her with a perfect thick lipped smile and smooth brown skin. "I'm Jake." He seems a bit older. Maybe sixteen or seventeen, but his confidence is spellbinding. His eyes aren't just brown; rather they have nearly a reddish tint to them.

"It's nice to meet you," Rachel says shyly.

"Well, you been catching anything good?" P.B. asks as he sits down.

"Not today. It seems that a beautiful summer day is all we're going to get."

"That'll do, won't it?" P.B. seems to be in his thirties, tall and lean, with kindness in his eyes.

"Rachel, these boys play at P.B.'s bar on the outskirts of town," Dick explains. "They came in the other day and I told them about you."

An intense panic grabs Rachel's gut until she has to look away, pretending to watch the water.

"Yeah, your pa was saying you have something special," Jake says kneeling beside P.B. "Is it true you sang with Eubie Blake?"

"When I was little," Rachel practically whispers.

"And James Europe!" Dick says quickly.

"Dad!" Rachel grumbles.

"That's amazing. I'd give anything to have that kind of opportunity," Jake says.

"We don't mean to be talking to you too much about it, Rachel. It's just that music is our life…" P.B. takes his shoes off and places his feet in the water. "It's all we do." He turns to Jake. "Grab your guitar. Let's show her something."

Usually, Rachel wouldn't want to have any part of sharing music with anybody, but she can't stop sneaking peeks at Jake. Dick stays quiet, smiling in his heart, but hiding it on his face. He doesn't want to push, but he also doesn't want her to stay so distant to something that seems so important to her. For the last several years, he's watched her stop and listen whenever music is playing, no matter where she is—along the street, on the radio, or she's singing herself.

Jake returns with his guitar in his hand and sits on a nearby rock. His dark fingers begin plucking and strumming so intricately that she loses sight of where his fingers are. As usual, the moment the music begins, Rachel can't help but pay attention. P.B. begins to sing and Carl, a man with pasty white skin, a mustache, and extremely long fingers, drums sticks on a can. They fall into rhythm, needing nothing more for fulfillment than this. Rachel is not that different. If music had a hold on anybody, it's her. What they play is different than Eubie Blake or James Reese Europe. It's less practiced, less refined, but still addicting. It sways more and instead of the hard beats, it rolls smoothly like hills in the countryside. When they stop, Rachel and Dick clap excitedly.

"You're great," Rachel admits, forgetting all reasons she shouldn't join in.

"It's the new stuff now. It takes Blues, jazz, ragtime, and adds a bit," Jake says as he strums something quickly to show her more of the style.

"You know any songs?" P.B. asks.

Immediately, Rachel feels the wall rise once again. She shakes her head. "No."

"It's alright . . . you don't have to sing . . . even though your father always talks about how great you are. Maybe if I know a song that you like---"

For the first time, Rachel frowns at Dick. She is desperate to act normal, to pretend there's nothing wrong, but it is written all over her face and she knows it. Her heart hasn't raced this hard in a while. Perhaps noticing that she's uncomfortable, Jake plays something anyway. Instantly Bernie's face appears in Rachel's vision, raising her hands in church as the song "I Surrender All" is played. They can tell she knows the song and P.B. sings a verse then stops, looking at the blonde beauty.

"You know it. Sing." It is strange the way he says it. It isn't forceful, but it isn't weak; it simply gives Rachel no room to argue.

Jake plays without anyone singing and then Rachel stares at the water ahead of her that lay still in the humid summer evening. She rubs her cheek, but strangely feels the urge. Soon, she sings. It is comfortable and relaxed and he follows her lead easily. The world rights itself and she forgets that anyone is watching, just as it used to be when she sang for Bill. No matter what he did to her, when she was singing, it blocked everything but her obsession with the art. Mr. Penny trained her for ragtime and jazz, but Rachel felt each kind differently and adapted easily. Spirituals are still her favorite. When the song ends, P.B. speaks first.

"Well, I'll be. It's a shame you ain't singin'. I have never seen . . . well . . . the only women I know that sings like you is as buxom as the day is long."

As the afternoon sun hits the sides of their faces, Jake nods. "Amazing," he says simply. His grin is enough to change the beat of her heart. With a gentle hand, he continues to strum.

"I..." she begins, but doesn't finish when they hear a vehicle approaching.

A policeman pulls up close to the dock and Jake immediately stops playing and groans. Two large officers soon walk steadily with their fingers in their belts to the water's edge where the group sits. Dick stands up swiftly and takes a step to the officers.

"Good afternoon, officers. What brings you here?"

The officers keep their mouths shut for a short time and eye P.B. and Jake.

"They botherin' you?" the officers ask Dick.

"What?"

"Them..." the officer asks, "those colored boys botherin' you?" His words cause a jolt within Rachel, but she's not surprised by it. Bernie always gave lessons when they met men like this, and it happened plenty. Being with Dick and Sylvia, it had been a while since Rachel had dealt with such things.

Jake drops his shoulders with exhaustion and P.B. eyes them angrily.

"You're speakin' about my friends, officer," Dick says. Rachel had never heard Dick's voice so harsh.

"They're your friends?" the officer asks condescendingly.

"That's right."

This time P.B. stands to his feet, which worries Jake so he swiftly follows. He walks to P.B. and rests a hand on his chest. "We're just playing the guitar and minding our business," Jake says confidently.

"You're lettin' them around that pretty daughter of yours?" The officer whistles and looks Rachel over a bit too long. She is only just in the last year changing shape and gathering the wrong kind of attention from men. The officer's roaming eyes makes her skin crawl. Still focused on her, he continues, "Ain't a smart move, fella."

P.B. speaks in a more controlled rage than Rachel can fathom. "We've done nothing to you, officers. Just having a fine time. Can we get back to it?"

"P.B., you can wait for me to finish with this gentleman here." One of the officers reveals they have dealt with each other before.

"This is a shit load of ridiculous," P.B. growls.

"What'd you say?" the officer asks nearly charging him. "You're supposed to be down at Chicken Bone so I'm doin' you a favor for not throwin' a rope over this tree branch."

Dick and Jake step in the way.

"Come on now. Just let us be. We're fine here. We're all fine. In fact, if I have any more trouble with you, I'm going to have to go to your commander. I know him well," Dick says clearly.

The officer seems to hold his breath and then looks at Dick with frustration. Just before they walk away, the officer runs his fingertips along Rachel's shoulder and under her hair making everyone tense and uncovering fear and discomfort that Rachel didn't know she could feel. Soon, they jump in their vehicle and drive away.

"They're always givin' us trouble." Jake shakes his head and grabs his guitar once again.

"Who are they?" Rachel asks.

"The tall one is Officer Finnegan and the other is Officer Hannah. They give everyone around a problem. I guess it's just their way." Jake responds and sits right next to her, placing the guitar on his lap.

Rachel turns back to the water and feels Jake's eyes on her.

"They're just afraid of your power," Rachel smiles, after repeating something Bernie always said. For a moment Jake looks at her as though he had never heard anyone else say this. After a while he smiles, making her drop her head sweetly.

P.B. lays his hand on Dick's shoulder as they walk back to the edge of the water. Then he kneels beside Rachel.

"You interested in meeting a friend of mine? You might like her . . . she sings like there's jewels on her tongue. Her name is Bessie Smith and she's doing well for herself." Carl and Jake nod in agreement. "In fact, I'm thinkin' she's only here for a while . . . got other shows to do, you know."

Rachel is hesitant. Not really knowing if it's good for her to immerse herself in music once again, but her desperation to meet another woman singer far outweighs any apprehension.

"When, P.B.?" Dick asks while he gathers his fishing gear.

"Did she say nine, Carl?" P.B. asks with a turn of his head.

"Yep . . . think that's right."

"Your place?" Dick wipes his hands after he sets the things in the car.

"That's right."

"Okay," Dick grins, "We'll see you there."

"Beautiful," Jake says as he climbs to his feet.

Jake walks beside Rachel, a bit slower than the others.

"What did he mean by Chicken Bone?" Rachel asks Jake quietly.

"What . . . oh, Officer Finnegan? We have our own place, our own beach. They call it Chicken Bone Beach. It's the place where we're supposed to stay." Jake looks at her with curiosity. "You don't know this?"

"I don't . . . I've never heard of it before."

"You're one of those that are up in your own world then, don't care much about the black folk," he says with a smile.

"It's not that."

"I'm just givin' you a hard time…" They reach the cars and Jake sets his guitar down. When he looks back at her, he smiles. "Nice to have you coming to our parts tonight." Jake leans against the car with his hands in his pockets. "I'll see you, right?"

"Yeah." Rachel grins. She watches Jake all the way down the road as she and Dick rush home to get ready.

1998

"I remember Rachel talking about Jake and how beautiful a man he was. I'm sure she didn't realize how young the two of them truly were, but at that time, he was a man to her," Gramma says. I was still angry from the story of the two officers and Gramma could tell. "What's wrong, Bobby?"

"I would have given those officers a piece of my mind."

"Would you have?" Gramma asks. "And risk your life?"

"Gramma, the risk is no longer what I'm afraid of. I'm more afraid, now than ever, to not do something. Not to mention the way the officer looked at Rachel and touched her. As if she didn't have autonomy in her life."

"Bobby, did you know that women couldn't wear pants on the senate floor until 1993?"

I gave my Gramma a curious look. "That can't be right, can it? 1993 was just five years ago."

"Oh Bobby, women all over the world followed rules for the sake of men not touching them. It wasn't law but it was conditioned . . . if they wanted to walk on the senate floor and not be turned away by a man choosing whether their attire was appropriate, then they did what was considered appropriate. Until one day someone chooses to break the rule."

My life was all about following the rules. Not the lawful ones, the ones set for me by my father. Some he didn't have to tell me; it was just assumed. I thought of the backlash of breaking these rules and it still makes me shudder.

"Hey Gramma, Rachel's going to meet Bessie Smith? My Ma plays her music when she is cleaning the house on Saturday mornings." Though Ma didn't have a voice like Bessie, she used to sing as loud as she could, never caring who might be listening or judging. Bessie's voice is like lemonade on a hot day—refreshing and strong.

Still outside the retirement home, we walk back and I immediately notice Mandy as she and her grandmother have found seats to watch a show in the main hall. Mandy looks up to find me staring in her direction and she lifts a small hand to wave. I throw my hand up instantly. I look at my grandma. "You wanna go back to your room?"

"Sure, honey. I could use a nap."

"Okay, Gramma."

In her room, I tuck the blankets around her and take off her glasses.

"Oh, now I'm not tired."

"You look tired to me."

"Nope."

"Well, then . . . Rachel's gonna meet Bessie Smith."

"Yes, that's right, but most importantly she is excited about Jake being there."

1923

The club is full—so much so that people are leaning out the windows to smoke. Bessie Smith has attracted her fans and more. A mixture of color from skin to clothes, Black, white, Native, Asian, and more from Atlantic City came with their dancing shoes. P.B. owned one of the hottest clubs and did so by way of choosing a location in the country. On a back road, with barely any signs, he built this place with his bare hands. It had room for a nice sized band, a large dance floor, a bar, and a stage. He broke a finger in the process and practically his back, but doing so meant that he could keep the doors open to whomever he pleased.

One of P.B.'s men from his band, Alquan, an indigenous man from the Lenni Lenape tribe, brought his entire family every weekend to dance to the music. This consisted of seven sisters and two brothers, with many cousins here and there. They all arrived with smiles and flowers excited about Bessie Smith.

"Good evening, Dick," Alquan says as he opens the door for his wife and sisters. Dick is fixing his shirt as he comes upon the family.

"Good evening, Alquan and ladies! Are you excited about Bessie Smith?"

"We are!" they all say as they hurry inside while the pluck of the piano pours out the open door and onto the wet grass outside. P.B. notices them quickly and comes to their side with his large hands held out.

"Glad to see you!" he says with a happy chuckle.

"Glad to see you, P.B." Dick smiles.

"Same here, P.B." Alquan says. Alquan's wife, Chepi, the same little girl who went to school with Simone and Rachel, hands P.B. a bag full of herbs from her garden just down the road.

"For your mother's fatigue. I believe this will help. Just a bit in her tea." Chepi's beauty is the obvious kind with not a lick of makeup.

"Thank you Chepi," P.B. says as he kisses her cheek. "I'll make sure she tries it. Come on in everyone and have some lemonade!"

Rachel and Chepi stare at Bessie as she enters. Bessie's dress is a greenish blue with glitter-like jewels around the waist. She has a large pendant on her chest that moves to the sway of her rhythm. It is clear that she feels the music all the way down to her toes. Rachel is caught up in her beauty until she notices Jake playing the guitar. He is waiting for her to notice him and when she does, her heart skips.

P.B. stands next to her and grins.

"She's good, ain't she?"

"The best." Rachel is mesmerized.

When the set is over, P.B. calls Bessie down and introduces her to Rachel.

"Rachel's got a voice, Bessie," P.B. says with his head cocked to the side.

Bessie looks Rachel over as though she is doubtful but then drops her playful skepticism and gives her a smile.

"You gonna compete against me, huh?"

"No, ma'am, I just want to listen."

"What the hell do ya mean, honey? If you're as good as me, there ain't no time to be listening. You gotta do it, don't ya?"

Rachel doesn't know what to say to the extraordinary woman.

"You're recordin' somethin' soon, aren't ya, Bessie?" P.B. asks her.

"Yep. Me and Clarence are comin' out with Columbia. Guess you should buy it, shouldn't you?" she asks with a wink.

"Yes, ma'am. I certainly will," Rachel answers.

P.B. laughs and wipes his sweaty forehead. In the middle of summer, with the swarm of people pressed together, it is downright nasty. Women and men are dressing down as much as possible, although P.B. is careful about keeping his place looking classy. He does what he has to, to keep people from stripping down too far.

"I even stand on my bar at midnight," he tells Rachel later as Bessie sings another few songs, "and I throw water over 'em if the party's just beginnin'."

"People like that?" Rachel asks.

"When it's hot enough, people beg for it."

"What's that?" Rachel points to a couple dancing. They are better than anyone else on the dance floor.

"They're doin' the Charleston."

"The what?"

"There's a Broadway musical that came out this year called Runnin' Wild. It came from that."

Finally, at 11:30, Bessie takes to the bar for a drink and rest, then leans against it to watch everyone continue the party.

Dick comes to Rachel. "It's time we go,"

"Okay," Rachel nods.

Before they leave, Jake makes his way to Rachel's side. "You leavin'?"

Rachel nods as she sips some water.

"Okay. Well, I hope you had fun."

"I did."

"Good. Maybe next time I won't be playing the whole time and we can dance or somethin'."

Rachel can feel her cheeks blush. Before long Bessie Smith joins them. "You know this kid, Jake?"

"Sure do, Bessie."

"Beautiful, ain't she . . ." Bessie places her arm around Rachel. "I hear she's as good as me."

"She's amazin'," Jake grins.

"Well, honey, do somethin' with it."

Bessie walks away, but not before she runs her hand along Rachel's cheek and Jake whistles once she's gone.

"Just add her to the list of people you've met..." he hesitates for a moment and then laughs. "I'm glad you came." Jake's eyes dive deep into her soul.

"I'll never forget meeting her," Rachel admits.

For years, Rachel heard about Bessie, the Empress of Blues. Sadly, her career ended after a car accident heading to Mississippi on Highway 61 in 1937. It was a tragic day for music, but until that moment, Bessie sang her heart out.

§ § §

Rachel waits nervously while tapping her foot on the grass just outside P.B.'s club. She thinks of walking away several times, but P.B. soon arrives and pulls his keys out of his pocket.

"Hello, beauty. Whatchya doin' here?" he says as he opens the door. He looks around the countryside. "How'd ya get here?"

"I walked."

"You walked? You're nearly four miles from here."

"Would you help me?" she asks quietly.

"Help ya with what?"

"Well, I'd like to start singing again."

He stops moving. "You would?"

"Yes. But just for fun, not on stage."

"Okay," P.B. says.

"Just for fun?" Rachel asks concerned.

"Just for fun, Rachel. I promise. Come in."

"Okay."

That evening, just her and P.B. sit at the piano and play a few songs. He keeps to himself all his thoughts about how good she truly is, just hoping she'll find herself again. Then as he drives her home, he invites her to come again. She arrives the next night and the night after, and so on. It takes a while, but her love returns and every chance she has to sit around with the boys and play, she does. The only thing that makes any of it better is that Jake is always nearby. He finds reasons to touch her. Yet nothing seems to make it concrete—a real relationship.

§ § §

In 1924, George Gershwin's "Rhapsody in Blue" premiers at Carnegie Hall, J. Edgar Hoover is appointed head of the FBI, and Hubble announces the existence of distant galaxies, but before anyone knows it, the year comes and goes.

Suddenly, 1925 is upon them. In a year when Babe Ruth is out of play for five weeks due to ulcer surgery and the Ku Klux Klan have their first National march in Washington D.C.; in this year Rachel's childish looks have melted away into a striking sixteen-year-old. Between school, Jake, and singing, there's something else that she's thinking about more and more every year. She's wondering where

Simone could be.

Dick notices Rachel's growing preoccupation and finally asks to share what is on her mind. "Just like Levi," she tells him, "I thought that I would see Simone again…"

"That's the way of life, Rachel. People sway in and out of it." Dick lays a fatherly hand on her shoulder. "Hey, listen . . . I have your papers . . . the ones from Bernie. I'll see if I can look at them and remember where you and Bernie lived. It's been a long time, but you never know…"

"You think we can find Simone?"

Before long, after Dick searches her papers, they are traveling down a dirt road and Rachel is grasping Simone's directions, scribbled on paper. Her nerves have made her sick to her stomach and her hands are sweating. As they barrel along the dusty road, things begin to grow oddly familiar.

"We're here," Dick says looking around at the quiet homes.

"Already? I've been living this close?" There is regret in her voice.

"It seems the place has gone down just a little," Dick says as he watches children play along the dirty street.

"No," Rachel says in an almost dreamlike fashion, "no, this is exactly how it was. It hasn't changed a bit."

"How on earth do you remember—you were only five?"

"I'll never forget this place." She closes her eyes as she breathes in the smells. The memories are permanently melted to her pallet. Dick parks just in front of a candy shop at her request. The roads could have been washed with honey and it wouldn't have been sweeter than when she steps from the car for the first time. It is another world. She has suddenly entered a glorious memory; only now she is looking with older eyes. After a minute she opens the door to the candy shop. The same sweet smell of chocolate and peppermint hits her nose.

Dick stays close by, enjoying every moment of her sentimental reminiscing. She buys a couple of chocolates and then they move on. They wander down the street as people sit and stare at them from their store windows and children running by stop to look at them. For a moment he feels out of place, yet when he sees the joy on Rachel's face, he smiles. She appears more comfortable than she has in years.

"That's it," Rachel says pointing down the street at a large house on a hill.

It seems out of place and he looks at her with confusion. "Bernie owned that?"

"No," she grins. "That was Mr. and Mrs. Ashton's place. We lived in the small one next to that one while Bernie tended after the Ashtons."

He sees the tiny backhouse just next to the mansion. Both homes have been boarded up. Across the street is the church standing just as upright as when Rachel left. She realizes, if there is a place that she might be able to find someone who knows Simone, it will be there. They enter the church from the large front doors and find a couple of people chatting in the front hall. The women in nice dresses look at the blonde teenager and her father. Their eyebrows lift out of curiosity.

"Can I help you?" one of the ladies asks.

It isn't until she speaks, but when she does, Rachel knows exactly who it is. Clarine is older with gray hair and glasses, but for the most part she is the same.

"Clarine?" Rachel asks.

"Yes?"

"It's me . . . Rachel . . . Rachel Anne Praline."

The woman throws a hand over her mouth and shakes her head with wide eyes that teeter back and forth as she stares at the blonde beauty. "Oh, my Lord, Jesus . . . honey, honey, honey . . ." Clarine throws her arms around Rachel and squeezes her tight. Then she takes her face with her well-manicured hands, "You are just a sight . . . look at you . . ."

"This is my . . ." Rachel hesitates as she thinks about what this might mean. The last time she was there, Bernie was her mother. She wonders if it is unfair to call someone else her parent as though she is mistreating Bernie, "Dick Jenner."

Clarine looks at him with suspicion. "You're not the man that took her from us?"

Just the reminder is enough for Dick to understand that this might be a difficult trip for Rachel, but he steps forward with a smile anyway. "I'm not. You have a beautiful neighborhood around here."

Clarine steps back. "Who in the world are you kidding, Mr. Jenner?" She laughs. "Come with me. You must see Affie. He is goin' to just go wild when he sees you. He still talks about you to this day."

"Really?" Rachel asks as Clarine pulls her to the sanctuary.

Just ahead of them, is an older and grayer Affie, standing at the pulpit and practicing his sermon. He looks up when they enter and quickly closes his Bible.

"Good mornin'." He takes his glasses off and starts down the stairs. "Who do we have here?"

"Affie, baby, this is Rachel. Rachel Praline."

He stops walking and nearly stops breathing. It appears that he doesn't know what to feel, whether embarrassed or excited. Finally, he shakes his head, "Of course it is! Look at you." He too, tosses his arms around her and gives her a kiss on the cheek.

When Affie notices Dick he reaches out his hand to introduce himself. "So you've been takin' care of our dear Rachel?" He turns back to her, "My goodness it is good to see you. Are you still singing?"

There is an awkward pause and a strange but vaguely familiar feeling rushes over Rachel. "Just a little."

"Oh no, no, no with a voice like yours, you should be doing much more."

"Well, I really just came here to find someone," Rachel redirects kindly.

"Of course, of course . . . come on, let's step outside and I'll take you anywhere you need to go."

"I'm looking for Simone."

"Oh, honey, Simone's still in the same place she was when you left. Hasn't moved an inch," Clarine says lightly. "Come on now, we'll take you to her."

"Okay."

They talk incessantly as they walk along the road. Rachel learns of the people that have come and gone, of those that have died—some old and some young. When they finally reach Simone's house, Rachel wonders how she ever forgot the way. It looks just the same and sounds just the same—screaming children that can be heard from down the street.

Affie knocks on the door. Jerry, Simone's brother comes to the door with a drink in his hand. "Mornin', Pastor."

"Good mornin', Jerry. You remember Rachel Praline."

He has become a large man with heavy brown eyes that look her up and down with surprise. "Rachel?" He turns his back on them and quickly yells. "Simone!"

"Yeah!" a woman's voice yells back.

"There's someone here to see ya!"

"Damion wet his damn shorts again. Tell them to come back!" Simone yells.

"I'll take care of it. Now you come and see who's here before I knock you upside the head," Jerry hollers.

The pounding in Rachel's ears has moved to her jaw and is now traveling all over her skin as she waits for Simone to appear. Rachel's not sure why she's so afraid, but even trying to shake it from her hands doesn't work. Dick touches her shoulder, but it does nothing to calm her.

Then Simone appears.

Her hair is no longer wild, her eyes have matured, and Rachel thinks she's the most beautiful woman she's ever seen. She appears tired and worn out from the day, but other than that, Simone is just as vibrant as before. She's quite tall, standing many inches above

Rachel. At first nothing changes in Simone's eyes, and Rachel is terrified she somehow won't remember her, but then there's recognition and it sends Simone's brows nearly to her hairline.

"Rachel?" she asks, stepping forward.

Tears start to flow from both women, and they begin to laugh. It is loud and boisterous. Simone lunges forward taking her friend in her arms. Together, they hold on to each other for what feels like an eternity almost as if they are afraid to let go.

"Where have you been? I've been lookin' all over for you!" Simone cries out when she finally lets go.

"You have?"

"Yes! I went all over the place trying to find you, but no one would help me."

"Well…" Rachel doesn't even know what to tell her, or how. Affie, Clarine, and Dick are listening as they stand behind them on the porch and she wishes she could pour her heart out to Simone, just as they used to. "I've been here and there."

"Girls, why don't you take a walk." Clarine winks at them. "We'll take Dick to the cafe while you catch up."

"Can you?" Rachel asks Simone.

Simone leans into her house. "Jerry, I'm going out and I'll be back in a minute."

Some more screaming falls onto the porch from inside, but she acts undeterred as she closes the door. The teenagers link arms with each other and scurry away. As they walk down the middle of the road, they repeatedly gaze at each other in disbelief.

"Oh my God, is it really you?" Simone laughs.

"Look at us, we're all grown up."

"I feel happy again. My best friend's back."

"Me too."

As they cross the street, many of the people who pass take a second look, wondering if this is the same duo who caused so much trouble when they were children.

"Tell me everything," Simone says. "I have to know, where did you go? Why are you back? Everything." Rachel takes in a deep breath and more tears flow. "Why are you crying?" Simone asks with concern.

"I've wanted this forever."

"That day you left and all I could see was your eyes over the back seat . . . well, I wondered about you almost every night." Simone looks her over, takes a breath and nods. "He wasn't who we thought he was . . . was he?"

The emotion bubbles to the surface and Rachel cowers behind the nearest tree. "Simone, I can't tell anyone."

"I'm not anyone. I'm Simone. I just knew it, Rachel."

"How'd you know?"

"You know, my feelings. I saw you, Rachel. In my dreams, I saw you. You and that bear of yours in a rundown house, in the dark. I prayed for you every night."

"You did?"

"Yeah, I prayed someone would see you and save you."

Rachel hugs Simone again.

Simone continues, "Just hear me out, Rachel . . . Not another day will go by that you and me don't see each other. For better and worse. Now tell me what that horrible man did to you."

For nearly an hour, the girls walk arm in arm. Both beautiful, both grateful, and not too different than when they took walks as children. They take the same turns, pointing out landmarks of their relationship, and never thinking about stopping. When they pass fences, they stick their hands out to run their fingertips along the wooden pickets and end up in their field of orange flowers. Rachel tells Simone things that she's never spoken to another soul. "And your prayers worked." She explains how Levi saved her and helped her get to Dick and Sylvia.

"I'm so sorry." Simone shakes her head. "But you've also done some pretty damn exciting things."

"I guess so…" Rachel rubs her friend's arm. "So come on. Tell me about you."

"Momma got remarried and had three more babies that Jerry and I are taking care of during the day when she's at work. But that won't last long because I finished high school." Simone smiles. "Yeah, and as it turns out, I made a name for myself. Some woman came by a few years back after my teacher turned in my paperwork and math studies. This woman wants to help me with school, hell she wants to pay for the whole damn thing! I leave for college next year."

"College? That's amazing, Simone. I'm still working through high school. You always were smarter than me. What are you going to do with a degree?"

"Well, the same year Bill took you, my dad was killed just outside the town by a couple of police officers. They blamed him for looking at a white woman. Turns out it was just a co-worker. And that's when I knew."

"Simone, that's awful. I'm so sorry."

"That's the moment I knew, I was going to law school. Because of my test scores and grades, this woman is paying for all of it. Can you believe that?" Simone clears her throat as they pass the haunted house they used to be afraid of as children. She whispers about the old woman who used to live there, "I saw her the day before she died. She looked at me and said 'walk beside him' and then died that morning."

"Walk beside who?"

"Don't know. Couldn't ever figure it out." Finally, she stops, turns to Rachel and touches her face. "I thought you'd never come back."

"Why?"

Simone seems to have to think about it, "I overheard Affie talkin' to my mom about what he'd done and I just figured you'd never forgive him. I haven't spoken to him since the day you left."

"Affie?" Rachel asks confused. "What did he do?"

Simone looks at her with surprise. "You don't remember? He

wasn't supposed to take you anywhere when Bernie was sick, but then he took you to the city to sing. He's never forgiven himself for the fact that it's because of him that Bill found you and if you told him what Bill did to you . . . I will never forgive him, Rachel."

Memory is a funny thing. It's like drawers in the mind that can be shut tight and we don't even hold the key, but songs, smells, and people do. One word shared, one note sung, one whiff resurrects parts of you whether you want them to or not. Rachel suddenly rec-ollects that Bernie had been sick when they had gone to the city and that she had always taken great care that no one take advantage of her voice. She remembers running into Bill on the sidewalk with Clarine and Affie and feeling uncomfortable just by looking at the man.

Nausea floods over her until she's sweating and pale. However, even worse than sickness is the weight of Affie's betrayal. It seems, for the first time in Rachel's life, she is feeling anger instead of fear. Simone distinguishes it well.

"I've never forgiven him, Rachel. Affie took you from me all because he wanted the money. Even though I wanted to find you all these years, part of me was glad that you had gotten away. But now I know what actually happened." She peers off over a field of workers and then lays her arm over Rachel's shoulder. "I'm here for you. You be angry with him. You tell Affie to go to hell."

"He's the pastor…"

"Don't mind that. He took you from this place and now he thinks that everything is fine that you've come back and you're look-ing nice and have done well. He isn't gonna know that he sent you off to some molester and abuser. It's our job to tell him."

"Please don't. I've never told anyone. Only you."

Simone hesitates. "I understand. He doesn't need to know it all, but don't forgive him, okay."

"Okay." Rachel grins. "You always did take care of me."

Finally, Rachel and Simone make their way back. Even though it has been a good day, Rachel feels like her insides have gone through war. Having Simone back in her life brings so much joy, but sometimes when the past is opened, pain is waiting in the wings. As they stand together in front of the candy store where their car is parked, Rachel stares at Affie and he doesn't look the same. She keeps quiet as she holds her best friend's hand. The sun begins to set and Dick appears concerned.

"I'm sorry, Rachel, but we really should be going."

Rachel nods. Affie and Clarine grab her for hugs yet she says nothing. When they let go, she turns to Simone who is silently crying. Rachel wraps her arms around her. "Now that I know where you are, I'm coming back. I promise you. You're only minutes away. It can be like the old days only now it's a drive rather than a walk."

Simone smiles. "It's just so good to see you."

Rachel kisses her and presses her hands against her friend's sculpted face. Dick is already standing at the car with her door open. As they drive away Simone gives Affie and Clarine an angry glare just before she heads home with her arms tucked at her sides. As she watches the sun set, a smile spreads across Simone's face. Her best friend came home.

In the car, Rachel is suddenly overwhelmed by tears and finds it hard to catch her breath. Dick pulls the vehicle over onto the side of the road and, without a word, he wraps her in his arms as she deals with old wounds. It's an hour before her tears subside.

Chapter Sixteen

1925

The rain is heavy as Simone makes her way across the college campus. Her hair and clothes are soaked, and she's convinced she'll never get her books dry.

"Simone!" Someone hollers from across campus. One of her friends named Whitney is standing under the overhang of a dormitory with a large smile and a towel. "Come get this!"

Simone smiles and rushes over, grateful once the rain isn't blinding her. "Oh my goodness. It was dry before I went to class."

"I know! It came on fast." Whitney grabs her hand. "There's a party upstairs and I swear it has your future husband."

Simone is appalled and looks up at Whitney in horror. "Shut your mouth. I am too young for a husband with too much to do."

"Oh I know all of that, but your husband is up there."

"Whitney!"

"What! I can't help that I know this. I just do. Come on."

Whitney grabs her hand and they run up the stairs, through the halls, and can hear the music for several floors before they get there. Finally, they come upon the end of a hall where several rooms have people pouring out of them, yet the music only comes from a band that has been set up in the farthest dorm. Several men and women are playing what looks to be band equipment, while everyone around them are all split up in groups chatting. Before she can stop her, Whitney pulls Simone across the room to a man with a hat and glasses on, as he leans over several people talking politics. When he looks up, Whitney can't contain her excitement.

"Reed, this is Simone, Simone, this is Reed."

Simone looks at her friend with annoyance, then back at Reed who is looking her over. She can't help but admit, this man is handsome. More than handsome, he is gorgeous with his dark brown skin and kind eyes under the brim of a fashionable hat.

"Hello Reed." Simone says with a grin. "Nice to meet you. Let's go," she quickly says to Whitney.

Simone hurriedly pulls her friend away, but when she reaches the hall, she feels a hand tap her shoulder. "Excuse me." She hears the deep voice and turns around. Reed is standing there with his hat in his hands rather than on his head.

"Yes?" Simone asks.

"You know Whitney worked really hard to introduce us. She even borrowed my towel to bring you over." He reaches out and takes the wet rag from her hands. "I have to admit, that's a lot of work and we owe poor Whitney to at least see if I truly am husband material for a beautiful and audacious woman such as yourself." He smiles, increasing his looks by a thousand and sending a hot flash through Simone.

"Whitney!" Simone yells.

With a proud grin and a strange wave, Whitney backs away, leaving Reed and Simone together. Once she's gone, Simone chuckles and looks up at the beautiful man, but she doesn't say anything. Instead, she crosses her arms in front of her.

"Well," he says, looking around. "You like music?"

"Oh, you are going to have to do better than that." Simone shakes her head and starts walking to the stairway in order to leave.

"Wait, wait, what do you mean?" Reed asks.

She reaches the first step but doesn't take it. Instead, she looks directly into his eyes. "Reed, I am a law major, and I will one day be a black female lawyer." She raises her eyebrows. "Do you know what it takes for me to do that?"

"I'm a black man and an engineering major."

Simone opens her eyes wide, surprised at the audacity, then heads down the stairs away from him without a word.

"Wait! That doesn't make us similar?"

"No! It sure doesn't. Wear a wig, Reed. Put on some heels and a dress, then go get that engineering degree." She continues descending past the next floor.

She can hear him hurrying to catch up to her and this makes her happy, but she hides it well.

"You're right. You're right."

She turns back to him, stopping on the second-floor landing. "You just gave that to me?"

"What?" He asks utterly confused.

She clicks her tongue. "Reed, I do not have time for someone, especially a man, who isn't going to challenge me in every thought and every idea, arguing with me until the morning comes, for the rest of the years I will be in school."

Again, she walks away.

"Simone!" Reed calls out, then just as she's about to step foot on the main floor tile, he jumps directly ahead of her and she is forced to retract her step.

"What are you doing?"

"I think I'm in love," he says with a hand on his heart.

"Oh, stop it. Reed, go home."

"You know what?"

"What?"

"It's raining outside, and you shouldn't walk home in the rain."

"I have a test tomorrow. You had better believe that I will be."

"Can you give me a second?" Reed lifts one hand and in genuine hope looks at her.

"How long?"

"Count to ten."

He rushes back up the stairs, but instead of counting and waiting, she hurries out the front door and back under the overhang where Whitney started this all, only now the rain is coming down even harder, until she can barely see a foot in front of her. Just as she's about to step in the rain, "Wait!" she hears Reed call out from behind her.

In his hand, he has three umbrellas, one blue, one pink, and one black, each with a different handle. Opening one at a time, with his large hand he holds all three of them together so that it creates a large covering. With a smile he walks to Simone, raises an eyebrow, and leans into her.

"Where did you get those?"

"I stole them."

"So, you're a thief?" she asks sternly.

"So are you." He says with a very serious expression.

"What? I . . ."

"You've stolen my senses. So, it's actually your fault, I did this. I'm not thinking clearly."

Simone shakes her head. "Oh god."

"Now let me walk you home before I return these to their rightful owner."

Simone looks at him with an irritated expression, but she doesn't say no.

§ § §

At the end of 1925, Rachel and some high school friends are taking a stroll. Their coats aren't doing much to keep them warm, so they hurry inside the café to study. After hours of unending lessons, when their brains feel like mush, they order tea to relax. However, Rachel catches sight of Jake walking down the street, so she rushes to the glass door with a smile.

"Rachel?" one of her friends calls out.

"Just a minute."

Taking her chances with the cold, she opens the door and runs to him. "Jake!" He turns and smiles. "I saw you walking by," she says out of breath. "We're in there studying for a test."

Jake catches sight of fresh-faced white girls staring at them through the café window, their eyes wide with obvious bewilderment. "Oh, I didn't see you."

"Are we getting together tonight?" Rachel asks. She seems to think nothing of the wide-eyed girls staring at them through the window, but Jake is as uncomfortable as ever.

"Of course. We've got a new song for you to try."

"Oh, great."

There is bit of an awkward pause as Jake looks away and stuffs his hands in his pockets. "You should probably get back to your friends."

"Yeah, I guess I should. Well, I'll see you tonight."

"For sure," Jake nods. Then hastily he turns and walks away.

When Rachel returns to the study table inside the cafe, her friends stare at her. "What?"

"You should be careful, Rachel. What will people think?" A girl named Claire shows her disgust.

Rachel stands, pulls her purse onto her arm and buttons her jacket. "It's a good thing I don't care what people think . . . especially you. Have fun, ladies."

Rachel never hung out with those girls again.

§ § §

Rachel walks into P.B.'s restaurant with her purse under her arm. P.B. always made sure that he had a small amount of time to jam with his buddies, so he closed early on Thursday nights just before the Friday rush. Over the last few years Rachel had become a regular figure in those get-togethers. Just across the room, a few of the men, including Alquan, are talking with each other as they relax on their chairs and smoke cigars. Over the phonograph is a Bessie Smith recording.

"Rachel, Rachel!" P.B. hurries from the back room and throws his arm over her shoulder. "You have to hear this new song we've got for ya." He hastens to his piano with the sheet music, then hands it to Rachel who reads it over with curiosity. P.B. begins to play. Before long all of the men run to their instruments and a concert begins. It's easy enough to follow and she fills the room with her rich and sultry voice. Halfway through, Jake walks in the door and crosses his arms in front of him and she can see that he's pleased with the sound. It's difficult to look at him, so she keeps her eyes averted elsewhere. When Carl hits the last drumbeat and the song ends, P.B. hoots and hollers. "I think it's time."

"Time for what?" she asks.

"Time that you sing in here, on this stage."

"Oh no, no, no…you're not going to be able to get me to do any such thing."

"Tomorrow night. I expect it, kiddo. Come on now…" he motions to his friends who are waiting with their instruments in their hands, "They all expect it too. So be here or be square. Let's catch a smoke down in the basement. I need a break."

They grab their liquor and smokes to head downstairs to the basement, but Rachel has never been. She refuses to go down there. As she leans over the piano staring at the sheet music, her body is throbbing as though her blood has suddenly thickened and can't fit through her veins. Jake leans over the piano beside her.

"He's right, ya know," Jake says.

"Why? Why do I have to sing for anyone if I don't want to?"

"It's not that people want to make you do something you don't want to do. Because in all reality, I think you do want to do it. I think that's the point…you want to sing, don't ya?"

"I love to sing, but I don't want to step foot up there."

Together they observe the stage as though there is a concert going on at that moment. "It's just wood." Still, they stare. "Is it the people? Do you have a problem with the people?"

"It's a long story." Rachel's thoughts briefly turn to Levi, even though the years have gone by in a blink and she has no idea where he is.

Jake steps closer to her as music suddenly floats up from the basement, filling the room with the sound of pounding piano keys. He covers her hand that is gently lying over the top of the piano. "You need to realize that you've got somethin' to do with that voice of yours."

"The only thing it brought me is trouble."

"I wish I knew what that meant." Jake steps into her so closely she can feel his breath on her skin. After years of catching eyes during rehearsals and brushing hands when reaching for a glass, Jake finally builds up the courage to kiss her. She's never been kissed before and the feeling of his lips on hers is surprising. It's soft, warm, and her belly is doing flips. He raises his hand to touch her cheek, as he pulls away just slightly. "I had to do that."

Then she raises on her toes and kisses his lips one more time. "I've been waiting for you to do that."

"You've been too young."

"I'm not anymore?"

"Well, you're still young."

"You're only two years older."

"Besides it ain't a smart thing . . . us getting together."

"Why?"

"You know why."

"No, I don't. Why?"

"Look…" He gets flustered by her naivete. "I know girls like you…"

"Girls like me?"

"Just listen . . . you've lived your sheltered life and you think that people will just let you get away with whatever you want, but that ain't the way it works. People are mean and cruel out there. People don't like little blonde girls with black men like me. They don't even call me a man; they call me a boy. They call me every nasty word they can think of and for years I've learned to stay away from it or just ignore it." He rubs his head knowing that he is getting more heated than he should. "It isn't like I can walk around with you on my arm or that I can kiss you in public. It doesn't even come close to that---"

She interrupts, "--And you think of me as that type of girl. Spoiled and stupid."

"No. Just protected is all. You don't know the real world and you look at it with bright eyes and colorful words, but…"

"I think you should stop," she says angrily, "I'm not . . ."

Before she can finish, he wraps his arm around her waist and kisses her more passionately than before. She's never felt something like this. It is sweet, deep, and makes her knees weak. After a while, he finally lifts his head.

"That girl," she says quietly beneath her fast-paced breath, "I'm not that girl."

"I just know what we're up against. Do you?"

"Probably not as much as you. But I think you would be surprised what I know."

"No matter what you've gone through, your skin color is desired, not hated. You can walk down the street and people look at you—not because they hate you, rather they want you. You'll never understand what it means to be hated for nothing. Or to be treated less than."

Heavy footsteps echo as someone climbs the stairs. P.B. enters the main room and smiles at the two of them standing near the piano. "We're all out of moonshine. Y'all should go down there. Carl's tellin' us stories of his war days."

"We'll be down in a minute," Jake says.

"Alright then," P.B. says as he grabs more and heads down the stairs again.

Rachel looks back at Jake. "I'd like to take you someplace tomorrow. Are you free?"

"I think I can figure something out."

"Okay."

The next day Rachel takes Jake to Bernie's home. She shows him where she lived and tells him the stories of her childhood. His eyes are as wide as silver dollars. She introduces him to Simone who has a break from college, but leaves out the part with Bill Manchuron, figuring there is no need for anyone else to ever know. As they drive back that evening, Jake takes her hand.

"Thank you for taking me. I just need you to remember when it comes to us . . . we're still different, you and me. Your skin will always be the desired color and that provides you with privilege that I'll never have. We can't just be out and about. I won't take chances with your life or with mine."

"I understand."

That night Jake watches from the audience as Rachel steps up to the microphone for the first time in years. This time she sees the crowd with a little more understanding than she had as a child.

"What the hell is this, P.B?" one of the women at his bar asks.

"Just wait."

The music starts and Rachel begins. Before a couple of songs are over the entire crowd is alive and jumping. She puts her hand to her chest and laughs. It feels good to be on stage again. She has been so afraid and yet now that she is there, she wonders why. It isn't that bad. It isn't bad at all.

1926

Keeping her love for Jake secret from the world isn't easy—it is nearly impossible. If it was her choice, she would have thrown out the worry and displayed their relationship with pride, but Jake has been around for too long and struggled too much to not know that all hell would take over their lives if they let everyone else in. They hadn't even told P.B. Although there wasn't anything that the club owner couldn't pick up on as they rehearse—the lingering hand touches and smiles that last longer than is safe. When they have a chance, they meet each other by the pier where they can be out of sight and talk, or Rachel would take him with her to see Simone.

Through the summer of 1926, a year when Walt Disney Studios is formed and Harry Houdini has his last performance; Rachel continues to sing at P.B.'s restaurant. People come from all over. A local reporter even writes a small story about her in the paper, although he doesn't mention the name of the club or that P.B. Nelson owns it. No one quite knew whether it was her sultry voice, her beauty, or maybe that she just understood music. Whatever it is, people flock to her. The only difference this time was that she did it on her own accord. No one was telling her how to sing or for how long. She chose everything. Dick and Sylvia come nearly every night to enjoy their child's gift, yet they never say a word pushing her one way or another.

During the day, Rachel works at a small shop on the far side of the boardwalk. On her breaks, she meets Jake under the pier and they skip rocks. It is comfortable and easy. She isn't sure whether she's in love with Jake, but she knows she can't be far from it.

One day, at the end of the summer, Jake and Rachel laugh as they walk down a country road heading to the corner store where they will keep separated while buying the things they need.

They don't see Officer Finnegan as he slows his car to a near stop and leans over the passenger seat with his eyes squinted. At that moment, Jake pulls Rachel in for a small kiss. The town knows

Officer Finnegan hates Jake Smith, P.B. Nelson and anyone involved with that group. In Finnegan's opinion, they're cocky and need to be torn down until they understand their place. With a shake of his head, Officer Finnegan leaves the two at the pier. He had heard that she was singing at P.B.'s restaurant. Plenty of white folks had come in to mention it.

"Now that just ain't right," one old woman said when she came into the precinct at the beginning of the week.

"I know ma'am, but some folks just ain't been brought up right," Officer Finnegan says with a laugh. "I'm taking care of it."

"I sure hope so."

§ § §

P.B. and Simone sit in the back of the club and simply chuckle at the crowd in front of them. It is larger than normal, and P.B. isn't complaining. The crowd claps as Rachel steps to the microphone. After several songs, the place is loud and happy. Rachel catches sight of the tall windows leading outside and notices several men in uniforms walking up to the front door. They peer through the glass windows with squinted eyes and when they notice her on the stage, they point and talk to each other. Something doesn't feel right to Rachel as she continues the song. She quickly makes eye contact with Dick who stands close by.

It isn't until one of the men relieves himself on the window as the group laughs that she stops singing. The band continues on as Dick stealthily makes his way to the front door. Before he can get there, one of the men throws the door open so hard it makes a loud crash against the wall. Instantly, everyone stops and turns. Rachel knows him immediately as the grocery owner across the street from the ice cream shop where she works, and his name is Al. He never was nice or welcoming. Just behind him eight men enter, all walking with their chests high and pushing people out of the way with their elbows and shoulders. Jake, Alquan, and the other band members stop one at a time leaving the music feeling increasingly empty until it altogether ceases. Sitting next to the bar, P.B., Simone, and Chepi hop to their feet.

"Oh ma'am, don't stop singin' on our account," Al says with a grin as he stands in the middle of the crowd.

Slowly, the audience backs away from him. It's obvious he's here for trouble, so Rachel steps away from the microphone.

"Come on!" he yells with a mischievous laugh, "We just wanted to see what ya folks are up to. In fact…" He stops for a minute and licks his lips. "In fact, we were wonderin' how ya got this pretty lady to sing for ya?"

P.B. confidently walks to the man's side. "Hey Al, let's not have any trouble."

"No, no! I wasn't gonna give ya any trouble. Was I now, boys?" The rest of his men shake their heads. "I just wanted," Al pushes P.B. out of the way and steps to the bar. "A drink. I heard you're serving alcohol in these parts."

Everyone knows this is the quickest way for P.B. to lose his club. It took him almost seven years to own it, then when prohibition hit, he thought business would be dead, but business only grew. He was one of the only clubs in town that allowed any and all, no matter their status. People didn't care that there wasn't alcohol; rather they simply wanted a place to hear good music and dance.

"No sir, we haven't for six years," P.B. says proudly.

Al looks at him with raised eyebrows making Jake step closer to P.B.'s side. Dick isn't far away either.

"Interestin'. That ain't what I heard." Al turns and waves his hand at the door. Eight more men rush inside with boxes in their hands. They hurry straight to the bar and set them up underneath the counters. Al walks to the bar, pulls out a bottle of vodka from under his coat and pours it everywhere. P.B.'s chest rises and falls, as he clenches his fists and jaw. Suddenly Simone gets courageous and hollers out from across the room, "We all see you. Don't think we won't tell them what we see."

Al smiles. "Tell who?" It doesn't matter the number of witnesses when the police are the devil's army. As the bottle empties, Al leans over the wood and sniffs it heavily. "Sure smells like there's been alcohol in here tonight." He then walks around the bar and pulls a bottle from one of the crates the men brought in. "Yep, look at all of these bottles. It seems we've been goin' to the wrong place to enjoy our weekends."

Dick's cheeks are the color of fire as he rushes to Al's side angrily. "What the hell are you doing, Al? You know there isn't anything but music and dancin'."

"I don't know nothin' about that. Look around, Dick, all I see is a bar being used . . . quite sufficiently."

Jake loses his cool, but P.B. holds him back. "There's nothin' we can do."

"Sure there is. I'm gonna get some satisfaction and pound his face."

"No, you ain't," P.B. says calmly.

One of the women in the crowd yells. "We know it was you!"

The rest of the crowd agrees with shouts and nods.

Al shakes his head and then looks out the window. "Well, I'll be. Look who it is."

Officer Finnegan strides in the restaurant with his thumbs under his belt. "What's going on here, folks? Are we having some trouble?" It isn't long before he walks to the bar and runs his fingers along the wood. Finnegan smiles, as he looks P.B. up and down. "Whiskey."

"Leave us alone, Finnegan!" Jake yells.

"You can't fix it, Jake," P.B. whispers into his friend's ear.

"You can't just stand around and let this happen, P.B. You have to fight for yourself," Jake pleads.

"I'll figure it out, Jake."

Officer Finnegan comes so close to P.B., it's as if he'll kiss him.

"I'm going to shut you down."

"He ain't done nothin'!" Chepi yells as she stands at the bar next to Simone.

"Hush up." Finnegan rushes toward her forcing Alquan to set his instrument down and jump from the stage. "How dare you speak to me like that. You best watch yourself, squaw." Finnegan has forced Chepi so far back that her back leans over the wooden bar awkwardly.

Alquan doesn't say anything, but he tries to come after Finnegan, only to be stopped by several men on the dance floor.

"This is between me and P.B.," Finnegan growls. "Come on, P.B. I'm taking you in for possession of alcohol."

Then, as if the line has been drawn on the old oak floor, everyone in the bar rushes to P.B.'s side. Men grab soda bottles from the tables, a couple of women grab their umbrellas, but most just squeeze their fists preparing to rip and claw. Instantly, Finnegan and his men stand with their chests out. Even the flies landing on the ceiling above stare down at the front lines of an impending battle.

"Am I gonna have to force ya?" Finnegan asks with a lifted chin.

P.B. steps to Finnegan.

"I've done nothing wrong and God knows. God knows," P.B. says, giving Finnegan a glare that he might never forget. P.B. turns his back on Finnegan and addresses the crowd. "Just wait on it, folks. I'll be okay and I don't want anyone fightin' over this, ya hear me? It'll be figured out."

Finnegan places handcuffs while P.B. winks at Rachel as she hurries from the stage. Finnegan and P.B. reach the door, but that is as far as they can get before two men push through the crowd and grab Finnegan with their large hands messing his uniform and pulling off several buttons.

"Hey!" Finnegan yells.

Instantly, the crowd erupts. The two sides clash as Rachel does her best to join in. Jake grabs her hand and pulls her behind him, but in the chaos, they are separated and they lose sight of each other.

Nothing is off limits as women use their heels and men use their keys. P.B. tries to yell to get everyone to stop, but quickly realizes it isn't any good. There isn't an end to this battle nor was this the beginning. This fight will be going on for months, years, and generations.

Within thirty minutes of the first punch, sirens scream. Men and women with their hats in their hands run full throttle down the road and away from trouble. Soon, the police cars screech to a halt in front of P.B.'s, who is now standing against his bar with his hands behind his back. Police race in with their batons high over their heads.

Finally, Jake flies past Rachel. "Come with me!" he yells, running to the back of the club and out the back door.

"What are we doing?"

"Let's get out of here."

Rachel notices his head is bleeding and she quickly places a hand on it. "Jake?"

"It's nothing," he says, shrugging off his wound. "Come on!"

They run through the woods far enough away that they know they won't be caught. The Ferris wheel can be seen above the cityscape, which tells them they aren't too far away from the boardwalk. Finally, he turns to her with sweat pouring down his temples.

"You okay?" Jake asks.

She nods. "But what's P.B. going to do?"

"I don't know. He can't do much." The tension in Jake's jaw shows there's more rage beneath the surface.

Rachel shivers a bit from the cold night.

"Let's get out of here," Jake says.

"Where are we going?"

"You need to go home and I'm going to find a way to figure things out with P.B."

Rachel stops. "No, Jake. Please don't."

"P.B. needs me."

"P.B. wanted you to be safe."

"Rachel! Enough. I have to do something . . . do you understand that? This is a fight I'm willing to die for."

Chapter Seventeen

1926

Rachel and Simone sit at Dick and Sylvia's kitchen table the next morning. Simone watches Rachel as she thumps her foot against the wood floor. Every time she places pressure on the old slats they creak and holler, until she can almost find a rhythm to it. Finally, at half past nine, Dick enters the front door and drops his hat on the foyer table. In seconds, Rachel is on her feet and at his side. Just his face alone tells her that something is not right.

"Where have you been?"

"The jailhouse."

"And?" Rachel says.

"At first they wouldn't let me talk to anyone, but I was finally able to get a hold of Finnegan's commander."

"What did you figure out?" She asks. Dick drops his head. "What did you figure out? Dad?"

"Rachel, I uhhhh . . . P.B. is gone."

"What do you mean gone?"

"P.B. is dead."

Rachel feels the pain clear through to her fingertips as she brings her hands to her mouth. Simone's eyes are wide and her chest rises and falls at a fast pace. Sylvia, who is coming down the stairs, drops the papers she's carrying until they spray across the room.

"What do you mean he's dead?" Rachel cries out.

"They said that he fought them and wouldn't stop. They said he was a danger to everyone else."

"They said?" Rachel shakes her head. "You saw him! You know he would have never done anything! He was trying to get everyone to stop." For the first time in their years together, she yells. Neither Dick or Sylvia know what to do.

"I know," Dick says and tries to reach out to her, but she pulls away.

"What about…" she stops with realization and looks at Simone, "Jake! I've got to get to Jake." With that she races for the foyer table and grabs Dick's keys.

"Rachel," Dick says.

"I've got to find him!" Rachel and Simone run out of the house, leaving the door open behind them.

Dick races to jump in the back seat as Rachel roars away in his new 1925 Chrysler Roadster. Cars and houses whizz by the window faster than usual and Dick watches the girls with concern. In Jake's neighborhood Rachel screeches to a stop and jumps out, running to Jake's mom's door. After three heavy knocks Jake's mother answers.

"Mrs. Smith, where's Jake?"

"He's just left to go over to the jailhouse to see P.B."

Nerves slash at Rachel's insides. Rachel turns on a dime.

"What's happened?!" Jake's mother calls out, but they don't stop.

They fly to the jailhouse where Jake—with fists tightly clenched, his body pushing forward—is being held back by Alquan and Carl as he growls at Finnegan on the jailhouse steps. The officer and several others stare at a glorious mixture of men and women from P.B.'s bar. Finnegan's hands are in his pockets while he smirks. Leaving the motor running, Rachel jumps out of the car, followed by Simone and they climb the stairs two at a time.

"Jake!" The tears in his eyes pull at her heart.

"Jake! Jake!" Finnegan mocks Rachel. "Yeah, Jake. Take this beautiful n***er lover back to your home and infect her," Finnegan curses with a grin.

Jake explodes forward nearly grabbing Finnegan's uniform. But everyone knows if he touches the man, there is no stopping his arrest. Several of the band members stop Jake from touching the officer. Rachel steps close to him, placing her hands on his face. Dick watches on, suddenly realizing the love that has secretly grown between the two.

"Jake," she cries.

Carl and the other band members see the writing on the wall. "We can't do anything about it right now. Come on, before you get hurt." Carl says.

"Yeah, come on, Jake," the others encourage. "This ain't over, Jake. But we can't do anything 'bout it now."

One large tear rolls down his cheek.

"P.B. deserved it. You know he did," Finnegan taunts.

"Keep quiet, Officer Finnegan." Simone says, poised and in control just as she always is.

"What did you say?" Finnegan descends the stairs swiftly.

But Simone doesn't back down. She points behind her at the crowd that has gathered. "You gonna attack me in front of everyone? Oh, I hope you do."

Finnegan clenches his jaw, but sees that people are piling up along the yard out front to watch.

"Come on, Jake…Rachel. Let's get ourselves out of here." Simone says, while staring down the officer. "I'm gonna turn around now and if I even so much as think you're gonna touch me, I'll make sure I give the best performance there is."

For nearly a week Rachel and Simone can't find Jake. No matter who they ask, he has disappeared. Finally, one day Rachel drives to his house where she locates him sitting on the steps outside.

"I was worried about you," Rachel says gently when she reaches him.

"No need. Just thinkin' is all."

"Are you okay?"

"Yeah."

"I'm sorry."

"For what?" he asks surprised.

"For asking you to go home instead of to the jailhouse that night."

"I would have just been killed with him and that wouldn't have done anybody any good. Rachel, I--"

His tone makes her shiver, and she quickly cuts him off, "--- Don't say anything. I know that I won't ever understand all that you have gone through or will go through."

"No you won't. But you understand more than most."

There is a bit of silence between them and then he shrugs. "The boys are comin' over tonight, so I can't see you. But, I want to give you something."

"Okay."

She steps forward and touches his chin with her hand. For a moment, he allows it until one of the neighbors comes outside and he pulls away. He ascends the stairs to the porch and reaches for a small stack of papers sitting on a table between two rockers. He hands them to her.

"It's a song, Rachel."

Rachel looks it over. "Where is it from?"

"P.B. and I wrote it. For you. No one would be able to sing this like you."

Her hands shake as she studies the notes. "I can't believe he's gone. I'll never watch him play the guitar or piano again." Under her fingers there is a second page. "What's this?"

"That is studio time. We figured out a way to get you some studio time to record it."

"I . . . I don't . . ."

"You have to. Nothin' is more wrong in this world than you bein' afraid of your gift."

"But..."

"Nope. You can go any time you like. Get this recorded, Rachel. Make something and do something with it." Jake takes her hand and pulls her around to the side porch where they can't be seen.

"Will you help me?" she asks.

He hesitates. "Yeah, sure."

Then as though he can't help himself, he leans into her and finds her lips. He wraps his arms around her, and she sinks into his chest. The kiss seems desperate, in a way. When he lets go, it is too soon. "I've got to go," he says holding onto her dress with just a finger.

"Okay. Will I see you tomorrow?"

"Yeah," he says.

She heads to the car as he watches. Then as she settles into the driver's seat, she finds it hard to relax. She can feel in her heart that he is ending their relationship. Quietly, she lets the tears drain from her eyes as she drives home.

1998

Gramma falls asleep, almost mid-sentence. I notice her words beginning to slur, then within seconds her mouth is open and she's snoring. I cover her up with a blanket, turn out the light, say goodbye to the nurses and begin the drive home. When the lights make glimmering rainbow colors on the wet cement, it reminds me of the many nights that I walked New York's sidewalks with women, talking about our relationship or our lives and yet here I am, in Atlantic City, alone. Not only that but I'm listening to Gramma for hours on end talk about a woman I will never be able to know.

A few weeks before my mom called me back to New Jersey for my dad, I ran into an old flame on the subway. We missed our exit several times because we were talking and I thought to myself, "What if I'd made a mistake?" What if I had ruined my chances with the one and now it's too late?

Am I that person that is so pathetic because I long for love so much that I'm willing to find it wherever I can? I fall in love with these stories—these ideals that give me the chance to be who I want to be in a relationship. Or I could be one of those people who keeps myself at the safest distance and fall in love with untouchable women.

"You won't be alone forever, Bobby," my ma says when I get home.

"How do you know that, Ma?"

We sit on the porch rocking back and forth in the crushing heat as we watch the kids around the neighborhood play baseball in the streets. My sister is at the hospital watching over my dad. He is making improvements day by day. My brothers are playing cards in the dining room.

"I just know, honey. I'm your Momma."

"Because you are my Ma, that is the reason you believe the best."

"What makes you think you can't fall in love?"

"I haven't yet."

She laughs her 'you've just said the stupidest thing' laugh, and takes a sip of her iced tea. "You always have been the worrier. Bobby," she turns to me with a serious expression, "give it some time. Stop thinking it has to look any specific way."

"Maybe I'm broken." I think of Rachel. Gramma used that word several times to describe her.

Ma seems to get an even bigger kick out of this comment and chuckles. "Who broke you?"

There is a temptation even if it is just slight, to tell her the truth, but I stop myself. She sees the change in my face and grows curious. "You think someone made you who you are—afraid of commitment?"

"I don't know, I'm just studying my history and finding my inadequacies. Maybe I'm afraid that I'm not good enough to make something work?"

Momma pats my leg and stands. "I don't believe it. Whoever told you that you weren't good enough?"

Dad.

"Bobby," she drops her face in front of mine, "you are a stronger man than you think you are." Then, she walks to the door and turns to me. "I think I should go see your father now."

That's how it always is with my family—always two cars away from a train wreck. At that moment I get up and walk out into the street. The little boys look at me like I am Sammy Sosa and I like it. They give me the bat and with my thick arms I crush the ball down the street. Two boys race after it and the others wait with hopeful anticipation as I round the paper sack bases. Before the ball makes it halfway back to me, I cross the home plate and the losing team cheers as I bring them one step closer to winning the game. I breathe in the moment of triumph. These boys are only a few years from Jake's age. They see the world through baseball and late nights in the summer. If only they knew of the fear in their momma's bellies as they watch them from the front yard. What happened to P.B. still happens today. I high five all the boys and two girls who continue to play even when I walk inside.

That night as I lay in bed, I think about Rachel. I know that Jake is up to something. P.B. was murdered for no reason at all. The last part of Rachel's story haunts me all night, as I think about the injustice. But then again, humanity seems to have a knack for unjust hatred.

The next morning, as I sit in the cafeteria while Gramma eats her breakfast, I explain that I have already been there to see her, and she has been telling me about Rachel for the millionth time. I can see that she enjoys telling me the story when she doesn't finish all of her pancakes.

"You're right," she says with a solemn nod of her head, "Jake was up to somethin'. He and Carl decided that they would rather get into trouble than let P.B.'s death pass by without a word. The night that Rachel came over was the night that they were headed out to find Finnegan. They knew—having lived in Atlantic City all of their lives—where Officer Finnegan lived and where Al, the owner of the market, lived. So, they waited until nearly two in the morning, when everyone would be asleep, and jumped in their car."

Chapter Eighteen

1926

The car engine mimics their racing hearts as it roars to life with Carl behind the wheel. They were able to convince a boy named Kyle, who often searches for trouble, and Lester, the drummer of P.B.'s band, to join them. Four is enough. Any more, they feel, might make it too hard to get away.

The streets are empty as they race along in Jake's mother's car. He prays that she will stay asleep and never notice that he is gone. Maybe he will have a chance in trial if his mother is an alibi? Jake scratches his head until it hurts when he anticipates what might happen—wondering if he'll come out of this alive. He reaches for the cross hanging around his neck that his mother had given him and brings it to his lips.

They drive swiftly to the other side of town—past Chicken Bone Beach, past the boardwalks and Main Street, and into upper class residential areas. They park the car next to an empty field and run the rest of the way.

"Right there," Jake says as he points at the large house in the cul de sac.

"How do you know?" Carl asks as he kneels behind a house across the street for cover.

"I sat outside the precinct two days ago and waited for him to drive home. That's his house, for sure," Jake says as he checks his pockets for his weapon. "Let's go."

They race across the street in the dark. Then, Kyle passes by Finnegan's shiny car, carefully opens the door without a squeal, and slashes the seats until the fluffy insides are gaping out. "Let's not waste time!" Jake whispers. "We're just here to scare him. That's all."

"We're here to get P.B. justice," Carl says.

"Obviously. But we gotta do it right." Jake walks to the front door, then with a heavy hand he knocks. It doesn't matter that it is the middle of the night, he knocks aggressively. He looks back at the rest of the men standing behind him and they're fired up. After a couple more knocks, lights begin to glow from inside. Jake tries to hide the fact that his hand is shaking, but he's never done something like this before.

Finally, Finnegan opens the door, completely unprepared with wild hair and tired eyes. Jake and the boys rush in pushing him until he falls to the ground exposing that under his robe that he sleeps naked. They grab the police officer's arms and drag him along the wood floor as he yells.

"What are you doing?! I didn't do---" Finnegan is angry as he struggles, but he doesn't finish what he's saying as he climbs to his feet.

"You didn't do what? Say it, cracker!" Jake yells in his face.

It isn't long before his wife comes out and screams when she sees her husband against the wall and the men with guns. They quickly grab her and set her on the couch.

"Keep quiet!" Kyle yells lifting his hand to slap her face.

"Kyle!" Jake says angrily. He turns back to Finnegan. "Just tell me to my face that you killed P.B. Tell me that P.B. did nothin' and you just wanted to hurt one of us."

Finnegan is now beginning to get his confidence back and he grins. "How would that help you, boy?"

Jake throws a punch that connects with Finnegan's cheek. His wife's cries grow louder.

"Tell me!" Jake yells.

"I don't need to tell you nothin'."

Carl and Kyle lose their temper and take turns hitting Finnegan until he is down on the ground.

"Get off my daddy!"

The men stop suddenly surprised by the small voice behind them. They knew that Finnegan had children, but they didn't expect the gun that fills the little boy's tiny hands.

"Drop your guns," the boy says, not seeming the slightest bit nervous.

"Come on, boy. Stay out of this. This is between us and your daddy," Kyle says clearly.

"I already called the police and you ain't gonna move until they get here," the boy says confidently.

Jake takes a look at the others and then at the bloodied Finnegan lying on the floor. Sadistically, Finnegan shows that he knows the men are in trouble by his smile.

Jake walks to Finnegan's wife. "You're married to a killer. He killed our friend . . . planted evidence in his club and killed him when he didn't fight back. That's who you're married to. Look at how easily your child holds that gun. Do you think that's right?" At first, she is angry and scared, but Jake waits to see the realization hit her deep set eyes. "And just so you know, Caroline Mansfield who works at your husband's office, I saw them kissing outside of the station a couple days ago when I was waiting. I know he's shown you who he is . . . it's about time you see it."

"Let's go," Carl says quickly.

"What about the kid?" Jake asks.

"You ain't leavin'," the kid insists.

"Don't believe him, let's go," Kyle yells suddenly taking a quick run for the door. Before he can pass the boy, a shot rings out, mixed with the high-pitched scream of Finnegan's wife. Kyle drops to the floor, instantly lifeless.

In a split second, Jake, Carl, and Lester head for the door while the kid has to reload. Another explosion and this time Carl falls. Jake turns to Finnegan who is now holding a gun in his hands, pointed directly at him. Jake lifts his hand as he reaches the front door and takes the shot. In milliseconds the bullet reaches Finnegan and throws him against the wall. His wife screams. Jake and Lester race out the door, but as they round the neighbor's yard, they run into three squad cars coming down the road. There is nowhere else to go when the cars screech to a stop in front of them. The two of them are forced to raise their hands in surrender.

§ § §

Rachel wakes the next morning with a renewed spirit, having decided that Jake would not be able to push her away so easily. It had been obvious, the night before, that this was his intention, and for a moment, she accepted it—crying herself to sleep. When the sun came up, so did her resilience. She threw off her covers, dressed, and hurried downstairs.

"Where's dad?" Rachel asks Sylvia as she's heading out the door.

"He needed to go to work early this morning. There's been a problem with the lion cage in the last two shows."

"Okay. Well, I'm going to try and see Jake this morning."

"Really? Are you sure?"

"Yeah." Rachel smiles. "I need to tell him that I love him."

Sylvia grins. "Okay, have a good day."

Rachel sings as she drives down the country roads and into the city, her heart feeling ready to battle this world with Jake at her side.

On the road near Jake's house, cars are strangely parked where they shouldn't be and people are standing about, staring at the church lawn across the street.

"What is going on?" Rachel asks herself out loud.

Finally, unable to continue past the crowd, she pulls over and parks behind a truck. Medford Willy is standing there with his old wrinkled hand rubbing behind his ear.

"Good morning, Medford."

"Morning, Miss Rachel." His voice is not nearly as upbeat as normal.

"Everything okay?"

"No . . ." he hesitates, "no, I don't think it is."

She comes to his side. "What's going on?"

Medford shakes his head and breathes heavily. "Well, it seems they strung up a few more."

Rachel looks at him confused. "Strung up? What do you mean?"

He points toward the large oak trees on the church lawn, but before she can even turn her head, the memory of that boy by the train tracks so long ago comes back to her. She turns her head toward the crowd of people and slowly steps to the middle of the road. The largest oak tree is blocking her view of whatever they're looking at. If she just takes two steps to the right, she'll be able to see, but she doesn't want to. With her heart already beating so rapidly it nearly makes her sick to her stomach, she finally reaches the moist green grass and pushes aside several people who are watching. Women from their church are crying and men's voices are yelling.

Finally, one branch at a time, she sees the men hanging from them. Tears instantly fill her eyes, and she doesn't know whether to get closer. Carl is first, then Kyle, Lester, and the last of the men is Jake. His neck is tilted at an awkward angle as he hangs lifeless from the largest tree branch there is. His feet and hands dangle so far away from the ground. The ropes are wrapped so tightly that several of the men around have backed their trucks up toward the bodies and are trying to stand tall enough to cut them free.

Rachel hears her sobbing before she feels the scratch of her throat. Then it comes, loud and hard. "Jake!!!!" Rachel screams. She races toward Jake and reaches out for his feet.

Standing on the bed of a Chevy truck, Dick notices Rachel and swiftly jumps down.

"Rachel!" he calls out. "Stay back!"

But it is too late. She has his feet in her hands, but they don't feel right. They're cold and stiff, so she drops to her knees.

"Get him down!" she cries. Dick reaches her side and wraps his arms around her. "Get him down!"

"They're trying, Rachel, they're trying," Dick cries.

Several of the men, finally get two of the bodies free and carefully carry them to the ground. But it isn't Jake. They've tied it too tight and too thick. "Jake!" Rachel moans.

"Rachel," Dick says in her ear. "I'm sorry."

This time her voice is pleading. "He's so cold. Jake!"

"I'm sorry, Rachel," Dick says.

Rachel pulls away from Dick. "Help him! Help them get him down! Please!"

Dick obeys his daughter's request and jumps up on the Ford farm truck. It takes several men and many minutes to finally get him down.

Then she hears crying, louder than her own, from somewhere behind her. She turns to see Jake's mother walking to him, desperately wailing. "No!" She wraps her arms around the child that she gave life to and begs God to undo what has just been done. A mother's cry can never be forgotten.

Rachel runs to her. They look at each other with lost eyes, hoping for understanding, and desperate for this to have been a bad dream. She pulls at Rachel's hands and clothes until they are both on the ground, holding onto each other.

Across the street, standing stoically and hauntingly, are the police squad, not lifting a finger to help. Alquan and several of the band members rush toward them. "Don't think we don't know what you did! All that you have done!" Alquan says. He alone knows this for his own people and feels for his friends who have become family.

"Can't help you," one of them says, his eyes full of hate. "They killed an officer last night."

"You're lying!" Several people call out.

Everyone knows there is no use. The damage is irreparable, and they will always have the upper hand.

An hour later, they help Jake's mother get home. Women from everywhere, in the neighborhood and beyond, leave flowers on her doorstep as she struggles to catch her breath.

Chapter Nineteen

1926

For five days Rachel stays in her room. Although Sylvia and Dick wait to hear footsteps coming down the stairs, they are saddened every day when it doesn't happen. However, on the second day, Simone, who has come all the way back from college, shows up at the door. When Dick opens it, he drops his head, thankful.

"It's okay Mr. D. I've got her," Simone says as she steps inside.

"She's not talking."

"And she probably won't." Simone starts to head up the stairs and looks back, "If you could just bring food every now and then, that would be great."

"Of course."

When Simone walks in, Rachel is sitting on her windowsill looking out at the men working with the animals. She turns her sad eyes to see Simone standing at the door with a raised eyebrow of sympathy. "You okay?"

Instantly, as though Simone's mere presence opens the floodgates of emotion, sobs shake her shoulders. Simone walks to her side and sits close enough to her best friend that her arms can drape around her neck. For the longest time they don't move. When Rachel finally looks up, her eyes are red and puffy.

"You look awful." Simone says.

"How did you get here?"

"My brother called me and told me what happened. So, I borrowed some money from my professor and jumped on the train." Rachel nods, on the cusp of falling apart once again. Simone continues, "Do you want to talk about it?"

"It's the worst thing I ever saw. You remember that boy at the train tracks so long ago?"

"The one I laid into? Yeah." Simone smiles.

"I don't know that I ever truly believed him. But there they were," Rachel sobs. "There was Jake."

"You were a child, how could you have known? In fact, I'm glad that you didn't know. That's somethin' that can ruin someone, especially a child…"

"I don't know what to do." She folds over Simone's lap.

"We'll figure it out, Rachel." For the next five days, Rachel and Simone don't leave her room.

In a strange twist, Finnegan's funeral is held on the same day as Jake's—showing how divided the city is. Every man, woman, and child, of all different races, who had ever been in contact with P.B. or been in his bar, walks the streets of Altantic City with the four men's caskets on their shoulders. Meanwhile, an entire procedural salute and honor, on the other side of town, is displayed for Officer Finnegan. The story about what had happened passed through many different filters, changing based on each person's affiliation. But all those who were there knew the truth about P.B.. If only the truth mattered more in this world.

Rachel tells Simone everything leading up to the murders as they lay on the couch. Simone just shakes her head. "Sure doesn't make sense does it? Where is any justice in all of that? But that's why I'm doing what I'm doing. I'm going to become a lawyer, just like Charlotte E. Ray."

"Really?" Rachel smiles for the first time in a week. "How is Howard? And who is Charlotte E. Ray?"

"I'm killing it, Rachel. You should hear me in debates. I can take anyone down and make them cry while I'm doing it."

"I believe that."

"Charlotte E. Ray was the first black female lawyer. She couldn't sustain a business because of being black, but she set a precedent for anyone like me for admission to the bar."

For two months, Simone travels home from Howard University on the weekends in order to come stay with Rachel. They lay under the stars, swim in the river, brush the animals, and, most importantly, never leave each other's side. Slowly, Rachel begins to come back to life.

"You need to learn Jake and P.B.'s song," Simone says one night as they lay out under the stars, their heads on each other's shoulder, their feet pointing opposite directions. "Have you even looked at it?"

"I can't bring myself to."

Simone rolls over and sits up. "Look Rachel, I love you. You're my best friend, but every weekend I come home and you're still in the same place. Do you know what I go through to be here with you on the weekends? Last week, a woman at the train station yelled at me because I touched her bag as I passed by. She accused me of trying to steal her bag. What do I do in that moment? If she's got it in her mind that I did that, there's no fighting it. Not only can I not sit in the same car as her, if she decides that I have done something wrong, there is no changing what my path will be as they carry me off to jail. You know what I have a problem with? I'm used to people hating me and holding me back for my skin, but sometimes I wonder . . . why does that exist between women? Hmm? With all of the men hell-bent on stamping us down, every one of us women needs to be reaching our potential and we can't do that without each other. But I turned around, looked her square in the eye, and said, 'Ma'am, I'm a woman, you're a woman, now treat me as such. You know I didn't try and take your bag . . . if you really look me in the eye, woman to woman.' And Rachel, something happened. She looked at me for a moment, picked up her bag, and walked away. But before she got on that train, she took one more look at me and I swear she was about to nod. She didn't, but I think she was about to. Why I say this is because despite those situations that happen to me on a weekly basis, I still choose to step outside, improve myself, and go after something that I know I'm meant to do."

After a moment of thought, Rachel breathes in. "You should've stuffed that purse somewhere where the sun don't shine."

Simone smiles and lays back down. "Yeah, I should have. But I put on my good girl panties that morning."

Both of them laugh and at that moment they see a shooting star. "I love you, Simone."

"I love you, Rachel."

"And Simone, I'm sorry for that. I know it doesn't make it right, but I'm sorry."

§ § §

1927—the year that Grauman's Chinese theater opens, Model Ts are replaced by Model As, and Ain't She Sweet hits number one on Ben Bernie's list—begins with Rachel's first recording. Holding hands, Simone and Rachel walk downtown to the recording studio at the end of the row. Rachel's hands are shaking, she's so nervous.

"Rachel get ahold of yourself. If I could sing like you, I wouldn't be having to study until all hours of the night. Besides you owe it to Jake." Simone says as she checks her dress in the nearest window.

"I know you're right." Rachel says, but her heart is still racing. "Jake once told me that music runs parallel to everyone's dreams, hopes, and struggles and it brings people together in a time when together seems taboo."

"Good ol' Jake. Sounds like he was trying to get something from you."

Rachel blushes, but doesn't deny it.

"Is this the building?" Simone asks.

"You have the paper in your hand," Rachel says looking at the sheet music.

"Well excuse me!" Simone looks carefully, "Ahhh, yep, this is the one."

"Okay," Rachel says reluctantly.

Simone pulls Rachel's hand with a smile. Since the recording studio's small office is quiet, they stop talking and Rachel links her arm with Simone's tightly. A young girl about fifteen sits behind the desk with a pen in her hand and looks up from her papers. "Can I help you?"

"I'm Rachel Anne Praline. I'm supposed to record today."

"You got a band?" she says going back to her drawing.

"A band? No. I just have a song and the sheet music."

"You gonna sing without a band?" The young girl appears confused.

"I guess."

Just then an old voice, sounding much like an old door that needs oil, makes the girls turn their heads. "You come to record?" An old man with hair whiter than snow appears from down the hall and, with a cane in his hand, and makes his way to them.

"Yes, sir. I made an appointment with you last week." Rachel feels like she will lose her lunch at any moment. Looking around, she sees the difference in this recording studio compared to the one Affie took her to when she was just a child. This one is much more humble with a few holes in the wall and a squeaky door.

"What's your name, honey?" he says.

"Rachel Anne Praline."

He looks up and she can see it in his eyes. "Oh, yes, Jake's girl." He looks her over with his small circle-shaped glasses sitting at the end of his nose. "I'm sorry, darlin', 'bout your loss."

"Thank you."

"I'm Corny Phillips." Just as he says that, two black men enter through the front door. One is blind and the other is directing him with his hand. The old man smiles and nods at them but then looks back at Rachel. "You ready to get recording?"

"Well, we don't really know." Simone says quickly. "She doesn't have a band. Just her voice."

Rachel continues, "I don't really know how this works, Mr. Phillips. You see Jake just gave me this song before he died, and he didn't tell me much about what to do when I record it."

"Oh honey, he was a friend of mine." Corny says it with so much respect that it makes Rachel's eyes tear up. "He worked everything out with me. I's just waitin' for you to call. If you're as good as he says, we should have no problem today."

The bell over the door rings again and this time a grizzly-looking white man walks in with instruments in his hand. Rachel notices that he knows the other two men from minutes before. He shakes their hands then joins them in the seats across the wall.

Corny looks out the window. "We're expecting one more."

Simone and Rachel glance at each other when the old man says nothing more. The men in the corner laugh and chat so fast neither girl can make out what they say.

"Ahh, there he is," Corny says, pulling away from the window and looking at Rachel. "Did you learn the song?"

"Yes."

"Good. Rachel let me introduce you to my boys here. This man," he points to the mountain man, "this is a friend of mine: Stanley. He may look a bit wild, but he's as down home as they come."

Stanley stands to his feet and dips his brown tattered hat that is missing part of its brim—it looks a little like teeth marks.

"And this…" Corny continues, "This is The Beast." He points to the man who is helping the blind man. "His name is really Tony, but we call him The Beast because well, you'd have to be one to cover keys of a piano like he does." Rachel and The Beast nod at each other. "And this…"

He helps the sweet-faced blind man to his feet. There's something about his presence that fills the room. His clothes are simple—a blue shirt with a darker blue pair of pants, and he carries himself with pride. Corny lifts the blind man's hand to Rachel's. "This, Rachel, is William McTell, people call him Blind Willie. He's just beginning, like you. But I believe he's gonna do real well. Aren't ya, Willie?"

Willie takes Rachel's hand in his and she can feel the calluses from his guitar. "That's right."

"It's so nice to meet you, Willie," Rachel says.

"Rachel," Corny says with a grin. "These are your boys for an hour or two. They're all doing a big favor for me, and I would love to hear what you all can come up with today. This song's real good. Real good."

"What? They're here for me?"

"Yeah. Jake set it up a long time ago. We all were friends with Jake."

"I can't ask any of you to--" Rachel begins but Corny interrupts her.

"--Rachel, you didn't ask anyone. Jake did and this was his wish."

"Say thank you, Rachel," Simone warns with her tone.

"Yes, thank you! From the bottom of my heart, thank you!"

"Not a problem. Let's get you practicin' so that you can get recordin'." Corny winks at her and leads the group to the back.

"You do anything, Miss?" Stanley asks Simone.

Simone chuckles lifting the side of her mouth. "I can't sing, if that's what you're asking."

"She's becoming a lawyer," Rachel interjects.

The men's eyes widen, and a whistle comes from Willie. "A

lawyer! Hm! That sounds nice."

They enter the dark room with instruments hanging on all four walls. Corny turns on some lights—just enough for the musicians to see their hands to play.

"I am sure interested in what you sound like. I've never really played for someone like you before."

Rachel smiles, "How do you know I'm different?"

"My blindness isn't too deep," is all he says.

The musicians test out their sound and tune quickly, and then they stop and wait for Rachel.

"Willie," Rachel says shyly. "Would you count it out?"

"Sure. One, two, three, four…"

Tony begins running his fingers up and down the piano keys and Stanley begins tapping on a set of drums, but it isn't until Willie starts strumming that the music changes. He rocks back and forth and she is nearly so mesmerized that she almost doesn't come in on her measure. Luckily, she comes to her senses just in time and she begins to sing. She follows the men, and they follow her. As usual, the moment the music starts, her nerves fall away, and it leads her. She can't help but think of Jake and his ability to write.

After just the first run-through, Corny claps his hands together and laughs, "I'm going to get this on the radio."

"What?" Simone asks with a smile, but Rachel says nothing. The idea sounds outrageous.

"Let's do it again. This time record it, Corny," Willie smiles.

"You got it, Willie," Corny says raising one finger and dancing out of the room.

Before long, they have recorded P.B. and Jake's song, as well as four others. When they are done, Willie walks to Rachel using the table next to him for guidance. She takes his hand when he is near.

"You a believer?"

"A believer?" she asks with surprise.

"Yes, in God, in Creation, in the Almighty?"

She hasn't thought about it in years, not since Bernie. "I don't know," she says with a smile.

"Because only God could have created a voice like yours. I'm glad we got to play together."

"Thank you, Willie. I'm so grateful for you to have come."

"Anything for Jakey-boy."

There is something about Willie's spirit that reminds her of Bernadette, and for a moment she longs to see the woman who gave her so much as a child. When all is done and the men have packed up their belongings, Willie comes to her side once again.

"You know sometimes I wonder why God made me blind, but I sometimes just wish that all people with sight could hear things the way that I do." He turns to everyone in the front office and looks at them as though he can see them. "Goodbye, folks. It was fun. I have to hurry back. I got a recording in Atlanta."

"Let me walk you to the train, Willie," Stanley offers.

They watch as the men glide down the street beside each other. Throughout Rachel's life she heard little things about Blind Willie McTell. He did well, but not as well as he should have. He was right—the world couldn't allow full success to a disabled man. Later in his life he gave up his quest for a career in music and took a career at the pulpit. It wasn't until after he died that his fame and all that he had done for music became known.

1928

Even though it had been years since she had seen Bill Manchuron, he still haunted Rachel. The night before Bill kidnapped her was her last uninterrupted night of sleep.

Since then, nightmares have been a common occurrence, and they have only grown worse since Jake's death. Waking with drenched sheets, her heart pounding, and visions of Bill Manchuron, or Jake hanging from the trees, is too much for her to bear and many days she stays quietly secluded within Dick and Sylvia's home. Dick and Sylvia's hearts break every time they walk past her room and hear her soft cries or restless nights.

Rachel gasps as she sits up in bed after feeling Jake's cold hands in her dream. It feels all too real. She clutches her chest as she struggles to take in a deep enough breath, while whimpers of fatigue and desperation bubble from within.

The next morning Dick talks to her about going to college, but the idea of having a roommate seems impossible. So instead, Rachel works for Dick. Even Simone, when she's home from college, comes to help as the crowds grow every year. Then one day in the theater as they prepare the animals for the next big show, Gregory sets up the radio and plays tunes so they can dance to the latest hits. On a break, Simone and Rachel lay together on the stage staring up at the beams above. A strangely familiar tune begins playing that makes Simone sit up. "Do you hear that?"

Rachel listens carefully, then, in a startling moment, her eyes grow wide as her voice echoes over the waves of the radio. "That's me!" she says with shock at the same time that Simone yells, "That's you!"

Dick runs onto the stage afraid that something has gone wrong with the animals but finds the girls jumping around with excitement.

"She's on the radio!" Simone bellows.

"What?" Dick listens for a moment and then proudly raises his hands in the air, unable to contain his exhilaration. "Rachel! That's you! I can't believe it!"

How Corny did it, they would never know, but he did it all the same. Two months down the road, P.B. and Jake's song, Somethin' Tender, sweeps the broadcasts and gains enough momentum that Rachel hears it almost everywhere. She doesn't even realize how far her success has truly gone.

§ § §

Across the country, Levi sits outside a café in a suit and tie next to a beautiful woman and suddenly hears a rich and sultry voice. The radio broadcaster comes on just at the end, "That's Rachel Anne Praline from Atlantic City."

Levi looks up from his menu as if he's seen a ghost from his past.

"Excuse me," he says to his date, as he quickly leaves the table and heads straight to the bar. The bartender looks at him with a smile as he wipes his hands on the towel over his shoulder, "Evening, Mr. Price. Can I help you with something?"

"Were you listening to the radio just now?" Levi asks.

"I think so."

"Did you hear the last song that was played? The broadcaster said a name after it. Did you hear it?"

"Uhhh, no, I don't know." He bartender replies, but just next to them an old man with silver hair smiles. "That's a new girl, Rachel Anne Praline."

"You sure?" Levi asks with a sudden rush of emotion that he hasn't felt since before the war. It makes him sentimental and curious about the child he once protected when he was only a child himself.

"I'm sure." The old man says. "They've not let it rest in weeks. Been playing it every day."

"Thank you." Levi says, then he walks back to the table.

"You okay?" the woman asks.

He thinks for a moment. "Yeah, yes, sorry. Just heard a name from my past."

"Oh, those are never good," she smiles.

"No, this one is good. It's really good." Levi says as he takes a sip of his drink.

§ § §

"Someone called again yesterday afternoon." Sylvia says as she enters the kitchen. Dick and Rachel are finishing breakfast at the table. "He was asking to speak with you. They all say the same thing, Rachel. People want you to sing."

"I met with the ones last week. That was enough."

Rachel had met with three men the week before who all wanted her to sign to their record label. The first man as he walked up said, "Well, well, well, and beautiful too. This will be an easy sell, Rachel." The second man waited until after dinner to tell her that he would be traveling with her everywhere she went. "I'll pick up the tab for anything and everything you want, Rachel. Can I just tell you, with your looks and your appeal, I'll make sure to keep a bat by my side and fight off the other men." And the last man waited until they were standing just outside the restaurant to wrap his arm around her waist telling her how rich he truly was and how that might benefit her.

"We're happy to support you, Rachel, in anything that you wish to do," Sylvia says as she sits down.

"I don't want . . . I don't want to . . ." Rachel begins, but she doesn't finish. She stands and without another word heads to her room.

Finally, in February of 1929, before the Stock Market Crash in October, and a new Pandemic in November, a woman calls the house requesting an appointment with Rachel. Rachel accepts and soon sits in a café across from this woman who arrives with a large man at her side. The woman looks like a cat. From her clothes to her hair, she reminds Rachel of a Persian cat—with white hair, dark eyeliner, bright red lipstick, and black clothes. She is sweet. Her tone, her mannerisms—everything is kind and thoughtful. Rachel likes her instantly, although she remains uncertain about the quiet man next to her who resembles an overgrown baby. His head is bald, his cheeks are chubby, and, if he isn't smiling, he looks sad as though he might burst into tears.

"Rachel, my name is Catalina. And this is my brother, Jeffrey. We're so glad that you could come and meet with us."

"I'm sorry my father couldn't come; he had a show to do,"

"That's no problem. We don't want to take up more of your time than we have to. I'm sure that you have been contacted by plenty wanting to help you in your career and I am here to do just the same," she says with a smile.

"Help me?"

"Well, I want to promote you. I want to take you around, manage your career, and hopefully record a few more songs. Don't worry, Rachel," she says with a smile. "I'm not here to take advantage of you, I just know that I can make you and me money with your voice. You have a number one song right now. It's being played from here to California, and I think we can figure out a way to keep its momentum."

There is something about Catalina that Rachel likes. She's strong, quirky, kind, and most of all straight to the point. Rachel finally looks at the woman, "Catalina, what if I hate it? What if I don't want to, one night, or two."

Catalina smiles, "Then Jeffrey here takes the stage and tells them there is no show tonight. He can handle a bottle or two being thrown his way. Look Rachel, I can tell you're nervous or scared, but I'm not into this because I need the money, I'm here because I love music, and I believe you have the talent needed to succeed."

By March, Catalina sets up touring dates for Rachel all across the United States and even some through Europe. Two weeks before Rachel and Catalina are to leave, Rachel and Simone sit outside watching the sun set on a beautiful spring night. The orange glow of the magical hour is upon them.

"What if you go with me?" Rachel asks with a grin.

Simone looks at her with a raised eyebrow. "Don't even tease me about something like that. These classes are zapping the last bit of strength I have left. I wish I could go with you, but I'm doing well and need to finish."

A tear falls down Rachel's cheek. "You've just been there for me through everything. I swore the last time that we got together I wasn't going to leave you again."

Simone places her hand over her friend's shoulder. "There will always be times when we leave each other, but we've clearly shown that it isn't going to trouble our friendship any."

"I'm scared. I don't know what I'm going do without everybody." Gregory walks past several yards away as he hauls food to the animals. "Even Gregory and Sandy."

"So, you think that just because you are leaving we aren't gonna be here when you get back."

"I'm just gonna miss you so much, that's all."

"Miss what?" Simone asks appalled. "Miss playing cards or reading when there's nothing else to do? Rachel, you're gonna be off traveling the world, seeing things you've never seen before, meeting people that you never would have met otherwise. Come on now, this is something special—something worth pursuing for sure."

Rachel glances out over the fields until the lowering sun blasts her eyes and she can only see white. "I've been movin' from one place to the next since I was a baby. I never seem to know where I'm going to be in the year to come."

"Well, I promised you before and I'll gladly promise you again, that I'll be there for you when you need me."

"Okay. I'll accept that promise."

1998

It is like Rachel's voice opened a portal that connected her world to mine. I had never spent so much time with my gramma, at least not since she was diagnosed with Alzheimer's. Perhaps that shows my selfishness, or perhaps it was simply devastating. My gramma was everyone's favorite person. The hooting and hollering gramma, the one with the big presents at Christmas, the hard lessons when needed, and the affection that meant all would be okay even if it wasn't today. I'll never forget the first time we took her to dinner, then I walked her home; but not five minutes later she was at our door again wondering when we were going to dinner. "We just got back from dinner, Gramma." "Oh that's right, baby!" But I could tell in her eyes that it scared her as well. My father grew worse after all of this, and I suppose our family separated more when Gramma was no longer leading the cause. I miss Gramma Johnson and her magical humor that could switch me from a bad mood to a good one in seconds.

"So, Jake and P.B.—as tragic as their deaths were—they gave Rachel something that changed her life," I say quietly with a nod.

"I believe Jake truly loved Rachel and Rachel truly loved Jake. It's still sad to believe they could have loved each other forever."

"Like you and grampa."

"Yes." She smiles, closes her eyes and raises her chin to the ceiling. "Just like that."

"Gramma, do you have the song they wrote her?"

"Well, it was called "Somethin' Tender" and I believe I have it on one of those CDs over there."

I jump to my feet and hurry to the stack. I check every CD and finally come across one of her earliest recordings. In seconds the song seems to color the white walls of the room with her mood, her vibe, and I close my eyes. It is obvious why this song led her to better things. "What I like most about it is the way she speaks about love—seeming almost optimistic that love can be the escape from dark places. She gives me hope. Man, what a sap I am turning out to be."

"You've always been a sap. Don't kid yourself."

"You think so, Gramma?"

"You remember that time in my yellow kitchen, when the summer heat was turned up hot, and that girl came by from a few doors down. Do you remember what you said to me?"

Do you, I thought to myself. This was the first actual memory that wasn't Rachel's story. "I suppose I don't."

"You said, 'Someday I'm going to find someone that makes

me care nothing about anything else. Someone that takes all my thoughts for her own.'"

"I said that?"

"Yes, you did."

"Rachel's not mine and she's not real."

"But Rachel's story reminds you that your life can change in an instant. She had moments of bliss, and moments of heartache just like us all."

"Was she bitter?" I'm not sure why I want to know—maybe because any real person would be, and I want her to be real.

"In some ways, you could say that. But Rachel began her life with this sweet aroma always following her, the one that makes everyone so intrigued by her, and I think, in some way, God just made her full of ease with an ability to move beyond."

"She doesn't care to ever search for her mother?"

"Give her time, Bobby. I have to tell you the story as it goes."

"Alright, just tell me the story as it goes then."

"I will." Gramma grabs her knitting again and begins moving the needles in and out. "Catalina and Jeffrey took Rachel all over the States. They were going to take a small bit of time at each stop and then when they reached California they would stop for one month. Everywhere she went there was a crowd. She often wondered where the people were coming from, but what she didn't know was that everyone knew her name now. Three songs of hers had been released—from recordings that Catalina had her do before they left Atlantic City—and every song went straight to the top. The three of them stayed in decent hotels and ate at decent restaurants. She actually got to know Catalina along the road. She found that Jeffrey didn't speak more than a word a day. Catalina was also born into humble beginnings and although Rachel never told anyone what she had gone through as a child, she was pretty certain that Catalina had gone through something of the same. The age difference—Catalina was nearly seventeen years Rachel's senior—didn't make a difference, they still laughed like old friends. She introduced Rachel to alcohol, even though Prohibition would last another few years.

'She actually began enjoying herself. I think she loved the partying and laughter, but the men's attention was a little overwhelming. After Bill and then Jake, her heart was a little worse for wear. Catalina on the other hand, had her share of men come back to her room with her. Every night, Rachel saw a new man enter as Catalina hung a stocking on her door handle. Rachel quickly found that Jeffrey was useful. He was the size of a large bear and kept closely by her side as she came on and off stage. Even though he didn't speak, she could see that he was growing to like her very much—maybe even a little crush. I believe close to the end of August they reached California."

Chapter Twenty

1929

"We're stopping in Napa Valley tonight," Catalina explains as she drives the car through the rolling hills of California's wine country. She suddenly grabs her stomach and scowls.

"You okay?" Rachel asks.

"I'm just feeling a little off. But don't worry about it." She changes the subject even though she keeps her palm on her stomach.

Rachel takes a quick glance at Jeffrey sleeping in the back seat. It would have seemed equally normal to see either his thumb or a cigar sitting in his mouth. Instead, he has just a small grin as he sleeps.

"Why doesn't he speak, Cat?"

"I'm not sure. I've never heard him speak and our parents died when he was young, so no one knew what the doctor said of his condition before that, and it seems no one cared enough to ask again. I suppose I should have done something as he got older."

Catalina passes by small homes until they gradually find themselves in a more happening area of town. Soon they turn down a driveway that leads to the most gorgeous hotel Rachel's ever seen. It is a Spanish Revival with white everything and accents of wood and black, surrounded by vineyards on every nearby rolling hill.

"This can't be it," Rachel whispers.

"I believe it is."

A circle drive leads them to the curved front doors, and they quickly step out once the car pulls to a stop. Two young bellhops come to their side and smile. "Can we help you, ladies?"

"My name is Catalina, and this is Rachel Anne Praline. The owner hired her to come and sing."

One of them, looking no older than fifteen, nods his head. "Yes, of course. May we take your bags?"

"Yes, please." Catalina turns to Rachel and shakes her head. Her skin is as pale as the white roses planted all over the grounds. "Rachel, I'm going to find a place to rest."

"Yes, go, Catalina. I'll check in."

"Thank you."

Jeffrey follows Catalina to the garden where a bench resides, and Rachel walks up the steps into the grand foyer. It is magnificent. A wide chandelier hangs above the long front desk. Windows line the walls toward the back of the hotel, displaying the miles of grapes that expand beyond. The colors are several shades of white with a very classic and elegant feel. After driving all day through hot temperatures, Rachel feels far from adequate to stand as a guest in the glorious hotel.

"May I help you, miss?"

Rachel turns to the man behind the counter and smiles. "Yes, I need to check in."

"Of course. Your name?" He looks in the books in front of him.

"Rachel Anne Praline."

For a moment he looks up as though he doesn't believe it. "I love your music," he says.

"Thank you."

He seems to have something to say beyond this, but his tongue sticks to the roof of his mouth as if he chooses not to. Rachel breathes in till her diaphragm expands, still not used to this kind of attention. Thank you, Bill, she thinks to herself with bitterness.

"You have three rooms?" The concierge shows his lazy dimple as he smiles while the chandelier above casts diamonds of sweat along his tall forehead.

"I don't really know."

"Will you be needing all three rooms?" He looks for the rest of her party.

"One of them isn't feeling very well. They're outside."

"Oh, I see. Please just give me a moment while I find your keys." The short and slightly chubby man with a double chin leaves the counter.

Several men and women, some coupled, some alone, saunter through the foyer. Never has she seen such regality, from their white linen suits to their very shiny, very expensive jewelry. The most interesting couple is dressed as if they are heading to a ball, she in a black gown, and he in a tuxedo. They don't look at anybody, or each other, so Rachel is able to watch them with curiosity. "I'm in a different world," she whispers to herself.

It doesn't take her long to realize that she's clutching her purse to her chest and questioning the very simple and very plain blue dress she chose that morning. Bars and restaurants are what she's used to—places where sweat is necessary to display your appreciation. Rachel peers outside as she wonders how Catalina pulled this off.

Finally, the man comes back. "Here are your keys and if you follow these stairs up two flights, the first three rooms on the left are yours. I hope that your friend feels better."

"I do too. Thank you."

Before Rachel can turn, she hears a voice say, "Can we have the nurse come to her room?" It paralyzes her instantly, as a flood of memories, both good and bad, nearly drown her. How long can she hold her breath? Even her hands start to shake, and she pictures the young seventeen-year-old face as she peered out from under the stairs in the dark basement. Eons seem to pass before she finally forces herself to turn.

It's desperately embarrassing when tears form beneath her pupils until her eyes are swimming. If she blinks, he'll see them, so she tries to battle the urge. A man looks back at her with kind eyes, chiseled jaw, and a knowing grin. His clothes aren't formal and restrained, rather liberated and a bit carefree. She would expect nothing less from the troublemaker teenager that he used to be. In wide-leg linen pants, and a button-up green shirt, the top three buttons undone—Levi has his hands tucked calmly in his pockets.

Finally, the dam breaks and Rachel looks away with the back of her hand hiding her face. He steps forward out of concern, but this only makes her panic worse. It's quite possible this is the longest she has ever gone without answering a question.

"Rachel?" His voice is deeper, more polished and supported, while his eyes are bluer than she remembers.

She laughs at herself, "I'm sorry. I just . . ." Every ounce of her wants to avoid his strong stare, just so she can compose herself, but before long it is impossible, and she looks directly into them. Just as she thought, she is swallowed by their knowledge of her or quite possibly the appreciation of what she is now. "I just never expected to see you again."

"I promised you."

"Forever ago."

He nods. "I'm sorry."

Deep down she doesn't know how to accept this. Should he be a reminder of the very desperate years of her life or the moments when she was saved by someone who took notice. She shyly wipes the drops from her cheeks and breathes out to compose herself.

The concierge seems to be mesmerized by the scene before him. "You know Miss Praline, sir?"

Levi reaches out behind her and takes the three keys from the counter, which makes him come so close that she looks up into his eyes and he looks down. "I used to."

"What are you doing here?" she asks.

"I'm staying at this hotel."

"You are?"

"Yes, for business. You?"

"Same," she answers, refusing to tell him too much.

He smiles again. "You have a friend that's ill?"

"Yes, she's outside."

"Well, may I help?"

"I think she might be embarrassed." Rachel doesn't want him to leave yet. "That would be nice, thank you."

As they walk outside, they continue to take quick glances at each other. "Over there." Rachel points to the bench where Catalina sits with Jeffrey. As they come near, it is obvious that Catalina is feeling dramatically worse.

"Catalina?" Rachel asks. "What can we do? I have the keys for you. Will you be okay walking?"

"Yes, I think so."

Catalina takes Rachel's hand and tries to stand, but the moment she gets to her feet her knees buckle, and Levi swiftly pulls her into his arms.

"Come with me," Levi says carrying her with ease back to the hotel, "Let's get you to your room."

Catalina looks up at the man holding her and although she feels awful, she smiles. "Wow. Who are you?"

"I'm Levi."

"Well, don't you know how to sweep a girl off her feet?" With that, she throws her arms around his neck and snuggles her nose just under his jaw.

Rachel grins when Levi doesn't seem to mind.

The hotel is beautiful with every detail thought about and

cared for. Windows line hallways so that the vineyard can be always enjoyed, and Levi seems to know exactly where to go. Before they've even reached Catalina's room, the nurse meets them. When Levi lays her on the bed, the woman quickly shoos them out. Jeffrey goes to his room, so Levi and Rachel are alone. Levi takes Rachel's key from her hand and opens her door for her without a word. He leads her inside the most beautiful room she's ever stayed in—her own veranda, a large, canopied bed, and bathroom with a deep tub. If only she could share this with Simone, but most importantly tell her who's standing across the room, looking more perfect than she remembers. Someone left the window open, and the sheer white curtains lift off of the floor from the strong breeze outside. Levi stays in the doorway as she studies everything. She runs her hands through her hair, suddenly wondering what she must look like after the long drive. "Are you really here?"

"I am." He grins.

"Thank you for your help with Catalina."

"Of course, anything." When he's quiet for a moment with his hands in the pocket of his slacks, Rachel compares this man to the boy across the street.

"It's hard to connect who I used to know . . . to you," she breathes out.

"I feel the same." He begins to walk toward her, which makes her heart race, but he passes her instead. With quick hands, he ties the curtain to the hook so that it doesn't knock over a vase. When he's done, he rubs his neck, breathes out and grins. "Well, I'll let you go."

"Will I see you again?" She's not sure what to say.

"That depends."

"On what?"

"Do you want to see me again?"

Afraid to be too eager she holds her tongue for a second, then it slips out too fast anyway. "Yes."

"We have a lot to talk about, don't we?"

"I want to know where you've been."

"You don't want to know that," he warns.

"I do."

"Are you free tomorrow?"

"Yes."

"Okay. Tomorrow then. After your show."

"Wait, you know why I'm here?"

"Of course. I heard your song all the way on the other side of the world. I'll see you tomorrow."

He leaves the room, and she stares at the door. Levi has felt like a figment of her imagination or a dream for so long. On impulse, she runs to the hallway, but he's already gone. So, she hurries to the next hall. "Levi?" She turns the corner and stops. In his slacks with his hair cut short, he turns around quickly when he hears his name.

"Is everything alright?" he asks taking a few steps toward her.

Then she realizes she has nothing to say. There is no real reason she just called for him. "No, I..."

He takes another step towards her and the concern in his eyes steals her breath.

She says, "I just needed to make sure that you are real."

"I am and I'll see you tomorrow."

§ § §

It seems the entire hotel, as well as the local residents, have come to see Rachel. She smiles at the crowd and says, "Just make sure you're having a good time, it's the sole reason for music," and after a while even the most well-behaved men and women are letting loose.

Catalina is still ill, and Jeffrey is by her side, so for the first concert Rachel is alone—until she looks up to find Levi watching her from the back of the room. He is different than she remembers. The suits he wears make him appear taller and more put together than the kid across the street. His face is serious, as though he has seen more than she might ever know. Afterwards the crowd surrounds her, and she signs autographs, as Levi waits at the exit.

"Thank you," Rachel says to the crowd as she maneuvers through them and crosses the large theater that is in the center of the hotel.

"Can we take a walk?" Levi asks.

"That would be nice."

They take the walking path through the vineyards and golf course, then around the garden that is lit up just enough.

"How long are you here?" she asks.

"I'll be here for another few weeks. The business that I came to do is taking longer than usual."

"Business? What do you do?"

He smiles, seeming as though he doesn't want to tell her.

"Is it a secret?" she asks curiously.

"No, it's not a secret. I buy real estate or businesses. When I see something that will be a good investment, and they need help…I help them."

"By buying their property?"

Levi stops for a moment and looks at her until she blushes.

"What?" Rachel watches his blue eyes, unable to look away.

An owl soars across the sky grabbing their attention. It lands at the top of a nearby tree and watches them walk slowly.

"What did you do?" she asks.

"I went to college, got a degree, then I found that I loved taking something that needed help and making it prosper. It started with small homes. My parents helped me with my first buy. It just so happens that I did my homework and bought the right property."

"Did it have gold or something?"

"Close; it had oil."

Her eyes grow wide.

"I know," he says with a laugh. "It seems the older I get, the more I realize that life is a lot about luck. I paid my parents back, studied a little bit more, and bought my second property."

"Did this one have oil?"

"No," he chuckles. "But I did have an inside tip that a very wealthy man was looking to buy it to build his golf course there, so I bought it first, did a couple of things to make the property worth more, and sold it to him for a rather large profit. Then it turned to businesses, and now hotels."

"So that's what you've been doing with your life?" A strange feeling comes over her. It's not that she never wished him success, it's just that he never came back to her like he said he would. She tries to push the feelings down, but can't.

"Yeah. I guess after the war I just had to put all my energy into something."

Maybe if she asked more about his life, it would go away. "And your parents, how are they?"

"My father died two years ago."

"I'm sorry."

"Thank you." Levi looks at her with sincere eyes. "He always asked about you. It was important to us that you were happy."

She says nothing, confused why he didn't just find out for himself. "And your mother?"

"Doing well. She lives near me in Italy."

"You live in Italy?"

He smiles. "Yes. I took some time to travel and found that Italy was really where I wanted to be. At least for now, it suits me."

They are just about to make a full circle back to the hotel, but she finds that she doesn't want it to end. "So, what are you buying here?"

Again, he laughs. It is obvious that Levi doesn't usually tell all of his secrets in such a short time with someone, but Rachel is different. Already they are involved in each other's secrets so heavily that he doesn't hold back. It is unusually easy to tell her what she wants to know.

"This hotel."

"You're buying this hotel?"

"Yes. The old man who owns it actually called me. He's in trouble financially and I told him that I would take it off his hands for a fair price."

She doesn't know whether to praise him for a good deed or laugh at his luck. "Okay. So when will you own this place?"

"Technically, I do now."

Something occurs to her, and she turns to him. "Are you the one that brought me here?"

He grins. "That depends. Are you happy to be here?"

"Yes."

"I might have had something to do with it." Everything about this night is memorable—the fragrance of the flowers and grass, the breeze that sweeps across their skin, the way the shadows are bouncing across their faces—providing the mystery to increase intrigue. He leads her into the lobby of the hotel from the back patio and says, "I'm up on the top floor. Would you come up with me?"

Rachel's heart speeds up, which she didn't think was possible, and even though she doesn't want their time to end, she wonders whether taking his offer is appropriate.

However, the more she tries to fight it, the more she wants to go. "Okay."

"Come with me." Levi leads her through the lobby and through a door that says 'restricted', where they arrive at an elevator.

"You have your own elevator?"

"Yes."

She steps inside with him, and he pulls the cage shut. Neither one of them says a word the entire four stories, yet they continue to take glances at each other. Before long, he pulls his keys from his pocket and opens the door to the suite. He is right—it is an apartment—it is just more beautiful than she's ever experienced. With a kitchen, two rooms, and a large terrace that overlooks the surrounding vineyards, it is perfectly decorated. "I believe this is where the old man spent too much of his money." Levi says, as he takes a couple steps inside. "He spent nearly two hundred thousand dollars on an interior decorator."

"It shows."

"Let me take this." He gently helps her remove her sweater and sets it on a coat rack. "Just to return to your question, I am the one responsible for bringing you here. First of all, you're good for business…" he says, then the smile falls from his face and his voice deepens, "but---" he doesn't finish.

"But what?"

"Never mind. A few months ago, I heard your voice on the radio, and I needed to see how you had grown up."

"Well, how have I grown up?"

He shakes his head. "Terrible." They both laugh. "No, it's unbelievable, really."

When she can't handle more butterflies, she walks to the nearest sofa and runs her hand along the expensive, emerald green material. She's aware of his every move and listens to him come closer. Finally, when she turns around, he is only feet away. "Do you want a drink?" he asks.

"No."

"You don't drink?"

"I do. Just not tonight."

He smiles as he pulls his jacket off and throws it aside while stepping behind the bar in his kitchen and pouring water instead. Then he leans on the bar, resting his elbows on the wood. When she does the same, their faces are not far from each other.

"Tell me that my father and I did a good thing," Levi says, hopeful.

"You did a good thing," she assures him. "Dick and Sylvia have been the best parents anyone could ever ask for." He blows the air out of his lungs with relief. "It was hard after they took me, but they were great and so nice compared to…" Rachel stops, wondering when she last said his name. "They didn't force me to do anything I didn't want to do. I spent most of high school taking care of his animals and helping him with his show."

"Did you finish school?"

"I finished high school."

"And after?"

Rachel hesitates. The story is long and hard, still stinging her heart every time she speaks of Jake. The clock on the wall chimes midnight, but she doesn't feel tired, if anything, she feels as if she'll never sleep again. She runs her fingers along the smooth wood just in front of his hands and can't help but notice that his hands are rough.

"Where did you get these?" she asks about his calluses.

"Back in Italy. I build boats and I fly planes."

"Boats and planes?"

"Yeah. It's become a passion, I guess. Gets my mind off work."

"If this is work, then I wouldn't mind thinking about it all of the time," she says, motioning with her hands to the ornate room around them.

"This is the fun after the work."

"Oh."

"And after high school?" he asks again.

"You first," Rachel says quickly.

"Oh, I don't think that's how it works. I asked you. Besides I've told you nearly everything. College, Real Estate, and now I'm here."

"Are you married?"

"No. I'm not married. There is someone back in Italy that I have a long history with, but at the moment, there is no one. Are there any men in your life?"

She looks away. "Not anymore."

"There seems to be a story there," he says studying, her every expression.

"I guess there is. His name was Jake."

"Is he still in your life?"

"No. And it's a long story."

"I have all night, unless you would like to go back to your room."

"No. No, I don't."

"What happened to Jake?"

"Our skin didn't match. So, people had trouble with that. He died…standing up for someone…someone that had been treated unfairly and he was hung on the church lawn." Levi is quiet as she explains. "I think I was in love with him if we had just been given more time, but…I don't know…" With a heavy breath, she finally turns to him, desperately wishing to change the subject. Her need to know why he never came grows within her, but she is hesitant to ask. "I thought you were going to marry that other girl."

"What other girl?"

"Vanity?"

He laughs. "Oh man, I haven't thought of her in years. No. She was just…I was too young…still in high school…no. But she's a writer now and has a couple of kids, I think."

"I liked her."

"Me too."

An hour later they sit on the couch beside each other, and she can feel her eyes fatiguing, but she wants to fight it more than anything she's wanted in a long time.

"Where are Dick and Sylvia now?" he asks.

"Still in Atlantic City. His show is doing well."

"Good. I'm glad to hear that."

"He helped me find my best friend from my childhood."

"Simone?"

Rachel looks at him with wide eyes. "You remember her name?"

"I haven't forgotten much of anything that you ever told me."

"Haven't you?"

"No." He reaches out and runs his finger along her hand, which makes every molecule in her body come alive. After a moment's pause, he continues, "You're a singer now."

"I guess I am."

"That's good. It was what you were meant to do."

A breeze comes through the doors of the terrace and blows her skirt up just a little bit.

"I should show you outside," he says, standing with his hand out.

She takes his hand as he turns, and he doesn't let go. They step out onto the balcony, where the stars are bright and the moon is full. For miles, the beautiful acreage he owns extends beyond what they can see, piecing together rolling hills of vines, that make the sweetest red wine. A phonograph sits on a table next to the door.

"Hold on just a minute," he says. He sets the needle down and the music begins to pour out of the large horn. Rachel covers her face when she recognizes her own voice.

"Oh no," she laughs.

"Come on." He takes her hand and pulls her in to dance. It is a slow song, and she lets him guide her. "Sing it to me."

"You've got the phonograph."

"I want to hear you."

"I'll have to charge you."

"I think I can pay."

She sings softly and before either is aware of it, he has pulled her even closer. After a moment she stops singing when the question still looms. Why seek her out now? So many times in her life, people have been careless. Using her for her voice, or now her beauty. This is all nice, but it doesn't take away the nights she cried for him. She finally gets the nerve to pull away and immediately heads inside. "I think I should go."

Soon the clock strikes two. He can tell something has changed. "Let me walk you."

"No, it's okay. You don't need to do that," she says as she grabs her sweater.

"I have always felt protective of you, Rachel, it's certainly not going to stop now that you look this way."

She feels her throat constrict and she hesitates.

"Rachel?"

"I don't understand." Her words come out louder than she expects. The expression changes on his face as though he knew this would be coming, but he doesn't say anything. "If you really felt that protective, then why did I spend so many nights wondering where you were? Wondering whether you were okay?" Once again, the tears are getting treacherously close and her face is hot to the touch. "You're the only one that knew what happened to me, you saved me from . . . him . . . only to disappear the moment you handed me off to someone? I just don't understand, why now?"

He takes a moment to breathe, then continues. "I ran away. After the war, I'd seen too much and done too much. I wasn't the same, if you can understand that."

"Who better to understand that?" The tears are falling now. "Everyone in my life before you disappeared. Do you know what that does to a girl? Is it me? Am I the reason? Were you hiding from me?"

They meet eyes and the memories of what they have gone through together pass between them as if they are fresh.

"I was scared of someone seeing me like that . . . of you seeing me like that."

Rachel shakes her head and wipes her face. There's no hiding now. "Somehow, I was more mature than you. I had no choice to run away. You promised that you would come to see me. Year after year I prayed that you would . . ." she stops when it will only turn her sadness into all-out crying.

He doesn't say anything, but walks to her. When he gets near, it still takes him a moment. Finally, he nods. "I deserve all of this. It tortures me to think of you, worried about me . . . when all you needed to do was heal." He reaches out and touches her hair. "I'm so sorry Rachel. You needed people to show permanence and all I did was the opposite. All I can say is that I was young and if I could go back now, I'd do it differently. I am desperately sorry."

As his hand touches her hair, it travels down to her hand—not reaching to hold it, but brushing it gently. "I feel better," she whispers.

He smiles. "Good." After a moment he helps her with her sweater. "Let me walk you back."

In the elevator, they watch each other as it drifts down and shadows run across each other's faces. When they finally reach her room, again, he takes her key from her hand and opens the door without a word.

"Good night, Rachel."

"Good night, Levi."

"Tomorrow?"

"Yes, tomorrow."

"Good."

He walks down the hall, but stops halfway. "I'll answer any questions you have. Hopefully, you can learn to trust my promises again." As he turns the corner, he glances back with a smile on his face as she holds her hands at her chest.

§ § §

The weather in Napa at this time of year is shaped by the warmth in the sun and cool in the shade, or the smooth stream of air that gathers speed through the vines and seems to slow between the hills. A consistent scent of sweet floral notes underscored by earthy tones is something that Rachel appreciates every morning as it wafts into her room. She is tired after another sleepless night, but when she sits up in bed and hears faint music coming through her window, it reminds her of the night before with Levi Price. It all seems too unbelievable to be true and she shakes her head as she covers her face.

Once she's ready she hurries next door to see how Catalina is doing and finds Jeffrey asleep in the chair beside her bed.

"There you are. I was wonderin' who took you," Catalina grins.

"I was just busy doing the show last night. I'm sorry I didn't come see you."

"Are you kidding? I'm your manager. I'd be upset if you were here instead of where I need you to be."

"Well, it went great."

"So I hear." Catalina turns her eyes to her brother.

"He was there?" Rachel asks, surprised.

"Yeah, I had him go check on our favorite girl."

Their communication, while not usual, works well between the two of them. Jeffrey may not speak, but he is able to communicate wonders with Cat.

"So, tell me…" Rachel sits on a chair on the opposite side of the bed as Jeffrey. "What did the doctor say?"

"It seems my promiscuous days are over."

Rachel furrows her eyebrows until she realizes what Catalina is saying. "Are you…" she doesn't know the polite way of asking such a personal thing, "having a baby?"

"Yes." Catalina forces a smile. "But don't worry, this isn't going to affect my job. We'll be just fine."

"Catalina, I am not worried about that."

"You aren't? I was." Catalina gives an awkward smile that makes them both laugh.

"What do you do now?"

"I don't really know. I've never been pregnant before." A knock sounds at the door and Rachel stands up to answer it. A nice-looking older man stands there, with a leather bag at his side.

"Good morning. I'm the doctor on call this morning. Is . . ." he pulls out a piece of paper, "Catalina here?"

"She is." Rachel opens the door to the handsome man and Catalina suddenly sits up straight and preps herself.

"Good morning, Doctor." Catalina says suggestively.

"I'll see you later, Cat," Rachel says with a laugh.

"Alright now. Have a fun day. I know I will." Catalina is paying no attention to Rachel anymore.

She reaches the elevator and just as the doors open, they reveal

Levi dressed in a casual suit. Rachel's breath catches.

"You running somewhere?" he asks.

"I'm not sure. Are you here to find me?"

"I am."

She steps beside him as he closes the door. "I still feel like a child next to you."

"I was just a kid too," he responds.

"Just two kids trying to survive," she whispers. Their bodies are so close that she feels the energy of her shoulder touching his arm and she presses her palm to her face, trying to cool her cheeks.

"How did you sleep?"

"Fine," she lies.

"Your room is satisfactory?"

"Yes, completely."

"Good."

"Although it doesn't have its own bar, or veranda, or living room, but I guess it will do…"

"There's only one of those. I guess I should switch rooms with you. Would that make you happy?" He turns to her.

"Not in the slightest."

"Why?"

"There would be something missing." She lets the answer slip but can't look him in the eye. There are but two inches between them.

They don't notice the doors have opened until they hear the clearing of someone's throat. Both of them turn to find an old man with sleek rimmed glasses.

"Mr. Farley! Good morning," Levi says, letting the gentleman in before he steps out.

"Good morning, Mr. Price."

"Things going well for you?"

"Just fine, thank you."

"Let me close this." Levi pulls the doors closed as Rachel waits behind him with a smile. When he turns around to her, he shakes his head. "Two 'fines' this morning. Guess I'm going to have to do some things differently."

They walk to the front desk and the same concierge is there.

"Can you make sure to hold all of my calls?" Levi begins to walk away placing his hand on Rachel's back, but then he turns to the chubby, friendly man, "Steve, figure out how we can make this place great instead of just fine. I'll expect the answer by the time I get back from breakfast."

"Will do, sir."

"Thank you," he says with a wink. He walks to Rachel's side. "You ready to go?"

"Where are we going?"

"Not very far. We can walk."

Rachel makes sure that her hat is on correctly as they pass a large mirror in the hall. When they step outside, the slight breeze feels good against their skin as they walk slowly. For a moment, they are quiet as the sun warms their skin. Napa Valley has a constant smell of fermentation which carries with the breeze and Rachel wonders whether she'll forever connect it with him. It's Levi, but at the same time, it isn't him. There's something so put together, so strong, so unbelievably powerful compared to the boy of mischief. He's still youthful in his face at only thirty-one, but even still, she finds it hard not to be slightly intimidated.

"Are you happy now?" she asks, having gone to bed wondering this.

"Why would you ask that?"

"Last night, everything you said about wanting to run away after the war and it made me curious. Are you happy now?" They pass a fashionable couple who nod in Levi's direction so he smiles.

"It took many years, but yes. It's more so today, than in a long time." He gives her a side eye which makes her grin shyly.

She's hesitant to ask the next question, but also eager—it's difficult to know which emotion will win. "You never married. Why?"

"I've been close. That girl I was telling you about in Italy. We were supposed to get married two years ago, but we were different. I don't think I was sure and she was."

"Why weren't you sure?"

"There was just something stopping me, almost as if I hadn't met the right woman yet."

When a group of young men pass by, he moves out of their way, and his shoulder brushes hers. She's more aware of his touch than any ray of the sun, the grapes, or anything else Napa has to offer. The night before she warned him of her anger, being clear that his absence was painful. The vulnerability makes her unsettled beside him, as though she should have said nothing.

When he unexpectedly turns down an alleyway, she continues the wrong way until he reaches out and takes her hand. His fingers slide between hers and she can't help but look up at him.

"This way," he says.

With a rapidly beating heart, she nods and follows him down circular stone steps along a hidden path, but as he leads, he does not let go. Instead, he holds her hand close behind his back.

After several feet, the buildings part, revealing a restaurant patio and beyond that, vines for miles. Greenery and succulents are perfectly planted from window to window, and round tables are covered by orange and white striped umbrellas. The cobblestones beneath their feet appear old but well-kept and several old brick buildings stand to their right. This is where waiters and waitresses emerge with decadent looking food and bottles of wine. A large fountain creates a constant white noise that muffles the conversations of every guest.

A young waiter rushes to Levi's side. "Good morning, Mr. Price. We've been expecting you. Please sit right here."

"Thank you."

They are led to a table so far away from the others, that it appears they won't have to worry about anyone hearing any of their conversation except for the birds in the bath nearby. Before long, they order and, once the waiter leaves, Levi looks at her.

"How did we get here?"

"I don't know," she answers truthfully. "Sometimes I didn't think I would."

"Me either."

He asks about her music and how it came to be that she tours with Catalina. She asks him about his college days, and this leads him into the death of his father. They talk about Simone and her success in college. The food comes and it's perfect. Every morsel is perfect.

"Do you think you will ever move back to the States?" she asks, as the waiter takes her food away.

"No, I don't think so. Especially, since I don't have family here anymore."

This bothers her, yet she doesn't know why—or at least she tells herself that she doesn't. "I feel like I moved around so much as a child . . . never having something solid, that I strive to stay in one place."

"That's just another demon talking," he says quickly.

"What do you mean?"

"I don't know anything that is truly stable. If you try and hold on to anything in this world, one of these days you're going to end up shorthanded, but if you find out who you are without all those things, without anything…then you might have a chance."

She looks at him with a strange expression.

"What?" he asks.

"You're just so grown up."

"Oh no, did that sound too mature?"

"A little."

"Well, how's this? I hate waking up in the morning for work. I still enjoy getting drunk every once in a while, and gambling a little, and I hate to read. Does that sound too grown up?"

"No," she smiles.

"What about you? What are the things that still make you young?"

"Beyond the fact that am I still young?"

"Yes, beyond that fact."

She doesn't know where to begin. "I still hate to drive even though I have been driving for years, I love to get my hands dirty, I can't stand the taste of alcohol—it makes my nose turn up, and I still have to sleep with a light on."

"You still sleep with a light on?"

"Yes." She chuckles as she takes a sip of water.

"Why?"

"Nighttime isn't good to me." He doesn't have to say anything for her to know he understands, so she continues, "I was doing better, but then everything with Jake. I burn out light bulbs pretty fast."

"Did Jake ever ask why?"

"Why what?"

"Why you had to have a light on at night?"

She looks up at him and takes a moment before speaking. "No." She clears her throat to stave off any emotion. "He never knew. We were never with each other at night." She sees the twist of his smile and she cocks her head to the side, "What are you smiling at?"

"I just can't believe that you're sitting here with me."

"I can't either."

"Shall we find something else to do?"

"Yes."

Levi lays money on the table and they saunter back. When they reach the front of the hotel, Rachel begins walking up the stairs, but Levi doesn't follow.

"What?" Rachel asks.

"Once we go in there I have to work," he walks the couple of steps to meet her, "but I want you to come with me."

"To work?"

"Yes, you don't have to, but…"

"I'd love to."

They walk into the hotel side by side, and women pass but stare at him, while men pass but stare at her. They pay no attention. Levi walks to the front desk.

"Has Mr. Huffman arrived yet?"

"Yes, sir. He is waiting over there." The concierge points to a silver-haired man sitting on one of the couches in the lobby with a paper in his hands.

In moments, Mr. Huffman, Rachel, and Levi take a walk through the vineyards as the old man talks about his love for them. Levi explains, "Donald was the owner of this hotel."

"Yes, but no longer," Donald says with an appreciative sigh.

"You seem pleased, despite how much you love this place," Rachel says.

"Well, I did love this place, Rachel, very much, but for the last few years it was quite a burden." Donald wears a white linen suit and a straw hat to polish off the ensemble that turns just slightly yellow under the cascading sun. "Unfortunately, at the same time that I lost my wife, Prohibition began. I wasn't in the mood to create something brand-new in order to keep this place running and I suppose I have never come back to feeling the same passion I once had for it."

She looks at Levi, "How does this place stay running with Prohibition?"

"Well, that's why Donald called me. To bring in new eyes, I guess. First of all, wine can still be used as sacramental or anything having to do with religious affiliations. We have changed the grapes to make jam, or raisins, or juice. These fields were perfect for the transition, but I just believe it was Donald's heartbreak that couldn't change."

Donald stops and stares at the clouds with utter sadness. "Yes. You're completely right."

Rachel reaches out and touches the man's shoulder as she says, "I'm sorry."

Surprisingly he turns to her and with a careful tone he says, "You know heartbreak, don't you."

It catches her off guard but finally she admits, "As well as my reflection."

It isn't long before they come to an underground wine cellar with two doors that sit inches above the ground. Donald pulls them open revealing a steep set of stairs with black walls all around. The rush of cold air sends a chill through Rachel, and she recoils.

"This is the wine cellar where we keep it all," Donald says proudly. He begins descending underground.

Levi follows but stops when he notices Rachel is frozen. "I think I'll go up to my room," she says softly.

He looks at the cellar and then back at her with a nod. "All right."

"Thank you for today."

"Here." He walks to her and places a key in her hand.

"What is this?"

"It's to my hotel room. Would you meet me? I'll be done within the hour."

"I will."

§ § §

Rachel waits on his balcony with music playing quietly on the phonograph, yet she finds it hard to pay attention to anything else but her irritation. She acted like a child, unable to enter the cellar and the thought of explaining to Levi seems unbearable.

He has a phone in his room that she didn't notice the day before. As she sits there waiting for him, it rings several times then stops. Repeatedly the phone rings, until Rachel wonders if it's Levi. Finally, she picks it up and the switchboard operator says, "I'm connecting you with 4225 in Italy." Before she can decline, a woman's voice comes on the line. "Levi, you haven't called in weeks. What's going on? I thought we were going to have a conversation."

"I'm sorry, Levi isn't here at the moment."

"Who's this?"

Just then Levi enters the front door and looks at her with question. She holds out the receiver. "I'm sorry, she called so many times I thought it might be you."

He takes the phone as if he already knows who it will be. "I told you I would deal with this when I get back." Rachel steps away, trying hard to not listen, but finding it nearly impossible. "We've already discussed this. You want everything the way you want it . . . when you want it. That's not how it works." He's quiet for several minutes, while Rachel can hear her yelling on the other line. "Don't call again. We will work this out when I get back. Goodbye." He hangs up, clearly upset.

Instantly Rachel is nervous that she's made a big mistake. When he turns around with flushed cheeks and furrowed brows, she knows she needs to fix it. "I'm sorry, Levi."

He looks up as if saved from himself. "For what?"

"I shouldn't have run off, and clearly I shouldn't have answered the phone."

He walks to her. "That was the woman I was telling you about. She and I still work together, in a manner of speaking, and she doesn't like that I'm here or that she heard a woman's voice."

It does more than bother Rachel to think about him with another woman. "I hope I didn't ruin things for you."

He looks at her strangely. "What do you mean? Rachel, I'm not with her. I told you, that was over last year." He shakes off the frustration with a twist of his head, while unbuttoning the top button of his shirt as if it's choking him, then he continues. "I'm sorry for not thinking about the basement. It didn't occur to me."

She reads in his eyes that he not only understands, but he also feels responsible. "I..." she begins, however, she can't continue.

"You what?"

"I don't want to be the little girl you needed to save."

They are quiet for a moment, then he comes so close that she can feel his warmth and his eyes stare deep into hers. The way he looks at her has changed, which forces the flush of her body when her heart races. After all these years, Levi is here and standing in front of her but most importantly, something has shifted between them. "Rachel, we can't change the fact that I was there . . . because I was. I know what he did to you, and all I've ever wanted to do was take it away. I should have broken in, I should've done something beyond what I did—but I didn't get there fast enough. If only I had listened to my gut."

"You were seventeen." Never once did she think that this would be his reaction. He looks away, so she says it again. "Levi, you were seventeen."

He places his hands on his head and breathes out with defeat. "My guilt kept me from you. I couldn't save you . . . then I went to war and I couldn't save anyone there either. I live with that guilt every damn day. It's no excuse. I should have kept my word, but I couldn't look you in the eye and tell you what a failure I was . . . again."

Rachel can't believe the emotion pulsing through him, from his clenched jaw to his tight eyes.

Despite her shaking hands and racing heart, she raises her palm to his cheek hoping that he'll look back. "You were just a kid yourself. It's not your fault." His chest rises and falls. "It's nobody's fault but Bill's." This is the first time she's said his name in a while. Finally, he looks at her, her fingers still touching his jaw. Obviously unsure, he lifts both hands and places one on each of her cheeks. It's an unexpected turn—what's happening, but neither is willing to stop, despite their surprise. When her gentle hand drops to his chest, she can feel the energy of time in their favor. There is nothing to do but exist in this room together. Carefully, his head falls, letting his lips land softly on hers. It's unlike anything she has ever felt. He's been with plenty of women, but there's something different here for him as well. Slowly and gently, he massages his lips on hers and when she reaches up to wrap her arms around his neck, their bodies connect.

Their mouths open a little wider and his hands wrap around her body, pulling her so close that she's on her toes. They shared something that no one else will ever understand and many years have passed with no fix, but strangely the moment he lifts her onto him, they have release.

Levi isn't impulsive, after being the teenager who did nothing right, but there is no resisting this urge today. He kisses her harder, as she matches his passion and her fingers brush through his hair, while his biceps press into her ribs as his hands roam her body. When she can't breathe, she gasps with amazement, lifting her chest until it presses against his. He hesitates a moment, as if he wonders whether she'll protest, or he's possibly waiting for his common sense to return. "You're here" she whispers, as a tear hangs dangerously off her bottom lash. Her body is on fire as he kisses her with perfection and experience beyond her own.

"I am," he whispers. He runs his hands down her back, then along her hips, until he lifts her all the way into his arms so that her legs can bind his waist. He carries her through the sliding glass doors, still holding her lips with his, as the curtains run along their bodies. When he lays her on the bed but stands above her, his lips are red and swollen. Just beneath her chest, he pulls the ribbon that holds her dress together and then un-wraps the smooth material from her body.

The sun is falling in the afternoon giving an orange glow to the entire room and somewhere music is playing, but it doesn't cover the sound of birds flying by. His apartment's large windows let enough light in that he can see the lacy slip she wears beneath her dress, and he shakes his head at the way it clings so beautifully to her curves. Then he lays on top of her without going further and stares directly into her eyes. "You've never been with anyone?"

"No," she whispers.

He kisses her lips, then her neck, and her cheek, but waits for more.

"I want to be with you," she says.

"Are you sure?" His thumb runs up and down her cheek.

She nods. He kisses her again, only this time there is no going back.

His tongue runs along the pink of her lips, and then down her bare skin. With just his fingertips, he runs them along her arm, then her palm and eventually laces his fingers with hers as he kisses her deeply. She wishes for him to never stop, now understanding such attention and care mixed with the greatest passion. He rubs his face along the silk slip as he travels down her chest, ribs, and hips. Then, his hands slide up from her thighs, artfully drifting beneath her silky undergarments and gliding them up until she must lift her body so that he can take it off. Before long the smooth material falls to the ground. He can't help but kiss her naked stomach while her hands tug at the buttons on his shirt and, quickly, she is able to pull it off. Her breath stops when she looks at the bare skin of his broad chest. He rolls over on top of her, holding himself up with his striated arms, then carefully lets his weight cover her as her leg naturally lifts and wraps around his. With a strong hand he pulls her thigh tighter which makes her inhale. The breeze from the open windows lands on all the right places as his fingers dance about her body, touching and caressing, forcing her to need more. Every second of their making love, he takes his time making sure that she knows he's there. She is protected in every way as he covers her with his own body and makes her feel brand new sensations. At this moment, nothing in the world can hurt her.

"I've got you," he says breathlessly, yet wondering how he will ever let her go.

§ § §

They lay in his bed staring at each other and she can't stop touching his face.

"I should probably go," she whispers.

"Stay here."

"Where?"

"This room. We don't leave."

She laughs. "I have a show tomorrow. I don't think that will work."

"Okay, if you must." He rubs her back and then kisses her shoulder. "But I do own this hotel."

"Yes, but I have fans now. They would be disappointed."

"I suppose they would. I'm having trouble caring at the moment," he whispers with a grin.

She runs her hand along his face. "You have to go back to Italy, and I have to finish my tour."

He keeps her silent by kissing her again.

Before the sun goes down, he gets up and looks at her bathed in his sheets. "I want to take you somewhere."

"You do? Where?"

"Get dressed."

Before long, they arrive at an airfield with military airplanes parked side by side. A man waits there with his hands behind his back and as they walk up to him, he smiles and reaches out a hand to shake Levi's. "So good to see you, Levi."

"It's good to see you, Colonel. So, you don't mind? I'll bring it down before the hour."

"Anything for you after all you did. Just don't tell the president."

Levi leads Rachel by the hand toward the planes and floats her a mischievous smile.

"What did you do for him?" she asks.

"Nothing I wasn't told to do. Come on."

They get so close to a specific plane, and he runs his hands down its nose as if he knows it well. "Climb those stairs."

"What?" Her eyes are wide with fear.

"What did you think we were doing?"

"I just figured you were showing them to me."

He laughs, "I am. But from the sky."

Her face gets serious. "Levi, I've never flown before. I can't." She backs away but he pulls her closer.

"I'm pretty sure today is a day to break some rules."

"Levi, I can't."

He comes close and places a hand on her neck. "Rachel, I've got you."

"He's the best pilot around!" The Colonel yells from several hundred yards away as he talks to several men in uniform.

Levi looks back at Rachel, "See. Thanks, Colonel," he yells.

Her body is shaking just as it did while they were making love and Levi runs his hand down her back, then holds her from behind with his arms over her chest. He whispers in her ear, "I won't let anything happen to you."

Together, they climb in, and he holds her close as the plane engines start to shake the warm metal. Then, she watches as his face becomes serious while he presses buttons, pulls levers, and before long, they're speeding along the runway until the nose climbs up. She's never felt the act of defying gravity and while she's afraid, it's also exhilarating. Before long they break through the clouds, heading directly toward the sun. Levi watches her awe as he effortlessly handles the large aircraft. She smiles at him and so many wrongs are making right from his life. He shows her tricks and the beauty of the world from miles above, until finally the sun sets and he easily sets the landing gear on the tarmac.

Within the hour, he's driven her back to the hotel where she starts to turn toward her room. However, he catches her hand and when she turns back, he grins. "Don't go. Come with me . . . stay with me."

They don't have dinner as they spend every moment with a new kind of hunger. Even a man like Levi, who has been with other women, has never felt this way. He kisses every inch of her, exploring and tantalizing, until she cries out in ecstasy. With heightened awareness of herself and him, she tucks herself into his arms and they fall asleep.

At nearly 2 am, Rachel's nightmares return as she walks through the dark hallways of Bill Manchuron's home. Her small feet tap the dirty floors, while she's desperate to get away from him as he chases her down the hall. Only now, the arms that hold onto her are suffocating and dangerous. She cries out in fear as she sits up in bed.

"Hey, hey, it's okay," Levi whispers while touching her face.

Taking in a deep breath, she closes her eyes. "I'm sorry."

He presses his lips to her temple, then she lays back, still shaking and he leans over her. "Was it worse tonight?"

Her heart has not slowed, so her chest rises and falls as she nods. He stares at her for a moment. "I'm sorry," he says. Then he wraps her in his arms until her cheek presses heavily against his chest. "We'll get rid of those yet."

For an hour after, Levi has yet to return to sleep. He stares at the gorgeous woman in front of him, in disbelief of who she's become. If only he'd known or perhaps this is the best way.

The morning comes with the call of the birds outside, but Rachel also feels his lips kissing her bare back until he pulls her to him. With his forearm wrapped around her chest she feels her body shiver as he runs his lips along her neck.

"What do you have to do today—more climbing around in dark cellars?" she asks with a grin.

"No, I don't think so. But I do think my day is busy."

"I should probably help Catalina. Then I have a show tonight."

"Come to breakfast with me first?" He kisses her, running his hand along her thigh.

"Is this breakfast?" she giggles.

An hour later they reluctantly separate, promising each other that it won't be long until they see each other again. Rachel spends the afternoon with Catalina, walking the grounds and talking about everything.

By nine o'clock, Rachel is on stage singing to an even larger crowd than the one before. People are standing in the doorways or seated along the stairs on both sides of the stage when there are no more seats available.

After the show, Rachel grabs some water from the bar, whilst a man with curly dark hair and a nice smile comes to her side. He looks at her for some time until she finally notices him.

"You watching me?"

"I'm sorry, I am."

"Why?"

"You're beautiful."

She has heard this before. "Thank you."

"My name is Chuck."

"Hello, Chuck. I'm Rachel."

"Yes, of course. I know." He turns and leans his back against the bar to watch everyone dance. "You bring quite a crowd."

"They have to come since they're staying at the hotel. It's part of the hotel requirements."

He chuckles. "Very funny. You know I think I've got something else for you."

"What do you mean?"

"Have you ever tried classical music?"

"No." She laughs. "It's not quite what I'm used to."

Again, he chuckles. "Sometimes it can be boring I guess, but when it's done well, I don't think so."

"You know I don't really know that I've actually listened to it much. I've been raised on hymns, blues, and jazz—they're in my roots."

"And you do it beautifully."

"Who are you, Chuck?" she says with a laugh.

"I am the leader of a group that travels all over Europe and the States and anywhere else that will have us. We sing classical and I just thought some day you might want to try it out. It's different, I know, but sometimes different is good."

"Well, I'm happy where I am, but I'll try it if anything changes."

"Okay. Here's my information. Just keep it with you. I have tour dates booked for years to come. It will take you through some of the most beautiful places in the world. Give you a lot of history lessons, only these lessons are given where they actually happened."

"Beautiful. Again, if all this ever changes I'll make sure to think of you."

"Okay. Thank you, Miss Praline."

"Thank you, Chuck…" She looks at his card one last time "…Chuck Gerber."

The crowd is so large that Rachel steps to the microphone for a few more songs and then she hurries out the back door before the throng can trample her. She tucks Mr. Gerber's card in her purse, just in case. Then as quiet as a mouse she hurries to Levi's suite. Using the key, she finds the living room empty, then turns to close the door. When she turns back around, Levi is standing across the room.

"I wasn't sure whether to expect you," he grins.

"Should I have come?"

"Of course. Every moment."

"Good." She hurries to him, throwing her arms around his neck.

He kisses her and quickly pulls her into his arms. Once again, they are lost in each other. They don't let a breath pass without touching and caressing. The rise and fall of their movements feels like an escape as small moans come from her throat, and he smiles, wanting to hear more. When he looks into her eyes as his body shakes, he whispers, "Stay with me forever."

"I'm tempted," she whispers.

"But not convinced?"

"To stay here in California?—no. To do this with you forever?—yes."

Once again, in the middle of the night, Rachel wakes from a

nightmare. The moment her eyes open she feels the pressure of his arms around her, and he pulls her tighter. Again, she crawls down until her cheek is against the top of his chest and feels him kiss her head. Never before has she felt so safe.

As time passes, Rachel and Levi never leave each other's side unless they have to. They make love every night and talk for hours afterwards without running out of things to say. Many mornings they wake up and make love again before they must separate. Not once do they talk about Levi going back to Italy or Rachel moving on to another city.

Catalina studies Levi from across the table one day at lunch with her finger pointed, "If you end my tour, you're in trouble."

"I have no plans to end your tour." He raises his arms in surrender.

"Good. I'm hungry."

Rachel can't help but think about the tour and how it will go on without Levi. That night—with only one week left until Levi is supposed to return home—they make love again. Only this time something has changed. Rachel holds onto him like she doesn't want to lose him.

"Rachel, I've got you," he says, out of breath.

A tear falls down her temple. As they lay beside each other, their hearts still racing, he runs his hand along her cheek.

"Do you remember that night you came for me?" she asks.

"Yeah."

"I thought about you just before you came down those stairs."

"You did?"

"I wondered if I would ever see you again. Bill said that the next morning he was taking me somewhere. We were going to move away."

"Where?"

"I don't know, he didn't say. But, when the door opened and you came into the basement I thought at first that you were him. He had a habit of waking up at night and coming to find me. You'd never believe the relief I felt when I saw you standing there."

Levi clenches his jaw. "I'd kill him if I ever saw him again."

She looks up at him, while she rests on her elbow, her bare chest against his. "I've never felt so much relief in all my life seeing you. But now you're here and I have no idea where we're going to be next week," she says as she runs her hand along his face.

"Come with me."

"To Italy?"

"Yes."

She stares into his eyes. "Would you really want me to come with you?"

"Yes, although I do worry about taking you away from your music."

"I want to be with you. People don't seem to stay in my life, but music seems to never be far."

"So, you'll come?"

"Yes," she laughs.

He wraps her in his arms and breathes out a sigh of relief. Then, he holds her as they fall asleep. She said yes, and although the thought of leaving Dick and Sylvia and Simone frightens her, she can't think of being away from Levi.

The days carry on in the same way, except now Levi and Rachel can talk about what they might do in Italy. He has plans for them and it makes her smile. She is completely in love, without question.

One night as they sit at the dinner table in the hotel restaurant with some of Levi's business colleagues, they laugh over coffee and dessert.

Their waiter comes to the table. "There's a phone call for you, ma'am."

"For me?"

"You are Rachel Praline?"

"Yes."

"Someone is on the line for you."

Rachel looks at Levi with curiosity and then stands. "Okay.

Where is the telephone?"

"If you will follow me?"

Levi takes her hand as it runs along his shoulders. "Should I come?"

"No. Stay. It's probably just Catalina."

Levi nods and Rachel follows the waiter out of one of the doors of the restaurant. He shows her the phone. "Hello?"

Far across the States, Sylvia stands at the house phone—her hands sweaty as she waits for Rachel to come on the line. When she hears her daughter's voice, all of her emotions begin to bubble over.

"Rachel?" she asks.

"Sylvia…mom?"

"Yes, honey."

Rachel laughs. "I'm so glad to hear from you."

"Rachel, something's happened."

Suddenly, Rachel is aware of the critical tone in her mother's voice.

"What—what's happened?"

"Your father is ill."

"What?"

"Very ill. The doctor is here, and I don't know what's going to happen." The weeping overtakes her, and Rachel pushes back the lump in her own throat as tears fill her eyes.

"I'm coming home."

"I didn't want to ask you to."

"I know. But I will. I'll come home."

"He's been asking for you."

After a few minutes, Rachel hangs up the phone.

"What will you do?" Levi's voice interrupts her thoughts as he stands just feet away with his hands in his pockets. With the look on his face, she knows that he has heard everything. Both of them understand instantly, their plans have changed.

"I don't know."

"Let me call someone. I'll see about travel arrangements."

"No, you don't have to do that."

"It's important, let me do this."

As they lay in bed that night, both find it hard to sleep. Rachel continues to stare at him as though he might disappear.

"What will we do?" she asks.

"You go home and be with your father, that's all you can do."

"What about Italy?"

"This doesn't mean that can't happen." He brushes her cheek with the back of his hand. "I can come with you."

Rachel inches her way closer to him. "No. You have things to do. You have people that are expecting you."

"None of that matters, Rachel. I'll come with you, just say the word."

"I have no idea what it's going to be like when I get home. I don't want you to be there for all of it. You've seen enough of my crazy life," she grins.

"I would gladly see more." He kisses her.

"Let's give it three months," she says.

"Three months?"

"Yes. I'll take care of my parents, and you'll finish what you have to finish. It will give me time to be with Dick and Sylvia and then I'll come to Italy."

"You call me in that time. I will come to you…or you can come to me. We'll figure it out."

Rachel kisses him, not sure that she can stick to this plan, then the panic starts to set in. "I can't do it." The emotion builds until tears are sliding down her cheeks. "I can't leave you."

When he rolls over onto her. "I love you, Rachel. Do you get that? I would do anything for you."

A tear falls down her temple and he wipes it away. "I love you."

He kisses her intensely, never giving her a moment to catch her breath. As they sit up together, their bodies entwined, she holds him with such force that he looks her in the eyes. "It's okay, Rachel. I won't disappear. I promise."

§ § §

Just hours before Rachel's departure, she stands with Catalina and Jeffrey in Catalina's hotel room. "I'm so sorry, Catalina."

"Honey, you have to do what's best for you. We all know that," she says as she packs their bags.

"Thank you."

"You've been a great girl to take around. It seems we both have bigger things to do, but never, ever, be afraid to reach out to me."

"Thank you." Rachel helps her fold a blue skirt. "Levi said you could stay as long as you need."

"He did now? Well, that's nice of him."

"Catalina, do you know that I was an orphan—given up by someone that couldn't take care of me?" Catalina is silent. "I sometimes wonder what my mom would have done if she'd been able to take me. Or did she regret giving me up? I don't know what you're going to do, but I do think you will be an amazing mother. And Jeffrey," he looks up with innocent eyes, "you'll be a great uncle."

Catalina stares into her eyes. "I never thought I was going to have a baby. Hell, never thought I wanted one. But I do. I want him or her."

"You do?"

"Yeah. I do. I just don't know what will happen if I can't afford her."

"You will call me if that should happen," Rachel tells Catalina.

Catalina's eyes widen with panic. "I'm going to have a baby!" The women laugh and hug, realizing they only have a few more moments together. "Your leaving doesn't mean you're done, Rachel."

"I know."

"No, I don't think you do. When something bad happens in

your life, it doesn't mean you have to give up your passion. Go be with your dad, and when you're ready, pick it right back up. That man is in love with you. I can see it." Catalina throws her arm around Rachel's shoulders.

"I know he is. But I really need to take care of Dick and Sylvia. He has work to do."

"Maybe you'll get married and have his babies someday."

This is the first time Rachel ever thought of getting married or everything that follows. After all that she's gone through, she's not sure what she wants, but she knows she wants him.

Together they walk to the lobby where Levi is waiting patiently at the main doors. Catalina grabs Rachel for one last hug. Just as they are letting go of each other, a man accidentally bumps into Catalina.

"I am so sorry," he says quickly, as he looks up, revealing his handsome face.

Not a day in Catalina's life has she ever held back a curse until now. For the first time she is speechless as she stares at him with wide eyes. "It's my fault."

"Are you sure? I didn't hurt you?" he asks.

"No, honey."

Levi interjects, noticing the explosive chemistry between them. "Doctor Charles Wimbey, this is Catalina—Rachel's manager."

"Catalina? What a beautiful name." He takes her hand and kisses it. He's quite a bit older than her, but there's something between the two of them that is dynamic.

"A doctor?" Catalina's voice floats as if in a dream.

"Yes. If you need anything, please tell me." He writes his name and room number on a paper, and hands it to her.

"This is your room?"

"Yes."

"Will I get your wife or a secretary if I bother you?"

"No," he chuckles shyly. "I don't have a wife. My secretary doesn't answer my door for me. But I'll be here for a few days." He takes the paper back and scribbles more. "Let me give you my name and phone number, should you need anything."

"Thank you." Catalina watches the doctor walk away and just as he steps into the elevator he glances back at Catalina.

When he's gone, Catalina turns to Levi. "Levi, do you know that man's routine?"

"I don't, however I think Steve over there," he points at the front desk, "has a better idea."

"Thank you!" Catalina reaches out and kisses Rachel's cheek. "I think I might stay here for a few days." She turns to the desk, calling out, "Yoohoo, Steve!"

Rachel kisses Jeffrey goodbye. "I'm sorry I have to leave so quickly."

With sad eyes, he nods.

"But my dad's sick and I need to help him."

Again, he nods.

"Take care of yourself and take care of Catalina." Rolling onto her toes, she kisses his baby face again.

It isn't until years later that Rachel speaks with Catalina again. She married the doctor. After all of those years of being alone, she found that she was simply waiting for the chance to meet the right man. Her little girl was born into the hands of her husband. They even learned that Jeffrey had something wrong with his ears and, in fixing them as best they could, he began to communicate more.

§ § §

Levi stands next to Rachel in front of the train. Her heart is eager to get back to Dick and Sylvia, however her heart is also standing in front of her. He takes her face in his hands. "Just three months. That's all."

"Three months," she repeats.

He pulls her in for one last kiss—neither one wanting it to end.

His arms wrap around her tightly, and his lips caress hers. The last call comes from the conductor and before she can change her mind she pulls away, grabs her bag, and jumps into the car, just before it pulls away from the station.

Levi watches until the train is no longer visible.

Chapter Twenty One

1929

Every time Rachel closes her eyes, she pictures Levi's body or the way he runs his hands up her thighs or through her hair, but most importantly she can't stop thinking about the safety she feels in his arms. The trees speed past the window, as she runs her hand down her neck and chest remembering the weight of his body on hers. The world is empty now without him. She's made a mistake leaving him and yet there's nothing she can do since Dick and Sylvia need her home.

Sandy meets her at the station with yellow flowers, igniting her suspicion that things have grown worse with her father. "Hi, Sandy."

"Hi, Miss Rachel." His eyes are forlorn, and she refuses to ask.

When the car pulls into the drive, Rachel rushes inside. She searches quickly but finds everyone gathered in Dick's room. The doctor and Sylvia are close to his bed where he lies dwarfed by the furniture and ghostly white. In an oddly familiar way to Bernadette's last moments on earth, Rachel kneels next to him, scared to even breathe.

"I'll leave you alone to talk." The tall and slender doctor glides out of the room.

When Sylvia reaches across the bed to touch Rachel's hand, her eyes are swollen and her face moist. "Welcome home."

"Thank you." Rachel touches Dick's hand, which is cold to the touch. For a moment she pulls back, suddenly reminded of Jake's foot. Dick opens his eyes and she smiles, "Hi, Daddy."

"Rachel," he says with a sudden spark to his eyes.

"What did you do?" she teases. "Couldn't you just be good while I was gone?"

"I tried." Every move he makes is weaker than the last and although he tries to swallow, he has nearly lost the ability.

"Can I get you something?" Rachel asks seeing his dry mouth. "Maybe some water?"

"No, no. It's just so good to see you home."

"I missed you two."

Sylvia stands up. "I'm going to talk with the doctor, I'll be back. Are you alright, Dick?" she asks bending over with such care and tenderness that it makes Rachel's heart ache.

"Go ahead," is all that he can get out.

"Okay." Sylvia walks out of the room and Rachel crawls up next to him laying her head on his bony arm.

"Are you in pain?"

"Not really."

She bites her lip to hold back tears. "Good."

"I'm sorry that you had to come back."

"No, it's fine."

"I'm sorry…" A moment passes and he breathes as though he is asleep, but soon he continues, "We bought your record."

"You didn't need to buy it. I could have given you one."

"Oh no, it was our pleasure to buy it, but we also heard your songs on the radio. Simone came over and we listened together."

"Really? Simone came to visit you?"

"Yes."

"Well, we went from city to city traveling by car and stayed in a lot of hotels. At first the crowds were small, but then they began to grow. The farther west we went, the more people showed up. People just love the song that Jake and P.B. wrote for me. It's the first and the last one that they want to hear."

"I do like that one."

"But Dad," she leans in closer with a smile, "you'll never believe who I ran into." He doesn't say anything. "I ran into Levi Price. Do you remember him?"

"Of course. He gave me you."

"That's right. He hired me at one of his hotels to sing for nearly a month."

"He did?"

"Yes."

"That boy owns a hotel?"

"Turns out he's quite the businessman."

"I should say so."

"We had a lot to catch up on."

Dick coughs slightly at first and then it grows into an uncontrollable wheeze. Rachel grabs his back helping him try to sit up.

"What do I do?"

He continues to cough until it seems it might hurt him, but then slowly it begins to subside. "I'm fine, I'm fine." He turns his eyes to hers. "He hasn't seen you since you were a child."

"I know. It was rather different."

"Different?" He raises an eyebrow. "Somethin' seems different."

"He loves me."

"He does?"

"Yes. And I love him." Rachel doesn't tell him about their torrid romance, but she does smile to let her father know that she is happy.

"Now you're here." There is sadness behind his words.

She wraps her arms around him. "I want to be here. I promise you. I want every moment with you that I can get."

"Rachel…" he pleads.

"What?"

"Take care of your mother."

There is no holding back. The thought of taking care of her mother without him sends her into sobs. For the first time in years since she was a child, she thinks of the things that Bernie said before she died.

"What do you believe?"

"What do you mean…about what?"

"About life after death?"

When she looks up at him, she is surprised to see a tear at the corner of his eye. "As a man you can feel invincible, like you don't need strength from anywhere else. It's not until you are too weak to stand that you begin to realize there has to be something more."

"Are you scared?"

"No."

They are silent for a while just watching the light from the sun move across the ceiling.

"What about the show?" Rachel finally asks.

"I haven't been able to do it since I got sick. I think we might have to shut it down."

"What about the animals?" In an unexpected turn, Dick begins to cry. He gave his life trying to make them healthy and safe. Rachel sits up quickly. "I'm sorry."

He takes in a withered breath, "When I die, I give them to you. Make sure that they find good homes."

"I will."

Dick holds on for two more weeks and on October 20th, 1929, he takes his last breath. The man who had given up a job for a dream and his home for a lost child. Simone and Rachel hold onto Sylvia as she falls to her knees after witnessing the passing of the greatest man she's ever known.

§ § §

Four days after Dick's funeral October 29th, 1929 brings Black Tuesday. It arrives uninvited, but there just the same—the stock market crash. People are instantly terrified, trying desperately to hold on. Overwhelmed with grief, Sylvia can concentrate on nothing, so Rachel throws herself into the care of their home, leaving no time for crying as she plows through their finances looking for ways to make ends meet. Because of Dick's illness, no income has been made, but the bills had piled up. Dealing with debt collectors became a way of life, almost as though she could fill eighty hours of the week with them.

One day Sandy, Gregory, and the other workers come to Rachel with soft eyes while she sits at the table, unable to eat her breakfast.

"We know you are having trouble, Rachel," Sandy says quickly.

"Everyone's having trouble right now, Sandy."

"Yes, well it's been a hard time for you and Sylvia and we don't want to make it harder. We are giving you our resignations tonight."

She looks up, mystified. "But what about your families?"

"Well," Sandy begins, "I've saved up quite a bit of money and my son called me this week telling me that his job has been doing okay there in Canada. He wants me to go live with him and his family. But please don't worry about me. I will be fine."

"And you?" Rachel asks Gregory. It is sad to even think about them leaving.

"Well, I actually wanted to talk to you, Rachel." He sits down in front of her, with a look of apprehension. "I've been thinking about something very carefully. But I would never do it if I did not have your complete acceptance."

"What's that, Gregory?"

"I want to take over the show."

"What?" It takes a moment for Rachel to understand beneath her fatigue.

"I want to buy the animals and continue the show."

For a while, the men just wait for her to combust with anger or weep with sadness, but instead she begins to laugh and claps her hands together with excitement.

"You're happy about the idea?" Gregory asks wearily.

"Happy? Gregory, I'm over the moon. It doesn't make any sense for Sylvia or me to try and take on this show and yet I have these animals that I have been so worried about. You know them better than I do, and I can't think of a better man for the job. I will warn you though, after all this chaos, I don't know how much people are going to pay for a show."

"Well, I know that. But I love them. They have been my life for almost eighteen years, and I cannot live without them."

Within moments and with a handshake, the deal is done.

§ § §

Early in the morning the day that Gregory is to move the animals out, Rachel stands in their cages saying goodbye to each one. She remembers the day that Dick introduced her to his magical world. Running her hands through the lion's mane, Oliver comes to her side and pushes against her with his hips as though he knows that something is happening. She says goodbye with a gentle touch, as Gregory comes to take them. Sylvia can't be there. So, all alone, after the animals are gone, Rachel sits on the ground against the back wall looking over the empty space. Dick's heart is gone from the building, and she stares silently.

"I don't know what to do." Rachel says to Levi over the phone. "Sylvia needs me to help."

"It's okay. I'll come to you."

"No, not yet. I still have so many things to take care of . . . I don't want you to miss your deals because of me."

"Rachel, I would miss anything for you."

"I know. Give me another couple of months. When you are finished . . . I'll be done here."

"I'll be traveling to France this week for the next month and a half, and meanwhile I'm selling my house in Italy to move closer to one of my hotels there. I won't have the same address or phone number. I'll call you next week to tell you the new information."

"Okay."

"Rachel, I love you. It'll be okay."

"I love you."

Rachel walks down the streets of New Jersey noticing the lines of men, women, and children waiting for food. The per capita income falls from $839 to $433, and banks begin closing almost immediately. This is just her small part of the country. Across America, people are starving and seeking shelter. Families who have never known poverty are without the means to live a normal life and even Sylvia, still struggling with grief, comes home one day with a paper in her hands. "Did you hear?"

"Hear what?" she asks as she finishes writing a letter.

"They've shut down our bank. There's nothing. We have nothing." Sylvia suddenly falls to the chair in sobs, and Rachel runs to her side.

The next day Simone and Rachel sit out on the back porch. "I've never seen my ma so grateful that she keeps everything in cash. Never really trusted banks. And here I am, done with school, and what do I do?" Simone asks with disappointment.

"I'd yell at you to stay with me and never leave, but it seems Sylvia and I are in a bind."

Simone places an arm around Rachel. "Rachel, your songs are played over the radio, you should be getting paid. Where's your money?"

"I really don't know. I'm not even sure how they ended up on the radio."

"I'm going to figure it out. You hear me? This is just all kinds of wrong."

"We're selling this house." Rachel says quietly.

Simone looks at her friend as the sun sets. "We'll get through this, Rachel. I just got a job doing research for John Ipson in the District Attorney's office."

"I guess owning your own law firm will have to wait? It's what you want."

Simone laughs. "Someday, I'll have my dream. Besides John isn't so bad. He's been treated a certain way his entire life too because he's Jewish, so I think he wants to help."

Rachel squeezes her hand then looks back up at the stars. "As long as we have each other."

"Oh, you have me honey. You have me. What about Levi?" Simone has been hesitant to ask.

Rachel shakes her head. "He hasn't been returning my calls."

"There's gotta be a reason."

"Yeah, the reason is it was too good to be true."

Simone looks at Rachel for a moment, then clears her throat. "Let's go have some tea."

Dick and Sylvia's beautiful country home sells for a fraction of what it should. Simone moves back to New Jersey and into an apartment with Sylvia and Rachel, while Rachel gets a decent-paying job at the docks, unloading and loading ships. One night with her dirty clothes and calloused hands, somewhere in the distance, she hears her music playing. She stops what she's doing and steps outside of the warehouse to listen while tears form within her bottom lashes.

"Get back to work!" the foreman yells at her.

Every night those nightmares that once disappeared while Levi was sleeping beside her, have returned. It has been months since she spoke with him and when she tries to call his old number the operator continues to inform her that he is no longer there. But she can't stop calling, hoping that it is a mistake. For months on end, she cries herself to sleep as Simone listens in the bed next to her. Her eyes are swollen in the morning, so Simone rubs her arm as she passes by, "He'll find you. I know he will."

1931 is soon upon them. It is a year when the Empire State Building opens, Al Capone is sentenced to eleven years for tax evasion, while the Great Depression still has its grasp on the country. In the middle of April on a cool morning, Simone returns to the apartment with a large smile on her face.

"What are you smiling about?" Rachel asks.

"I have some news."

"In this crazy world, how does anyone have any news?" she says resting her hand on the sink as she looks at Sylvia sleeping across the room.

"I'm getting married."

Rachel turns with shock. "Married? I didn't even know you were in love."

"I suppose I'm not quite yet, but I refuse to let that stop me. I have things to do. Babies to make. You and I are not getting any younger."

"Babies? Oh, Simone how can you even talk about bringing babies into this world?"

"I was made for motherhood. His name is Reed, and he has a small business that's making a decent living compared to most, so with my duties at the DA's office, we'll be just fine."

Rachel turns back to Simone, "Wait, you're serious?"

"I am."

"Simone?!" Rachel cries out and hurries to her friend with her arms out. They holler and squeal until it wakes Sylvia who then joins them. "Just promise me this . . ." Rachel says suddenly. "This man will allow you to be everything it is that you want to be. You have big goals. Just tell me he's okay with that."

Simone smiles, "He's my biggest fan."

1932

Adolf Hitler obtains German citizenship, James Chadwick discovers the neutron, in Iowa there is a farmer's revolt where farmers try to block dairy products from Sioux City over rapidly declining farm prices and high tariffs, and Mahatma Gandhi begins a hunger strike in Poona prison, all within the days of 1932. Meanwhile, Simone, under the trees and stars, gets married to Reed while many people watch from under several canopies as Rachel stands at her side as Maid of Honor. Simone, Sylvia, and Rachel all cry the next week when she packs up her things to move in with her new husband.

Now, all alone again, Sylvia and Rachel play cards at their small table in their even smaller apartment. Rachel finds it hard to smile as every day she tries to call Levi, and every day he cannot be found. "I have something for you," Sylvia says with hesitation. "It is something that I found when going through Dick's things. I know that he didn't want you to have it until he knew that you could handle it."

"Okay."

Sylvia leans over to the table and grabs some familiar papers. In an instant, Rachel is reminded of Levi when he took them from her room in Bill's home. That was the last time she had seen them.

"You know what these are," Sylvia says with a nod.

"I only know that this is the reason they knew I wasn't Bill's."

"Listen to me, Rachel, this tells you your start in life, not your end. Do you understand that?" Sylvia says carefully and Rachel nods. "You don't ever have to read them. But I know that you probably will and I just want to remind you that these are only papers."

That night as Sylvia sleeps, Rachel stares at the thick folder lying beside her pillow. Why does everyone act as though these papers are so important? The thought of discovering their contents frightens her. For a moment she toys with the idea of reading them and she runs her fingertips down their edge, but her hand is shaking, so she slides the stack under her pillow instead.

She has enough to think about with Levi missing.

§ § §

"There has to be a reason that he just never found me. What did the hotel say?" Rachel cries.

It is obvious Simone doesn't want to be the bearer of bad news, so she looks down. "I've sent them letters and each one returns to me unopened."

"Oh." Rachel's eyes appear to be near tears, but she looks away to hide them.

Simone grabs her hand, "We'll find him."

The ladies, despite Simone being married, spend most of their time together, struggling through the economic crisis. By 1933, the world needs entertainment so desperately that they get it in the form of Bonnie and Clyde. Their sensationalized string of robberies and murders makes them famous. No one realizes that Nina Simone and Quincy Jones are born this same year and will someday offer the world a true reason for fame.

At the docks, Rachel waits for her name to be chosen for a night of work. They don't always take everyone, and a woman is the first to be denied, so she spends the hour reading a newspaper that sits beneath her masculine boots on the dirty gravel. On the paper, it reads, End Of Prohibition! and A New German Chancellor Named Adolf Hitler. The hour turns into two, but Rachel is desperate.

"Excuse me sir," she says to the man in charge, "I really need to work tonight. You didn't take me all last week."

He looks her over, his gruff beard and hard eyes, irritated that she would even stop him.

"Please, I've been without work for too long. Let me work tonight."

Finally, something changes, and he shrugs. "Come with me."

She follows quickly behind him, anxious to get the money at the end of her shift.

"You been here before?" he asks.

"You've seen me nearly every night."

"You don't look like you should be doing this stuff."

"I can." She is nearly running to keep up with him.

He grunts instead of saying anything.

"Well, I've done a good job . . . every night that I've been able to work."

He smiles a wicked smile as they enter a large warehouse, "I'm sure you do a good job at many things." She ignores his insinuation when they soon stop in front of a large stack of boxes—more than anyone could ever move alone. "I want you to move these over there on that truck." A green truck is parked inside the quiet but very large warehouse. Boxes piled nearly to the ceiling are make-shift walls. Rachel finds it interesting that she hasn't seen a soul but him.

"That's a job for just me?"

"I thought you said you was good."

"I'm a hard worker, not a miracle worker."

He laughs at her joke even though she keeps a straight face. "You can do it. Get to it. You'd better just feel lucky that I picked you. Not everyone's going to get to work tonight."

Immediately, she begins hauling boxes from one end of the warehouse to the next. Three hours go by, and she is exhausted, but it doesn't look like she has even made a dent in the pile. The man with his red cheeks and dark beard comes back to look at the progress she's made.

"You tired?" he says with a smile.

"I'm fine." She obstinately carries another box to the truck trying to cover any effort on her face.

When she returns, she bends low to pick up another box, but as she tries to pull it up, he places his foot on it. "Do you mind?"

she asks.

"There's a way that you can still get the money and not have to do any of this…"

She has heard this many times before and shrugs it off. "I'll earn it the easy way, thank you." But he still doesn't lift his foot. Instead of fighting back she moves to another box, but this time when she turns around with the box in her hands, he is blocking her way.

"You don't have to get paid for this, you know."

"Well, if I'm not then just tell me so I can drop this and go home." He reaches across and moves some hair off of her shoulder. Instantly, she knows the look in his eye and wants no part of it, so she drops the box. "Alright, I'll just go home. Keep your damn money."

Before she can walk away, he grabs her arm and pulls her back. "You're not goin' anywhere." He yanks her arm until she falls to the hard cement floor, hitting her head, and she sees stars. This gives him just enough time to climb on top of her while unbuttoning his pants with one hand and holding her down with the other. When her wits return finally, the panic begins to set in, and she fights him with everything she has. "Get off of me!" She screams, but he is so big and so strong that she cannot get out from under him. "No!" she screams again.

"Be quiet!" he yells, then punches her in the face.

Her hand frantically reaches for a board that is near them as he manages to rip her clothing in his attack. Anger explodes inside of her as her fingers finally reach the wood. She swings it using everything in her body and hits him across the head. He groans and rolls off of her as blood seeps from his nose.

"Keep the money!" she yells.

"You bitch! Don't ever try and work at the dock again."

"I won't ever be back," she says as she heads out the doors. It isn't until she is halfway home that her emotions catch up with her and she sobs. Instead of going home, she heads to Simone's instead. Sylvia wouldn't question her staying out all night for work. Reed answers the door half asleep. "Rachel, is that you?"

"Yes, Reed, I'm so sorry."

As he wakes up, it's obvious that he notices the bruising beginning on her face. "Yeah, okay, come in! Come in!" She enters and he hurries to the back room of their cute but small house to get Simone. When Simone comes out, Rachel can't help but fall apart.

"I'm going to murder this man," Simone says angrily once she knows the story.

"What do I do?" Rachel cries out, knowing that they already have nothing to live off of. But Simone and her husband don't have the answer; no one does except the rich who get richer from everyone else's disaster.

The next morning in Simone's kitchen, Rachel turns on the radio to hear one of her songs playing. Simone drinks her coffee while shaking her head. "You should be singing, Rachel." Something occurs to her suddenly from what Simone says, and she grabs her purse. She sifts through the items, trying to find a small piece of paper and when she does, she opens it with Simone watching. On it is the name Chuck Gerber and a phone number in New York. For a moment, this only reminds her of Levi and California, but then her hope turns to the curly-haired man that talked to her about classical music.

"What is that?" Simone asks.

"Possibly my only hope for salvation. Do you know of a phone that I can use?" Rachel asks.

"Come with me to my office," Simone says, "I'm leaving now."

As they walk along the sidewalk, Rachel explains the story of Chuck Gerber and his bid for her to sing with his choir. "It's all I can do."

When Simone walks into the DA's office, people treat her like the President. So much so, that Rachel smiles. "Well, don't they love you."

"Oh, sure they do. They love to talk to me, but give me equal pay, or let me actually do the job that I have a degree to do, nuh uh." Simone rolls her eyes. "People show me they love me by their actions, not a morning hello."

Rachel nods, "I hope someday, Simone."

Simone takes it one step further and says, "White people get in the way at every turn."

Rachel playfully hits Simone's shoulder as they reach the office with the phone, then Simone closes the door. As Rachel picks up the receiver, the operator comes on the line. "Yes, may I get Bentley 5587 on the line please?"

"Hold, one moment," the operator says.

"Don't take too long." Simone warns.

"It's probably a dead end anyway," Rachel says while rubbing her swollen eye.

The operator comes back on, "Bentley 5587."

"Thank you."

"Hello?" an older woman asks.

"Hello, umm yes, is there a Chuck Gerber that I may speak with?" So much time has passed that she expects nothing.

"Yes, who's calling?" the woman asks. Rachel pauses with surprise and the woman grows annoyed. "Hello?"

"Oh, I'm sorry, this is Rachel Anne Praline."

Before long, he comes on the line. "Rachel?"

"Yes, Mr. Gerber?"

"Well, my goodness. I didn't expect a call from you after all of this time."

"I know it's strange, Mr. Gerber, but I came across your number and I just wondered what might be happening with you."

"Well, things were rough for a while, but it's funny that you called because things are starting to pick up again."

"It has?"

"Yes. I have several dates in the works through England and Spain…" he pauses for a moment, "oh and a couple in Greece and Italy."

"You do?"

"Yes. The choir is just about ready, and we'll leave in the next couple of weeks."

"Oh," she says lowering her voice in disappointment.

"Can you get to New York?" he asks suddenly.

"Would you want me to come to New York?"

"That's why you're calling isn't it? You want to be a part of my choir?"

"Yes. I would love to try at least."

"Okay. Can you come tomorrow?"

"I will."

"Good. I look forward to meeting with you. Hopefully we can make this work."

"Yes, of course."

When she hangs up, she smiles for the first time in what feels like years. Simone shakes her head. "Music is going to take you more places than you ever knew."

"Maybe so."

"Okay, well let's figure out how we're going to get you to New York tomorrow. And you can't go with this..." Simone picks up Rachel's sweater from the chair and sticks her fist through a hole in its side.

"Oh, I don't care as long as he gives me a job."

"Should you tell Sylvia?"

"No. Not yet."

The next morning Simone and Rachel have come up with enough money to buy a one-way train ticket. Neither woman knows how she might get back, but that isn't the most important thing on their minds. Simone waves goodbye from the platform as Rachel waves out the window. It is an all-day ride with numerous stops and when she finally reaches the station, she recognizes Chuck Gerber instantly. His hair is still just as curly as before and he wears virtually the same suit.

"You made it!" he says as she steps off the train.

Although it isn't a new dress, Rachel borrowed one of Simone's from her closet that definitely has more charm than any of her worn-out clothes.

"I did."

"Well, first things first. Are you hungry?"

She is starving after not eating all day, but she doesn't wish to act too eager.

"I'm alright."

"Well, I'm starving. Let's grab some dinner."

He takes her to a place where only the richest people can afford to eat and they drink their tea with their pinkies in the air. He orders for her before she can object. It is difficult to keep a slow pace when finally tasting the rich and decadent steak that they set down in front of her.

"You're still just as beautiful, Rachel," Chuck says as he watches her finish her food.

"Thank you."

"The last time I saw you, I heard a rumor that you were with… what was his name…the hotel owner, Levi Price?"

"Yes, I guess you could say that."

"You still together?"

"No. We lost contact a while ago."

"Oh, I'm sorry to hear that." He pays quickly for the meal, and she repeats her thank you three times. "Now let's talk about music. Have you listened to any more classical?"

She pauses, wondering if she should lie, but knows he will probably see right through her. The last thing she wants is to give him a reason not to hire her.

"No," she chuckles softly, "I haven't, but I'm sure that I would like it."

"Well," he leans back in his chair and looks at his watch that he pulls from his pocket, "we might catch the end of it. Why don't you come with me?"

They stand up and reach the door before she asks, "Where are we going?"

"Just down the street. My theater is there."

"Your theater?"

"Why don't we walk, and I'll give you the story." They head down the sidewalk, "My family founded a theater back in the late eighteen hundreds just down this row of buildings. It was a beautiful place, meant for live performances, but my father had a passion for classical music. So, he bought the theater, and he renovated it to have the greatest acoustics. My father was rich, so it didn't matter that it didn't bring in enough money at the beginning—he could support his passion. People began to come, and the next thing we knew, we'd had generations of this amazing choir. So, we meet in this theater, and we call it the Gerber Church."

Rachel looks at him with surprise.

"I know. My father was so passionate about this music that he felt like it was more of a church than a theater. His exact words were, 'We are a part of the greater connection between this realm and God's. Nothing transports you quite like our choir.' It probably all sounds crazy to you since you're a blues woman yourself."

"It doesn't sound crazy—it's probably not far off from how I feel when I'm singing no matter the kind."

"Do you have time to listen?"

"Yes," Rachel says wondering where she might sleep. It is already nearly 8 o'clock.

They reach a large, gray stone building with massive wooden doors and Chuck pulls them open. A sound, so ethereal, so angelic, floats past them and she realizes Chuck might be right. They stop in the hall just below an ornate archway to listen to the perfect eight-part harmony. Although she isn't trained, she can pick out certain parts. One is the bass, a guttural and beautiful straight note hanging below all the other voices. The other one she can hear is a high voice and it holds strongly in the middle of the others. Then the last is the top. She hears a soft, gorgeous, high voice. It is so beautiful the skin on her arms rises and she looks at Chuck completely moved.

"Unbelievable, isn't it?"

"Yes. It is."

He walks to a door off of the hall and opens it making the voices even louder. Just ahead of them, standing all over the room in a circle, is a group of men and women. Chuck and Rachel proceed into the middle of the circle and then the conductor drops his hands and the voices stop.

"Hello, everyone!" Chuck says with enthusiasm.

"Hey, Chuck," a chorus of unique-sounding voices ring in the air.

"I want to introduce you to a friend of mine. Her name is Rachel Anne Praline. Has anyone heard of her?"

Several hands lift in the air and Rachel drops her head shyly.

"Well, you all are done for the night. I expect you back here at 10 o'clock tomorrow."

Everyone claps, proud of the rehearsal they have just had. Then slowly they leave Chuck alone with Rachel and the conductor. "Paul, this is Rachel. Rachel, this is Paul Levinson. He is the mastermind behind this beautiful sound that we always get with our choir."

"It's nice to meet you," Rachel says with a nod.

"And you."

Paul seems serious, but gentle. His nearly bald head glistens under the lights of the chandeliers and when he smiles, he has two deep dimples in both cheeks.

"Would you mind singing with Paul?"

"I guess I could try," she says, feeling inadequate.

"I think you might surprise yourself. With your smooth tone you should have no problem." Chuck winks. "I have a knack for this, please just trust me."

"I will try."

Chuck backs away and Paul comes to her side with sheet music in his hand.

"Let's begin with what you know and what you don't." His voice, strangely enough, seems to be as high as hers and bent at the ends with an English accent. Immediately, she thinks of Levi, and she has to shake him out of her head. "Do you read sheet music?"

"I do, but I'm not sure whether it's the same for your kind of music?"

"It is, only there will be two sets of bars. The top is the Treble Clef, and the bottom is Bass Clef." His shaky fingers point out the two sets of five bars. "Now…the difference you will see is the eight separate notes."

"Yes, it looks very crowded on this paper."

He smiles, but continues on without a beat, "A choir is made up of eight parts. You have first and second soprano, alto, tenor, and then baritone followed by bass. Soprano is the highest, and bass is the…" he pauses, expecting her to answer the simple question.

"Lowest."

"That's right. As you get used to the music it will all become easy. You will begin to concentrate on just your line."

"That's good to know."

"Follow me. Let's go up on stage to the piano. I would like to check your range." As they walk, he stiffly turns to ask her questions. "Has anyone checked your range?"

"I don't think so."

"It just means," he is a little out of breath after reaching the last step onto the stage, "figuring out how high you can go and how low you can go."

"Oh, okay."

"Have you done exercises to warm up your voice before?"

She thinks back to the effeminate man who used to help Bill get her ready for gigs—she couldn't remember his name.

"Yes, I have."

"Good." He sits down at the piano and runs his fingers quickly along the keys. "Try this." His voice bounces up and down the scale. She pulls her face back when he sings, surprised to think that if she closed her eyes, she could be listening to a woman. When he stops, he points at her to start, and she follows his cue. "Good," he says quickly and then moves her to higher octaves.

She does the same thing over and over, rising and falling from notes like he asks. As he gets higher on the piano, his eyebrows rise and she unintentionally makes the same face as she sings, like it will help her get the notes out. Her range never really mattered for the hymns and gospel music, or for the blues and jazz, P.B. taught her to scat and that often helped her range. To Rachel, singing comes as naturally as breathing. She feels the sound deep in her stomach and pulls her muscles from within.

He stops her for just a moment suddenly, "Now, try…when you're at the end of your notes, try not to use much vibrato or drop off at the end like any show singer might do. See if you can jump into each note without scooping into them. Now, continue from this range." He plucks the notes again in the higher octaves and she follows, trying to hold back her vibrato. The scooping into the higher notes seems to be the hardest, but the more she does it, the more she gets the hang of it. Finally, he reaches a height she can't sing, and she laughs at how awkward it feels to try and reach it.

"Good, good, good," he says with a smile.

Chuck, from his seated position in the audience, calls up to the stage. "What did she reach, Paul?"

"High A."

Chuck's eyebrows rise and he writes it down.

"Now, look at the paper I gave you and let's see if you can read the top line for me," Paul says.

"Okay." Rachel looks it over, nervous that she might let Chuck down terribly.

"Here is your starting note."

She tries to follow the line as best she can and when she is done, she looks at Chuck, but he says nothing and keeps his head down, fervently writing on his notepad.

"Good job," Paul says. "Now let me play it for you." He proceeds with the top few measures and when he is done, he looks at her.

Her eyes are wide. "That didn't sound at all like what I just sang."

"Yes, it did. I think you would surprise yourself. You actually did very well. Let me play the line one more time and then I want you to sing it back to me."

She nods, feeling confident with this task. When he is done playing, she sings it back to him always keeping in mind the things he has already asked her not to do.

"Wonderful!" he smiles. "Now, I am going to sing the second soprano notes while you sing the first soprano."

"Okay."

"Try to concentrate on your line and don't worry about me. It's going to be difficult if you have never done it."

He counts the three-four beat and then together they sing. No matter what has ever been happening in Rachel's life, music has been her rescue and as their harmony blends, she closes her eyes feeling the emotion draw from a well of sadness deep in her soul. Bernie, Jake, and Dick are gone, but it is Levi who creates the ache within her. Whatever she needs to do to keep her mind off Levi, she will do it. Music will once again be her catalyst for revival.

"No, it's not difficult. Not at all, is it?" he jokes as he turns to her on his bench.

"I guess not. I just heard it," she explains. "The harmony nearly made it easier."

"I understand that because my lower notes are giving you a base to keep the key up. That's great . . . exactly what you should be hearing."

"Thank you."

Suddenly they hear the door to the theater open grabbing their attention. Coming down the aisle are seven people—four men and three women walk onto the stage to stand around the piano. Chuck is just returning to his seat as though he had been the one to gather them.

"Now, Rachel, I'm going to add each part separately. By the time the bass joins in, you should know the line well enough to be okay." He raises his hand to direct the group. Rachel finds that she quickly and easily catches on to the bounce of his hand. If she follows, it leads her in the exact time. "Here are your notes."

He plays eight notes one at a time and then all together. With a flick of his palm the group begins to sing and as it progresses, Rachel has never heard anything like it. Everything comes together to make a crisp and perfect sound. Every time she hits a different note, the others do as well, changing the sound from one chord to the next.

Paul stops them after the line and turns to Chuck sitting in the audience. "Is there anything else you want me to try with her?"

Chuck runs up the steps and onto the stage. He comes to Rachel's side taking her forearms in his hands. "I knew you would be good. But I had no idea. Did you know that you could be a soprano?"

"No."

"Do you want to go home, or can I have Paul work with you for a while tonight?"

She is the only one who knows she has nowhere to go. "I would love to work with him more."

"Wonderful. Paul, are you able to?"

"Of course."

For several hours, Paul works with Rachel on a beautiful piece in Latin. He teaches her technique, holding her breath, and the way she should say each word. Rachel can't get enough. When he teaches her something new, she wants to repeat it until it is perfect. The hardest part is getting the pronunciation correct, but he reassures her that it will come.

"You've done beautifully, my dear," Paul says with a grin.

"Thank you."

"I look forward to working with you." The conductor shakes Chuck's hand and leaves the stage.

When they are alone Chuck shakes his head with a smile. "I'm amazed, Rachel Anne Praline. You've lived your whole life never singing what you were meant to sing, what a shame."

"I've enjoyed learning this, thank you."

"No, I don't think you understand..." he puts his hand out in front of his face as though he wants to emphasize his point—his voice rising just a bit, "people can't just do this, Rachel. Women that I have brought in here with classical training have not been able to create the sound that you gave us tonight. You need to see how special you are—or at least grasp how truly exciting this is for me. Your range expands forever, your tone has the richness of," he closes his eyes trying to dream of the exact metaphor, but he grows agitated when he can't find anything to compare, "your coming here and being able to do this for Paul and me, is like bringing the perfect wine to a connoisseur."

"I feel honored, but I..."

"I won't allow you to finish that sentence," he interrupts.

"Does that mean that I can come with you?"

"It means more than that. It means that I don't allow you to leave my sight," he says laughing and coming closer to her, "and I don't allow you to speak unless it's in practice."

"Really?"

"No, but I'd like to think I have that power," he laughs again. "You are what I need today, Rachel Anne Praline. I was having a horrible day, and our soprano section has never been so aggravatingly wrong."

"Wrong?"

"I haven't the right women. I've been looking, but you see we're at the top, Rachel. No other choir from around here compares to us and I have to look for a specific level. Every performance I have planned, they are expecting the best. Did you know we are singing in some of the most beautiful cathedrals throughout all of Europe? We'll be singing for kings, and princes, presidents, and the most influential men and women on the planet. Now…" he says happily, "…Now I feel as though we can reach the expectations that are on us."

The pressure is daunting and she realizes how tired she feels the more he speaks. "All because of me?"

"Don't worry, we have two weeks to work really hard. Are you tired, you look tired and…," he pauses as though he isn't sure whether to say what he feels, but he continues, "…thin. Have you been eating?"

"Yes," she says as more of a question than an answer.

"Where are you staying tonight?"

"To be honest I didn't know what I was doing, and I thought I would just be on the train again when you found out I wasn't what you wanted."

"Oh, I want you." He places a hand on her shoulder. "You have nowhere to stay?"

"No, I don't."

"You may stay with me. Come on. Let's get some sleep and tomorrow we'll start work. You have a lot of songs to learn in a very short time."

They step out into the cold spring air and Rachel immediately begins to shiver.

"Your jacket isn't thick enough for these New York springs," he says as he opens the door to his car. She hurries inside, but isn't sure what to say. When he climbs into the driver's seat, he looks at her with concern. "Rachel, have you been okay?"

"Yes, I've been fine."

"Alright then."

"I do need to know what I will be making, Chuck."

"Of course. I pay each of my singers about three hundred dollars a month, plus I pay for your travel and accommodations."

"That is very generous of you." Rachel immediately begins doing the math in her head. If she can travel with the choir, then she can send Sylvia all of the money she is making, keeping just a small amount for food. No more working at the docks and no more starving and she drops her head in her hands.

"Are you okay?" Chuck asks.

"Better than okay. Thank you, Chuck, for allowing me to come."

Everything about Chuck is lavish from his car to his suits, even down to the perfection of his wavy hair that has been so carefully cut and styled. He's a good-looking man in his forties who comes from wealth; Rachel is sure that many women would be happy to be in his car. When they arrive at his apartment, she sees it is also an exclusive building in a great part of the city with a fancy foyer and a protective doorman. Never has she slept with such relief when Chuck is a complete gentleman.

Chapter Twenty Two

1998

As Gramma Johnson sleeps, I stare out the water-spotted window on a rainy day with dark clouds for miles. It isn't until the clock chimes that I realize I haven't moved for nearly forty-five minutes with my hand on my chin as I think about Josephine . . . the ex-girlfriend I ran into just before I left. She's a beautiful woman, but more than that, she's one of the most talented women I've ever met. It makes me sick what I did to her and my anger gets the best of me every time I think about it. I breathe out trying to forget how I acted.

"What are you thinking about?" Gramma asks.

I don't try and figure out who she thinks I am anymore. Instead, we just continue no matter if, in her mind, I'm Tom, Dick, or Harry.

"My mistakes."

"Oh Lawd, that's dangerous."

I chuckle, "Yeah, I know, Gramma. Rachel and Simone have made me think of it." Gramma furrows her brow as she does every time she has to be reminded. "You've been telling me about them and

Gramma . . ." I turn to her with my arms crossed. "These are women who were very successful for their time, despite all their troubles."

She chuckles with pride. "Yes, they were."

"I had a girlfriend, Gramma . . . named Josephine. She was one of the most brilliant, strategic, and successful women."

"That's a beautiful thing," Gramma says.

"I didn't think so."

Gramma looks up from her cup of water as if glaring at a stranger, but she has always been my one—the one I can be the most honest with. So I continue, "I know, Gramma. I made her feel bad for it. When she was promoted, I stepped in and said she wasn't giving me enough of her attention. I made her feel bad at every moment she climbed the ladder, not because it was true, but because I didn't feel adequate."

It thunders somewhere in the distance as though the earth shares in my revelation. "Oh, honey," Gramma says.

"I don't know that I even realized this until now. Josephine felt stifled by me . . . this is what she always said and I didn't understand. But I loved her, Gramma. I wanted to be with her."

"You didn't love her," Gramma says.

I'm startled by what she says, and I look at her. "You loved you and that's why it didn't work. She needed someone that loved her and that person would have held her hand on the way up."

I nod and breathe in heavily. "I'm sorry about it."

"Don't be sorry, be active. Figure out where that came from. Honey, women need each other because oftentimes the world does everything they can to stamp out their power. You know how many times your girlfriend was dismissed in a conversation as though she had nothing to contribute, or how extra prepared she needed to be to win over a room with her mind and not her face? How many times have you been dismissed like this? You should understand better than most."

"I know. I know. Every time Josephine would come home with

good news it felt like I was losing."

"We can't compete with each other. We need to hold space for one another because everyone's story is so very different. Rachel and Simone, despite living separate lives, did this well."

Josphine and our last moment together is replaying in my mind. She reminded me that she loved me, but until I was able to recognize her successes as my own, we couldn't be together. My answer to her was, "You see! You don't see what I've done," to which I now shiver with embarrassment.

"Why didn't Levi and Rachel just find each other?" I finally ask, switching the subject.

"It wasn't easy back then. People barely had phones and when the depression hit, people barely had anything. It would have had to be a miracle for them to find each other."

"She was a strong woman."

"Yes, she was. Sylvia, Simone, and Rachel all were. Most women facing the depression had to be…You look upset," Gramma says.

"Nah, I'm not upset."

"What did you do, Neil?" Neil is one of her brothers.

"It's Bobby, Gramma."

"Oh, Bobby, that's right. This head of mine."

"You should worry more about my head."

"What, honey?"

"I love her."

1933

"I need to go home to make sure everything is okay before we leave." Rachel tells Chuck at dinner two days before they head to Europe.

"Rachel, it's not possible," he insists. "How about this, I'll set up a call with Simone and Sylvia."

Above the candlelight of the fancy restaurant, she can see that he quickly moves on to the check and doesn't truly care. But then again, Chuck is busy with all the preparations for a tour. It might just be that what she's asking for is ridiculous and she breathes out. Finally, he hears her sigh and smiles. "You're sending her your money, and I can set up a call. Rachel, she's a grown woman and will be fine without you. I really just need you to finish out rehearsals with the others. If I let you go, I must let everyone go."

"I understand." Even though the words come out, it does nothing to contend with her heartache over not seeing Simone and Sylvia before she flies overseas.

Just then, he reaches out to touch her hand. It's obvious that Chuck is used to demanding excellence and getting what he wants, but it has also been the reason he is as successful as he is. As his fingertips gently stroke her hand, she misses Levi. Letting a smile part her lips, Chuck doesn't realize that she's thinking about another man. "Let's go home." He stands, fixes his jacket, then leads her outside with his hand on her back.

The next morning, she stands amongst the choir making sure everyone is ready and at their best, but her mind is thinking about Sylvia.

"Rachel will get that solo," Chuck calls out from the audience.

The woman with thick fingers, thick hair, and a square face named Vonna, who had already performed the solo several times, looks at Chuck in horror. "What do you mean?!"

Chuck raises an obstinate eyebrow. "Vonna, I told you before that it was not yours yet."

Vonna had already made it known by sending glares from across the risers at Rachel from the moment Rachel arrived and this was just an added insult. "Vonna really knows it better," Rachel says quickly.

This now upsets Chuck, and he runs his hand angrily through his hair. "Everyone will listen to what I ask and make it happen. Do you understand?"

On most days, very few people speak to Rachel. She is grateful during one break when Minnie, the brown-haired alto with uncommon green eyes, walks up to Rachel in the city park with her coat wrapped tightly around her. "It's not exactly warm out here," Minnie says with a grin.

Rachel is cold, with her fingertips and nose feeling the greatest chill, but she doesn't want to sit with the rest of the choir after Chuck has, yet again, given her another one of Vonna's solos.

"I know. I just love this area of the park."

"It is great, isn't it?" Minnie looks around at the block of buildings built mainly in the past century and aging to perfection with ivy- covered brick and tarnished copper accents. When she looks back, her eyes wander to the seat next to Rachel. "May I sit?"

"Of course." Rachel scoots over just a bit, even though she doesn't need to, as Minnie is nearly six feet tall, but weighs but a hundred pounds.

"I think if Chuck gives you one more of Vonna's solos, you may need to sleep with one eye open," Minnie says matter-of-factly.

Rachel smiles. "I tried to tell him."

"He won't listen. Besides it doesn't help that he sets you up in the best hotel rooms and takes you to dinner most every night."

Rachel looks at her with concern. "Wait, what? You're in a hotel room?"

"Three people to each one. You get your own."

"Really?" She breathes out as things become very clear. "I thought he was just taking me to dinner because he saw that no one talked to me."

"Nobody talks to you because he takes you to dinner every night. Listen, I was worried at first that Chuckleberry, don't tell him I call him that because he hates it," she smiles and shivers at the same time, "was giving you every solo just because he loves you, but then I heard you sing. I understand. It was just a relief when you opened your mouth, and you weren't ghastly. In fact, I figured if you weren't good, I was going to have to throw my body over yours to keep everyone from stoning you."

"Things are making so much more sense now." Rachel eyes are wide as she looks at her new friend and they laugh eventually. "Well, how do I fix it?"

"Can't. It's the way Chuck is and there's really no stopping it."

"So the choir stones people?" Rachel asks as Minnie just smiles.

"Don't worry. Vonna's just been around for a long time, so people are quite loyal. But I agree; you're better for the solos. And besides, none of these people are worth catching a drink with. Do you drink?"

"Sometimes."

"Want to share a room in Italy? We all have to have roommates. Do you want to be my roommate?"

"I'd love that."

Minnie stands up. "Let's see if Chuck allows it. He may just want you for himself."

Rachel looks at her swiftly, "Well, he can't have me."

"I'm freezing out here. My bones can't handle this." Minnie turns away, thinks of something, then turns back. "You'll win the men over quickly, which I'm sure you already know…but the women may take just a bit longer. For now, I'm here."

"Thank you," Rachel says with a smile.

Minnie nods and heads back inside. From that moment on, Minnie and Rachel spend very little time apart; on the plane, the car ride to their first hotel, and Chuck even allowed them to room together. Very quickly once they are on European soil, concerts begin. They are thrust into a calendar of matinees and evening shows with practice in the mornings till curtain call. The rich and famous come backstage after each performance and Chuck immediately introduces her to an adoring public. Articles are written about her in newspapers and Chuck brings them to her with a proud smile on his face. At an afterparty in Paris, Rachel and Minnie are sitting on a green velvet couch with cocktails in their hands, enjoying the most

Parisian décor in one of the most elegant hotels in the city called The Peninsula Paris.

Minnie drinks from Rachel's drink, since hers is already gone, when she stops and freezes. "It's unbelievable."

"What?" Rachel looks up, trying to see through the crowd.

"Clark Gable," Minnie whispers.

"Who?" Rachel asks.

"Clark Gable . . . an actor." Minnie stands.

When Rachel looks at the crowd once more, a man is making his way through the throng of people with a drink and a smoke in his hands, heading straight toward them. Rachel's eyes fall on his dark features and his masculine eyes, and she pops up from the seat like there is a fire underneath her. He doesn't look familiar to her, but that doesn't matter. There is something about him that is simply perfect.

When he reaches them, Minnie is still staring, but she sticks her hand out to shake his. "Mr. Gable, it's so nice having you here."

He smiles. "Well, thank you so much. I wanted to introduce myself to you," he looks at Rachel and reaches out for her hand, "Your talent is unmeasurable. From Somethin' Tender to now this…" he shakes his head with a smile, "well done."

"Thank you," Rachel whispers. "You knew Somethin' Tender?"

"Did anybody not know Somethin' Tender? My name is Clark." He kisses her hand.

"It's nice to meet you, Clark."

For hours Rachel and Clark talk and laugh as he takes her up to the hotel rooftop so they can enjoy the view of the city. He is more handsome than any other man at the party, but it is more than that, it is charisma—pure and beautiful magnetism. They sneak out of the party together as Rachel hides from Chuck's watchful eye. Clark holds her hand as they grab a drink in a small café and then walk the streets of Paris. It is chilly, but Rachel barely notices as they talk about anything and everything. He is due for several movies back in the States, and she tells him that she would love to record again. All night people want to see him and talk to him, but his attention is on her. Finally, at nearly six in the morning, they make it back to her hotel. He stands outside of it and stares intently into her eyes. Rachel smiles. Then he leans in to her and kisses her lips. It is sweet and gentle. When he lets go, he smiles. "Please look me up when you are in the States once more."

"Of course," Rachel nods.

He watches her as she walks through the hotel lobby and onto the elevators. Soon the doors close and the night ends.

It isn't until later that he becomes the famous Clark Gable, one of the most classic actors of his time, but she always remembers the night they shared.

Chuck takes away her solos for two weeks because he is so angry that she left with Clark. Yet Rachel doesn't seem to mind—even when Vonna smiles.

§ § §

"Is there something going on with you and Chuck?"

Rachel looks up from her magazine, appalled. Minnie is standing over her with her hands on her hips. Her eyes are nearly sideways from curiosity. "Heavens no. Why would you ask that?"

"It's the rumor. From the way he looks at you, I guess."

"How does he look at me?"

"Like I want someone to look at me," Minnie laughs and throws herself back on the bed.

"Believe me, there is nothing there. I can't get him to leave my side."

Suddenly the thought occurs to her that growing old without Levi is horrifying.

As the fans buy out the concerts requesting specifically to be introduced to the beautiful soprano, Paul works with Rachel even more. At times she wishes to simply be one in the crowd. More solos come her way, and she tackles them with as much tenacity as anything else—because it's music. She doesn't know how to sing any other way.

Finally, they reach Italy, the place she always wanted to see. As the train enters the station, part of her wonders where Levi is. Before, he said that his home was in Naples, but that was years ago. Ephod, a young and flamboyantly gay Jewish man in the choir notices her distraction as they step off the train. They too, had developed a friendship. "You expecting to see someone?"

His question catches her off guard. "No."

"Because you look as though you might know someone here."

"No." She slips her arm through his. "No. I suppose I'm hopeful."

"Oh," he grins and leans in to her. "You have a story to tell."

"I have many stories to tell, but not very many with happy endings."

Chuck gathers the choir in the crowded station and stands on a bench in his new suit to talk to them. "I have a list. For every four persons, you will have one host family. They are prepared to take care of your food and housing and get you to every concert for the next month. I'll pass this list around. They will be waiting just outside. Please be careful…" His stern eyes fall on specific people who tend to be troublemakers, "I'm prepared to hear all of the problems you get yourselves into…just follow the rules I've set in front of you."

Minnie comes to Rachel and Ephod's side to wait for the list to come around.

"He better not have split us up," she whispers with a pout.

"I asked him to put us together."

"Oh, good. He'll grant you any request."

Minnie is right. Rachel and Minnie are together and, surprisingly, no one else. Chuck comes to her side with a grin. "We had plenty of room, so I simply kept it you and Minnie." He presses his shoulder against hers and then walks away trying to make his infatuation less obvious.

"He wanted to keep it just you and Minnie because that means less people he has to sneak around when he comes to see you," Ephod whispers.

"Oh, hush up. Let's find our hosts."

People hold signs up with names written on them as they wait by their cars and Chuck yells over the crowd about rehearsal the following morning. Minnie sees an adorable old man standing by a black car holding a sign that reads Praline and Costa and she pulls at Rachel's hand. "Come on!"

They hurry over together and the darling Italian man smiles. "Praline and Costa," he says in a very heavy accent.

"Yes."

"Beautiful! Come with…uhhh…me," he says seeming uncertain as to whether he is saying the English words correctly. "My name is Raul." He throws their bags in the back compartment and then opens the door for the girls.

"It is a…short…drive uhhh…to the home so just… uhhh…relax."

Chapter Twenty Three

1933

Nothing is more beautiful than the rolling hills of Florence that make Minnie and Rachel look at each other excitedly from the back seat of the sedan. With not a soul for miles, Rachel never imagined so much space and so much color, broken up by ancient towns along the way. She breathes in, deeply enjoying the cool air from the open window. "I can't believe where we are," she whispers.

"I know." Minnie nods.

They are about twenty minutes from the station before Raul turns the car down a long gravel drive that seems to be out in the middle of nowhere. Another five minutes and the automobile is sandwiched by stone walls as they enter a sturdy metal gate that opens without a squeal. A large Italian Villa is just ahead, and their eyes widen as they gawk out their windows. Every inch of this land has been dutifully landscaped with gardens, fountains, pathways, and several other smaller homes—more than likely for the employees. Rachel and Minnie hold each other's hands with excitement.

"This is where you stay," Raul says as he pulls the car to a stop and jumps out at the smaller villa along the dirt drive.

They follow him inside and suddenly realize just how small the place is. Two bedrooms and one tiny bath is the entire layout of the cottage. There is no kitchen or icebox. When Raul sets down their things he smiles and walks to the window. "Nice, ehh?" He opens the shutters to the large window and, when he does, both Minnie and Rachel suck in their breath. Just behind the cottage is a gorgeous stone path that leads directly toward the colossal villa.

"Yes, it is magnificent," Rachel agrees.

"Your family," referring to the host family, "lives there and they would…uhhh…like you to come…uhhh…to eat. Breakfast, dinner, and supper, they will provide you."

"What is that?" Rachel asks about another home just to the right of the large one.

"That is…guest house." He looks at the girls, "Mrs. Rizzo likes to have visitors. Her daughter is staying there just now." Everyone is quiet for a time and then Raul pats both of the women on their backs. "I will go. Dinner…be ready shortly."

"Thank you, Raul."

Minnie looks at Rachel with a dumbfounded smile on her face. "Can you believe this place?"

"No. I've never seen anything like it."

"If only we could stay longer than a few weeks."

After some time, the dinner bell rings. They follow the long path to the main house. When they near, Raul comes out to greet them as though he has been waiting. He introduces them to the workers around the property and then leads them inside. The house is old, yet extraordinarily cared for. Everything about it is fluid with color and detail. Rachel finds it hard not to stop and explore as they pass book-shelves and knickknacks. Raul takes them to a living room where he motions for the girls to sit on a couch, then he disappears, and, before long, a beautiful, well-dressed woman comes down the stairs. She is a stunning Italian woman with dark skin and dark eyes. Her hair is graying, but it has clearly—at one time—been black.

"Oh, this is wonderful," she exclaims. "I have been waiting." She comes to their side and when both of them stand quickly, she hugs them. "I don't know what Chuck told you, if anything," she says in a mild Italian accent, "but my family has been housing his singers for years. In fact, most of my family still comes to Florence when they know that your choir will be here. It's become quite the tradition."

"You know Chuck?" Minnie asks.

"Yes, for years. I know his family well." She stops to touch Rachel's blonde hair with a smile. "So, which one is the new soprano I've heard so much about?"

Minnie quickly points to Rachel with a grin.

"I am so excited that I could care for you while you are here. How is your voice? Do you need some tea or anything?"

"No, thank you. I'm fine."

"Oh, good. Well…," she says as though things need to get done, "…while you are here, Raul will take you where you need to go. When you have rehearsal or a show." She grows excited. "I have a ticket to four of your concerts in the next month. You would be surprised how difficult it can be to get one of the tickets, let alone four."

"If you know Chuck, he should have helped you," Minnie says quickly.

"Yes he did, wonderful man. He just knew how much I love the romance of the music you sing. Are your accommodations suited to your liking?"

"Yes, they're beautiful," Rachel says quickly.

"I'm sorry it doesn't have a kitchen, but you see my family has owned this place for generations and the thought of changing anything just…well…makes my fingers ache so I don't change much. But we have a wonderful cook here…actually it is Raul's wife, Ginnie." Soon Mrs. Rizzo walks them through the house and points out the things that mean much to the family line.

"Just after Chuck's choir visited two years ago, my husband died, so I wasn't sure how I would feel about having you stay with me, but now that you are here, " she sighs and shakes her head with a smile, "It's good for me...yes it is..." Slipping from one conversation to the next makes it seem like the woman is starving for companionship as she holds on to the girls' arms and leads them through the house to the dining area. "You must be hungry . . . are you hungry?"

Minnie speaks up first. "I am, Mrs. Rizzo."

They enter a large dining area that looks like it can feed an entire army. The table is desperately long and made of a heavily ornate wood. One wall is made of stone and the other of birch wood.

"Mrs. Rizzo," Rachel asks thinking of something that she has forgotten, "I have a letter that I would like to send. Is there somewhere that I may do that?"

"Oh, of course. Anything you want to send, just bring it to me and I will see that it gets where it needs to go."

"Thank you. Do I have time before dinner to go get it?"

"Yes, of course."

Rachel quickly ascends the small hill, along the stone walkway toward their small cottage. Several times she stops just to smell the fragrance in the air that must be wafting from a nearby flower. It is warm enough to just wear a light sweater and she hums along the way. The sun is setting, turning the sky a tricolor of pink, orange, and purple while flocks of birds in V-formation fly past. She finds the letter quickly and then returns to look at the horizon that faces the gravel road. Past the stone wall, the landscape rolls like frozen waves extending to the horizon and bunches of trees grouped together on different parcels of land. It is all so mesmerizing as she watches the last little inch of sun fall behind the multitudes of grapevines. On one of these family-owned vineyards, an elderly woman carries a bucket down a winding path—probably ending her day of hard work.

To explore the world is a gift, and she thinks of Sylvia back home suddenly hoping that she isn't lonely. Chuck had never let her call, so she stays in touch by letter; which is the very reason she caught the sunset and she looks down at the soft paper in her hands with Sylvia's name and address on the front. Inside the envelope is one for Simone as well. However, Simone is on a big case or so she said the last time she wrote.

Just past the stone gate is a dusty road and Rachel looks up as a 1933 Stutz Monte Carlo—the largest and most expensive Stutz—hurries along, sending puffs of dust into the air from just underneath its belly. She expects it to pass, but instead it slows as the metal gate opens, then turns onto the drive just beside the small cottage.

As it passes, she looks down at the letter to make sure that all is written correctly, but the cut of the engine catches her attention. The driver has stopped midway along the gravel path in an unusual spot, then steps from the car. She pays no attention, assuming there must be something wrong with the vehicle itself and starts making her way back to the Villa. However, the person's silence and stillness sparks her curiosity, so she turns to him. Just after sunset, the light is expectedly dim, yet the sprays of orange and pink are splashed across the sky making it difficult to see his face. He is tall and broad and, for some reason, is staring at her. There is something very emotional about his stance even though he is completely frozen.

"Can I help you?" she asks, taking a couple of steps.

"Rachel?"

Everything stops, including the earth's turn. Except her hands. They begin to shake when a thousand questions attack her mind. Has she heard correctly? She wants nothing more than to hear this man's voice again-- to prove to herself it is not who she thinks it is. Her heart, quite possibly, might not be able to handle another break. Please speak again, she thinks to herself. As if she's willed it so, he does and this time she can hear the shock in his voice. "Rachel?"

Before she can stop them, tears flow down her cheeks as her knees grow weak. "It can't be," she whispers as she shakes her head and covers her face.

He takes two more steps, "Rachel."

His voice finally matches the sweet recollection of his hands running down her skin, his lips making her quake, and the pressure of his body offering her every bit of safety she's ever known. Instantly, her memories return to California, visualizing them in his bed, making love like never before and never since.

In this twilight hour, she chides destiny, begging that this is not some sort of cruel joke.

"Levi?" She places her hand on her stomach.

"Yes," he says deeply.

The earth could have swallowed them and they would not have known.

"Levi?" she asks again.

"Yes."

With a force as natural as breath, her feet run to him. His arms are already open, and she falls hard and fast. He holds her so tightly they can feel each other's hearts beneath their skin. It is a strange twist of fate that neither can understand. Why are they suddenly in the same place at the same time and able to touch each other again? Out of superstition or fear neither one of them wants to challenge fortune's choice. Some might say that it is rare for love to find its match, but some would argue that love's power can't help but draw itself to the place it belongs. Many have lost love, and only those lucky enough know what an extraordinary feeling it is to have it return.

Unable to stop, she presses her hands against his face and looks at him as though he will disappear. Finally, now that her eyes have adjusted to dusk, she can see the striking lines of his face and she takes his hat off to get an even better look. His eyes are just as brilliant as always and his tears match her own. Then, he kisses her. His lips hungrily wrap around her thick bottom lip and it's as if there has been no time between California and now. All those nights of desperation are forgotten even if for a moment. It's nearly impossible to stop. The years of separation have become an entity that controls their every move. It doesn't take them long to be out of breath, and before they've parted, her crying has worsened.

"I'm sorry," he whispers, pressing his cheek against hers. "I'm sorry."

Levi looks up the road as if concerned about something, then he hurriedly pulls her hand guiding her to inside her cottage. A small night light allows them to see each other just a bit better.

"I can't believe it!" Rachel says as a tear falls off her chin.

He runs his hand along her cheek as he shakes his head. "I thought I would never see you again."

Rachel hesitates. "Why didn't you call? When you said you would, you didn't."

He breathes heavily, "I know. Some things happened that made it impossible for me."

"I can't believe I'm touching you," Rachel says gently, a smile starting to appear.

"But I have to tell you what happened, Rachel . . . you need to know."

"Right now, I just want to look at you." She kisses him again and he wraps his arms around her waist. His lips are just the same—just as perfect. She has forgotten how good it feels to be held. They can't stop. When they finally let go, they keep their faces just inches apart. "This is not happening," she whispers.

"What are you doing here?" he asks in disbelief.

"I'm singing," she smiles. "I've been traveling with a choir."

"Chuck's choir?"

She is suddenly surprised. "Yes."

He nods like this has suddenly reminded him of something—almost fearful. "You're staying here?"

"Yes, Mrs. Rizzo has given us her home to stay in."

He looks at her, yet she can't read him. She tries, but his focus seems to bounce around.

"She does that every year," he finally says.

"I know. She told me. How did you know that?"

"Rachel, I…"

Suddenly they hear Raul calling for her from the main house.

"Oh, I should tell him where I am." She has forgotten the length of her disappearance.

"Rachel," Levi says, quickly grabbing her hand before she can leave. "We have so much to talk about."

"I know, but they think I've just gone for a letter and I need to…"

"Rachel, you can't say anything about this just yet."

"About what?"

Raul's voice is coming closer, but Levi won't let her go. "Rachel, I'm here, because this is my wife's family's place."

All noises and sensations—good or bad—are too loud. The sun and then all sight, in fast succession, disappears, making it nearly impossible to see Levi's face. Raul comes around the corner of the cottage with a lantern and finds the two of them standing there.

"There you are." He sees Levi, although Levi has already dropped her hand. "Mr. Price, we didn't know you were home."

"Hello, Raul," he says calmly.

"We were worried when you didn't come back, Rachel. Is everything alright?" Raul looks at the two of them suspiciously. "Dinner is on the table."

Levi's words don't make sense to her—the sound of them is like a scream when woken from a bad dream.

"Miss Praline?" Raul asks.

She can't speak. Levi's horrifying words have caused everything in her body to crack, especially her heart. Once again, she has found a new depth of brokenness. Raul comes to her side and she nods to show him that all is fine. Only because of the darkness is her nod believable.

Rachel doesn't know the anguish that is happening in Levi as she walks away. She will never see that when she walks out of sight, he grabs his head and bends at the waist, growling with anger. There is nothing he can do. Everything is wrong, but nothing can change.

Back at the large house, Rachel is numb as she walks into the dining room where several new people sit around the large table. It is unexpected and she tries to act composed, giving everyone a smile, but Minnie can see on her face there is something wrong.

Mrs. Rizzo stands to her feet and motions to Rachel. "Rachel, honey, you may sit anywhere you like."

"Thank you." Rachel's voice is so quiet she isn't sure that anyone has even heard her. She feels her shoulders slumping down and the skin under her eyes seems to have dropped to her mouth. There is a seat next to Minnie and she is quiet as she makes her way to it. Mrs. Rizzo is at the head of the table, standing as if to direct the conversation for the night. She wears a silky dress that hangs long under her arms so that, when she points, the material nearly touches the food. Just beside her is another woman, much younger, but they look the same. Her eyes and hair are dark, but her skin is smooth and fresh. There is an empty seat beside her and then three men who look American. The only other two are Minnie and Rachel, and they sit across the table from the Americans.

"Rachel, did you get lost?" Mrs. Rizzo asks.

She wavers, wondering what to say. "I'm sorry. I was so caught up watching the sunset."

"Aren't they gorgeous here?"

"Yes, they are." Rachel tries desperately to keep a smile, but it is impossible.

Just then, everyone turns when Levi walks in hurriedly. His eyes first fall on Rachel and although the others don't notice, she can see that he feels the same way she does—in a cage from which they can't break free. Now in the lighted room, Rachel notices that he is still as handsome as ever, if not more. A room loves him whether he cares to give it much at all.

"I'm sorry I'm late." He sits at the table beside the beautiful woman who looks like Mrs. Rizzo.

"You've come just in time," Mrs. Rizzo says with a grin. "Everyone, we have new visitors with us for the next month—Rachel Praline and Minnie Costa. Aren't they just wonderful!" she says gleefully. "Rachel, Minnie, this is my daughter Kendra, her husband Levi…"

While Kendra—looking very proper and beautiful smiles at the two girls, Levi doesn't fake a nod of introduction to her; he simply stares with intense emotions that seem to make his chest thicker.

"And these gentlemen are staying down the road. Ladies, they are here on business and have been friends of the family for years. There's Daniel, Carlos, and Alan." The three men either say hello or nod. "I invited them to come to dinner. Besides, one of them . . . Alan, is it you . . . that has been to one of their shows?"

"Yes, ma'am." The young man, a little younger than Levi, has a nice face and a genuine smile.

"Please, call me Carlotta."

"Well, then . . . yes, Carlotta, I have. I went to one when you were in Paris," he says to Rachel and Minnie. "I even went to an after party and although I wished to talk with the lovely soprano," he smiles at Rachel, "you were slightly preoccupied with a rather well-known actor." Alan winks at Rachel and she gives him a smile.

"Oooh, what actor?" Carlotta asks.

Rachel is suddenly aware that the answer belongs to her, so she momentarily leaves her wallowing and looks at Carlotta. "Clark Gable."

"Oh my, he is handsome, isn't he?" Carlotta says, letting her eyebrows drop and shoulders raise as she nearly purrs.

"He was very sweet," Rachel says looking down at her plate once again.

"Oh, I was able to see Red Dust last year when I visited New York. He was just magnificent," Carlotta continues.

"I've never been to one of his movies," Rachel says quietly.

"Oh well, he must have loved that," Alan says with a cackle kind of a laugh.

"He didn't seem to mind."

"Well, Rachel is the new buzz in town," Carlotta says brightly.

"She certainly is the talent in Chuck's show. There is one song, Rachel, where you start out so beautifully with this high seamless voice. I nearly fell in love," Alan says making both Rachel and Levi look at him at the same time.

"I just can't wait to see it this year," Carlotta says.

"Rachel," the sound of Kendra's voice makes Rachel insecure, "I believe you have been a radio performer for the last few years, is that correct?"

"Not really. Some recordings just happened to get into the right hands."

"Well, it's nice to have you here. My husband and I are looking forward to seeing the concert."

At the wrong time Rachel looks up to watch Kendra run her hand through Levi's hair and smile. Surprised—even to herself—Rachel jumps up from her seat hitting the table with her leg and making everything bounce. Rachel hesitates as Carlotta looks at her with alarm. "Are you alright?"

"I'm so sorry. I'm not feeling well. I think I should go back."

"Oh sweetie, can I get you anything?" Carlotta asks.

The men at the table, led by Levi, stand.

"No, please, no fuss. I'm fine. I just think I'm tired."

Hurriedly, as though she can't get out of the room fast enough, Rachel bumps everything on her way and finally makes it outside. She doesn't even say much of a goodbye because she is afraid at any moment that her voice will give her away.

After just moments, Levi comes running from the house to chase after her. He grabs her hand when he nears. She stops and sucks in a sob as he turns her around.

"Rachel, I'm so sorry."

"What are you doing out here, Levi? You can't run after me."

"I'm going to tell my wife about us."

"What?"

"I'm going to tell her what you used to mean to me. I'm not a coward," he says with serious eyes. "She deserves to know. Besides, I suspect there will be no hiding it."

"What I used to mean to you?"

He stops.

"Rachel, I don't know what this means. Years have passed. I have not seen you for more than three years."

"But I still love you," she whispers.

He is quiet. "We must talk…tomorrow?"

"I have rehearsal tomorrow."

"After."

"There is a concert after."

"When your concert is over."

She finally nods.

"I am so sorry." Levi shakes his head.

Rachel can't breathe, especially with him standing so close to her. She now believes wholeheartedly that life is cruel. No matter what you give it, it takes from you. She feels so far from the little girl at Bernie's side.

"I have to be alone," she says trying to breathe.

"Rachel…"

"Don't tell her anything," she sobs.

"What? Who?" Levi asks.

"Kendra. Don't tell her anything until we have time to talk."

"She's going to ask why I ran out after you."

"I don't care. Make something up. Tell her something . . . just don't tell her anything about me." She can feel the lump deep in her throat, "Oh God, I don't know what to do." A deep pain begins in her chest when she forgets how to breathe.

"Rachel, just wait. We'll figure things out."

Just then Kendra stands at the door. "Levi?"

"I'm here," Levi says. Rachel hurriedly walks into the shadows.

"What are you doing?" Kendra asks him.

"I'll be just a minute."

"But what are you doing?"

Levi turns angrily. "I'll be just a minute."

Kendra gives him an annoyed glance and then walks back inside. He takes her face in his hands, "Tomorrow, Rachel. We'll figure it out."

It is difficult to rehearse the next day. Even Chuck grows concerned when he sees the distance in Rachel's eyes, but she assures him that it is nothing. That night in a large and glorious church, every seat is full with people dressed in gowns and tuxedos. Chuck stands at the door greeting everyone as they come in. Finally, the time comes for the concert to begin and the lights are lowered. Quietly, the choir fills the halls surrounding the audience. With soft notes played just once, the men begin to sing, and then the women join in. Instantly, the room is bursting with the most magnificent sound.

For the next hour the concert proceeds without error. On the very last song of the night, Rachel stands on the stage alone as the others take their place in the surrounding aisles. The song begins and she falls into the dream of it all. Women and men within the audience are mesmerized. Her eyes survey the room and suddenly they land on Levi who stands at the door. He is watching with almost a bit of surprise as she sings—the other voices perfectly streaming beneath her. It is in this moment that the emotion tumbles clumsily from her soul. There is silence when the song ends for just a moment until the crowd erupts in applause and they climb to their feet. It isn't long after the concert ends that Chuck finds her.

"Beautiful, Rachel," he says holding a flower in his hand as he walks to her, but her attention is toward the door overlooking the stairs. At the bottom of these, that's where Levi waits. She doesn't know how to take the first steps. "Come with me," Chuck grins.

"Where?"

"Come with me . . . somewhere . . . I don't know. We need to celebrate after a concert like this."

"Chuck, I can't. I have something to do. I'm sorry."

He is bothered by her refusal, but he doesn't try to change her mind. "Alright. Soon then?"

"Yes, soon." As the words slip out, Levi comes to the top of the stairs and her heart trembles. He is so handsome in his black suit that she bites her lip. Chuck looks and instantly Rachel sees him withdraw. It is obvious he remembers Levi from California.

"Oh, I see. Well, I'll see you tomorrow."

"Okay."

He walks away taking one last look at Levi. Finally, Rachel slowly makes her way to him.

"Is your wife here?" Rachel asks.

"No. I told her I had things to do."

"Okay."

"Come with me?"

In just minutes, they walk the sidewalks of Florence, not saying much of anything.

"You're quiet," he notices.

"Am I?"

"I thought you would have a lot to say."

"I don't know what to say."

They walk beside the busy cafes, yet even the chaos can't tear their attention from each other. Among the ancient and perfectly weathered buildings—that most would find it difficult to turn their eyes from—Rachel and Levi seem not to notice. They watch each other, only turning their eyes ahead of them for seconds at a time to keep from walking into anything. Few people are on the streets in the late hour, yet restaurants are surprisingly full. Levi and Rachel continue for nearly a half-mile, not saying much, but noticing the bit of excitement that each touch brings them and finally Rachel stops.

When she does, he turns to her.

"What?" Levi asks.

"Where are you taking me?"

"I can only walk with you, Rachel. I don't trust myself going anywhere else."

"You don't trust yourself?"

"No. Just walking next to you, I feel as though I'm doing something wrong."

"You have been in my life since I was a child, how can we just pretend that we don't feel a connection?"

"We can't . . . which is why I'm struggling."

"Oh."

She starts to walk away, but he stops her with a gentle hand on her forearm. "This," he points to the café to their right, "is a place where I know the owner well. Would you like to stop here?"

"Is that a good idea to be seen by someone that knows you well?"

"He's a friend. He would never say anything unless I wanted him to."

"Okay."

For a moment Levi's hand lands on her lower back as they walk in together and she sucks in her stomach desperately hoping he doesn't move it. A young man comes to Levi throwing his arms around him in a bear hug.

"Levi! When did you come into town?" He has dark eyes, dark hair, and speaks English well.

"Just a week ago."

"You staying long?"

"About three weeks."

"Oh, well it's good to have you."

The man notices Rachel. "Who's this, Levi?"

"This is Rachel."

"Rachel?" He looks at Levi with shock and then back at her. "You have shown up?"

"Rachel," Levi says with a grin, "This is Pablo. He's been a friend of mine for years and he knows everything about us."

Pablo laughs. "I had to hear about you nearly every night." He steps in between Rachel and Levi and throws his arm over Rachel's shoulders to lead her farther into the restaurant. Pablo winks at Levi. "I remember this tortured soul," he says of Levi, "would come and sit at my bar. I could only serve him lemonade, but he would drown his sorrows in the sour drink. I've never seen anything so pitiful."

"Oh, come on now. I wouldn't say pitiful." Levi quips from behind them.

"You're right, Levi," Pablo says with a laugh, "What about pathetic? Does that work for you?"

Levi laughs.

They reach a booth in the back corner of the restaurant and Pablo helps Rachel take a seat. He stands in front of them. "Drinks?"

Levi sits beside her. "Would you like anything?"

"I would. What will you have?"

Pablo leans forward.

"Whiskey, straight." Rachel says quickly. Both men look at her with surprise. She shrugs, "It's been that kind of week."

Before long, Pablo has given them two small glasses and pours the brown liquid from a heavy bottle. Then, finally, they are alone. For the longest time they simply stare, until Levi suggests they drink, hoping it will calm their tension. As they look at each other, they both gulp it down. Instantly, Rachel's eyes water and she coughs when it finally slides to the pit of her stomach. Levi doesn't make a sound as the liquor seems to go down his throat like water. When they are finished, Pablo fills their glasses with more.

"I have to go help the others. Your drinks are on me tonight."

"Thanks, Pablo," Levi says.

The shot of liquor warms them through, so much so that Rachel takes off her sweater.

"For a moment," he says, "let's forget about where we are. I just want to hear what happened to you after I left you at the station that day in California."

"Can we really do that? Forget where we are?"

"What happened, Rachel? Start with the reason you went home. Dick. What happened?"

"He died two weeks after I got home."

"I'm sorry."

She nods, then downs the second glass of liquor. "I didn't expect Sylvia to be such a mess after he died. But she was and I guess I just felt like I owed her all of my time. She didn't want to take care of anything, so I did. Then the stock market crashed, and we found ourselves with a lot of debt and no money saved."

"You were hit hard by that."

"Well, I wasn't," she chuckles. "I already had no money to my name, but Sylvia was. Dick wasn't there to do the show and so I sold the show. I sold the animals." Her eyes get misty. "Then I had to sell the house. In the middle of everything, you never called and I would ask myself why, but there wasn't a lot of time to be angry and try to find you. Every time I rang, the operator said you were no longer there. Simone sent letters to the hotel, but they came back." The emotion starts to get the better of her and she tries to hold back the tears but it doesn't work. "Where were you?" she cries out. The anger heats her face, or maybe that's the whiskey. "Why didn't you call when you said you would?" Unexpectedly, Levi reaches out and runs his finger along her cheek. She can't help but take his hand and press it against her face. "Was it me? Was it her?" He runs his thumb along her chin.

"You have to tell me that it wasn't me. It wasn't because you didn't love me."

Levi swiftly pulls himself close to her. He wraps his arms around her until she can't breathe. "Rachel, I love you."

"Then why? Where were you?"

He pulls away just slightly and pushes a curl away from her face.

"I was in an accident."

"What?"

He takes her hand and guides her fingertips in his hair. Just below his dark waves, she can feel a long scar. "I was traveling just like I told you I would. But I woke up after the accident and it was weeks later. By the time I could reach out, you were gone. I searched for anyone to find you, I even started contacting radio stations that would play your music, but no one seemed to know."

"Are you okay?"

"I am now. It was a bad accident and killed my mother who was in the car with me."

"Oh, Levi, I'm so sorry."

"I had my money in so many different places and remember the oil..."

"Oh, yes, that oil."

Pablo comes back and fills their glasses once again. He hears the end of their conversation and shakes his head. "You want to know what this fella's been doin' with his money?"

"Yes."

"There's no need," Levi says quickly.

"No, come on." Pablo lifts his hand to stop Levi, "This is Rachel. Your love. She should know what you've been doing in a time when everyone is struggling..."

"Tell me," Rachel says.

"He has a hotel in California..."

Rachel turns to Levi with question. "The hotel?"

"Yes, the hotel," He nods.

"So, you know it?" Pablo asks.

"Yes, very well."

"He's been letting families live there...scot-free...if they don't have no home...he let's 'em stay. He never asks anyone to pay or leave..."

Rachel looks at Levi. "Is that true?"

Levi avoids her eye contact. Pablo continues, "It isn't just that… they are treated like guests at the hotel. He still pays for all of the workers…waiters, gardeners…"

Just then a woman calls to Pablo from a table behind them and he excuses himself again. When he does, Rachel looks at Levi.

"You're always the philanthropist, aren't you?"

"It just didn't feel right doing anything else."

Suddenly, Rachel becomes very sad. This is the very reason she fell in love with him and now, even though he is sitting just feet from her, the barrier keeping them apart can't be greater.

"What's wrong?" he asks.

"I can't believe what has happened. I wish you had just come with me."

"I did come to find you." He studies her eyes.

Her heart drops. "You did?"

"Yes. I went to your house, but like you said it was sold and there was no record of where you were staying. For months, any chance that I could fly to Atlantic City, I walked along the Boardwalk just hoping that I would run into you."

"You did?"

"Yes. Then I had to stop. I just couldn't keep chasing what felt like a hopeless dream."

"I'm so sorry, Levi. I hadn't a dime to my name. Then Sylvia got sick and I had to work longer hours to get food on the table.

"I would have taken care of you."

"I know you would have."

"Did Sylvia get better?"

"Yes, she did."

With a quick change of subject Levi smiles. "You never cease to amaze me."

"What?"

"Your voice. How did you get in with Chuck?"

"I lost my job." For some odd reason she laughs when she says it.

"You lost your job?"

"I was working at the docks, day and night, moving cargo, until one of the managers attacked me just a month or two ago. I was able to fight him off, luckily, but in doing so, I hurt his ego. I'm not allowed back." Levi breathes in heavily as he touches her neck. "There's just something about me, I guess. First Bill and then this guy."

"I'm sorry. You were able to fight him off?"

"Well, he was going to do much worse if I didn't," she says with a grin.

"Good for you."

"Chuck had given me his information in California and I ran across it and called him. Turns out I'm pretty good."

"Pretty good does not give justice to what you sang tonight."

"Thank you."

He reaches out and takes her hand. They are quiet for a while and then she asks the question both of them know has to be answered.

"You got married?"

"Yes. She was around while I was recovering, and Kendra has a way with things. While I was searching for you, trying to get better, and still having a large corporation to deal with, Kendra took care of the company. Her mother helped me get connected with some people and then Kendra got pregnant."

"Oh." The darkness crashes over Rachel. "So, you have a child with her?"

"No. We got married because I care, but a month after the wedding she lost the baby. I held out hope that you would call for so long, but the more time that passed, the more impossible it felt. I suppose I jumped into it hoping that it would make me feel better."

"Did it?"

He sucks in a deep breath, then turns to her, "If you're asking if it made me stop thinking about you…I think about you every day of my life. Then I saw you standing there yesterday and I thought I was seeing things. I got out of the car and when you turned around I almost hoped it wasn't you…"

"You did?" she says sadly.

"You standing there meant that I'd made the biggest mistake of my life."

The bar around them is beginning to empty, but they don't notice. Pablo—a romantic at heart—doesn't care that he'll have to stay late.

"What do we do?" Rachel finally asks.

"I don't know."

"Does Kendra know about me?"

"No," he says calmly. "She knows about the woman that I call the love of my life from California."

There's a moment of silence when the cruelty of what he just said can puncture her heart a bit deeper.

"Are you happy with her?"

"We've had our troubles. She's not you. I've thought about telling her and now that you are here, I believe I have to. But it's tricky. Kendra and her mother have shown me, since getting married, that there was more to their pursuance of me than love. These women are ruthless and will do anything to get what they want."

"Don't tell them then."

"She's in love with me, Rachel. She deserves to know my history with you."

"I'll leave you alone. Just don't tell her. I'm living next to her, and I would hate to think what my presence would do." There is a long silence and suddenly Rachel feels her tears pile high. "I can't be so near to you and not be with you."

"I know."

"Maybe I'll leave."

"Leave Italy?"

"No, I have concerts to do. Maybe I'll leave Mrs. Rizzo's place."

"Where will you go?"

"A hotel."

"This month is the busiest time for Florence. If I could, I would stay at a hotel instead of Carlotta's home, but hotels are full during your choir's tour."

"Chuck would let me stay with him."

"You cannot stay with Chuck," he says with no option for argument.

"Why do you say that?"

"I see the way he looks at you. You can't stay with him."

Rachel laughs. "Are you telling me that I can't stay with another man because you will be jealous?" He looks at her halfway serious and halfway grinning, but he doesn't say a word. "You're married and you don't want me to work with Chuck."

"No. I don't."

"You have no right."

"It doesn't feel that way." He takes her face in his hands. "It feels as though I should be able to have a say in it. I'm in love with you and it feels as though I should have that right."

She can't argue.

They both bring the glasses to their lips and take another shot. She is beginning to feel it everywhere in her body—the tingle and warmth. But he is large and it will take several more before anything has an effect.

"I've still been hearing you on the radio—your old recordings," Levi finally says.

"I know. They still play them often."

"What about that music?"

"I don't know. Right now, I'm enjoying what I'm doing, but it's the music that Bernie taught me. I'll always come back to it."

He chuckles. "My wife…" he watches Rachel cringe as he says it, "Kendra and her mother have tickets for several nights. Now I won't try and think of an excuse as to why I shouldn't go."

"Kendra seems lovely," Rachel finally says although the words feel strapped painfully to her tongue.

"She's a good woman. She's strong, stubborn—a little too stubborn for me and she knows what she wants."

"Already she sounds like a better woman for you than me. I always used to wonder why you loved me. I wasn't the picture of the woman I thought you should be with."

She suddenly grows frightened that he might agree with her so she drops her eyes. He lifts her face with his palm to her chin. "In every single way, you are exactly what I need."

"You know what I'm most afraid of?"

"What's that?"

"That you'll be happy." She doesn't wait for him to say anything. "I know it's horrible. It's selfish and awful, but it's how I feel."

"The worst thing that I could do right now is act on how I feel," he says honestly. "Kendra and I have done a lot of great things in business together. It's one of the reasons that we got married. We worked well together. But how I feel right now is that none of that matters and I have to have you, but that could potentially ruin so many lives."

"I know."

"How can I not see you while you are here?"

"I don't know."

"Listen, you do what you came here for. I'm busy with work anyway. I always try and keep myself busy while we're visiting Florence since we don't come very often and I have business associates here. I'll see you when I see you."

"Can we do that?"

"We're going to have to."

"Okay."

Levi and Rachel help Pablo close the restaurant then they walk to Levi's car. He drives her home and by the time they pull into the driveway, the liquor has made Rachel extremely tired. He stops the car just outside the cottage and she looks at him. The alcohol makes her emotions well up easier than normal and tears fall from her eyes.

"Don't cry, Rachel," he says, unable to stay away from her. He reaches for her and takes her head in his hands. Suddenly, as though saying goodbye is giving them an idea of what the next few weeks will be like, both of them change their minds. "I'll figure something out."

"I can't live my life without you."

"I know. I'll figure something out."

He kisses her forehead and then kisses her cheek. In the dark car with the rumbling engine beneath them, he brings his lips within inches of hers. His hands hold onto her face and his fingers dig into her hair. They want to surrender and just give in to desire. It is only one kiss and one night. The beating of their hearts is painful as they try to decide whether it is worth it. But finally, Levi lets go without making that one last dip to feel her kiss. Rachel grabs her purse and hurries out of the car.

§ § §

For several days, as Rachel and Minnie go to and from rehearsals, Levi remains nowhere to be seen. He made it clear that he had plenty of work to do and he sticks to his word. Kendra, on the other hand, is always near. She stays much of the time with her mother and lounges around the house. At times, she is dressed in business attire and leaves with Levi, but, besides these outings, Rachel runs into her quite often. Rachel finds it hard to look past her beauty. They are so completely opposite.

One morning while Rachel is eating breakfast alone before she leaves for rehearsal, Kendra comes in and sits down at the table with a smile.

"Rachel, I am so excited to see your concert tonight."

"Oh, are you coming tonight?"

"Yes. I've been coming to these since I was a child and I just love them."

"I'm so glad."

"What an interesting life you must lead," Kendra says with a wink.

"What do you mean?"

"You travel from one place to the next, meet new men every-where . . . not just new men, but men that adore you for your voice. What a life!" she says, laughing as she spreads butter on toast that Raul's wife brought her.

"I wouldn't say that there are all that many men out there to meet."

"Oh, I don't believe it. You met Clark Gable," she pushes her chair closer to Rachel, "What was he like?"

"Very kind."

"That's it?"

"I try not to look at men." The sentence sounds awkward the moment it comes from her mouth. "I just mean I'm a little shy."

"Well, Alan asked me about you yesterday."

"Alan?"

"Yes, the other American at dinner the first night you came."

"Oh, that's right."

"He would like to see you on a more formal basis, I think."

Rachel stands to her feet and moves about the kitchen clumsily as though she can't find her footing.

"I just don't think I have time for that, right now..."

"But—," Kendra says furrowing her eyebrows at Rachel.

"I'm sorry," Rachel interrupts. "I'm running a little late this morning. Thanks for breakfast."

They come to the show that night and Rachel finds it horrible when Kendra comes to congratulate her, but Levi says almost noth-ing at all. That night she cries herself to sleep.

Italy flits with excitement over the new soprano. People come from all over to hear her. Chuck is forced to schedule more concerts so that the choir might stay longer.

"But why, Chuck? I don't understand. Haven't we already booked ourselves in other cities?"

He finally turns to her with a smile that he seems to want to keep secret. "Rachel, you mustn't let a soul know. But I have just been contacted."

"What? By whom?"

"Benito Mussolini."

"Benito Mussolini called you?"

"No, his assistant, but she bought thirty tickets for him and his family."

"Benito Mussolini wants to come to the concert? Why?"

He seems insulted by the question. "You just don't understand, Rachel. Europe is in love with us…you…they want to hear you. How can you argue that? Why don't you seem happy, Rachel?"

Suddenly there is no holding back. Rachel drops to the couch in Chuck's hotel room and throws her face in her hands. Tears begin to fall even though she tries to hold back the sobs in her chest. He rushes to her side.

"Rachel, Rachel," he says like he is speaking to a child. He wraps his arms around her, and she lets him. "What has happened?"

"It's nothing."

"Does this have to do with Levi?"

"Yes."

"I'm sorry."

He brings his eyes down to look into hers and runs his hand along her face. If she expected it, she might have had the chance to dodge his pass, but he made his move too quickly. Before she knows it, he brings his lips to hers and kisses her.

Rachel has no feelings for Chuck Gerber. He is kind and has given her so much. Maybe, had he come into her life at a different time, she might have been able to give him the chance, but Levi's kiss is imprinted in her memory. She pulls away, but before she can say anything he jumps to his feet and walks to his desk.

"We have a concert tonight. Go get some rest," he says forcefully.

"Chuck, I…"

"Get out!" he yells at her, his face red with anger.

"Please let me explain."

"There's nothing to explain. You're in love with a married man." His tone is accusing.

"It's not my fault."

"Rachel, you'd turn down someone who has given you so much for a man who has a beautiful wife like Kendra." For a moment, Rachel had forgotten that Chuck knew the Rizzos. When she starts to say something, he cuts her off. "You are a fool, Rachel. An absolute fool."

"Chuck…"

"Please leave, Rachel. I must get ready for tonight."

"Fine."

Rachel walks out of Chuck's room and down the hall silently. She lets out an aggravated sigh as the elevator doors open, then keeps quiet in the back seat as Raul drives home.

"Miss Praline?" he says, as he looks in his mirror to see her. She is so lost in thought she does not hear him the first time. "Miss Praline? Rachel?"

Finally, she looks up. "Yes, Raul? I'm sorry."

"No, it is fine, Miss Praline. Are you alright?"

"I'm just having an off day, Raul."

"You don't have to be at the concert for another couple of hours and Minnie has gone home to shower. May I take you somewhere?"

"I don't know." All she really wants is to sleep, forever.

"Ahhh, please, Rachel. I insist. You will love it."

"Alright."

Soon they are heading down a dirt road, which leads out into the countryside. The grapevines pass outside her windows and Raul seems to know exactly where he is taking her. They finally pull onto a stone driveway where just ahead is a medium-sized house with large barrels stacked along one side and a large barn on the other.

It is beautiful. The plants bloom in every color on a small patio just beyond the front door.

"What's this, Raul?"

"You will see."

The sun is beginning to grow weaker as the night takes over. Raul sees that Rachel is looking at his gold watch that lays on the seat next to him.

"Don't worry, I will get you to the church on time," he says, speaking of their concert in a few hours.

It isn't until Raul pulls to a stop and Rachel begins to climb out that she sees that Raul is not intending to stay. She looks at him strangely until she hears footsteps behind her and turns. Levi is walking up a steep hill alongside the grapes. His boots are filthy, but it's obvious by the smile on his face that he's happy. Just before Raul drives away, he calls out, "I will be back to pick you up for the concert tonight, Miss Praline."

A cool breeze blows her hair out of her eyes, while she debates jumping back into the car, but by the time she decides, Levi is too close to back away, especially once she smells the soap on his skin.

"Should I blame Raul for me standing here?"

"I do pay him well."

After a moment of weighty hesitation, she looks away. "Yesterday was the first day that I didn't think about you every second."

He breathes until his chest puffs up and then he lets it go. "So, I've made a mistake then?"

Instead of responding, she tries to hold back any answer and hide the deep sadness that wants to drag her knees out from under her. With one foot in front of the other she takes the small stone path down the hill he just climbed, perhaps to give her time, perhaps to see if he'll follow. It does both. However, the sound of his shoes just behind her means that soon he'll close the distance between them which places her right back to the confusion from where she started.

"Wine is a distraction." His voice is an even tone, not too

aggressive and not too passive, but it still pulls at her breath, nonetheless.

"I didn't think successful men like yourself allow distractions."

He looks at her with such intensity, it says more than any words. Finally, he takes a step forward and lays his hand so close to hers on the fence, that she closes her eyes. She isn't surprised when she feels that he's now stepped behind her, pressing his chest against her back, as he subtly wraps his hand around her waist. Just this act alone drives a small gasp from her. "Right now, distractions are my only lifeline," he says quietly, as his breath skims along her neck and shoulder as it used to when they were making love.

"It's been so long," she whispers.

"Do you want to see it?"

This forces her eyes open with surprise. "What?"

"My distraction?" he grins.

"Oh." They walk side by side, through the long rows of vines, each wanting to touch the other, but neither reaching out to do so. For many minutes they travel his acreage, returning to the small home on the property. He opens the door for her and they step inside a desperately simplistic, in a very aged sort of way, one-bedroom home with a fireplace, a kitchen, and a bathroom.

"Don't know that I've ever known you in something so small," Rachel nods.

"This is how I would live if I had the choice."

"Do you not have the choice?"

"Some are good at making them, and I'm not," he says.

She thinks of what Bernie would want for her as she stands there staring at the man she loves. He's a married man, and Bernie would have warned her to run, run far away. The turmoil in Rachel's sigh curls her stomach.

It takes only moments to walk every inch of the small place, and before long she doesn't know what else to do but look at him with question. "Why am I here, Levi?"

"I had to talk to you."

"I hope you take no offense, but talking to you doesn't feel good for my soul and I'd prefer to go home." One tear, careful and crafty not to fall for some time, finally runs down her cheek and she quickly tries to brush it away.

His eyes tell her he's sorry, his chest rises and falls with confusion, but even still, the floor creaks as he comes closer. When he's within a short enough distance, he reaches out and touches the line of moisture along her skin. "You asked me before if I am happy…" She says nothing, so he continues, "It's not possible. Not since California."

For a moment she almost allows him in, then steps back. "You chose to marry another woman!" As the heat rises from her chest to her cheeks, he doesn't respond. "Why!" After a moment of silence, she comes toward him angrily. "Why!" Again, nothing. "Why!" This time she shoves his shoulders back, but he's like a dense wall and will not budge. "You ruined everything!"

"I know," he says confidently, and when she goes to push him again, he grabs her wrists with his hands. "I never loved her."

"Then, why?" Rachel slows down, hoping for a response that will take all the pain away.

"I thought she would help me forget you. Then she got pregnant and with our business dealings . . ." He shakes his head.

"It's done. There is nothing---"

He interrupts her, "Rachel, although you make my desire to be out of this marriage worse, it is not because of you. I haven't been happy for a long time and neither has Kendra."

"Marriage is forever, right?"

"I would like it to be . . ." he looks directly into her eyes.

"I mean we don't get the choice to just say it's not working for us right now and get out."

"You're right."

Frustration builds as her heart beats rapidly. "Why am I here, Levi?"

"Not for what you think. I will not be unfaithful to my wife."

Even though she doesn't want to be the cause of an affair, the fact that he has brought her here just to tell her this, enrages her.

"Then what are you doing, Levi! I don't need to be here for your mistakes. Make a choice and stick with it, but don't bring me here to torture me." Rachel turns to race out the door, but he fights to be heard.

"Rachel! She's having an affair."

With her hand on the door handle, she stops, closes her eyes and breathes.

"She's having an affair. I'm sorry, Rachel. I didn't…that wasn't my intention. I just had to be with you. You're a friend as much as my lover and . . . my wife has been having an affair."

"How do you know?"

"I've known from the beginning. I knew when we were getting married that she was in love with someone else, but…" he grins, "…I was, too."

"Levi, I don't understand. How would you just live like this? You're okay with her having an affair?"

"No. Never. Don't get me wrong. I knew she was in love with someone else when we got married, but she promised she would be faithful, and I expected her to do that."

"Levi! I'm so confused. Why did this happen?!" She cries out as her throat clenches. "Why is it never simple?"

He hurries to her, but she pulls away. "Rachel."

"No, Levi. It's too much."

"Rachel," he says again, this time softer than before. Slowly he comes behind her running his hands along her arms. "I don't know why all this happened. With you, it all came so easy. Everything worked. But with her it's always been on her terms. And it's shown me that I don't want this anymore. I just wanted to tell you that I'm ending it with her. I want to do the right thing."

Rachel turns and places her hands on his chest. For a moment they are silent as the birds sing outside. He drops his lips to just an inch above hers, but smiles instead. "One day, this will all make sense. We have to believe that." Dropping just slightly again, she's anxious for him to finish, desperately hoping to feel his lips again.

"What are you doing?" she asks, more breathless than she'd hoped.

He grins, "Trying to help you understand why you belong to me. Do you feel it?"

"Always."

Just then, Raul's car hurries down the dirt path, telling them, they only have a few minutes. "Just one kiss," he requests.

Finally, Levi kisses her, quickly opening her mouth with his tongue and cleverly convincing her that she needs more. Immediately, they both realize it's not a good idea, but it's too late now, especially when he begins to wrap his fingers within her hair and pull. He lifts her in his arms, but then, he stops—but still holding her tight. They are both breathless, as he stares at her. "How long do you think Raul can wait?"

She quickly smiles, "I wish I could feel your skin."

He chuckles, then groans, "If only you knew."

"Then why not?" she says getting closer to his mouth.

"Rachel . . ." before he can finish, she kisses him again. This time they lose all of their senses. He wraps his arms tighter around her waist. Their bodies melt into each other and Rachel tears at his shirt to get it open. Neither one of them notices when a couple of his buttons hit the floor, followed by his shirt. He lays her on the couch never lifting his mouth—both afraid that if they take any time to think, they will have to stop. He is gentle with the buttons of her dress and finally it comes open revealing that in the warm weather she hasn't worn a slip, only her undergarments. He kisses her neck, then her chest and runs his hand down her stomach to her thighs. It isn't until Raul honks the horn that they both look up. Both of them chuckle and take a second to breathe.

"I won't be like her," he whispers.

Rachel nods. "I know. Just lay here with me?"

"No," he smiles.

"Will Raul tell?"

"He knows about Kendra. Not only that, but everyone knows about you…"

"What?"

"They know about my past with you. Raul knew from that first night when he saw us together."

"He did?"

"Yes. I think it was rather obvious by our faces and I spoke to him long ago of our story."

"Do you trust yourself to be with me again after the concert tonight?"

He sits on the couch hoping that he can resist. "I can't. I'm supposed to go with Kendra."

"Oh."

"But we'll figure something out."

Raul honks again since the time is getting scarily late. Rachel jumps up to work on her dress. She looks up when Levi laughs. "I don't think there is much hiding it," he says lifting the side of the shirt where there should be buttons. Rachel laughs. She walks to him and before he opens the door she gives him one last kiss, to which he growls for her being so cruel.

§ § §

Carlotta Rizzo, along with Kendra and Levi, appear extravagant as they sit in the theater in the most expensive seats. Rachel's voice is, as usual, miraculous and Levi can't help but lean forward in his seat. It doesn't matter than Kendra notices.

Meanwhile, Chuck's usual praise after the show doesn't come, rather she finds him staring at Levi when he and Kendra come to give their greetings.

"Rachel, you were just wonderful," Kendra says with a smile, her long dark hair shining under the lights and her makeup accentuating her perfect Italian features.

"Thank you."

"I have a surprise for you," Kendra laughs with pride when she turns around and Alan, the American from the very first dinner at Carlotta's, is standing at the door of the church.

"I was hoping that we could all catch a drink tonight," Kendra says happily.

Levi and Rachel stand like stone as Alan saunters over.

"Rachel, you were amazing as always," Alan says, taking her hand and kissing it.

"Kendra, I think that Rachel should be able to rest after her concerts." Levi suggests.

"I am quite tired," Rachel admits.

"Oh, nonsense!" Kendra laughs. "I know for a fact that you have no rehearsal tomorrow! I spoke to Chuck myself. I do my homework."

"You spoke to Chuck?" Rachel asks with her heart beating out of her chest.

"I did." Kendra says, and she looks Rachel directly in the eye. There's something there. It lasts just a second, but whatever it is, scares Rachel. "Chuck gave you up easily. Don't be shy, Rachel. Alan's a good man. Just one date. How hard could it be?"

"Just let me change?"

Soon, the two couples are sitting side by side in a quiet restaurant in the heart of town. Rachel finds herself being overly cautious. Every look at Levi she wonders if Kendra has noticed. They try to keep from speaking to each other unless it is called for in the conversation. Alan pays the utmost attention to Rachel and she is kind. He is a good-looking man with a lot of wit and she can appreciate this about him, but the man she loves is sitting across the table.

Kendra orders food for all of them, but Rachel isn't hungry. Instead, she wants something to drink, heavy and strong. Rachel raises her hand to get the waitress's attention and as she does, Levi does the exact same thing. The waitress laughs when she wonders which one to answer first.

"Ladies first," Levi says with a grin.

"Okay. I would like a shot of whiskey if you wouldn't mind," Rachel says quietly.

"And you, sir," the waitress asks.

Levi smiles, "Same thing, please."

Levi and Rachel finally look at each other, but before long they notice that the talking at the end of the table has stopped because Kendra and Alan are watching them. Instantly, Levi leans in to Kendra, lessening the distance between them.

"I was just telling Alan about the new hotel you've just bought in New Jersey," Kendra explains.

"Yes, it sounds fascinating," Alan says as he moves his chair closer to Rachel. "Why New Jersey?"

Rachel can't help but hold her breath at this information. "New Jersey?"

"I've always had a heart for the boardwalk in Atlantic City," Levi says uncomfortably. "I've been looking into this property for quite some time now and the owner just recently decided he would like to sell."

"A hotel in Atlantic City," Alan says with envy. He turns to Rachel, "Can you believe that?"

"No, I can't," she says softly.

"Have you ever been?" Alan asks.

She should have lied, but strangely she doesn't want to. "I was born there."

Suddenly Kendra is interested. "You were?"

"Yes, I was."

Alan—captivated by everything she says—leans in closer and places his head on his fist as his elbow rests on the table. "So where do you live now, Rachel, when you aren't traveling?"

Rachel hesitates and looks at Levi for just a second, but he only smiles. "In Atlantic City."

"Well, I'll be," Alan chuckles. "I'm in New York. I should come see you sometime. Then, maybe Levi, I could stay at your hotel."

"Of course. You're always welcome," Levi nods.

Kendra seeming to be stuck on a bit of information looks at Rachel. "Have you always been in Atlantic City?"

"Yes, unless I'm traveling." Rachel's hands are beginning to sweat and she is happy when the whiskey comes to their table. Swiftly, both Levi and Rachel gulp down their liquor.

Levi grabs his glass and hers before the waitress can leave. "Bring us two more."

"So, your family is there?" Kendra prods deeper.

"Yes."

"Who?"

"Excuse me?"

"Who in your family is there?"

"My mother."

"You have no other family?"

"No."

"Where's your father?"

Levi interrupts, "Kendra."

"I'm simply getting to know her, is all. Where is your father?"

Rachel hesitates, "He died a few years ago." Once again, Rachel can see that there is something off in the way that Kendra is looking at her.

"I'm sorry about that," Alan says sympathetically.

"Was he your real father?" Kendra asks—her face showing an even better understanding.

"Kendra!" Levi is now angry. "You don't ask these personal questions. You hardly know her."

"I'm just trying to get to know her," Kendra says sounding angry with him. "Answer the question, Rachel."

"No," Rachel stops, but Levi nods for her to continue. It is only now that Alan notices the strange exchange happening at the table. "I was an orphan and passed on to a woman named Bernie. After she died, I was taken to New York to live with a horrible man who did horrible things to me. Do you need me to continue? Tell you everything?"

"I think I would." Kendra's eyes are pinched with jealousy.

Alan uncomfortably speaks up, "Rachel, you don't need to share this. Kendra, what is going on?"

"Alan, be quiet." Kendra is no longer beautiful, rather her foul expression changes everything.

"Do I need to tell you more, Kendra? My birth mother killed my father, perhaps, so nobody knew what to do with me and no one wanted me? That Bill Manchuron assaulted me and forced me to sing until I stopped talking for many years? Which part of my story are you most interested in?" Rachel can feel the flush of embarrassment from her ambush.

"I'm not sure you didn't deserve every bit of it." The words come out like the hiss of a snake.

"Enough, Kendra!" Levi now yells. He jumps to his feet nearly knocking over the tables.

Kendra grabs her purse and smiles. "I'm not feeling well, I think I should go." She walks out of the restaurant with angry steps.

When they sit back down Alan shakes his head. "Is she always like that? She's a rather difficult woman. No offense, Levi and I'm sorry Rachel."

"None taken. She is just that."

The waitress brings more whiskey to the table and this time Alan joins.

"Should you go after her?" Rachel asks.

"Just give her a few moments," Levi answers.

"I would really love a smoke right now, but I seem to have run out. There's a little market on the corner," Alan says. "Would you like to come with me?"

"No, I'm fine. Thank you," Rachel replies.

When he is gone Rachel looks at Levi with serious eyes. "What just happened?"

"It seems she's just connected the dots. She's a grown woman and we haven't done anything, Rachel." Rachel lifts an eyebrow, and he laughs. "Okay, we've almost done nothing, but I know where I stand and I did nothing to bring you here. You came on your own."

"You wanted her to find out about me?"

"Rachel, I'm not playing games. If she wants to figure out that you're the one I've talked about, then she has all the right to."

"Now what do we do?"

"You don't have to do anything. I'm figuring out my marriage, you don't have to be a part of it."

"Levi, you bought a hotel in Atlantic City?"

"Yes. It's been in the works since before I was even married. I thought that it would give me a better chance of finding you. Besides, I got it for a steal since the owner lost nearly everything after…"

They both know he is talking about another victim of the stock market crash.

"After you steal these properties from these people are they upset with you?"

"No. I don't do it maliciously, Rachel. In fact, most of them are grateful since I try and do it without dealing nearly as much with the banks. I like to keep it as personal as possible. This man just sent me a thank you letter. I'll let you read it."

"You know, I would have been leaving tonight."

"What do you mean?"

"We were supposed to be done tonight, but Chuck has extended our shows."

"Good." Levi stares at Rachel for a moment, but as Alan walks back to the table, he stands up and closes his jacket. "I think I need to go find Kendra."

He never comes back to the table. Days later, while the choir prepares for Benito Mussolini, and Chuck ignores her, Rachel and Minnie walk arm in arm wherever they go.

Finally, when Benito Mussolini sits powerfully in the VIP section, he watches the concert with a straight expression until the very last number. Only then is he the first to stand after Rachel's solo and hollers praises for a job done well.

Chuck comes to Rachel's side as they walk off stage. "Rachel!" he says excitedly. "He has asked to meet you."

"Who?"

"Benito Mussolini."

Rachel places her hand on her stomach as the nerves explode before she meets the Prime Minister of Italy. Swallowed by several agents surrounding him, Benito Mussolini walks across the stage with affluence and pride. He seems soundly confident and when he sees Rachel, he lifts his hands in the air and begins to clap above his head. A man next to him whispers something in his ear just as they reach her. He nods and immediately begins speaking in English.

"Very good," he says in a deep Italian accent. "I just had to come to meet you. Your voice is beautiful."

"Thank you."

"What a beautiful woman you are also."

Chuck, who is standing next to her, is bouncing with excitement as he looks at the famous leader.

"I am pleased that you could come," Rachel says softly.

"Very good," he says like a proud father, "very good." He speaks to her for some time and then quickly hurries off with a swarm of men behind him.

At this time, when all the rumblings of power in Europe are just under the surface, it is believed that Mussolini would side with France, but in the end, his fascist regime joins forces with Nazi Germany. Years later, she sees pictures of his hanging body in the newspaper. It is difficult for her to imagine this dictator as the same man who once told her of her beauty.

After Mussolini walks away Rachel and Chuck stand motion-less, until Chuck walks away without so much as a word. "Chuck?" Rachel calls out.

"I have to go. It's late, Rachel. Good night."

Later, Raul drives Rachel and Minnie home. When they pull into the drive, Mrs. Rizzo is sitting on a bench outside their cottage door. Carlotta never visits them here.

"I wonder what she wants?" Minnie says with concern.

"Yeah," Rachel agrees.

As Rachel and Minnie step out of the car hesitantly, Mrs. Rizzo stands. "Well done, ladies!" she calls out.

"You were there, Mrs. Rizzo?" Minnie asks.

"Of course. I always go to the last concert of the season—espe-cially if our Prime Minister plans to attend. My, wasn't that amazing?"

The girls agree. Then, she comes to Rachel's side and places her arm over her shoulders. "I want you to come with me," she says sweetly.

"Would you like me to come?" Minnie asks with concern.

"No, why don't you stay here. She'll be back in just a little while."

Minnie gives Rachel a nervous eye, but Rachel ignores it. Car-lotta doesn't seem upset. Together, at nearly midnight, Carlotta leads Rachel along the stone path. "Rachel, I know that you are a sweet girl, and I have loved having you here and listening to your voice, but it seems we have a problem."

Rachel's heart grows wild and tramples the rest of her insides. "A problem?"

"Yes. You know what it is."

They reach the front door and instantly, Rachel can hear voices from inside. When Carlotta opens it, the muted voices turn into furious tones, so Rachel plants her feet forcing Carlotta to push her.

"Carlotta . . . I can't."

"Yes, you can, my dear." For the first time, her sing-song pitch turns sour, and Rachel can see the rage in her tense lips.

Kendra is screaming in Levi's face while he crosses his arms, refusing to engage. Just as Kendra reaches up to strike him, he catches her wrist with his quick hand. "Don't touch me, Kendra." That's when Carlotta clears her throat, informing them that they are being watched. When they turn, Rachel immediately notices Levi's red face and the resentment in his eyes.

"I shouldn't be here," Rachel says quickly and tries to leave. However, Carlotta blocks the way and forces Rachel farther into the kitchen.

"No!" Levi yells. "What the hell are you doing, Carlotta?" Levi hurries to Rachel and takes her hand, while standing between them.

"We need her here."

"Absolutely we do not. Rachel, let's go." He protectively walks with her past the kitchen and into the dining room where the patio door is standing open. But Carlotta throws herself in front of him.

"Levi!"

"Carlotta," he says with very controlled offense, "I suggest you let us go. This is not about her."

"I think it is, Levi," Carlotta says smoothly, unmoved by his anger.

"I shouldn't be here," Rachel whispers again.

"We must figure this out," Carlotta states.

"No, we don't. It's figured out." Levi clenches his jaw, doing his best to not let his rage take over.

"You see! You still love her," Kendra yells accusingly. "Are you going to tell me that you haven't had an affair?"

There is a pause as if Levi knows the truth doesn't matter to them. "You know that I haven't. I've told you over and over, Kendra."

"But what about Chuck? Is he wrong?"

"Chuck?" Rachel asks, surprised.

Just then, as if he's been hiding, Chuck emerges from the dark corners of the kitchen. "Rachel, I . . ." he begins.

"What are you doing? You know the truth," Rachel berates him.

"I don't know that I do."

Rachel stops, takes a breath, then shakes her head. "Chuck, I see right through you. I turn you down and here you are." Levi looks at her with question and unease as he squeezes her hand. Rachel looks at Kendra, then Carlotta, "Did he tell you that he kissed me and I said no? Then he kicked me out of his office."

Kendra looks directly at her. "Why did you say no?"

"Because I don't feel for him that way. Chuck, tell them that I was not with Levi."

"I don't know that," he whispers.

Levi keeps his hand protectively around hers. "I don't give a damn what Chuck wants to say. But what does it matter, Kendra? I'm leaving anyway, I talked to you about it months before Rachel came. You've stolen from me, from my businesses. You and your mother. And you used my accident to get what you wanted."

"I'll take everything from you!" Kendra screams with anger.

"That's all you've ever wanted anyway." Levi turns back to Carlotta. "Let us leave, Carlotta."

"Are you afraid? Are you afraid that she'll see what kind of man you are?" Kendra hisses.

"I know what kind of man he is," Rachel says quickly, then looks at Chuck.

"Oh, you do?"

"Yes. More than you ever will."

Suddenly, Kendra shoots across the room reaching for Rachel, but Levi blocks the way. He struggles to keep the wild woman away, without hurting her. "Get ahold of yourself, Kendra!" Levi yells.

"You bitch!" Kendra yells.

"Carlotta, take your daughter before she hurts herself or someone else."

Carlotta shakes her head. "You married my daughter. You get yourself out of this mess."

Levi glares at the mother and daughter. "I have been faithful to every woman in my life. You know that? Let's bring Fernan over here and talk about Kendra's indiscretions."

Kendra stops suddenly—enough that Levi can let go of her—but her eyes are still severe with anger as if at any moment she will lose control again.

"I don't know what you are talking about." Kendra lies.

"I'm talking about the man who told me one month after we married that he had never stopped sleeping with you and didn't plan to. The man whom you left for Paris with last month and he answered the phone when I called your hotel. You'll be speaking with my lawyers from now on." Levi pulls a few pictures from his pants pockets and throws them on the counter next to Kendra. Even Carlotta leans over to see what they are. Both women's eyes widen with surprise.

"That's right. I hired someone and he followed you to the hotel with Fernan. If you think you have anything on me, you don't. Let us go or I'll make it worse for you." Levi maintains his composure, then leads Rachel out the back door, past a silenced Carlotta. Without a word, they walk through the gardens listening to the screams still coming from the house but heading straight to the vehicle.

"Grab Minnie," he says, "I'm putting you up in a hotel tonight."

"Levi?" She can feel the rage through the shake of his hand, so she pulls him to a stop once they are close to her cottage. At first, he won't look at her, then finally, he does. She hadn't expected to see sadness.

"I made the biggest mistake of my life. What have I done?"

She reaches up and runs her hands in his hair. Then finally, he pulls her into his arms. "Are you okay?" Rachel whispers.

"I am now. I've had the divorce papers for six months and brought them over tonight. This was why they are so upset."

"If she's in love with someone else, then why is she fighting so hard?"

They walk the rest of the steps to her cottage. "Carlotta lost their family's wealth. Bad business decisions, gambling, drinking. If I go, they have no more income and these are women who rely very much on money."

"Oh."

"If I divorce her then I will pay alimony, but she wants more than that. She started screaming that you and I have had an affair."

"Is that why you stayed away from me?"

"No." He sighs. "Rachel, I've made a lot of mistakes in my life, but I'd like to think that I'm a decent human being. I stayed away because I couldn't bring myself to cheat." He rubs his face, "Rachel, I don't care about any of this money."

"You don't? But you've worked so hard for it."

"My intention was never to get rich, only to do what I love."

They are quiet for a moment. "Go get your stuff and Minnie. Let's get out of here."

"I'm leaving tomorrow."

"I know." He says, "If I can get her to sign the papers, I will leave with you."

"You will?"

"And if I don't, then I'll come later."

"But we'll be sure that actually happens, right?" she smiles.

He grins, but then grows serious. "What happened with Chuck?"

"He kissed me . . . the other day."

"He did?"

"Yeah. It was completely unexpected and when I told him that I didn't think of him that way . . . he threw me out and has been horrible ever since."

"It's taking everything in my power not to walk back into that house for Chuck."

"Levi? Chuck doesn't matter. If I haven't crumbled from the other things in my life, then I certainly can handle Chuck Gerber. You don't need to save me again."

He grins now that things have calmed and he places a palm on her face. "I will always try."

Levi pulls her into him and wraps his arms around her. "I'm sorry Rachel. This is just chaos. Listen, you go and pack. I'll take you to a hotel, then tomorrow we'll figure everything out."

Before long, Minnie sits in the back seat, while Levi drives them to the nearest hotel. He pays for a room with two beds. At the door, he kisses her, then her forehead.

"Where will you go tonight?" Rachel asks.

"I'll stay in your cottage. I have to get the papers signed. Then I'll try to meet you at the train station. Sleep well. I'm going to fix this."

§ § §

The next morning, there is a knock on the hotel door as Rachel and Minnie sleep. Rachel pulls herself out of bed. It surprises her when Kendra—prim and proper—stands on the other side of the door. Her face is serious, but not angry like the night before.

"Kendra?"

"Sorry to bother you so early this morning, but I felt as though you needed to know something."

"Why are you here?"

"I am pregnant," Kendra confides as tears come to her eyes. "It's Levi's."

Rachel hears nothing but the tearing of her own heart. Her body feels as flimsy as paper and she holds the door tightly to keep from collapsing. A baby. Kendra suddenly looks more vulnerable than ever with a tear in her eye.

"I must ask for you to think of this child."

"How do I believe you?"

"Here." She hands Rachel a sheet of paper.

Rachel opens it and reads the doctor's confirmation that Kendra is indeed pregnant.

"How am I supposed to know that it is Levi's?"

"I can promise you that it is. The dates match."

"Does Levi know?"

"He does now. I told him this morning. I knew he would take you to this hotel. We own it." Something deviant passes within her eyes, but Rachel is trapped, as is Levi.

"Please leave," Rachel says softly—too close to tears to be comfortable with Kendra standing there. Rachel shuts the door. Quietly, the wood clicks into place with Kendra still standing on the other side.

Minnie is watching Rachel in disbelief. "Rachel? Do you believe it?"

Rachel falls to her knees, the pain consuming her until she can't speak. Minnie runs to her and wraps her arms around her. "I'm so sorry, Rachel."

"I can't breathe," Rachel whispers. Her sorrow is beyond measure. A baby is the one thing she can't stand in the way of, and before long her sobs turn into wheezing as she tries to suck enough breath into her lungs. "I have to talk to Simone!" she cries.

Within an hour Minnie and Rachel have found the nearest telephone and when she hears Simone's voice on the other end, this is the first time she can properly breathe.

Once Rachel tells her the entire story, Simone's deep and confident voice responds with, "Come home. You have to let him handle it. Just come home. And tell this Chuck I'll be reaching out."

No one answers things like Simone. Rachel wipes her eyes, writes a note to Levi then she gives it to the woman at the front desk. Within the hour, Ephod and Minnie stand on each side of Rachel as the rest of the choir congregates around them, completely unaware of the night she just had. Every few minutes Rachel looks for Levi, wondering if he'll rush in and tell her that none of it is true, but by the time the train horn blows and the conductor calls, he hasn't come.

"What did you say in the letter?" Ephod asks.

"He is free to do what he needs to do," she whispers.

Ephod nods sadly, then places an arm around her as they climb into the train car. She doesn't even look up as the train begins chugging along the tracks.

"It will be alright," Minnie says compassionately.

"I know," she whispers—afraid that if she speaks any louder, she'll break into a thousand pieces.

"Rachel, you said it yourself. Levi is a smart man and he's someone you respect. There must be a reason that he didn't come."

"We know the reason."

Not too long into their journey, Chuck walks down the aisle and stops in front of Rachel. "We need to talk."

"I have nothing to say to you." Rachel says, emotionless. Ephod and Minnie sit closer to her, showing that he cannot have their seats.

"Rachel, I had no other choice to---" he stops before he says more.

"To what, Chuck? To tell someone lies about me?"

"I didn't tell her, she just assumed."

"And I'm sure you had nothing to do with that."

Everyone around is pretending that they aren't interested in this conversation as the smell of roast beef sandwiches wafts in from the sandwich cart, but even the waitress keeps eyeing Chuck with a sideways glance. Chuck notices but he's needy enough to continue anyway.

"Rachel, I can't lose you."

Rachel finally looks him directly in the eye. "You can. You have."

He leans forward to keep what he's about to say private in a group of thirty people. "I had it on good authority about you and Mr. Price."

"Good authority; who would that be?" Rachel looks around the car and her eyes fall on Vonna who sits beside the window a few feet back with a smug expression.

"Minnie…you shared a room with me every night…did you see a married man in my bed?"

"No, I sure didn't."

"Rachel, now please let's talk about this like rational adults."

"Rational, like when you kicked me out of your hotel room after I wouldn't kiss you." The entire train car seems to suck in air all at once and hold it so that they don't miss another word. Rachel watches the eyes of everyone around widen, but she doesn't care. She is tired of games and she doesn't want to play anymore. How was she so wrong about Chuck? "Is that your version of rational…because I can play along if you'd like?"

"Rachel…Rachel," Chuck begs.

"Was it Vonna that saw me with Levi?" Rachel calls out over the passengers. The older woman glares at Rachel and although Rachel knows she is making assumptions, she can see by Vonna's expression that she is right.

One of the choir members has on her lap a magazine with Rachel's face on the cover. She reaches out to take it from her and shows it to Chuck. "Let's be clear, this is why you don't want me to quit. Vonna?" She turns to the older woman, "Every solo is yours now. I give my resignation."

"Me too." Minnie agrees.

Chapter Twenty Four

1933

Simone is waiting for Rachel and Minnie at the dock, dressed in her navy-blue business dress, and a matching hat. In a slow and burdened walk, Rachel reaches her best friend and grabs her for a hug as Minnie follows closely behind. "Come on, let's get you home." Simone says with compassion.

Minnie sticks her hand out to Simone, "It's nice to meet you, I'm Minnie."

Simone smiles. "Welcome, Minnie. Hold on for the ride."

Later that evening as they sit around the table in the same tiny apartment with Sylvia, they drink until their heads are fuzzy. "I can't believe all that happened," Sylvia whispers somberly.

"We're going to be broke quick if I don't figure something out," Rachel laments.

"We don't need to worry too much." Sylvia says as she gets up with a small wobble from the table. "Two hundred dollars is a lot of money each month and, since you've been gone, I have been saving everything I could." She pulls out a small box from under her bed. When she opens it, a pile of bills is neatly stacked inside. "I didn't want you traveling forever, so I saved everything I could."

Minnie, Simone, and Rachel all chuckle at her resourcefulness. "Besides, I got a job working for Simone!"

"What?" Rachel says.

Simone shrugs, "She's my assistant. Her phone and typing skills are top notch."

"So, you're a lawyer?" Minnie asks a bit in disbelief.

Simone looks her straight in the eye. "I am. Even if the state doesn't recognize it." Rachel smiles and clinks her glass with Simone's. "I'm working on a case right now with John Ipson for a woman who wants to divorce her husband. Of course, the man is horrible and of course they're trying to make sure she can't get it done." Simone smiles, "But we're helping her."

"Can she do that?" Minnie says with wide eyes.

"Divorce him?" Simone asks.

"Yes."

"Not at the moment, but she will. You can trust me on that."

Sylvia lays down on her bed and closes her eyes. "I'm tired, ladies. Don't mind me. Oh, and the room is spinning."

They all laugh and decide with a quick nod to move out onto the creaky old patio. Outside the stars are out, kids are still playing on the street, and Mrs. Farley is hitting her hanging throw rugs with a fireplace poker sending dust billowing out from two doors down. "Hey Mrs. Farley!" the ladies holler.

"Oh hello, ladies!" The small woman who was brought over by ship from Cuba just a few years ago has a thick accent. "Cards tomorrow?"

Rachel looks at Simone with question. "Yep!" Simone answers. "Tomorrow!" Then she turns to the other ladies as she fills their glasses again. "Sylvia got so bored, she started a card night or two a week."

Rachel chuckles and shakes her head, "I can't even imagine."

"Well imagine it. Women sit around playing cards, drinking, and talking about their husbands. It's become quite a hit. I just can't stay as late as the others because I have to work."

There is a moment of silence and then Rachel becomes serious. "I hope you can help her get a divorce."

Even though she's speaking of Simone's client, it's obvious that this means more to Rachel than some woman she doesn't know.

Simone takes in a big breath. "Why didn't he come to the train station?"

Tears form in Rachel's eyes, but she's too drunk to care. "It doesn't matter. I'm sure he's doing the right thing."

Simone raises an eyebrow at her friend. "Oh, hush up. It does matter and I wish I could give him a piece of my mind."

"And her." Minnie chimes in, then looks at Simone, "Simone, this woman is just awful. After his accident she took over his businesses while he was hurt. He never knew some of the damage she had done until after they married. She's continued to have an affair all while they have been married and now she's saying she's with child."

It suddenly occurs to Minnie that Rachel might not want to be hearing it all again, so she quiets quickly. "I'm sorry, Rachel."

"Everything you said is right." Her words are slurring. "Let's just see if I can move on."

As a tear falls down her cheek, Simone and Minnie reach out and touch her hand with theirs.

§ § §

Six months after returning from Italy, it is February of 1934. This is the year when Alcatraz becomes a federal prison, the Flash Gordon comic strip is released, the majority of Germans elect Hitler as Fuhrer, and the Indian Reorganization Act aims at decreasing federal control of American Indian affairs and increasing self-governance and responsibility.

"You'll never believe who moved in downstairs," Simone grins as she walks Rachel to a door and knocks with her knuckle. After a moment, Chepi, opens the door. Her husband, also from her tribe, sits in the living room reading.

"Chepi!" Rachel hugs her.

"She has the fastest hand," Simone laughs.

Before long, Chepi is the dealer to nearly eight women from all different walks of life in Sylvia and Rachel's apartment. Most of them poor as church mice, sit around the small table playing cards, while they drink until their minds ignore their poverty. So far, Mrs. Farley is winning the pile of pennies.

Widows, wives, or never married, they all look forward to Thursday nights, but they tell no one, not even their husbands. What lie these women tell, no one ever asks. If men knew about it, they would be appalled, so they all keep it secret. Even some women with children are able to sneak away from time to time, leaving their children with their mothers. Every Thursday from 8 o'clock until midnight.

During the day, each of them work until they can barely see straight and their clothes seem to become more haggard as the days progress. When Rachel is still, she finds it hard to keep her mind off Levi, which is the very reason she stays as busy as possible. As Chepi pours herself another glass of wine, Simone declines a refill. Everyone in the room stops talking.

"What?" Simone asks. Still no one says anything, then finally she grins. "I was hoping to tell Rachel first but since you are all such busy bodies . . . fine. Reed and I are expecting."

They are quiet for a moment then everyone screams. Only when the old lady, Miss Percy, from below hits the floor with the end of her broom do they quiet down.

"Don't you be telling people. I still have my cases to work on and I won't have them stripped from me," Simone warns them.

"Why would you ruin your life like this," Carla Mae, a straight-shooting woman says as she shakes her head.

"Children are a blessing," Chepi says as she deals the cards again.

"Is this what you wanted?" Carla Mae asks.

Simone turns abruptly to the brown-haired woman from Cuba, "Carla, would you shut your mouth? Of course I want this. Reed can hardly see straight, he's so excited. He believes it's going to be a boy, and I'm convinced it's a girl."

The next day, Rachel, Simone, and Minnie walk arm in arm down the boardwalk, finally getting to discuss the secret. "I can't believe it." Rachel says.

"Honestly, neither can I." Simone admits. "We tried for a while, but I had given up hope, then one day . . . everything was different."

"Maybe someday it'll actually be you and me, Rachel," Minnie grins.

Rachel nods, "I don't know that I want kids or to even get married for that fact."

Minnie and Simone both stop and look at her.

"What?" Rachel exclaims. "Why would I want to? More heartbreak? I don't know. Besides, I'm already an old woman. I think my time is done," Rachel says looking out into the ocean as the sun sparkles along the waves.

"Oh hush, now." Simone shakes her head. "Just because women tend to have babies at nineteen does not mean your time has passed. You've traveled the world and met people, which is more than what most can say."

"That's right, Rachel." Minnie grabs Rachel's arm as though she too is invigorated by what Simone just said. "We have seen the world. We are what you call, bona fide…"

Rachel grins.

They soon pass an empty restaurant Rachel and her parents frequented when she was younger. "It seems they went out of business," Simone says with a shake of her head. "It seems the world is going to be out of business soon."

Rachel and Simone both notice a man in a police uniform walking their way.

"Oh, here we go." Simone growls.

"What's wrong?" Minnie asks.

He reaches them but before he can speak, Rachel cuts him off, "What is it we can do for you?"

He chuckles and places his thumbs in his belt loops. "You know damn well . . . What are you doing?"

"What do you mean? We are here to enjoy the sun and sounds of the boardwalk," Simone says with a roll of her eyes.

"Well, people don't want you here." he smirks. It isn't until he speaks that they recognize his voice. Officer Hannah, the officer who had been Finnegan's confidante, is much older now. "It's just the rules."

"They don't want me here, or is it the rules that I can't be here? What exactly are you saying, Officer Hannah?" Simone asks, specifically calling him by name.

His expression changes and he looks the women over, "How'd you . . ." However, he stops, and it is obvious that he has connected the dots. He looks Rachel up and down suggestively. "Well, you turned out didn't you?"

"Don't know what you mean by that, Officer Hannah." The anger is building until her hands are sweating.

"What was his name . . . that nigger boy who you liked that we hung on the church lawn?"

Rachel is praying that he doesn't say Jake's name. Again and again, the thought repeats, Don't say his name, don't say his name. Simone's hand is squeezing Rachel's until it hurts.

"Oh yeah, Jake. That's the kid you gave your soul to the devil for." Officer Hannah steps closer to Rachel, but she stands firm.

"What's happening here?" The three ladies turn to see John Ipson, the District Attorney who Simone works for, coming out of a nearby restaurant. It looks as if he was not yet finished eating, as he wipes his hands with a napkin. Rachel and Minnie still have no idea who this very Jewish looking man is.

Officer Hannah steps back suddenly, giving them space. John takes place beside the women. "Are you ladies okay? Simone? Is Officer Hannah bothering you?"

"As a matter of fact, he is." Simone stares directly into Officer Hannah's eyes.

"Officer Hannah, is there something I can help you with?"

"Nah, nah," he brings his hands up as if in defense and shrugs. "Just making sure everything is safe. It's my job, Mr. Ipson."

"Well, I'm sure you can tell now that they are doing just fine without you."

Officer Hannah breathes out in frustration and turns to leave when he says under his breath, "Whatever you say, kike."

John steps forward, "Excuse me, Officer Hannah." Officer Hannah turns with a bitter expression as John has pulled out his pad of paper from his shirt pocket. "I'll make sure to reach out to your superior."

With that, Officer Hannah walks away angrily. When John turns back to the ladies he has a smile on his face, "There's a reason he's still just an officer at his age. I've been keeping a close watch on him for a while now after he gave my sister trouble here."

"Thank you, John." Simone says.

"Of course. I'm sorry about men like him," John says as his eyes fall on Minnie and her tall thin frame.

"It just lets men like you shine," Minnie says with an unexpected smile.

Simone and Rachel look at each other as the sparks fly between John and Minnie.

"Not sure I've ever met you," John says with his hand out.

"I'm not from here, that's why. I'm Minnie."

"Minnie, it's nice to meet you." He takes her hand and kisses it gently. "Can I help you get somewhere?"

"No, we're fine now," Simone says, then Rachel and Simone laugh. This takes John and Minnie out of their laser focus and they chuckle themselves.

After they say goodbye and Minnie can speak of nothing else but John, they pass a nightclub with a big band playing and Rachel hurries to the window. A woman with a beautiful red dress and black shawl is singing into the microphone and swaying back and forth.

"I've never heard you sing this music, Rachel," Minnie says.

"I miss it." Rachel can't help but focus on the beautiful singer and the muted trumpet. "Although this is more proper than I'm used to if you ask me."

"What do you mean?"

"Everyone's white," Simone chuckles. "That's what she means."

"Is that what you mean, Rachel?" Minnie asks, surprised.

"No!" Rachel gently nudges Simone's shoulder, "No one's dancing and the rhythm is losing its bounce, you know what I mean?"

"Yeah, because they're all white." Simone laughs.

Minnie laughs.

"I heard Jake's mom," Simone says knowing this will grab Rachel's attention, "kept going with P.B.'s place. She turned it into a speakeasy during prohibition and now that it's legal to sell alcohol, I heard she's doin' pretty good. It's called Ada's!"

"Really?" Rachel is still staring at the band through the window. "You wanna go?"

Rachel finally looks at her. "Yes!"

§ § §

P.B.'s place has been completely remodeled from top to bottom until one wouldn't even know there is a bar inside. The city has moved farther out, until other businesses surround the small remnants of the building where P.B. invited anyone and everyone. Clandestine drinking establishments were no longer forced to hide but their mysterious locations still remain tucked away behind unmarked doors.

They make their way through the familiar door that is P.B.'s old bar and stage, but it is now a bakery, and the scent of bread and scones is decadent. Simone calls them over to a door with her finger and when they get close, the tiniest amount of music can be heard, coming from somewhere.

Simone knocks and, before long, a large man in a black suit with a white tie opens the thick door letting a sudden burst of music, hustle, and conversation take them back to the old days. He sees Simone, then looks at Rachel as though he recognizes her and finally, he lets them in. Through the hall is a large sign that says Ada's in a swirly style cursive. Simone leads down a flight of stairs and a magical world opens up. Minnie and Rachel gasp at the beautiful bar, stage, and leather chairs sitting beneath crystal chandelier sparkles. It is smokey and loud, but not one person seems to have a frown.

"Look," Simone says, "I've been helping Ada for years on this . . . even during the prohibition. P.B. always wanted all kinds to come together here and with a little help from Tittum Doosy's money, Ada was able to create it."

The black community is dancing with the American Indian community, speckled with a few Asian and low-income white crowd.

"Who the heck is Tittum Doosy?" Minnie asks first, even though Rachel is wondering the same thing.

The band is wailing as they make their way to a back room where it's a bit quieter. Simone knows exactly where she's going. "Tittum? He's a wealthy man who wants nothing more than to stick it to those he feels defy our constitution. He's about ninety-two and called up Ada after P.B. and Jake died."

In the corner at a circular table, Ada, Jake's mom is there. It takes a moment for them to see each other, but when they do, Rachel and Ada embrace. She looks different—dressed well and her hair is perfectly high on top of her head. Even her makeup is thicker and brighter than ever. Instantly, Ada takes Rachel's face in her hands. "My goodness, Rachel! Is that you? You're all grown up."

Simone continues the introduction, "Rachel and Minnie, this is Tittum Doosy." The old man has a cane, a hat, and several rings along his fingers. "Tittum, this is Rachel Anne Praline," Simone says.

Instantly his old wrinkly eyes light up. "I cannot believe it."

"This is beautiful, Ada and Mr. Doosy. Just beautiful." Rachel looks around and breathes in the joy of it.

"Yes, well, someone had to do Jake and P.B. proud!" Ada sucks down some water in the hot club.

"They are Ada, they are."

Ada looks her directly in the eye. "I hear Somethin' Tender even now and I just can't hold back. Jake always did know what he was doing."

Later that night, when everyone is slow dancing, Ada sits with her skin glistening. "Jake's death was a turning point for me. I had lost my husband and my son and what do you do? But I was determined to continue on. Jake would have wanted me to. Who knew I was such a businesswoman? P.B.'s momma sold it to me for a fair price. Then once it started doing well, Tittum became a regular and that's how it turned into this."

Some of the old band members notice Rachel. "Rachel Anne Praline!" Joey, P.B.'s trumpeter, yells from atop the stage. The crowd looks her way, and she raises her hand to wave hello. He tries to wave her up on stage with his hand, but it isn't until Ada and Tittum ask her to sing that she stands.

In the past, she might have been scared, but now there is no hesitation. It had been clawing at her like she was starving for it. Rachel leaves the table and hurries up on the stage. She says hello to the band members that she remembers and meets the newbies. They quickly pick a song she knows well and she comes to the edge of the stage. Joey speaks into the microphone, "This is Rachel Anne Praline everyone. She's the voice of Somethin' Tender."

Instantly, the crowd roars and she is welcomed back.

"Good evening, everyone."

§ § §

There is a crescent moon that hangs just above the dodgy apartment building in early May as the card game begins. Each woman comments on it as they come in with snacks and liquor in their hands. These nights have been known to get loud as they drink and smoke while beating each other for money. By 9:30 the tiny room is full of thunderous laughter as two women talk of the affairs they are having with married men in the city.

"They just aren't happy with their rich and snobbish wives," Hannah, a tall woman with the lightest green eyes, says as she throws a card on the table, "These men are just getting tired of buying coats for their wives that ain't good enough cause it ain't mink."

"Oh, I know what you mean, honey," Helen chimes in. She is a widow three times over, but carries herself like she owns the world—or at least the men in it. Her boyfriend in the city spends his days with his wife and children, and his nights with Helen. "My man says he gave his wife a new car the other day. Now we all know that cars aren't being bought right now, but he did, and she said it wasn't the right color. If I were his wife---"

"---Keep dreaming, Helen, you ain't gonna be," comes a shout from the eldest lady in the room, Ruth Bower, a black woman who gives every one of them advice whether they want it or not. "And besides, all you are asking for is trouble."

"Shush up now," Helen says with a grin. "If I were his wife, you know what I would give him if he brought a car home to me?"

"But you see he doesn't have to bring you a car. You give your you-know-what for free," Ruth snaps her fingers in the air as the rest of the ladies give a loud "oooohhh".

"Oh!" Helen grabs a handful of peanuts and throws them at

Ruth who sits across the table. Everyone laughs but continues playing right through the conversation.

Rachel, her hair down and her face free of too much makeup, pictures Kendra and Levi and she must shake her head to take away the pain of it as she says, "Breaking up a family isn't what I call a good time."

All the women know her story. In fact, these women know everyone's story who sits in the room. The laughter quiets down quickly until Rachel notices and continues, "I'm just saying, you waiting for a man that has vowed his life to someone else is worthless."

Chepi continues the thought when Rachel doesn't, "It doesn't matter what you say, it is women that you defile by being with their husbands. If we are not one with each other, we will never be strong. I would never stand against a fellow sister."

Helen shakes her head, "Oh, I stand with you, Chepi, it's the rich that I am against. Besides we're drunk at this moment, we don't know what we're saying."

"Rachel, what's going on, honey?" Helen asks.

"What do you want to know, Helen?" Rachel takes another shot, feeling the need to forget her own thoughts.

"Heard anything from your man?"

"No," Rachel says, "but I'm sure it's for the best."

A strange look comes over Helen's drunk face that makes most of the woman pay attention. "Rachel, I saw your man."

Rachel sets her cards down and looks at her. "What?"

"I saw your man," Helen says again.

Rachel recoils, not wanting to listen.

"I was there with John yesterday. You know, at the hotel that you said was his. They bought some of our paintings." The entire room stops and is able to achieve the unthinkable—silence. "We were walkin' through the lobby and he passed right by me."

"How do you know? You've never seen him in person," Sylvia interjects, noticing the look on Rachel's fragile face.

"When I was passing, he looked familiar and I asked John—John says, that's Levi Price, the owner. But I didn't need him to tell me that, Rachel. I knew it was him."

The news is disturbing and confusing, but not impossible. He would have to visit the hotel since it is his. Rachel takes her fourth shot of the night.

"Why ain't the man comin' after ya?" Helen asks.

"No, ladies he's doing the right thing. Every baby deserves a daddy." Rachel says, doing her best to believe the lie she just spoke.

"You need to go down there." Chepi speaks confidently. "I'll go with you."

"I'm not going down there."

"You have to. I checked around, Rachel. Everyone says…" Helen hesitates, "…he's not married."

Rachel stands on shaky feet. "That's impossible."

Sylvia chimes in from a nearby table. "You made sure of this, Helen?"

"Yes, ma'am. I was careful about it. Didn't want John to know why I was interested."

"He would have come to me if he wasn't married." For the first time in four hours, no one is holding cards in their hands.

"Does he know how to find you, Rachel?" Simone asks.

Rachel's heart is racing as she rubs her temple.

"I'll take you," Chepi stands with force.

"Good God, Chepi, I ain't never heard you be so loud before." Ruth crosses her arms with a cigarette dangling from her lips.

"You should be loud too," Chepi says.

"Rachel, maybe you should," Sylvia suggests, and no one can believe it. "I know you're scared, but he loves you. I can't stand the two of you apart."

Rachel turns to Simone. After just a moment, Simone nods at the same time that she rubs her belly. "They're all correct, Rach. If Chepi is adamant, you need to do something."

Within an hour many of the ladies and Rachel, walk the two miles to his hotel on the boardwalk. Soon, they stand outside just staring at the tall hotel.

"We shouldn't be here." Rachel second guesses everything as her fingers and toes have grown numb.

"The hotel sure is big," Minnie whispers.

"You should see inside," Chepi says.

"The only way I'm getting inside is if I find a rich husband like you've got…" Minnie says.

Chepi laughs, "John Ipson can't take you?"

Minnie blushes. John and Minnie had become quite inseparable since he stood up for them against Officer Hannah.

"Go inside." Chepi suggests.

"I can't." Rachel rubs her palms along her pants.

"I will," Helen says. "Come on!" She reaches out and takes Rachel's hand.

They cross the street and enter the main doors. The hotel is much like the one in California, only the colors of this one are brighter, to fit the scurry of the boardwalk. Helen walks up to the main counter. "Excuse me, can you tell me if Mr. Price is here?"

The man behind the desk smiles. "Oh, welcome back. He is."

"May I speak with him?"

"Can you remind me of your name?"

"Just tell him an old friend is here. No name."

The man hesitates, and then he turns to the boy standing near a window to which he whispers in his ear just before he runs away. "Please wait over there. It will be a few minutes."

Helen and Rachel walk to a bench where they wait and watch everyone who passes and every person who exits or enters the elevator. Rachel's not sure what will be worse, seeing him again and finding out he's still married, or never seeing him again. Finally, from out on the patio, Levi enters with a beautiful woman on his right. It's not Kendra but they look all too comfortable with each other. Rachel holds her breath.

"Who's that?" Helen asks quickly.

"I don't know." With a shaking hand, Rachel lays it on Helen's forearm. It's obvious when Helen looks back, she can see the panic and leftover pain returning to Rachel. "Let's go, please."

"Are you sure, Rachel? Why don't you just talk to him?"

"I can't." Rachel rushes to the door as Levi walks to the counter to speak to the concierge. "Hurry," Rachel calls to Helen. The man behind the counter points to the ladies, but they are nearly gone.

"Excuse me?" Levi calls out.

The women rush through the crowd and down the steps as the other ladies notice them. "I don't think this was a good idea." Simone whispers as she reads her friend's panic.

"What are they doing?" Minnie asks.

"I don't know," Sylvia replies, until they notice Levi exiting the hotel doors and all of the women, in unison, gasp.

Helen holds on to Rachel's arm as they flee. The women watch from across the street as Levi's eyes fall on her. His hand flies to his forehead and he breathes out with exasperation. "Did you see that?" Minnie asks them all.

"Yes," every one of them says as if they are watching off-Broadway theater.

"Rachel?" he calls out.

Thinking better of running, Rachel stops walking but doesn't turn to look at him. As Levi gets closer, Helen steps away, placing several feet of distance between them.

"Rachel?" He comes to stand only feet away.

Finally, Rachel turns but she doesn't speak. It's impossible to know how to feel. He chose the other woman—even though it's what she said to do. Being upset isn't an option, but she is upset.

He looks into her eyes, "Why aren't you saying anything?"

"I didn't know you were here."

"Rachel, I…"

"Levi, don't you think it's strange how we can never be together? At every chance, life provides a reason not to. Maybe it's just time we listen." For the first time, Rachel is seeing everything clearly.

"It may seem like that…"

"Levi, it is like that. Maybe there's something else for both of us. Maybe there's someone else."

"Rachel, you don't mean that."

"When I feel this way, I think I do." None of them, not Rachel, not Levi, not the ladies, can believe this is happening.

Across the street, Simone's body is so tense her shoulders sit up to her ears. "I can't believe what we are watching."

Finally, Rachel surrenders, "I can't do this anymore."

"Rachel."

Rachel turns away from him and Helen wraps her arms around her. Levi stands alone and perplexed.

Everyone views regrets differently. Is chasing love a waste of time or is it a waste to let love go? In Rachel's life she has never been given the choice. From her mother and father, Bernie to Bill—from Jake to Levi—everything has happened without her having a choice. Instead of floating through life, it has seemed to drag her along, kicking and screaming. She can't do it again. It is her choice, and she walks away from Levi.

Chapter Twenty Five

1998

The entire nursing staff have joined in on a night out for Gramma. First, I asked her doctor if he thought it would be alright to take her on a date. "She's been doing so well; I don't see why not. I would simply make sure you don't go too far and don't have her out too long."

That was several days ago and today, as I pull into the parking lot, I see several nurses gathering at the entrance, including one named Matilda who has been eyeing me closely since I started visiting Gramma. I can't tell whether she finds me good looking or whether she thinks I'll steal from my family, but either way, I try and steer clear of her. However, tonight she seems to be the ringleader for every nurse's excitement.

As I walk up to the hospital, in my best slacks and shirt that I brought, the nurses all begin talking at once.

"We've dressed her so nice!" one says.

"She is just not going to believe this," another says.

And another, "We tried to warn her as best as we can!"

And another, "I think she knows exactly what is happening!"

All of this is happening while we are all pushing through the entrance doors. I brought my gramma chrysanthemums since they were always her favorite flower, and they are wrapped in a thin green tissue paper.

"Oh, you brought her flowers!" Every lady swoons until I can't help but smile. People are watching from every corner of the retirement home, even a couple of janitors are watching and practically salute me as I pass. It appears as though they have even decorated with flowers and streamers from the entrance all the way back as far as I can see.

"Do you have something else going on?" I ask as the women still surround me, moving past the front desk, then through the hallway where we have to wait until someone buzzes open the door to the memory wing.

"Okay," Matilda finally stops me just before we reach Gramma's room, "did you bring what we asked?"

I have to think for a second, then remember. "Oh yes," I say as I pull several pictures out of my back pocket. The women grab them, then oooh and aaah as they look through the pile of Memorexes of childhood milestones where I stand next to her. Matilda holds both sides of my collar as if she's fixing it, but she's looking directly in the eye with very firm awareness.

"You will use these to remind your grandma who she is. If she has trouble, then you simply pull those out and show them to her. Just keep talking gentle and calm and remind her of the same story she's been telling you for the last several weeks. Don't talk about your father, and if you have trouble, here is my phone number." The look on her face makes me think she's giving this to me for other reasons, but the woman is nearly my mother's age.

"Matilda," I finally say to keep her from saying another word, "I got it. Thank you."

"Okay, well, then you just go on in."

Finally, they let me go and, as I round the corner, I can't help but smile. Gramma is surrounded by three nurses who have helped her into a beautiful dress with multitudes of colors, and they've even tied flowers together and wrapped them in her hair. Gramma is beaming with pride. As I hand her the mums, you would think I've just given her the world, until she says, "Oh my goodness, Joe . . ." One of the nurses quickly whispers in her ear, and Gramma quickly scrambles to say it right, "Bobby, of course! Bobby."

"Are you ready to go?"

"I certainly am, honey. This is the most exciting thing that has happened to me in years."

No pressure. The heat at my collar starts to choke me so I pull it away. Rachel can sing to thousands or even stand up to the man she loves, and I can't handle the pressure of my gramma's hope for a good night. Who the hell am I going to be if THIS is what sends me into a tailspin?

I stick out my elbow for her to wrap her arm around and then we head out into the hallway. Lined up along the walls are every staff member, including the CEO and CFO of the home. They clap for Gramma, not me, and I shake my head. This is unbelievable how much they love her here and how much they care. I'll safely be able to tell my ma that she's found the right place for Gramma.

The line of staff zigzags through the halls, then through the cafeteria where many patients are also sitting at tables and clapping. Gramma is eating it up. You would think she was going to prom again. Although I actually don't know if she ever went to prom. In fact, I'm not really sure I know much of Gramma's life. She was the kind of woman who made sure everyone else in the room was being praised and cared for. That's just the woman she was. Although I'm not sure it helped my father or made him feel like the golden child who could do no wrong. I guess it doesn't matter since I know the way I felt with her was always loved.

When we're driving to the restaurant, she's looking at my car as though it's a spaceship, touching every button, and then when she was done with that, she sniffs the chrysanthemums so deeply there's yellow dust left on her nose.

"How did you know these were my favorite?" she asks.

"Grampa once said, 'I won her over with daisies'."

"He did? Well . . . that man. What a wonder he turned out to be. Behind our house growing up, there was a field of daisies. It grew every summer only to die off. We didn't mind since it warned us of the changing of seasons."

We reach the restaurant and it's very obvious by their service that the rest home has warned them of our visit. They walk us through the crowd and I keep close to Gramma to make sure that she's okay. Finally ,we sit down and I order for us when she asks me to. I'm not sure how well she can see in the dim light, or without her glasses since she didn't want to wear them all dressed up.

Eventually, we get back to Rachel's story. "She can't do that," I say bitterly.

"What, honey?"

"She can't leave Levi. After all of this time, after everything, she can't just walk away from him."

"He had gotten married, honey, and had a child with the woman. What was she supposed to do?" Gramma looks at me with a sideways glance.

"But she just took control. She made that choice to walk away from him."

"Why did she do that, honey?"

There are so many things going through my head at this moment. Number one, I think my grandma is calling me honey to avoid having to remember my name—I've noticed she says it to nearly everyone in the restaurant. Number two, I am beginning to see the parallel from my life to Rachel's and I don't like it. And number three, I instantly think of the moments in my life when a woman looked at me with those eyes and walked away. That's why I hate this. I know what it is to be Levi.

"It doesn't matter what she says, she loves him," I say with a shrug.

"Yes, she did, but I think Rachel was tired of working so hard, Jimmy." She calls me my brother's name.

What must it feel like for everything to become so cloudy? How unsettling to never know who you're with or where you are? When I was a child, there was nothing more uncomfortable than being without my ma. She was my protection from the world when the world felt too big. I reach out to Gramma, but suddenly, she drops her head in her hands.

"Are you alright, Gramma?"

She looks up and I can see that there is nothing behind her eyes. All is lost for a moment.

"Who are you?" she asks quietly.

"I'm your grandson: Bobby."

"Where am I?"

"We're at a restaurant, Gramma. I took you to dinner."

"I don't want to be here. I want to go home. 84 Maple Ave."

She hasn't lived there since before I was born.

"Alright, Gramma. I'll take you home."

"Please, take me home. Take me home. 84 Maple Ave."

"Don't worry. I will."

Tears come to her eyes, and I can see the panic. She staggers to her feet nearly knocking her chair over and it causes me to jump.

"It's alright, Gramma. Just give me a minute. I'll take you home."

She walks through the tables in horror as everyone looks at us, so I quickly throw money on the table and follow her. A man walks close to her and she starts screaming, over and over again. The man is so caught off guard he hits a potted flower, knocking it over, sending dirt and leaves everywhere.

"Gramma, shh, it's okay." She continues to cry while rubbing her hands together and looking from left to right in fear.

"Sir, can we help?" the hostess asks.

"No, it's okay." I take my gramma's face in my hands and bring mine close to hers. "Look at me. Look at my eyes, do you recognize them? They are yours, Gramma. I have your eyes."

She continues to holler until I say it one more time. "It's me, Bobby. Remember your yellow kitchen and you would have fresh tea made every day?"

Finally, her scared eyes look into mine. "Take me home, Bobby," she cries.

"Yeah, let's go home." When we get back to the complex, she looks around as I park in the loading zone.

"This isn't 84 Maple."

"This is where you live, Gramma."

"I don't live here. Take me home!"

Getting a panicked woman out of the car when she thinks she doesn't know you is not as easy as it sounds. When I open her door, she leans away as if I'm a highjacker, and even my most soothing voice doesn't bring her back to me. So, I decide to let her have her meltdown. With care, I slide onto the hood of my car.

"I hope that Rachel finds happiness," I say calmly under the canopy of stars. "I've been listening to her voice every day, Gramma." She screams and wails, but I talk anyway. "Sometimes I wish that I can allow myself to let go like you're doing right now. I might just figure out a thing or two. But unless you're losing a little bit of your mind, there are boundaries that you keep."

"I was supposed to do so much more with my life, Gramma. Why didn't I become what I thought I would be? My father was able to reach his goals. He was able to be a man. I guess that bit of manhood skipped me. He loved what he did; he worked hard and moved up the ladder. People loved him, Gramma. I go to work and nobody even knows my name. What happened to me? You know, our old reverend once said I was going to be like an eagle. Like I was supposed to soar to great things. I'm not soaring and I'm not doing great things."

I remember the pictures in my back pocket, albeit too late. Even still, I pull them out, reach over the passenger window and drop them onto her lap. Then I sit back against the window and continue to talk, "When I think about the love of my life that I let go, I wonder if it's me. Am I more like my father than I want to admi-- but even he found a woman to marry."

Suddenly, I realize that it's quiet. I look over. She has climbed out of the car, holds the pictures in her hands like they are gold, and is now looking at me. "What makes you think you are old?" she asks as if she wasn't just wailing.

"What do you mean?"

"You're talking like you don't have a lifetime ahead of you. Silliest thing I have ever heard, Bobby."

"Well, I'm glad to have you back."

"Where would I go but sit here and listen to my grandson mope about how he isn't anybody special. You know your father isn't all that he says he is."

"He's not?" I raise my eyebrows. I've never heard this woman or any woman in my life say a negative thing about him. This should be interesting.

"Nope. You know your Ivy League college? He couldn't get into it on the first try like you did. Then one semester he came home letting me know that he failed a course and was going to retake it. Nah, honey, it wasn't until he was well older that things started to come together for him—even though he'll never admit it."

I smile as my gramma picks up her purse and starts walking to the doors.

"Levi wasn't having it," Gramma says as I run to her side.

"Levi?"

"Yeah. He wasn't going to let Rachel's dismissal stop him. But neither was Simone. That night, Simone runs to Levi as he watches

Rachel walk away. And you what she does? She whispers Rachel's address."

1934

Even more women show up, the night after the hotel predicament, with their poker faces on, but also too interested in the story to stay away. Gambling and gossip seem to be the only things keeping these women alive, so now they do it nearly every day.

Everyone's laughing and trying to cheer up Rachel as she sits silently at the table with a long-lost look, until a knock sounds on the door. Sylvia heads to it, "How could there be anyone else? This room won't fit anymore."

Rachel pays no attention until the sound in the room drops to near silence. When she looks up Simone and Sylvia are staring at her. A man in a coat and hat has entered.

"Rachel," Levi says quietly.

She sits up suddenly, her chest rising and falling with the untamed beat of her heart. Her fingernails are digging into her wooden chair and that might be the only thing keeping her from running away. Every woman stares at him with their mouths dropped open like a kid seeing Santa Claus for the first time.

He reaches up and takes his gray hat off. "I told you that I would come. I'm not going to stay away."

The women in the room can't control themselves. Whispers become roars. "You'd better explain yourself, sir," one of the ladies bellows and one by one they begin to stand. A wall of women now stands between them.

"These are my friends," Rachel whispers.

"Hello, friends," he says with a grin. Rachel's heart melts. "Would you like to talk outside?"

"We know your story," Helen calls out, "just say what you have to say."

"Ummmm,hmmm." Ruth grunts as she wraps her arms around her chest.

Levi breathes out, "Okay."

"You don't have to," Rachel says quickly.

"No, it's alright," he pauses, "they deserve an apology from me too. I'm sorry that it took me so long to come."

"But why are you here?" The burning in Rachel's chest hurts so much she places a hand over her heart, actually afraid of the answer.

"Yeah, honey, why are you here? And who is that woman you were with at the hotel?" Helen calls out.

"Shhh, Helen," Rachel warns her.

"That woman is my cousin." He tries to look every woman in the eye to show his honesty. Not much seems to win them over. Then he turns to Rachel, "The baby wasn't mine," he says softly. "I knew it wasn't, but I had to make sure for the very reasons that you wrote me that letter. I knew that if I left my own child, you would never forgive me . . . or yourself. So, I made sure just as you would want me to. I'm so sorry for all this time and all this trouble. If I just ..." but he doesn't continue and looks away.

Everybody is silent as Rachel walks through the mob of women ready and willing to stand up for her.

"I'm sorry, but nothing is going to stand in the way again," Levi says carefully. "Please, come with me."

Rachel looks at Simone for her to be saying no, but instead she is grinning. When they lock eyes, she nods and mouths, "Go."

Finally, Rachel takes the last few steps toward him and when she is close enough, he places his hands on her face.

"From here on, you're not leaving my sight," Levi whispers as he looks at her.

"I can't believe you're here."

"I'm here and never leaving you again."

She finally runs her hands down his chest, then grabs his collar. Without warning his mouth is on hers and as the room erupts with applause, hoots, and hollers, they kiss as if they are alone. There have been very few things in Rachel's life that have felt as familiar and yet as exciting as Levi.

When he finally lets her go, he looks around the room at the women as they watch on—some with tears in their eyes—and he smiles. "Can I take her somewhere?"

The women all look around at each other before they finally nod with approval.

Rachel looks at the rest of the women. "Don't wait up."

He takes her hand and they step outside onto the patio just as Mrs. Gerber yells angrily at her son from the second story. "You said you were getting jello not hostess cakes, you dummy!"

"That's Mrs. Gerber and this is where we live," she says, as he looks around at the neglected apartment building.

"I love it," he answers, and she laughs. When they reach the bottom of the stairs, he turns to her. "I'm really touching you. Come with me," he says as his lips brush hers, then he kisses her again.

They climb into his car and head down the streets of Atlantic City. She refuses to go anywhere bright enough that he might see her clothes and hands, so they compromise on a dimly lit café in front of the pier.

"You were already gone when I reached the station," he explains as he runs his thumb along her palm. Her skin tickles from his touch.

"You came?"

"Of course. I got your letter, but I already partly knew the baby wasn't mine."

"How did you know?"

"I was her husband. I knew."

"Oh."

"When you showed up, it scared her, Rachel. If I left, she had nothing. I didn't stay because of the baby, in fact, the next day I moved out. I went back home to Sorrento. But she and her lawyers immediately came for me. She tried to drag you into it, but because you left, we were able to tell the truth and make it clear. I couldn't come to be with you. Not then. I had some work to do."

"Are you divorced?"

"No. She's one of the most stubborn women I know. She's fighting me for everything."

Rachel stares at him and he smiles. "You're beautiful."

"I'm tired."

"I know. You don't have to be tired anymore, Rachel."

The waiter comes by and fills their drinks. "Does she deserve anything?" Rachel asks.

"Not in my mind," he grins, "but I'm offering her a lot, because I want to be free—free to marry you."

Again, Rachel hasn't thought of marriage, even to Levi.

He continues, "I want to be with you. I have wanted to protect you my entire life, and I'm getting the idea that this won't change."

"Levi . . ."

"Kendra admitted to me and the father that the baby isn't mine, but she won't to the court."

"What does she want?"

"Anything she can get her hands on. She wants the California hotel."

Rachel looks up quickly. "Don't let her have the California hotel."

"It's the reason we have yet to get divorced." They smile. "I was surprised to see you in my lobby. I assumed you would still be traveling with the choir. In fact, I tried to call Chuck but never heard back."

She tells him the story about Chuck and singing at P.B.'s restaurant, and the other odd jobs she's done to make ends meet. He looks at her ragged fingers when she wants to pull them away, but he won't let her.

"They look awful, I know."

"Rachel, you don't have to do anything you don't want to do anymore."

"That all sounds great, but Minnie and Sylvia rely on my

paycheck to make ends meet."

"Listen, I don't want to come in and change everything and tell you what you have to do. I'm not trying to be the savior on a high horse, but Minnie and Sylvia, as well as Simone . . . they will be taken care of, Rachel. I promise you."

"Simone doesn't need your help. She's gonna have a baby and her boss who's dating Minnie actually . . . he just promoted her and gave her a raise even though that's unheard of right now."

"Simone's a lawyer?"

"Well, as much as she can in a white man's world. But she's gonna do it. She just won her case helping a woman divorce her husband." They smile at the irony. "Only this husband was angry and volatile. The way Simone knew how to argue everything and made sure she was an expert at every little detail. A man named Frank Jenkins just contacted her about getting better representation for the International Longshore and Warehouse Union all the way in Seattle. Simone doesn't back down for anybody or complain about anything."

"Good for her."

They are quiet for a moment, until Rachel breathes out, "Levi, you know I've been in love with you for a long time, but it's never worked."

He pulls her closer, "It will now. I promise."

"No more Italy?"

"No, not for a while."

"I thought you loved Italy."

"I do, but there's a lot of unrest in Europe right now, so I think it's best to be in the States until it blows over."

After they talk for hours, they step out onto the sidewalk at nearly midnight. "Where do you want to go?"

"Where are you staying?"

"At the hotel."

"That's where I want to go."

He looks at her for a moment. "Anything you want, Rachel Anne Praline."

"Good."

It is nearly one in the morning when they reach the hotel. Standing outside, Rachel peers up at the beautiful and expensive building. "I think I've changed my mind."

"Why is that?"

"Look at my clothes. People are going to wonder who you brought with you."

"Well, then they'll think I'm more of a goodhearted person than I really am."

He walks proudly through the lobby, waves at the men and woman at the front desk, and then leads her into the elevator. They reach his beautiful suite. It is just as big as the one in Napa Valley.

When he tries to kiss her, she pulls back. "Not yet."

"What?"

"I worked all day and came home to a room full of smoking and drinking women."

"Alright." He takes her by the hand and leads her to the bathroom. Before long, a hot bath is waiting for her. As he leaves to get her a towel, she steps into the warm water and breathes heavily.

"I was a bit surprised tonight as I walked in to find so many women in one place." Levi says, smiling as he walks back into the steamy room.

Rachel laughs as she runs her hands along the surface of the water.

He sits on a stool next to the bath. "Was it your idea?"

"A little, and a little bit of Simone's. Life has been hard for all of these women and every one of them looks forward to our nights when they can get away to our small and dirty apartment."

"Cigars? I didn't know you smoked."

"Oh, I don't. I tried, but I wasn't very good at it. Sylvia on the other hand has done very well with it."

He laughs at the thought.

Rachel lifts her fingers and takes the soap next to her. For a moment she runs the yellow bar along her fingertips, but when that doesn't clean them, she grabs a brush lying next to her. She begins scrubbing until it makes the tips of her fingers raw. When she is done, the grime from all her laboring has disappeared. "I look like a woman again."

"It's not possible for you to look any other way, dirty fingers or not."

"The water is getting cold. I think I'll get out." She steps out onto the bathroom mat wrapping the towel around her body. For a moment he stares at her. Then he runs his hands up and down her wet arms. He places his hand under her chin and lifts her mouth to his. It begins softly and then progresses quickly until she's in his arms wrapping her legs around him as he carries her to his bed. As he lays her down, he pulls the towel from her body, then runs his hand down her skin. Her muscles contract from his touch.

"It's been so long." His fingertips run down circling her nipples, then her belly button. Never before has he wanted to move so fast but also take his time. Instead of stopping at her belly button, her skin still wet from the bath, his hand glides along her hip bone, then makes a turn inward. Slowly, he waits for her reaction, and soon she arches her back and sucks in a breath. The small whimper as his finger circles and circles sometimes hard and sometimes gently, makes him feel out of control, but he holds back knowing it's best. Leaning over her, he takes her nipple in his mouth and sucks it until it grows hard. Again her soft moan drives him crazy, but he waits still. He bends his knees until he's between her legs and can kiss the inside of her soft thighs. Just this alone makes her desperate for him to find the sensitive inner workings of her body, and as he gets closer, she sets her hand on his head. Finally, his tongue presses against her soft flesh, sinking deeper into the layers, until he hits a spot that makes her body shake. He pushes in and out of her until she cries out.

"Levi!" she begs. "Come up here."

Finally, he climbs on top of her as she unbuttons his shirt, and she runs her hands down his perfect body until she unzips his pants. He lifts himself higher as she pulls his clothes off. Before she can do anything else, he lowers himself onto her, then grabs her mouth with his. As he kisses her, the muscles on his arms tighten when he lifts his body to meet hers. He watches her as he enters her and for just a second, they stop as he runs his hands through her hair, "I love you," he says breathlessly.

"Promise me that you'll stay."

"I'm here. I promise you." He drops his lips back down to hers and wraps his arms around her. For the first time in years, they satisfy every touch and every need.

§ § §

In the middle of the night, Rachel wakes with sweat pouring from her skin and panic tightening her chest. She reaches across the bed but finds no one there. Suddenly she sits up with confusion, but there's a shadow in the doorway coming closer.

"You okay?" Levi's deep voice asks.

"I thought you were a dream."

He crawls across the bed to her and instead of falling asleep, they make love again.

The earthy aroma of coffee fills the room as Rachel opens her eyes. Rolling over, Levi is sitting up in bed reading some papers and when he sees her awake, he reaches out to touch her face. She smiles for a moment until she notices the time on the bedside table clock. "I'm late for work!" She leaps to her feet, but he hurriedly grabs her hand to hold her back.

"I think it's time to change careers."

"I'm not going to just rely on you, Levi."

"I'm not asking you to, I promise. What I am asking you to do is slow down, take a moment and find what you want to do, not what you have to." He grins, then winks at her.

"Do people do that?"

"Those who get the opportunity."

A long drawn-out sigh of relief fills her lungs and she falls on the bed beside him. "I don't know that I've ever thought about what I just truly want to do."

Before long Levi and Rachel drive back to the apartment where they inform Minnie and Sylvia they are to pack up. Within days, the women have moved into another suite on the same floor as Levi's. Minnie runs into the room and looks out the window that overlooks the boardwalk. "Oh my, I've never been in something so beautiful!" Sylvia is just as she usually is, reserved, but Rachel can see the release in her eyes—something that hasn't been there since Dick was alive.

"You'll stay here until arrangements can be made?" Levi says as he opens the curtains to let the sun in.

"Levi, I don't want us to be a burden." Sylvia's voice is so quiet that Levi walks to her and sets a hand on her shoulder to give her comfort.

"Sylvia, you spent your life taking care of Rachel. I can never repay you, but let me try."

A tear falls down Sylvia's face, so Levi hugs her.

Afterward, Levi walks to Rachel, takes her hand, and they head to the door. "Oh," Levi says as he turns back to Minnie and Sylvia, "all of the women are welcome here for cards. Please invite them all."

When Levi and Rachel step into the hall, they hear Minnie cry out in joy, which makes them laugh. He sets his arm over her shoulder and leans over to give her a quick kiss.

Two days later, seventeen women, from the old apartment and around, sit at round tables in a private room off the restaurant. Nothing changes as they are still rowdy and vulgar; the only difference is that now, they are waited on hand-and-foot and treated no different than the wealthy instead of the tired, working women that they are. Levi loves spoiling them and comes in every once in a while, to kiss

Rachel while they play Blackjack and Spades. Each time he does, the women tell him how he should fix the state's politics and how he needs to demand change. Levi's one requirement is that Helen keeps her hands off the men staying at his hotel.

Every chance they have, Rachel and Levi make love and talk until the sun rises.

Finally, in the middle of August on a beautiful sunny day, Rachel and Simone walk down the sidewalk. Simone stops mid-step and grabs her back with a pained expression.

"What's wrong?" Rachel asks.

"Oh, I don't know. My back is giving me trouble."

"Can I do something for you?"

"Well, I…" She pauses. "Oh my Lord," Simone says fearfully, "I'm having a baby."

"Right now?" Rachel cries out.

"Yes, now calm down before you give me a heart attack."

People see what is happening, but hurry by anyway. "Okay, Simone, don't worry. We'll figure something out. Can you walk?"

"Yes," she says as she takes a few steps forward still gripping her back.

"Good. There's a hospital around the corner. Just two blocks. Can you make it there?"

"Let's just hurry it up," Simone groans.

They walk, but every few minutes Simone stops to breathe and grab her side. "Tell me what you need." Rachel's panic sets in as she looks down the street for a taxi, but late morning on a Tuesday the streets are empty. Once they reach the hospital, Rachel helps Simone through the doors.

"Excuse me," Rachel calls out to the front desk. "Excuse me, my friend's having a baby."

Two women, dressed in nursing uniforms, immediately stand from behind the front desk and rush around, although the moment they see Simone, they stop. "We can't take her here," one of them says.

"What?" Rachel asks angrily while Simone holds on to her as sweat drips down her forehead. "This woman needs your help. You have to take her."

"No, we don't have to do anything," the first woman says.

The second nurse leans closer to Rachel with regret in her eyes. "We're not allowed; I'm so sorry."

"You're going to throw us out?" Rachel asks as Simone lets out a cry of pain.

"We're just not going to let you in."

"Oh, clever," Rachel says sarcastically. Simone lets out another groan and Rachel holds on to her tighter.

Then, finally Simone has a moment of reprieve and stares the women directly in the eyes. "Then you best let us use your phone and you will call the hospital that we will be going to."

The older nurse wants to talk back, but there's something in Simone's tone that doesn't allow it.

"Simone?" Rachel asks.

"I don't want them touching me anyway. Don't let those women come near me." Simone warns as she leans on the counter to look at their name tags. "It's best that you don't infect my baby anyway, Fannie and Patricia."

"What phone can I use?" Rachel says angrily.

"You may come back here and use it, but she may not."

"You want me to leave her here, while she's in pain?"

"If you want to use the phone, ma'am..."

"Oh hell," Rachel says furiously. She takes Simone to a chair in the waiting room. "Just sit a moment and I'll call Reed or Levi."

"You'd better hurry." Simone says with her eyes squeezed shut.

"Ma'am, she can't sit in those chairs," one of the nurses says quickly.

Finally, Simone turns to the lady with sharp eyes despite her pain, "I swear to you that I will sue you so fast you won't know what's hit you. I didn't go to law school for nothing."

This makes the nurses hesitate, then finally, they lead Rachel to the telephone. The operator tries to connect her to Reed, but he isn't answering, so she quickly connects her to Levi.

"Hey, baby," he says happily, "Where are you?"

"Levi, I need you to bring the car."

"What's going on?"

"Simone's having her baby, but we are at the hospital on Hickory Street, and they won't let us in."

"They won't let you in?" His business voice has taken over suddenly. "What do you mean?"

"Levi," she says.

"Okay, just wait there and I'll come get you."

Faster than either of them expects, Levi appears, racing his car up to the entrance. Simone stands, but as she does, her water breaks, splashing everywhere. With a grin, Simone looks up at Patricia and Fannie, "Oops sorry. Which one of you gets the honor of cleaning this up?" Simone gives a sadistic chuckle which makes Rachel and Levi grin. Patricia and Fannie's faces show exactly what they're thinking. "Come on, sweetie." Levi says as he pulls Simone into his arms and carries her out to the car.

"We don't have the time to get her to a hospital and hassle with them. The nearest is Kenney Memorial and it's over an hour away." Levi says from behind the wheel. "I'll take her home."

"My neighbor is my midwife," Simone gasps.

An hour later Reed rushes through the door in a panic, as scatterbrained as a child who has just been twirled. Rings of sweat darken his shirt at his neck and his armpits. "I ran the entire way home," he hollers as Levi takes his briefcase. Luckily, he makes it in the room just as Simone is about to push. Levi, Rachel, Sylvia, and Minnie stay out in the living room until the door opens, and Reed looks at Rachel, "She's asking for you."

Rachel runs in and notices the sweat drenching her best friend's forehead. Instantly she takes a towel and pats her dry. "You're doing amazing," Rachel whispers.

The room is dim as Simone makes her last attempts at pushing the baby out. Finally, with the last bit of her strength, the baby comes. Nothing could have been more beautiful as Rachel watches her friend finally relax and enjoy the first cry of her newborn. The instant love in Simone's eyes is breathtaking.

"You did it," Rachel whispers.

"What is it?"

"It's a boy."

"It is?" Simone says happily.

"Yes. A beautiful little boy."

"Reed!" Simone yells suddenly.

"What, honey?" he quickly turns to her in the small room.

"Where were you?!" she hollers at him with irritation.

"I got called in to work. But I ran all the way here!" he says with urgency.

"Yes, I know. I could smell you." Reed comes closer and Simone grabs his shirt, but then a switch flips. "We have a son, baby." Reed smiles from ear to ear and leans over to kiss her gently. "What are we naming this child?"

"Whatever you want, darling…"

§ § §

A few weeks later, in the middle of the night, Rachel feels Levi's hand on her shoulder.

"Aren't you sleeping?" she asks.

"No."

"Why not?"

"I have something to show you."

"Right now?"

"I'm sorry, baby, but I can't sleep until I do." He kisses her then quickly jumps out of bed as he pats her thigh. "Come on, lazy bones."

"It's 2 o'clock in the morning."

After they dress, he drives her to the outskirts of Atlantic City, ironically not far from where she grew up. He pulls onto a dirt road and parks with the lights of the car shining on a large, beautiful house.

"Come on," he says quietly. He grabs her hand and pulls her up the porch of the yellow-slatted house. From his pocket he finds a key and unlocks the door.

"You have a key? What is this, Levi?"

"Just wait," he grins. He pushes the door open and they enter. Everything about it is breathtaking. They stand in the entryway as he turns on the lights.

"What are you doing?"

"I found this place. Just behind it is another home just as big and just as nice. I want them."

She smiles, "You want them?"

"Yes. I want this to be our home."

"What?"

"I didn't buy it yet because I wanted you to see it first. I know the owners."

"It's beautiful."

"I knew you would think so. Come here." He grabs her hand and leads her up the stairs. Small pieces of furniture are left scattered about the house from the previous owners. When they reach the main bedroom, Rachel walks in with a smile.

"I love it."

After a moment, she walks to him and he quickly wraps his arms around her. "I want to grow old with you here," he says quietly. He looks down and sees that she has missed a button on the top of her dress. With his fingertips he pulls the next one open.

"What are you doing?"

"Making it feel like our home."

"But it isn't our home yet."

"Just say the words and it will be. Say you want it." He sets her down on the couch along the wall.

"I want you," she whispers.

1998

In a sea of white-haired folks, I'm trying to drink some god-awful coffee in the cafeteria while Gramma sleeps. My computer is set out in front of me and I'm agonizing over my notes when suddenly, Mandy appears from around the corner holding a cup of coffee and searching for an empty table. Luckily for me, there are none, so I quickly raise my hand.

When she notices me, my heart shifts a bit, as if it hadn't been in the right place until looking at her. With a quiet and shy demeanor, she comes over, yet, when she speaks there is confidence in her voice.

"Good morning," she says.

"Good morning to you."

"There aren't a lot of tables."

"I have one." I kick myself for stating the obvious, but I'm relieved when she smiles. "Won't you sit down?"

"Okay." She takes a sip of her coffee and cringes as she sits down. "Oh, that's awful."

"Isn't it, though?"

After another sip she shakes her head. "Nope, I can't do that. Hey," she leans toward me, "Do you want to go get some coffee somewhere?"

Trying to cover my smile I scratch my head. "I'd love to."

We find a coffee shop two blocks down where the line is long and when we finally sit down, both of us share the artwork within the foam. Finally, she takes a sip and I hear the sweetest moan. "That's better. I needed this."

"Been a long day?" I ask.

"A bit." After she takes a sip, she taps my computer with her pink painted fingernail. "So, you're a writer?"

"How'd you know that?"

"You seem to carry your computer with you wherever you go. My father does that and he's a writer."

"I am a writer."

"What kind of writer?"

"I work for a magazine in DC doing small stories here and there. Nothing exciting."

It's clear that she's surprised by this comment when she looks at me sideways. "Bobby, that is exciting."

"No, it's really not, but thank you."

"Okay, well, what would make writing exciting?"

"Well, traveling articles, sports articles, even political articles, for starters . . . but I guess my true desire is to write novels."

Mandy has a way with her eyes to draw me in, casually and coolly sharing with me, somehow, that she's interested in what I have to say. "I love to read. What kind of novels?" she asks.

"Any kind…fact, fiction, it doesn't really matter. I like it all. I just haven't completed one yet."

"Well, let me know when you do. I'd love to read it, and, with the connections my father has, I might be able to get someone to look at it."

"That's putting your neck out there. How do you know I would be any good?"

"Well, I don't. But that's why I'd read it first."

"Gotcha."

We both laugh.

For two hours, we talk. Hardly anything about our lives comes out, but we discuss our goals and dreams. I have too many to count. She does as well. But then it comes—the dreaded words I don't want to hear.

"My boyfriend went to Europe last year, but didn't take me. That was tragic."

I agree—tragic. I quickly change the subject away from her

boyfriend. We stay another hour, and then finally, head back to the retirement home. Once we get there, she turns to me.

"Thank you, Bobby. I needed this. My grandma hasn't been well and I've been spending so much of my time here. It was nice to get away."

"Good. I'm glad."

"You wanna do it again tomorrow?"

I hesitate on accident and quickly wish I was better on my feet. "That would be great."

As she walks away, I'm unable to keep from stealing subtle looks, then finally she disappears around the corner, but not before she gives me one last smile. "Well, well, well." I say to myself.

Chapter Twenty Six

1934

Her tiny feet tap the floor of the dusty hallway, while her hands run along the dirty wall, as hunger pangs force her to the kitchen. There's a large chance that this will all go wrong, the way it has many times before, but she's quite sure she might not live through the night without food. Slowly and cautiously, she peeks around the wall into the kitchen. The lights are off so it's hard to see, but usually that means that Bill Manchuron is asleep in his room. Rachel takes a relieved breath and walks to the icebox, but after a few steps, his terrifying voice sends shivers down her spine. In seconds, tears fill her eyes from panic while she searches the darkness, and finally she sees that the moon has outlined him sitting at the kitchen table. He flips the light switch on, but the bulb is old and dim. By the amount of cigarettes in his ash tray, he's been sitting there for quite some time chain-smoking as if waiting to catch her. Her body shakes knowing what's coming next.

"Come here," he demands with a scratchy voice.

She wants to do nothing less, but cannot disobey. As a tear rolls down her cheek, she comes closer and just as she's within arms distance, he swings his hand around slapping her to the ground. "What have I told you about taking my things?" He stands up and kicks her, until everything goes black. With no idea how long it has been, Rachel wakes up as she's being dragged through the halls, then he drops her by his bed while he grabs his belt. With each swing the buckle breaks her skin. When he's done, he pulls her like a rag-doll down the stairs into the basement and throws her on the hard cement floor. She begs God for him to leave, but instead, he walks to the table where he keeps his tools . . .

Rachel gasps and sits up in bed. Her heart races so fast that she's sure the pain won't end. With a hand against her chest, she strains to suck in and out through her spasming diaphragm, wondering if this is what it feels like to die. She tries to remember where she is. Boxes sit along the floor, and a moon, no different than the one that lit Bill's silhouette, shines through an unfamiliar window with no curtains.

Only when a large hand slides up her arm, does her brain start connecting the dots. It is Levi. He sits up and presses his chest against her back, dropping his lips to her neck. With a gentle hand, he lays his palm on her chest, and whispers in her ear, "It's okay."

"I'm sorry," she says.

"Shhh, you don't need to say that."

"I think it's the move," she whispers, and he nods.

She climbs out of their new bed, steps over some boxes, and looks out the window of their new home. Her heart still hasn't settled, and every beat shakes her body. Levi comes to stand behind her, and her tears fall as he wraps his arms around her.

"He's where he should be," Levi whispers.

"Sometimes it feels as though he's everywhere."

"I know for sure he's not." Levi says this with such confidence that it forces her to turn around and look at him.

"What do you mean?"

He wipes her tears from her cheeks. "I make sure of it. Every year."

Rachel drops her head into his chest as he wraps his arms around her. "Levi," she cries.

"He's still in prison and will be for a long time."

"How?"

"Friends of my father and I keep in touch. I'll know if he ever gets out."

When she looks up at Levi, he takes in a deep breath, expanding his ribs in her arms as if to teach her how to breathe again. Finally, by mimicking his breath, her heart slows down. Then he kisses her gently. "You never speak of that time," he says softly. "It'll never go anywhere if you don't. What happened just now?"

She tucks her head into his neck, but says nothing. A few minutes later, as they lay in bed, she breathes out an untethered breath. "He used to starve me, then he would sit in the dark, smoking cigarette after cigarette just waiting for me to come to the kitchen to steal his food. It got to the point where I was so hungry, I would risk it." Levi runs his hands through her hair and shakes his head. "Are you sure you want to hear this?"

He takes a moment to think. "No . . . but yes."

"His brutality was one thing, but it was his mind games that made everything worse. He wanted me terrified and worked hard at it."

"Did you ever tell Sylvia or Dick?" Levi asks.

"No. Simone knows almost everything . . . almost."

"Why not everything?"

"It's too terrible as if I don't want Simone or you to look at me different."

He draws closer. For several hours she tells him stories he doesn't want to hear, and she doesn't want to relive, but then she asks about the war, and he has his own. By 2:00 am, they fall asleep, but this time, she doesn't wake until morning.

Their new house is beautiful and just behind Levi and Rachel,

Sylvia has moved in with Minnie. Simone brings her baby over as often as she can, and even leaves the little man with Sylvia and Minnie during work hours. Minnie has found a new job that she loves, working at a small bakery where the owner is teaching her how to cook. She often brings the food home.

One evening, Levi walks into the new house while Rachel is covered in paint from head to toe. She doesn't hear him since he sets his things down quietly and tiptoes across the room, grabbing her from behind when he's near. She cries out in surprise, then laughs her deep guttural laugh as paint covers his nice clothes and he doesn't seem to care. Without a word, he kisses her, paint sliding up and down their skin, then he lifts her into his arms. It's time for dinner, but he's hungry for her. With the afternoon sun filtering into the wall-sized windows of their living room, he looks her body over as the light casts perfect lines across her and they don't even make it to their bedroom. Instead, he makes love to her right there on the sheets that cover the floor.

As they breathe heavily, he lies beside her, their chests rising and falling with satisfaction. "This is my favorite part," he whispers as the sun starts to set.

"What?"

"Coming home to you. Things are finally simple."

One weekend, Rachel takes Levi to Ada's speakeasy. He's always been obsessed with architecture and as they walk in through the hidden entrance, he touches the walls and smiles at the grandiose club.

"This is amazing. Where did she get the money?"

"A man who loved P.B." Ada comes dancing up to Rachel, which allows Rachel to introduce Levi. "Ada, this is Levi."

"Well, I've heard so much about you." Ada says as she takes his hand.

"You as well. You've done a beautiful job here." Levi says as they watch the mixed crowd bounce to the beat.

"It's packed for Rachel." Ada says with a clap of her hands.

Rachel gets onstage, giving a great show as the sweat pours from dancers and hardly anyone remains in their seat.

"The club is packed on the nights Rachel sings." Ada says to Levi as they stand at the bar. When Ada turns to Levi, she lifts an eyebrow. "Jake loved her."

Levi notices the lost look in Ada's eyes return. "I assumed."

She nods. "He couldn't show it or get 'em both in trouble, but he did. If that damn officer hadn't done what he done to PB, it would've been someone else." She takes a swig of alcohol from a nearby shot glass, then breathes out as if to blow away the pain. "I told him to stay away from her."

He looks at Ada with understanding and nods.

"Don't tell her that, but I did. It wasn't her . . . you know that, it's everyone else. This world has pain Levi. Pain! And I outlived my son." Her chin wobbles, then she smiles. "But look at this place."

"This is one of the best places I've ever been," Levi admits. "You've done well."

Ada chuckles. "I suppose I have. You see that woman up there?" She points at Rachel.

"Yeah."

"Take care of Jake's girl."

Levi grins, then he touches Ada's elbow that leans on the bar. "With every part of me, I will. Tell him that."

"You know what? I believe you."

Across the room, Rachel descends the stairs to find a man standing at the bottom, so she smiles. "Hello."

He reaches his hand out to shakes hers, "Rachel, you are so wonderful."

"Thank you."

"My name is Ernie Peck." His dress shirt is pulled tightly to his Adam's apple and his hair is perfectly swirled as though he has somehow flattened out his curls and pasted them to his head.

"Ernie. It's nice to meet you."

"Rachel, do you know Tommy and Jimmy Dorsey? Have you heard of them?"

She smiles. "Yes, I have."

"They've just put together their own band called The Dorsey Brothers. Well, you see, they're lookin' for some talent. They have several shows comin' up and are in need of a singer after the last one . . ." He makes a curve around his belly to indicate that the current singer has gotten pregnant. "Could I entice you to come and meet Tommy and Jimmy? You'd need to travel with them, but it will be well worth your while."

"I'm not interested. Thank you though." She starts to walk away but the man hurries to catch up with her.

"Wait, Rachel," he says with a kind smile. "Listen, they asked specifically for you. And I believe it would be great for your career..."

Her career. Years ago she'd been known for Somethin' Tender, then she was the choir soloist, and now, she's the happiest she's ever been with Levi, in their house on Apple Road. Had she followed music, or had it followed her? Did she care that people would no longer know her name?

"I'm sorry, you'll have to find someone else." Rachel says again, but as she walks away, his deep voice calls out.

"You owe it to your fans."

Before she can answer, Levi comes over once he notices them speaking. He instantly sees the confusion in her eyes. "Everything okay?" He slides his arm around Rachel's waist.

"I am." She smiles at him. "This is Ernie Peck. He's asking if I'd like to work with Tommy and Jimmy Dorsey and their new band."

"Your wife would be paid handsomely, and we would take great care of her while she's traveling," Ernie insists.

"She's not my wife and it's up to her." Levi says.

"Ernie," she says softly, "Do you have a number? I can't answer you now and I'd like to take a moment to think about it."

"Of course." He hands her a card, but before he walks away, he leans in closer. "If I can just say one thing: you belong on a stage."

That night when Levi lies asleep, Rachel walks down the stairs and out onto the porch to sit in one of their rockers. Within a few minutes, Levi comes out wiping his tired eyes and sits in the rocker next to her.

"Why are you up?" Levi asks.

"Do you think you have control over anything that happens in your life? Or is there something somewhere deciding everything for you?"

Levi looks at her, then at the stars as the crickets chirp, and the grass sways. "I believe we have a choice for many things, but do I believe there is something guiding me? Yeah."

Rachel looks at him. "How do you know?"

"A feeling . . . I guess. I believe I was meant to meet you."

"I was meant to be taken by Bill? Jake was meant to die?"

There is quiet but for one of Levi's deep breaths. He reaches his hand out and touches her arm. "I believe this world is hard to understand and not everything comes from what makes miracles. So, we have to lean into the parts of this world that exist in the realm of truth and goodness, not into the darkness. And don't get me wrong, the darkness is there . . . but I must believe that something better than I could ever imagine gave me you."

It isn't long before Rachel is singing with The Dorsey Brothers and separated from Levi by hundreds of miles. On the road, without knowing the significance of it, she meets Glen Miller—a young man who is playing in the band. Little does she know of the impact this shy man will have on music altogether, but they often speak backstage.

By the end of 1935, Tommy and Jimmy Dorsey split up when Tommy walks offstage during a live performance because he and his brother couldn't agree on the tempo of the song. Tommy asks her to come with him, but Jimmy wants her to stay. Unable to choose, she instead decides to go home, but doesn't tell Levi.

The door is open at the Apple Street house. When she walks in, Levi is sitting at the table working while the record player is softly playing big band music. For two months they have been without each other, but she resists the urge to run to him. Instead, she quietly leans against the wall and waits for him to notice. Once the record skips again and again, he turns and catches sight of her. A smile spreads across his face as he jumps up to grab her in his arms.

"What are you doing home?" he asks as he runs his hand along her face.

"I've decided it isn't for me anymore."

"What?"

"Being without you."

He smiles with a sigh and kisses her. Before she has a chance to move, he wraps his arms around her. In the middle of the night, they lay with each other as they listen to a night owl just outside. "Are you ever going to marry me?" he whispers.

She's heard him mention it before, but this is the first time that he has been this clear. With a deep breath, she smiles. "I love you. Isn't that enough?"

"Why are you against marriage?"

She takes a moment to think about his question. Finally, she answers, "Do you know why I was with Bernie?"

"You were an orphan."

"Yeah. But do you know why?"

"Why?"

"My mother got pregnant with a traveling salesman's baby. When her husband found out, something happened and she killed him. People said it was self-defense, but she gave birth to me with handcuffs on."

Levi protectively touches her face but stays quiet.

"The first time I heard this story was when I was in Bill's house. He was angry at me for something and found my papers. Those papers that you stole back for me when you were just a teenager, I still have them and I've never read what's inside. While Bill had his belt off and he was whipping me with it, he said that my mother was a killer and he was never going to allow me to turn out like her. He also told me that we would marry when I turned ten and there would be nothing that I could do to get out of our marriage because marriage bound us together forever." Rachel realizes from the pain in her throat all the way down to her stomach that she has never told anyone this story. Just telling it seems to wound her again.

It takes Levi several moments to say anything. "There are so many stories I haven't been told."

"I'm so happy now, I don't want anything to ruin it."

"Nothing is going to ruin this." Levi leans toward her and kisses her forehead, then her lips. "I love you, Rachel, more than I've ever loved anyone. You never have to marry me . . . ever. You hear me? I will never make you do something you don't want to do."

"Don't make a promise that you can't keep."

He rolls over onto her and stares into her eyes as he reaches out and entwines his fingers with her hand that lays on her pillow. "You have my word." Then he kisses her, hoping, deep down, that he can heal her every wound.

By 1936 Simone is pregnant again and Minnie becomes a baker—she doesn't even seem to mind that she's gained sixty pounds. But mostly, everyone is good, everyone is happy. Rachel wonders when she feels the weight of the world on her shoulders, wondering when the other shoe will drop.

One morning, Levi has the early news on the radio as he leans against the counter with his coffee in his hands. The bright sun is radiating through the windows when Rachel walks in from outside, but it's the look on his face that concerns her.

"What is it?" Rachel asks as she pours her tea.

"You remember Mussolini?"

"Of course. I don't think I could forget. Very nice man."

Levi chuckles and raises his eyebrow as though he doesn't agree.

"It seems that Adolf Hitler and Benito Mussolini have now become allies."

"Okay." She doesn't quite understand.

"It's not going to turn out well."

"Really?"

"It's just a hunch. But we'll see."

1937

In the year that William H. Hastie becomes the first black federal judge, Amelia Earhart and Fred Noonan disappear over the Pacific, and J.R.R. Tolkien publishes The Hobbit--one night in December, Levi and Rachel are lying in bed. Rachel is nearly asleep when she feels Levi run his hand along her back.

"What?" she says casually as she rolls over to him.

"I'm a divorced man."

She rolls over quickly. "It's official?"

"Yes. She finally signed the papers."

"Where is Kendra now?"

"I don't know and I don't care to know. She finally signed the papers because the man that she had a baby with left her and she has now found a new wealthy benefactor to target. She wrote me a letter and gave up her quest to take the hotel."

"Finally." Rachel smiles at the weight that is lifted. "I guess now it's our turn."

This shocks Levi and he looks up with surprise. "What are you saying?"

"I'll admit that I'm scared to change anything because I'm so happy right now. I don't want to jinx it."

"I know. So am I. But I want to make a family with you."

"Then let's make a family," she grins.

"You'll marry me?"

"Soon."

"Alright then. I'll wait. But you may wake up one of these mornings with a ring on your finger."

"I don't think that's legal."

"I have a lot of connections."

His hand runs down her body and he wraps her leg around him. Softly, he kisses her neck nearly sending her into a ticklish laughter. But as his lips reach her chest, she feels the heat rush to her cheeks.

"What if I said I wouldn't make love to you until you married me?" he says as his hands and lips roam freely along her skin.

"I would say you're a little late and I don't believe you could."

Suddenly, he pulls his lips away. Levi isn't the type of man to back away from a challenge and it shows in his eyes. Quickly he lifts himself off of her and steps out of bed.

"What are you doing?" she asks quickly, feeling the desire.

"You should always believe that I can do anything—just because I can."

He starts to walk out of the room, but she stops him quickly.

"Levi! Come back. I was just kidding."

"I don't think you were," he grins.

Within seconds she is out of bed and in his arms pushing him back into the room. "You can't kiss me like that and then not give me what I want." His grin is now an itch she can't scratch.

"Yes. I can. I think I'll go get some water."

"Okay. Okay. You win. I'll marry you."

"I don't want it because I win. You have to want to marry me, you have to need it. But I can wait until you get there."

She jumps up and wraps her legs around his waist. "I do. I promise you, I want to marry you." Suddenly, she grows serious. She can see in his eyes what he really wants. "Levi, I would marry you tomorrow if I could."

"You're not just saying that?"

"No, it's the truth." She kisses his cheek and then his lips as he lets his hands come back to her body. "And I desperately want you right now."

That is enough for him; he turns around and lays her back on the bed. Within seconds he has touched every part of her.

§ § §

Time passes quickly. Simone has two children—the second is a little girl and she names her Thandie. Sylvia spends most of her time playing games, reading, and walking downtown, while Minnie continues to bake—until John Ipson offers to open her a bakery. The sign is the last thing that hangs from the hooks outside and on the first day, a line of people are waiting outside.

By late spring in 1938, Edward R. Murrow, an American broadcast journalist and war correspondent, organizes daily news reports and Bob Trout, a journalist in New York reads them over the radio. People are eager to listen to the news. Small bits of information come to America regarding the strange new power that is developing in Europe.

One morning, Levi and Rachel listen to a broadcast.

"I am glad that you don't live there anymore," she says.

"Yeah." He nods.

In early August, the phone rings and Rachel hears Levi answer it. The conversation lasts nearly an hour with Levi's voice unusually hushed. Finally, after he hangs up, Rachel stands in the doorway. "What was that all about?"

"We have to talk," he says solemnly.

The sudden feeling of her heart dropping nearly sends her to her knees with a familiar panic, so she holds on to the wall as he walks to her.

"That was my old captain. We called him Captain Nel."

"From the army?"

"Yes."

"Levi, just tell me. What's happening?"

He reaches out and runs his hand through her hair. "There's been a lot going on in Europe." She nods. "They're concerned, Rachel. It seems that there's more going on than some want to admit. This man, Hitler—he's gaining a lot of power in a very short time and no one really knows what to do with it. I guess." She looks down at the floor, knowing what's coming next, while the tightness in his chest grows. When she won't look at him, Levi knows there isn't much to say. "Can you look at me?" Finally, she brings her eyes back up to his. "I guess that Britain has decided to prepare. Nel's asked me to go."

"To Britain?"

"They've made an order for four hundred planes, and he wants me over in England to train and fly one."

"What did you say?"

"I have to go, Rachel. I've had this feeling for a while."

"Levi?" Rachel steps away from him.

"I want to do this. Nel told me things . . . things that are happening over there that I can't tell you . . . I don't want to tell you. But this has to be done and if we don't, then who will?"

Rachel's tears come to her eyes thinking of the first time that Levi disappeared from her life. She feels him come near and wrap his arms around her. "The last time you went to war, it changed you so much."

He drops his lips to her neck and kisses her gently, then he turns her to him. "Listen to me. I'm not the same as I was back then. I promise you, I will come back to you."

In less than three weeks, she takes him to the train station. He's handsome in his uniform, but with his pristinely polished shoes, and perfectly ironed pants, his appearance doesn't foretell of the danger he might experience.

"I'll come back, Rachel."

"But what if you don't. What do I do?"

"I promise you if you promise me something." He leans over her until his lips touch her ear. "When I return, you will marry me?"

Suddenly, she wishes that they hadn't waited so long. She wishes that she had a ring on her finger at that very moment. "I'm sorry, Levi. I was stupid. We should be married."

"Shhh. When I come home." He kisses her, long and deep, still thinking about the way he made love to her the night before. Finally, he pulls away, lifts his bags over his shoulder, and walks to the train. With one last look, he disappears as she waves goodbye.

§ § §

Rachel reaches across the bed to the place where Levi's head usually lies, only to run her fingers across the emptiness. A tear runs down her cheek, then she closes her eyes trying to remember how she got through her life without him. Tucked in her hand is the first letter from him that she's been able to receive. Nearly a month had gone by without word, until that morning, when the postman set it in her hand.

"I know you've been waiting for this." The old man, Hank, says with compassion. Rachel reaches out and gives him a hug.

"Thank you."

She sets her hand along her stomach as she walks through her kitchen and into the backyard just staring at the letter with his handwriting. Sitting on the back porch, she opens the soft envelope, wondering where he is.

My lovely Rachel, he begins.

On the other side of the world Levi walks out to the large, green bomber plane, and runs his hands along the smooth metal as he wonders what he's doing there. The field is full of military planes lined back to back and side to side, on a soggy day despite the sun shining through a few clouds. Admiral Nel finds him at the early hour and comes to stand at his side.

"It's good to have you here," Nel says.

"You'll have to convince me of that, because at this moment all I want is to be home with her." Levi turns and smiles, but it's weighty and broken. "It used to be a lot easier to leave everything behind."

Nel nods, "Only something this important could take me away from my family. Levi," he says in such a way to encourage Levi to look him in the eye. "The cause is worthy. I wouldn't have asked you if it wasn't."

Days turn into weeks, as they learn to maneuver these new fighter planes. It takes time for the men to grow accustomed to the way the Supermarine Spitfire flies. Levi appreciates its top speed and agility, as he finishes his hours of training.

By mid-1939, the people of Great Britain flee to the countryside in order to escape the threat of German air raids targeting London, and the risk of war increases until Levi can feel its urgency.

Back in Atlantic City, Rachel relies on Levi's businessmen to keep things afloat with his hotels while still having a gambling night with the ladies. Every day she stands at the mailbox waiting impatiently for letters and every day it is like Christmas morning when the mailman arrives. One by one she places his letters in a wooden box with decorative metal straps and a hammer lock that Sylvia gave her when she was a child. It fills to the brim until she searches a nearby store for another. If one day passes without a letter, she re-reads the one from the day before.

As Nel predicted, the Battle of Britain arrives in 1940 when heavy fighting plagues overseas. Finally, after a few weeks, Simone and Minnie arrive at Rachel's house with one mission. "Turn off the radio," Simone says.

"It's not helping you, Rachel," Minnie agrees.

On August 17th, W.M.L. "Billy" Fiske is the first American soldier to die when his plane is damaged in battle. Initially, his name is not released, forcing many family members to dread what may come. Rachel stands at the radio waiting for the announcement of the first death. Finally, it is publicized, and she falls in her chair with relief. This is only the beginning. Men continue to lose their lives battling in the skies over Europe. Levi writes about how he is doing and how sorry he is that he can't be there with her. Even though he is convinced that his presence there is to serve a greater purpose, he tells Rachel of his wishes to be home.

Rachel smiles sometimes, but only when Simone brings the kids over or when Minnie talks about her expanding waist size. Daily walks fill her afternoons and she dreams about Levi touching her. She spends countless hours in the warm sun thinking about his voice and the way it feels lying next to him.

If only she knew at those very moments, Levi is thinking of the very same things. When dirty and tired, visions of her lure him out of his torment.

Then, the letters stop. The horror of what might have happened is unbearable. Many nights she drops to her knees begging God to send her word that Levi is alive. But day after day, there is nothing.

"What am I going to do?" she cries out one night. That morning, she wakes to a knock at her door. It is Hank, with a bag over his shoulder.

"Good morning, miss? I'm sorry, but there has been some mistake. Somehow someone messed up and we have been unable to deliver these letters to you for a while now. We only just found out."

She looks in his hand to see a stack of letters with Levi's handwriting on the front. Poor Hank hasn't a clue what to do when Rachel drops to the ground in sobs and laughter as she pulls the letters one by one from the strands of twine.

"I'm sorry, miss."

"No," she chokes with a sob, "It's alright. I just…I just…"

"She's been waiting for those." Minnie says as she runs up from outside. "Thank you," Minnie says to Hank, assuring him by her look that he can leave, so he walks away hesitantly. With a hand on her shoulder Minnie sits down beside Rachel and wraps her arms around her friend. "He's alive, Rachel."

§ § §

One morning, in July of 1941, Rachel runs down the stairs to answer the phone. "Hello?" Rachel asks.

"New York Westing 3045 is on the line for you."

"Thank you, operator," Rachel says, not recognizing the number.

"Rachel Praline?" a man's voice asks.

"Yes?"

"Rachel, it's Chuck. Chuck Gerber."

"Chuck Gerber?" She sits down on the table next to her. "What are you doing calling me?"

"Rachel, I need to apologize for everything that happened before. It is my fault and I know I was wrong."

"My goodness this came out of nowhere."

"Oh, I know, Rachel. This is probably making no sense, but I'd like to come see you tomorrow."

"See me? Why would you want to do that?"

"Well." He pauses, undoubtedly with something on his mind. "I have some work for you."

"Work?" she asks, shocked but curious.

"Yes. Please let me come see you and I'll tell you all about it."

The next evening, she sits in a restaurant looking across at Chuck Gerber—a man she hadn't expected to ever see again. He looks just as he had before, only this time he comes with a smile—and this time, she isn't desperate for money—which she shows by wearing one of the finest dresses she owns and insisting she buy her own dinner.

"So, what is this, Chuck?"

"You've heard that our military is massing for war?"

"Yes."

"Well, President Roosevelt has expressed a desire to have you come and perform for the men."

Rachel nearly chokes on her drink. "What?"

"That's right. President Roosevelt himself. You see, he and I know each other very peripherally and he saw a picture of you. I also played him some of your music and well, he thinks you're just what the men need."

"You know President Roosevelt?"

He changes his words ever so slightly, knowing that he is on shaky ground. "Well, a friend of my mother and father's knows him. But it is absolutely true that he requested you himself. He's a true fan."

"Chuck, I . . . I don't know what to say."

"I think all you can do is say yes. How do you argue with the President? Come on now?"

"I'm not meaning to argue with the President, but I just don't see how this would work."

"Are you married?" Before she can answer, he throws his hands in the air, "I am not interested. I am simply asking to find out so that I may have a better argument."

"I might as well be."

"But you are not?"

"No, I am not."

"You would be getting paid well. We'll take wonderful pictures of you and there is an entire entourage that will be at your side making everything easy and perfect."

"Chuck, this is crazy. What would I be doing?"

"Well, you see, there are USO dances going on all the time on military bases across the States and England, and there are lonely men that need a little bit of a pick-me-up." He sees that she's not convinced and finally his tone changes, "Rachel, I know that Levi is there. Why sit around wondering about where he is. Perhaps this would be a good distraction?"

He's right. She feels it through to her bones.

"Here is the contract." He passes a packet of papers over the table and smiles. "Take as much time as you need to read it over. Especially take a look at the section that tells you how much you are going to be taken care of." He winks.

"I thought you loved choir music."

"Yes, well . . . I also love Big Band music, but most importantly I love traveling and my tour with the choir has stopped. If this war keeps escalating…" he hesitates with a smile, "it will take us all over the world. Think about it, Rachel."

"Alright. I will."

"Good."

Within one week, Rachel makes up her mind. She has to do something or she is going to go crazy, so she signs the papers and sends them back to Chuck. He gives her a date when she will meet him in New York on November 14th of 1941.

Just three weeks before she is to leave, she wakes in the middle of the night. The darkness is broken up by stray bits of moonlight, but she furrows her brow and listens. She has heard something and waits for it to come again. She can tell that someone is in the house which makes her jump to her feet.

Before she can investigate, yelling fills the house. Rachel races to her door. Standing in the hall, naked as a jailbird is John Ipson, Minnie's fiancé, with a lamp in his hand as though he is ready to swing it like a baseball bat.

"What's going on?" Rachel asks, trying to avoid looking at him.

A voice comes from the stairs in front of John. "Rachel, what the hell is this?"

Instantly, she flies to John's side. Levi, in uniform, with his bag over his shoulder, is staring at the naked man in his house with all of the lights in the house off.

"Levi?" Her heart pounds with relief. "What are you doing home?"

"What is he doing here?" Levi asks as John drops the lamp to cover his private parts.

Minnie comes out and instantly flips the light switch. Both Rachel and Levi cover their eyes. "Oh my God! John, this is Rachel's Levi. Go put clothes on!" Minnie yells.

John lowers the lamp and nods with a smile seemingly a little insecure because of the handsome man in front of him. "Sorry, Levi. It's nice to see you," he says as he reaches for Levi's hand.

Levi doesn't take it. Minnie hurries to him, "Get in the room. You're naked." She pushes him into the room and closes the door, leaving them in the hallway alone.

Rachel is standing just a bit taller than Levi at the top of the stairs.

"You brought other men into my home?"

"Well, you were gone and . . . what if you had been someone else? You would have appreciated that John came out with a lamp." They're silent for a moment, then they finally laugh. "Sylvia wanted it. She didn't like that I was alone."

"Sylvia's right, I guess. I just didn't expect to see a naked man blocking my way to you." He smiles and reaches out touching her nightgown with his fingertips.

"God, Levi." She falls into his arms, and he walks up the last step as he holds her. "What are you doing home?" He squeezes her tightly. It has been too long since he last touched her and neither of them wants to move. "I was given a little bit of leave since I've been there for so long," he says.

"I miss you," she says with her face nearly touching his.

Finally, together, they walk into their bedroom. He drops his bag on the floor and begins pulling off his uniform. When his chest is bare, she walks over to him and places her hands on his skin. "I can't believe you are here."

"I'm so sorry I've been gone for so long."

"How long do you have?"

"Just a few days."

For the three days he is home, they don't spend a moment apart. They lie in bed together until noon, and at night they try not to fall asleep. The phone rings one afternoon and Levi answers it. Instantly, Rachel knows by the tone in his voice that something is off. She comes around the corner with a rag in her hands as she dries them.

"It's for you," Levi says looking confused as he hands her the telephone.

"Hello?"

"Rachel, it's Chuck."

Suddenly, Rachel looks at Levi with concern. "Chuck, what's going on?"

"I just wanted to say that I received your papers. Everything is in the works and the dates haven't changed."

"Alright."

"I will see you then?"

"Yes, of course. I'll be there."

When Rachel hangs up the telephone Levi stares at her.

"Why is Chuck calling you?"

"Well," she says hesitantly. "There's something that I haven't told you about."

"Okay." His eyes are more serious than she has seen in some time.

"Chuck Gerber contacted me a while back. It seems that I've been requested."

"Requested? What does that mean?"

"Well, I'm going to travel and sing for the troops."

"You're going to what?" He is angry.

"The President wants to entertain the soldiers and I've been chosen as someone to do that."

"And Chuck Gerber is the one heading this up?"

"Yes. He is."

"Rachel, you are not doing this."

"You don't understand, Levi. I've been so lonely here without you and I just thought this might get my mind off of the fact that you are gone."

"To send you overseas where there's fighting. You are damn well kidding me!" He is yelling as he walks into the kitchen. She doesn't know what to do as she follows him.

"I won't be where there is fighting. I'll have plenty of people around me."

"You don't understand what's going on over there, Rachel. There is no playing around. Men are dying and you want to go there? What are you thinking?"

She is quiet as she grips the table behind her back. He's never yelled at her before and frankly, it scares her. "I'm sorry, Levi. I didn't know you would feel this way about it."

"Get out of it."

"What?"

"Tell Chuck you can't."

"I've signed papers."

"You what?" Levi turns around and grabs the kitchen counter squeezing until his arms bulge beneath his shirt.

Slowly Rachel walks to him and wraps her arms around his back. "I'm so sorry. I didn't think this would bother you."

"Did you not question it when it was Chuck Gerber who called you?"

"I did. But he told me about it and all I could think was that I would be closer to you. And the thought of not staying in this house without you anymore…"

"You can't go there," he says through gritted teeth.

"I have to, Levi. I can't get out of my contract. Besides, I don't want to." With that, he pulls away from her. Now, she's feeling heat in her cheeks and the anger is rising from a hidden place within. "You have no say in this! I want to go. I will not be alone again　!"

"I forbid it! How dare you do this without telling me."

"How dare I? You made a choice to be a part of this war in any way that you could, now why can't I?"

"Rachel!"

"Don't yell at me!"

He walks out of the kitchen and slams the door behind him as he furiously heads outside. His chest rises and falls with such intensity that he has to set his hands on the top of his head. He closes his eyes but faces toward the sun letting the heat warm his skin. Every thought going through his head panics him.

Suddenly a soft voice calls to him, "Levi."

He turns to her instantly; her red cheeks and glistening tears. Her eyes are red from emotion and whatever anger he has calms. With strong steps he walks to her, pulling her into his arms. Before long he kisses her, lifting her feet off the ground and carrying her into the house. As if it's the last time, they make love, knowing that he returns tomorrow. For a moment as he relishes in her bare skin against his, he looks her in the eyes. Out of breath, he says, "I love you, Rachel." Then he kisses her again until he can't stop. As he lay with his arms around her, he kisses her neck. "I'm sorry. I just can't lose you."

"I don't want to be here without you anymore," she whispers.

He holds on to her, as both are silent. By the next day he is gone.

Chapter Twenty Seven

1941

One's life is comprised of chapters—periods of time that, when memory serves, were happy and easy, or strip us to the bone until we wonder if we'll ever be the same. Sometimes there seems to be no in between—only good and bad.

When Rachel is about to step onto the train, heading to New York and back into Chuck Gerber's care, Simone and Rachel are both crying. She said goodbye to Minnie and Sylvia at the house, but before Simone headed to the courthouse while her kids stay with her mother, she decided to see Rachel off. Everything in Simone disagrees with her friend's choice, but as usual, she stares into Rachel's beautiful blue eyes with compassion.

"Be safe, Rachel."

They look at each other, ignoring the stares from every direction. "I'll get home as soon as I can, but Simone, if anything should happen---"

"Shhhh." Simone shakes her head. "Not one word."

"Simone, if anything---"

"I said not one word. Get on that train and get home just like you've always done before."

As the conductor calls out, "Final call!" they hug one last time.

A few minutes later, they watch each other through the window as the train car picks up speed.

By mid-afternoon in New York, Chuck and Rachel ride the elevator to the top suite of a skyscraper. When the doors open, Rachel is rushed into the large and open room by an array of industry people—to clothe her, photograph her for publicity, discuss music detail, schedule, housing, eating, and even protection. Nearly thirty people are gathered in one room all for her.

Chuck doesn't say much about what she should say or do, but he follows her closely and speaks when he feels it is important. For two weeks they stay in New York, laying the groundwork for England. Everywhere she goes she is treated like a star. They hold press conferences for reporters to ask questions about the tour.

Simone, Sylvia, and Minnie collect every piece of publicity they can find from newspapers articles, despite their nerves. They listen to the radio every chance they can when Rachel is to be heard, and the stations have even begun playing her older songs more frequently.

On December 7th, Levi is pulled from his bunk in England while Chuck and Rachel hear the news from a photo-shoot in New York, and Simone listens while she and John Ipson are researching their next case at the office—Japan attacks Pearl Harbor leaving devastation in their wake.

The next morning, Chuck and Rachel sit in a café as the owner turns up the radio so they can all hear. President Roosevelt begins . . .

"Yesterday, December 7, 1941...a date which will live in infamy...the United States of America was suddenly and deliberately attacked by naval and air forces of the Empire of Japan.

The United States was at peace with that nation and, at the

solicitation of Japan, was still in conversation with its government and its emperor looking toward the maintenance of peace in the Pacific."

When President Roosevelt finishes, the café is silent, but for a woman crying in the corner. Rachel looks at Chuck.

"No plans have changed, Rachel. These boys need you over there now more than ever."

1942 comes quickly as the entire world seems to be suffering. Sometimes it feels as though there is nothing but military, fighting, and at home, talks about the destruction. In England, Rachel sings often, and the boys are happy to have her around. They couldn't have been more excited if the President himself had come to see them. Rachel Anne Praline, the beautiful cover girl, exits each plane to the rejoicing of large groups of waiting soldiers. She laughs, hugs, and takes pictures with them and her rich voice fills places like the Royal Opera House, the United Merchant Navy Club in South Shields, and the Grafton Rooms in Liverpool, and even many large airplane hangars. The press called it the "Dancing Boom" and Rachel felt lucky to be a part of it.

Every move that Rachel makes, Chuck is not far behind. Her every move is coordinated to perfection, while he stands at the base of every staircase to hold her hand and follow the timeline to the tee. He constantly whispers in his assistant, Carla's, ear what she will wear both clothing and jewelry. There is no doubt that Chuck Gerber is smart and a true publicist. His family had known this art for decades. Rachel's name blows over the regiments like wildfire, all because of Chuck's exhaustive efforts.

One night, Carla comes to Rachel's side with a towel after her last song with Conner, the photographer, in tow. The three of them had come to find solace from the crowds with each other. They watch as the floor vibrates with soldiers, nurses, and civilians dancing, while others watch from the surrounding tables with red, white, and blue tablecloths.

"You need a break," Conner says quietly.

"What makes you say that?" she asks sarcastically.

"As if Chuck will let her out of his sight," Carla quips.

Rachel is caught off guard, while she towels the sweat from her forehead. "What do you mean?"

Conner chimes in, "We've never seen someone so controlled. Chuck tells you where to go and what to wear . . . I'm surprised he doesn't tell you how to eat."

Carla laughs, "He does tell her what to eat. Through me. He tells me and I make sure she gets it."

"Well, there you go," Conner chuckles.

Rachel furrows her brow as the smell of newly baked bread fills the room, coming from the nearby kitchen and caterer. She then sighs. "Yesterday he told me that I shouldn't be putting butter on my bread. Does that count?"

Carla and Conner cross their arms in unison while Connor continues, "Yes. That absolutely counts. Why don't you come with me?"

Rachel can't remember the last time she made a decision that wasn't Chuck's. "I'm afraid to say yes."

Conner takes her arm. "Carla, watch for Chuck and distract him. Come on," he says to Rachel. "Trust me. I snuck out of my mom's house enough to know how to do this. Watch." Conner pulls them off the dance floor, through the crowd and out the side door while Carla heads toward Chuck in order to keep him distracted. Once they are outside, they hurry along the field toward the barracks, even though Conner has to stop to take a quick picture of the last bit of color leaving the sky.

"Where are we going?"

"You'll see!" he says as he pulls her across the open field. The moon is bright, and the air is fresh after being in the smoke-filled dance. They soon reach the sixth barrack, while staying pressed against the walls when a few soldiers pass. Conner tells her to be quiet with his finger to his lips. Once they are gone, he opens the door to the sixth barrack where five men in incomplete uniforms sit around a table or lounge on their bunks. At first, they notice Conner, "Conner!" one of them hollers as he throws a baseball in the air for it to land in his leather glove while he lays on his bed with no shirt on. "Come to take more pictures?"

"No, I thought I would bring a friend this time." Conner pulls Rachel in behind him, surprising every one of them so badly that they jump to attention. One of them nearly falls from the top bed when his foot gets caught in his sheets. Two of them nervously begin to throw clothes on.

"Oh, you got to be kidding me!" One of the boys smiles as he grabs his chest.

"Hi, boys," she says calmly.

"Rachel, this is Gerry, Howard, Pasty, Jack, and Killer," Conner says.

"Killer?" Rachel looks at the seemingly harmless man.

"Not the best nickname, Miss Praline, for a soldier. I'm good at baseball."

"Oh, is that it?" Rachel laughs.

"Yeah. He keeps busting the guts out of our baseballs," the boy named Jack says.

Rachel steps inside the room, which makes them shuffle about. Jack quickly brings her a chair. "Please sit, Miss Praline."

"Just call me Rachel."

"Oh, alright."

They hurry to surround the beautiful woman, unable to take their eyes off her.

"Why are you in here? Shouldn't you be at the dance?" Rachel asks.

"We would have liked nothing more than to see you sing, Miss Praline, but we're not allowed," Gerry, a boy with curly, blonde hair answers. "We're supposed to be sleeping. 0400 hours comes fast."

Jack, who has small eyes and a deep dimple in his chin, explains.

"We set out tomorrow at four o'clock am ma'am. Heading to the fight."

"No wonder you can't sleep," Rachel says.

"Yes, ma'am," all of them say.

Conner sits on a military chest next to Rachel. "I've seen this woman play cards. She's pretty good."

Rachel looks at him quickly. "Don't give away my secrets."

"You wanna play?" Jack flies to his feet and searches through a box at the head of his bunk. "We'd be happy to lose our money to you, Rachel."

Rachel plays games with the boys. She laughs more than she has in a long time. The numbers in the barracks grow and soon there are nearly twenty men asking her questions.

Killer brings her a poster and a marker. "Would you sign this for me, Rachel?"

Rachel looks down with surprise at a long poster of her dressed in a form-fitting gown and looking dolled up from head to foot. It is sexier than she remembers. "Where did you get this?"

"They're everywhere," the young soldier answers with a grin.

"Well, Killer, don't be showing this to everyone."

"There's no need, everyone has one."

"Oh, God. I'll sign it once I get your real name."

"Willibald C. Bianchi."

"Willibald?"

"Yeah, my mother liked it, therefore I had no choice."

Rachel runs the pen along the shiny poster.

"Miss Praline," he says as she writes. "You don't understand what you are doing for the troops here. I can't believe you are here, right now, in this room."

"Sometimes I can't either."

When the clock in the corner strikes midnight, Rachel and Conner bid them farewell. The boys rush to get a hug from Rachel before she leaves.

"Be safe, boys," Rachel says as she steps from the small building.

When Conner closes the door, they hear them hoot and holler. After just a few feet, the door to the barracks opens and Killer comes running out to stop her and Conner. "Thank you, Miss Praline. May I say, nothing could have been better before we ship out."

"You're welcome, Willibald."

Willibald C. Bianchi is captured by the Japanese on April 9th, 1942, then forced to be a part of the Bataan Death march and imprisoned in many Japanese POW camps, after a valiant fight to save his brothers-in-arms. Willibald barters with his captors for extra food and medicine, which he gives to his fellow prisoners. Sadly, Bianchi is killed instantly when an American plane, not realizing there are American prisoners in a Japanese prison ship, drops a bomb in the cargo hold. After his death in 1945, he and three other soldiers are awarded the Medal of Honor.

§ § §

"Be careful as you go around this corner," Conner says to Rachel as they head back to her room. "He always seems to be out on his balcony."

Rachel and Connor peek around the corner of the nearest building next to their hotel and look up to the fifth floor. Chuck isn't there, which allows them both to take a sigh of relief.

"Come on," Connor says as he begins running to the back door of the hotel. Before long, they laugh as the elevator climbs to Rachel's room on the eighth floor and, when it lands, Connor opens the gate for her. "It was good for those boys to meet you. Thank you for coming."

"It was good to get my mind off of things. Have a good night, Conner."

"You too."

He closes the gate and soon he disappears to the next floor.

Feeling relieved from a night away, Rachel smiles as she opens her hotel room door and drops her jacket on the nearby chair as she reaches for the light, but before she turns it on, she notices the light from the balcony is shining through the glass doors. Chuck is leaning on the doors, still in his suit, with his hands in his pockets.

"Where have you been, Rachel?"

"Chuck? What are you doing in my room?"

"I pay for this room."

"No, my sponsors pay for the room, and I do the work."

"You don't believe that what I do is important? You wouldn't be here if it weren't for me." Chuck's eyes darken over. It's obvious that this rich kid has never been told no in his entire life.

"I needed a night off, Chuck." Rachel says as she takes in a deep breath.

"With Conner?"

"I didn't say with Conner. Were you watching me?" She and Conner hadn't thought to look at the eighth-floor balcony, only the fifth. "Conner's a friend and I needed to enjoy myself for a while."

"You're not here to enjoy yourself, Rachel. You are here because you have a job to do. Now do it and stop flouncing around like a whore."

Rachel throws her purse on her bed. "A whore?"

"I seem to recall that I had this problem with you before."

"What problem is that, Chuck? That I need time away from you?"

He stomps to her and takes her arm forcefully. "You listen to me, Rachel. The contract is signed. You are mine for the next six months. I will hold you for breach of contract if you so much as look at me wrong. You got that!"

Rachel's heart beats heavily until she can't feel her lips and she stays silent. She doesn't really know what he can do with the contract, but Simone will. Without another word, he marches out of the room.

By the next morning, as Rachel heads to the cafeteria, an army jeep drives by and honks. On the very back of it, with his camera gear over his shoulder, and his legs hanging over the side, is Conner. Without smiling, he lifts his hand in a small wave. Their little getaway seems to have cost him his job.

1942

Levi walks to the airplane hangar, with several of his men, after one of the most dangerous landings he's had to make. The left side of the plane was nearly obliterated by flak until most of them were praying under their breath.

"Only you, Captain," one of the soldiers said with black oil all over his face, "could have done what you just did. Did you know you could do that?"

Levi pats his shoulder as he passes him. "Nope."

"Well, you did!" The soldier hollers as he heads the other way while one of his men kisses the ground nearby. Levi smiles then takes a deep breath of relief as the adrenaline starts to dissipate and he rubs his forearms in pain. Just across the tarmac, at the entrance of the hangar, he sees a man waiting whom he's never seen before. It is obvious that he's looking at him.

"Can I help you?" Levi says as he walks closer.

"You're Levi Price?" the man asks.

"Yeah, that's me."

"My name is Sykes."

"Okay, hi Sykes. What can I do for you?"

"I've had some guy calling me, asking for you."

"What do you mean? Some guy?"

"I've got a number for you that I think you're going to want to call," Sykes says. "It's about your girl."

Levi furrows his brow with worry. "What do you mean?"

"Someone that says he worked with her."

Levi grabs the paper he's holding out and reads the number. It's a New York number. Five minutes later Levi hears a man's voice on the other end while he wipes his dirty face with a rag. "This is Captain Price."

The other end crackles as Conner responds. "Oh, man, Levi Price. Rachel Praline's Levi Price?"

It isn't the first time that someone is interested in talking to him about his girl. He hesitantly responds. "What do you need?"

"I'm worried about her, Levi."

Levi's instinct to protect Rachel rushes to the forefront of his thoughts, as usual. "Who are you?"

"I'm sorry. My name is Conner. I was her photographer until I was sent back to the States a few months ago. I'm sorry. I won't waste your time. You're probably wondering what I'm doing. Look, do you have just a minute?"

"A minute."

"Do you know Chuck Gerber? The man—"

Levi despises even the sound of his name, so he interrupts, "Yeah, I know him. What's he done now?"

"I just wanted to warn you. There's something not right about him. He watches her every move. I'm not sure what to say except that he thinks he owns her. I don't know what the contract said…"

"Who the hell cares what the contract said, what's he doing?" Levi's blood boils.

"Well, she and I snuck away. I know that sounds bad, but I promise you, just as friends . . . and the next day he sent me home. I wasn't even allowed to see her before I left. I've been working for a long time trying to get ahold of you. Back and forth they sent me, until I was just about to give up. Finally, some man by the name of Sykes allowed me one call to where you're stationed."

"How do I know I can trust you, Conner? How do I know you don't just want my girl?"

"Well, sir, to be perfectly honest, I don't feel that way about women."

There is a bit of silence. Levi gets the idea.

"I appreciate that you called. Thank you, Conner."

"You're welcome. She's a great girl, Levi."

"Yeah, she is."

Levi hangs up and rests his hands on the desk in frustration.

"Something wrong, Levi?" one of his men asks.

Levi says quickly, "I have to find Rachel."

§ § §

They wake early and catch a ride on a Douglas C-47 Skytrain, used to transport troops and supplies across various theaters of war. From the moment they arrive, it is obvious by the way the soldiers react to Chuck's crew that they aren't happy about this mission. Rachel watches the side eye of the soldiers as Chuck tells them where to place things and how to be gentle with the sound equipment. Finally, one of the men barks, "Just because you know the right people doesn't mean we should be wasting our time with you."

A whistle rings out from nearby and the irritated soldier closes his mouth and continues to haul Chuck's equipment, as a handsome man in a pilot uniform passes by Rachel. Chuck hurries toward him with a hand out, but the man doesn't take it. Rachel and Carla stand beside each other as they suddenly understand the situation better. Once again, Chuck is never told no.

"Thank you, for letting us catch a ride," Chuck mentions.

"We'll get you where you need to go. You understand the danger here?" the handsome pilot asks.

"I understand the danger of low moral," Chuck jokes.

"Yeah," is all that the pilot will say.

A few minutes later as the sound crew and stage crew climb on, Rachel looks around at the uncomfortable faces, then finds her own seat beside Carla. Her heart can't help but race when she notices parachutes in the corner.

"It's fine, Rachel. They're doing us a favor to let us tag along," Chuck says when he notices the concern on her face. "It's what the President wanted."

Immediately as they head down the runway, the shaking begins. Sounds that they have never heard, and the toxic smell of oil fills their nose, until Carla reaches out and takes her hand. "Conner would be going crazy right now."

When they hit a long bout of turbulence Rachel checks her seat belt several times.

"I think it's as tight as it's gonna get," a good-looking soldier says from the seat next to her.

"I just don't know how much I can trust it," she smiles through nausea from fear.

"Would you like me to check it?"

"That would be wonderful, thank you."

The man checks the complicated metal clasp and runs his hand along the strong woven nylon. "It's secure."

Just then the plane drops twenty feet, forcing a gasp from both Carla and Rachel, so they both close their eyes until it stabilizes.

"Sometimes when it looks like this outside," he points to the gray skies through the small oval windows, "it causes a bit of turbulence. But Whipple's good."

"Whipple? Who's Whipple?"

"The pilot. I'm Nick." He puts his hand out for her to take it.

"Rachel." It is hard to hide her trembling of her hand and he takes it with both of his.

"You'll be fine, Rachel."

His brown eyes are genuine, and she appreciates it. After so many months with Chuck, she almost doesn't know what true compassion looks like anymore. A thin scar runs along his chin and it creases when he smiles. Rachel quickly looks at Carla who still has her eyes shut, then searches for Chuck. He is preoccupied with his paperwork in the far corner of the plane while yelling at the stage manager.

Soon, Nick pulls out his wallet and shares a picture of a beautiful brunette woman with almond green eyes. "She's waiting for me. When I get home, we'll get married."

"She's beautiful . . . and thank you. I know you're trying to distract me."

"Listen, these planes aren't easy to feel comfortable in unless you're used to them. Not sure why you're getting so close to all that's going on here anyway," Nick says honestly.

"I'm starting to feel the same way. I'm not sure I was given enough of a choice now."

He chuckles. "Well, hopefully we are able to deliver the package peacefully."

Another wave of the plane through the clouds and Rachel's heart beats rapidly as she squeezes her eyes shut. "Please distract me."

"Are you married, Rachel?"

"No," Rachel answers.

"Why's that?"

She shakes her head, reprimanding herself for making Levi wait until now. "We should be married. But now we're both here, so we may never get the chance."

"He's here?"

"I'm not sure where. But he's a pilot."

"What's his name? I'm also a pilot—just not today."

"Levi Price."

Nick laughs and looks up for a minute. "Small world." He shakes his head, "I was stationed with Levi. I got to fly with him once." He pauses for a moment and looks at her, "So when he talked about Rachel, he was talking about you? That's funny. He doesn't seem the type to be okay with you being here."

"That's because he's not."

They both laugh.

"Then why are you? Tell me…why do women do what we don't want them to do?"

"Women deserve to have a say about their own lives and not have to abide by every rule you have for them," Rachel checks him.

"Hmmm, are you sure you had a say in this adventure?"

Rachel smiles. "Honestly, I don't know why I'm here. Levi was gone and I needed something to keep me busy until he got back. And it has been good. I mean the soldiers have worked so hard, and the singing is always fun. You're right though, there's something I'm not understanding about myself to let him pull me onto this flight."

"That guy?" Nick says, pointing his head at Chuck.

"Yes." She looks at him with a raised eyebrow. "Why aren't you flying this plane?"

"I'm waiting for my plane to be fixed. That's actually where we're headed. It should be ready when I get there."

Nick's handsome brown eyes look her over as the plane shakes. On each cheek he has one deep dimple and when he smiles, his straight teeth shine white. He has more of a baby face than Levi, but overall, he is just as handsome. She shivers just a bit and he looks at her. "You cold?"

"I didn't expect to be-- in June."

"Well, up in these planes it can get that way. Here." He unfastens his seat belt, giving Rachel a shock.

"Oh, don't do that. Not for me."

"I'll be okay." He smiles as he stands and carefully walks through the belly of the plane. When he reaches the other side, he bends low and pulls a blanket from the nearest box.

She smiles until the plane makes a large dip forcing her to grab the arms of her seat. She looks up to find Nick holding on to the railing above his head.

"Whoo, that was a bad one," he laughs as he finally reaches her side again.

"Get your harness back on. Hurry," she demands as he sits beside her.

"I promise, Rachel, I'll be fine."

With the warmth of the blanket, Rachel soon falls asleep. Her head slides comfortably down on Nick's shoulder. It isn't until the plane begins to sway like a ship on the sea that she wakes. Nick appears concerned.

"Don't look like that," Rachel warns him.

Suddenly there's a loud crash. Rachels fingernails are clawing the metal armrests and Carla comes out of her sleep with a gasp. One of the pilots hurries out. "Make sure you all are completely fastened; we've hit a bit of a snag." With that, he turns and hurries back into the cockpit.

Rachel looks at Nick.

"Don't worry, Rachel."

The plane bounces and sways until a couple of boxes and bags get loose and slide down the middle aisle. Chuck's crew are rightfully afraid, but it's the look on the soldiers' faces that tells Rachel something isn't right. Again and again, men check their belts.

Then, suddenly the plane dives. Faster and harder than any of them can handle. Even with her belt tight, Rachel finds it hard to stay on the small metal seat, so she grabs the wall above her head. "Nick!"

"Don't worry. Just hold on tight." Nick takes his belt and with one hand unfastens the clasp.

For the first time since this began, Chuck is silent. Pressed against the wall, he desperately tries to tighten his belt, but he won't open his eyes. His papers are now flying in the air and his clip board is beneath his feet.

Nick practically slithers out of his chair, keeping close to the floor, and, with strong arms, he army crawls to the cockpit door. He gives a significant knock and just as the door flies open Rachel can see Whipple yelling while trying to keep the plane steady.

"The wing's been tipped by a blast and now the left engine is jamming," Whipple yells as Nick pulls himself inside the small nose of the plane.

Faster it falls and the pressure of the air pulls the skin on her face. Carla grabs her arm and won't let go, while their ear drums nearly pop with the roar. Tears begin to stream down her cheeks, as she prays under her breath. Rachel pictures Bernie in her favorite hat, pointing her finger with a slight grin. "God is bigger than this airplane, Rachel."

Whipple yells. "We're taking this down in the nearest field."

Rachel's throat turns to dust and her jaw hurts from clenching as she stares at the square fields outside the windows that are rapidly approaching.

Whipple, Nick, and the other pilot in the cockpit cry out in anguish as their arms burn. One of the soldiers named Daffy yells at Rachel from his seat across from her. "When Whip lands, Miss Praline…," Daffy yells, "…stay close to us. We've strayed over the Channel and might be landing in enemy territory."

She nods and then closes her eyes trying to think of Levi or Simone. Whip rocks the plane to make sure the landing gear is down. Nick, now sitting securely in a chair in the cockpit, yells, "Thirty seconds!" The plane tilts just a little and they wait for the impact. As the men pull at the controls, the plane shakes so hard that it seems it will break into pieces.

Chapter Twenty Eight

Simone sits at the desk trying to read the papers in front of her, but for some reason, she's read the same paragraph fourteen times. Something doesn't feel right.

"John, I have to go." Simone calls out.

John runs from the back room, spilling his coffee on the tile floor and all over his sleeve. "What do you mean?! What about the CORE meeting?"

"I'll be there. Just gotta check on something."

Simone runs to her car and jumps inside, only to dash home while still maintaining 35 miles per hour. As she reaches her front door, she can hear her mother's loud laugh and the cackling of her children playing. They are surprised when she bursts through the door.

"Well, goodness, something's made you all sweaty," her mother says. "What are you doing?"

"Is everything okay here?"

The babies run to her legs and wrap their arms around them, so she pulls them into her arms for kisses.

"Everything's fine, honey."

Simone breathes out, but still she can't shake the feeling within, so her mind vacillates to Reed. He would be deep into the inventory at the nearest machinery where he's climbed the ladder over time. It takes her eight minutes without speeding to get to the machinery and several men look at her as she screeches to a halt in front of the main doors. Leaving the car running, she runs inside, turning every corner as she calls out Reed's name. Rob, a close friend, nearly crashes into her as she hurries toward the offices.

"Simone? You okay?"

"Where's Reed?"

"He's back there."

Not waiting for him to say another word, she races toward the back doors and throws them open. Reed is standing there with his hard hat on, talking to his boss in his favorite white button-up shirt. When he sees her, the concern instantly tightens his shoulders. "Simone? What's going on?"

Simone breathes a sigh of relief again. "You're okay."

"I'm fine? Are you?"

Simone looks down as she places a hand on her heart, then she shakes her head. Reed places a hand on her face, running his thumb back and forth on her cheek. "Baby?" he asks.

"I'm okay. Go back to work," Simone says, but instead of doing so, Reed walks her through the halls and out the door, even when she says nothing.

They reach the car that is still running, so he pulls the keys from the ignition, then returns to her side. "Simone?"

A tear falls down Simone's cheek as she stares at the ground for several moments. Finally, she shakes her head. Deep in her soul, she knows something has happened. Without saying a word, she looks up into Reed's eyes as tears run down her face. Never asking for a reason, he pulls her into his arms.

§ § §

Finally, the plane crashes. The screeching and grinding of metal is painful to their ears, while their bodies slam against the belts across their chests, when the wings tip to the side. Sliding along the ground with one hard lurch after another, the pilots hold on for dear life as the plane continues through the field of high grass. The lights flicker as parts of the plane collide with others, or scrunch like an accordion, or completely separate.

Passengers are thrown from one side to the next. One of the engines bursts into flames. Suddenly, as one wing tips, the velocity of the plane sends it into the air and onto its roof. Several more seconds pass as they roll upside down through the field. Metal strips away and the large aircraft begins to crack. Rachel hits her head and everything goes black.

When Rachel wakes up, the plane has stopped, but she can smell burning. Next to her, Daffy is hanging lifelessly by her side with blood streaming down his face and on the other side Carla is making no movement or sound.

"Let's go! We have to get out of the plane!" Rachel hears Nick's voice before she sees him.

Soon, several soldiers drop to the roof of the plane with loud thumps as they unbuckle. Rachel tries to pry hers open, but realizes that something has hit it, causing it to jam. Her head hurts from the crash and now being upside down, which makes her panic. Just below, she sees Chuck scurrying out with his bag in his hand. "Chuck!" she calls out, but he doesn't respond. Instead, he hurries to the exit as one of the soldiers kicks it open. "Chuck!" Rachel calls out again. This time he turns back just long enough to show Rachel he has no intention of helping her. "Nick!" she yells out.

"I'm here, Rachel."

Just below her, he is trying to find something he can stand on to get to her level. Finally, he places two metal boxes on top of each other and climbs them.

"Get everyone out of the plane, Whipple!" Nick yells as he touches the belt to Rachel's seat.

"What about Carla?" Rachel asks, panicked. He continues without responding, trying to pry her free. "Nick? What about Carla?"

He looks up at her, then reaches to the girl with her hair hanging over her face. Carefully he assesses Carla, but stops when he sees the injury to her head, then checks her pulse. After a moment, he shakes his head.

"We've got to concentrate on you right now." Nick looks at her belt. "This is going to take too long. It's completely bent." He looks around. Rachel feels the pressure in her head and puts her hand to it. "I'll go as fast as I can," he promises. Whipple begins working on Daffy just beside her.

"Whipple I'm going to need something to cut the seat belt," Nick says calmly even though his arm is bleeding and it's getting hotter within the metal belly.

Through the windows, Rachel can see the other soldiers hurrying away from the burning engines. Her head starts to spin and she's seeing stars, so she tries to tilt her head to get some of the blood to move down her body. She places her hand on the wall behind her to help her regain some stability, but pulls it away in a flash with burnt fingers.

"Don't put your hand against anything right now," Nick yells over the cracking. "It's on fire. It's too hot to touch."

"Help," Rachel says as her breathing grows sporadic.

Nick looks at her face while trying to cut her loose. "I'm almost there," he whispers. He places his shoulder under hers to try and release some of the pressure while her hands try to grab anything, but she doesn't have much strength. "Whipple!" he yells out.

"Yeah, here. Got it," Whipple yells back. He holds an M3 Trench knife up to Nick. Whipple then climbs the boxes to Daffy.

Nick finagles the knife under her belt. "Don't move, Rachel."

"Nick, I can't…" Her voice starts to fade.

"Come on, Rachel. Lift yourself up by holding on to me," he orders her.

"I'm trying."

Soon Nick has the first belt cut, quickly followed by the second. Rachel drops to his shoulders. "Come on. Let's go," Nick says as he lowers her carefully to the ground. She feels herself rock just as her feet touch down, but he keeps his arm on her. "We have to run!" Nick says as he helps her from the plane. They race through the darkness, side by side, as the last of the plane goes up in flames.

Chapter Twenty Nine

1942

Levi can feel the tension in his body and his knuckles are white as he flies lower than ever allowed in military operations. Having very little information leaves them without coordinates—searching as best they can along the coastline. Behind him, in the belly of the plane, his men keep their sight on the open fields, but also have one hand on their weapons from fuselage-mounted guns to the smallest man in the ball turret, tail guns, anti-aircraft guns, and even their own individual pistols. This is unheard of to be taken off the front line in order to find a fallen crew, but it's obvious that Levi gave no options—nor did Nel fight it.

"Does anybody see anything?" he asks calmly into his mask.

"Negative, sir. Not yet," one of men from the back responds.

"Okay, yell out if you see anything."

Levi doesn't want to say it, as though the words might make it true, but he doesn't know whether he's looking for their plane or wreckage and he wipes the sweat from his forehead just thinking about it.

"Levi?" his co-pilot, Max, a man he's known since he first came back to England, calls out. Levi turns to him. "Where were you just now?"

"In hell."

Each time they speak it sounds like they are speaking into a seashell while the crackle of their voices nearly tickles their skin.

"We'll find her, Levi."

"Sir!" both of the men hear.

"What?" Levi asks quickly.

"Down! Just below us, there's a plane . . ." the soldier hesitates for just a moment, ". . . or remnants of one."

As they pass, Levi's heart drops when he sees the black, charred wreckage, that would never be able to have survivors. Max looks sympathetically toward Levi, but this only angers him. "We don't know anything yet. Let's land on the other side."

But the truth was that Levi could never live without her.

§ § §

Rachel tries to catch her breath in the darkness. She sits carefully on a tree stump as the flames from the plane continue to pop, hiss, and explode, a half mile away. Several did not make it out, including Whipple and Daffy, and she can see the look in the men's eyes as they kneel and stare.

"Miss Praline?" At first she doesn't hear the man asking for her attention. "Miss Praline?"

She turns to him with an apology already escaping from her lips. "I'm sorry."

"It's okay, Miss Praline. I just wanted to ask you if you are hurt," a young man, looking no more than eighteen, asks. On the front of his helmet is the sign of a medic.

"No. I think I'm fine," she says quickly.

"What about your side, ma'am?" he asks with concern.

She looks down and there is blood on her blouse. "Oh. I don't really know. I don't feel anything." She lifts her shirt just a few inches to see whether there is a wound or if she has happened to touch someone's else's blood amid the chaos, but there, along her left side below her ribs is a long cut.

"May I take a look at it for you? It's adrenaline ma'am. You'll feel it soon. We have a bit of travelin' on our feet to do now and we certainly don't want that to get infected out here," the medic says in his Southern accent.

"Uhhh . . . yeah . . . yes . . .," she says with a nod of her head.

"Why don't you just lay down here and let me fix you up?"

"Okay." She lays back in the tall weeds. From where she is, she can only see the medic who kneels over her with a serious expression and the stars. "I'm real sorry about all of this, ma'am." He has curly blonde hair and bright eyes but looks like a child.

"You mean this isn't supposed to be part of my experience traveling over Europe?" she asks while wincing.

He laughs and shakes his head. "I suppose it won't be worth it if you don't get a little adventure out of it." He apologizes as he cleans the wound. "I must say that I am a bit surprised that you might want to come to Europe durin' all of this fightin'. It was a dangerous trip even without the plane crash."

"Yeah, I know."

"Ahh well, that's alright, ma'am. Maybe they'll just send you home now. That's a better place for you to be," he grins.

"I suppose it is." She looks up at the young man's kind eyes and smile. "Can I get you to stop calling me, ma'am?"

"Now, I don't think so. I'll just have to apologize in advance before I throw out a ma'am on accident."

"Well, just try and call me Rachel even if I'm older than you."

"I was nineteen last Wednesday."

"Well, nineteen-year-old medic, what's your name?"

"Dell Moore," he answers with a nod. "Rachel, we're going to have to keep a close watch on this." He helps her sit up.

"Thank you, Dell. I will."

Suddenly, they hear a voice behind them. "Miss Praline? I thought you might need this." Together Dell and Rachel look up at a dark, Italian soldier standing above them with a black bag in his hand.

"My bag? How did you?"

"Yeah, I knew you probably wouldn't have time to get it," the soldier says, his deep voice resonant.

"Good job, Pacey," Dell says.

"Pacey?" Rachel asks.

"Yes, Miss Praline. My name's Pacey."

"Thank you so much, Pacey."

Commotion erupts from a group not too far off.

"Dell!" the soldiers yell. Dell hurries over to them. Rachel can see Daffy lying on the ground, covered in black soot and struggling to breathe. Whipple is bent over at the waist out of breath, having just carried Daffy so far.

Dell presses and prods, hoping to find what he can fix, then pulls his bag to his side. "What happened to him, Whip?" Dell asks Whipple.

"He was hit in the head during the crash," Whipple says as he throws his pack to the ground with a thud.

Nick comes walking back after talking with the rest of the men, including Chuck and his crew.

"What about you, Captain Nick? Are you okay?" Dell asks as he studies Daffy.

"I'm fine," Nick says.

"And you, Captain Whipple?" Dell asks.

"My shoulder hurts like hell. But, other than that, I think I'm fine."

Suddenly, with a guttural cough as though he had not breathed for hours Daffy comes to life. His body convulses as Dell tries to hold him down. "Daffy. Relax, buddy. I have to fix you up," Dell says calmly.

"Does it look like he'll be okay?" Nick asks.

"Yeah, Captain. He just took a good hit to the head, but his eyes look good." Dell reassures everyone.

Nick creates a perimeter of protection with several soldiers, while everyone recovers. Rachel stays quiet in the corner, but notices Chuck out of the corner of her eye, slowly making his way to her. She refuses to look at him, but he's but feet away.

"I'm sorry, Rachel. I saw Nick helping you. I wouldn't have left if he wasn't there."

"I can't believe I trusted you again," she says to mostly herself.

"Don't blame me for all of this. There was no way I could know this was going to happen. We'll get this all taken care of and then we'll get back to our tour."

Rachel finally looks at him. "Chuck," she stands up to look him directly in the eye. ". . . the tour is over."

Fear shows in his eyes and Rachel suddenly realizes there's something more he isn't saying. "It can't be. Rachel, just let some time pass. You're just upset."

"No, I want to go home."

"We have a contract."

She allows a bit of silence, then she steps toward him. "What did you do? Who did you promise?"

"People love your story. They really do."

"What are you getting paid Chuck? Is this a story to you?"

"I didn't know this would happen."

"But you knew the world would be more entertained the more dangerous our path was." She can see the truth in his eyes. "No choir means no money so you had to figure something out." She shakes her head with irritation. "Leave me alone, Chuck, you Son of a Bitch.

I don't care what contract you have; I won't be a part of it. Not anymore."

"Is everything all right here?" Nick interrupts their conversation and comes to stand next to her.

"I need a favor, Nick." Rachel and Chuck continue to stare at each other.

"Anything," Nick answers.

"I need you to keep Chuck away from me."

Without hesitation Nick nods and turns to Chuck. "Will do."

She walks away, but it isn't long before she hears footsteps behind her. "Rachel," Nick calls. She stops. "Whatever you need out here just tell me."

"Thank you."

"You're welcome." For a moment they are quiet. "We have to start moving. We're not exactly sure where we are so we have to find the nearest town." She looks at his guns and ammunition across his chest. His hand instinctively runs down the leather. "We have to be careful, Rachel. Just stay next to me. Okay?"

They walk all night in the pitch black, through weeds and mud. Suddenly she sets her foot in a hole, but Nick catches her before she falls. When she looks up at him, he nods. "I owe it to Levi to get you home safe. I promise."

Chapter Thirty

1942

Levi bends low in the weeds as he runs with Max next to him, and his men following closely. When they are near enough it is clear, very little is left to this plane as it has burned to ash and metal fragments. His heart pounds against his chest and he closes his eyes, no longer staying low and out of sight. His men pass him on the left and right with their firearms ready. Just behind them is a dramatic orange sunset, yet they pay no attention to it.

"Levi!" Max calls out quietly. "You should see this."

Levi takes slow steps as though he is heading to his own funeral while he lets his rifle drop and it falls like a brick on his thigh. When he finally enters the burned hull of the plane, Max is standing in the cockpit. In his hands he holds the Pilot's log that is nearly untouched by the fire.

"This is it . . . It's Whipple's plane," Max softly relays the news.

Levi looks behind him, recognizing the charred remnants of several bodies. Hanging from the blackened metal ceiling, is a burnt body—or what's left of it, still fastened to the chair. He reaches down when he sees a silver object below, and he pulls from the ash a bracelet. "There were women on this plane."

Max sighs. "I'm sorry Levi. It's definitely the right plane. Is that hers?"

"No."

"Well, that's good news, Levi." But when Levi says nothing and passes beside Max, Max sets a hand on his shoulder with compassion. "I'm sorry. Maybe most of them got out."

Just then, they hear a loud and bellowing voice carry across the field, so they race out of the debris. Across the field, as the nighttime draws closer, one of Levi's men, Donovan, has his hands raised above his head. Being one of his best marksmen, Levi relies on Donovan's presence behind enemy lines.

"Look at this, sir." Donovan points to several green army bags and tin boxes set about in the grass. "They were here for a while. There are some of the medic's used bandages over there and a couple of cigarettes. I sent Murphy over to find some tracks. And he says he found 'em."

Murphy stands three hundred yards away as he points along the grass. "They lead that way, sir."

Levi looks at everyone. "Let's go."

§ § §

On June 12th, 1942, Anne Frank receives her diary as a birthday present. Two days later, she begins writing the words that one day will be published worldwide. In that month alone, 144 U-boats are sunk in the Atlantic. The war in Africa, the Pacific, and Europe is in full swing. Yet, life continues to move on for those untouched by the ravages of war. On the other side of the world, Walt Disney releases Bambi, Bing Crosby records Silent Night, and Capitol Records opens for business.

Five of Chuck's crew and ten soldiers scatter about the deep green hillside with groupings of trees here and there. When they come across a town in the early morning hour, the moon is sliding down the sky and the sun is peeking through. This allows them to see that whatever village they have reached is left with mounds of rubble and a few buildings still standing. They keep quiet, with only their boots crunching the earth below and the mist of morning has created droplets on their skin, clothes, and helmets. Nick clears his throat to gather his men's attention before they cross the borders. "It'll be morning soon and I don't want to be walking along the road in broad daylight."

Whipple, who is ahead of everyone else, places a hand over his head to signal them to stop which quickly forces the company to its knees in order to wait for direction. Nick and several other soldiers tell Chuck's crew to kneel.

"Give me a minute, Rachel," Nick says as he quickly hurries to talk with Whipple.

Just next to her is Dell. "It's probably nothing, ma'am . . . I mean . . . Rachel."

She turns to him. "Did I seem scared?"

"Just a bit," Dell admits. "They'll talk and figure out what to do next. Then we'll just keep right on goin' I suspect."

"Do they have a plan?" Rachel asks.

"These captains always have a plan. Maybe we can hear what they say?" The two of them move a bit closer.

"We've reached a town. There's a small sign with a name that I can't make out," Whipple whispers.

"We have to hurry before the sun comes up," Nick suggests. "Send someone to read it."

The soldier they choose runs down there, then runs back. "LICQUES," the soldier says. Whipple pulls his map out, but can't find any indication of where they are. "Let's go. We don't have much choice."

They hike through white flower-covered grass just beyond the old, stripped and splintered, wooden sign of the small village. It seems to be abandoned, after whatever strike affected them.

"Wait here," Nick suggests. "Garrison and I will find us a place to stop for the day."

Garrison, a friend and soldier Nick relies on, follows closely behind as they come upon the homes that are lined up along the dirt road. Their boots stomp on moss-covered rocks. As soon as they pass the first home, they know the town is not abandoned. Clothes are hung on the laundry lines outside and washbasins with leftover water in them sit under the porch overhang. A large barn with half of the roof sunk in sits on a property where the home appears vacant. "Let's take our chances here," Nick says to Garrison.

By the time the sun casts its rays on the small village and dries up the dew, the group takes refuge in the ramshackle barn. Rusted tools hang from the ceiling and moldy hay covers the floor.

"Get some sleep," Nick tells everyone as they lay with their packs under their heads.

Dell hands Rachel his blanket and Daffy gives her some water. "Rachel," Daffy whispers. "Do you suppose when all this is over, I can get your autograph?"

"It won't do you any good. As soon as this war is over, I'll go back to being a nobody." Rachel answers as she lies on the hay.

"You really believe that?"

"I know that. I was just sitting at home before all this."

"There's no way. I've heard your name for years," Dell says with a smile. "This is the best unexpected mission any of us boys have ever taken."

"Dell?" Rachel says.

"Yeah?"

"This is the worst singing assignment I've ever had." They all laugh.

Just then, Whipple tiptoes over them and Dell looks up, "Where are you going, sir?"

Whipple has his gun in his hands. "I figure I'll stand watch by the door."

Rachel watches Nick make his way around the barn, searching it thoroughly. When he sees that she isn't sleeping, he kneels beside her with his pack in his hand.

"You alright?" he asks.

"I thought I'd fall asleep immediately. You think we're safe here?"

"For a while."

Rachel moves up onto her elbow to look at Nick, but stops suddenly when she feels pain jolt her senses. She sits up quickly and grabs the back of her shoulder just below her neck. With Nick's soft brown eyes he furrows his brow and moves just a bit closer.

"Are you alright?"

"It seems I might have found something," she says quietly.

"May I take a look?" he asks calmly.

She nods and then turns her back to him. He comes close until she can feel his warm hand on her neck. Carefully he pulls her blouse down until it reveals the wound. "Yep, you have a hefty bruise the size of a baseball. It's purple and a bit swollen."

"Wonderful," Rachel says.

"And your other wound? How's that?" Nick asks.

She shows him and together they recognize that her cut is swelling and angry, so he moves in closer. Nick is a calming presence. His gentle approach and soft touch helps her nerves. He grins, showing his dimples. "It's important to be careful out here. Let's keep our eyes on it."

"Thank you," she says quietly.

Before long, Rachel is trying to fall asleep while staring at the collapsing roof. A gaping hole lets sunlight hit her arm and it warms her skin. Her eyes feel tired, but her mind is reeling, and her wound is throbbing.

Nick notices she's not closing her eyes. "What are you thinking?"

he asks quietly.

She turns over to look at him. "How did I get here."

"I'm sorry, Rachel. You shouldn't be here."

"It was my choice." Rachel hesitates. "There's very little in my life that I've actually had any choice about, but I knew what I was doing. I suppose coming . . . I knew I'd make him mad."

"Levi?"

"Yeah. But I also love singing more than breathing."

"And you're truly amazing."

"Thank you." She pictures Simone in her mind. "All I can think about is home."

"Honestly," Nick says, "This war . . . many of us chose to come, but now all we can dream of is home. Besides, it was not your choice to fall from the sky."

She grins. "No, you're right. That was not my choice." She looks at Nick's hands and notices that he's holding a letter. "Is that from your fiancé?"

Nick clears his throat uncomfortably. "She's no longer my fiancé."

"What? Why?"

"I knew it was coming. She wasn't happy and I suppose I live in denial. I don't blame her. I'm here and she's there. This last letter informed me that she would be moving on."

"I'm sorry, Nick."

"I guess I have to believe it's for the best. How can I believe any different? If I let myself question all of this . . . I'll try and control it. And I can't control her, just as much as I can't control this." He points to the war-ravaged barn with pain beneath his strong brow. He looks past her suddenly. "Shhh."

A shadow is coming toward the large door where Whipple is pressing himself against the wall with his weapon at his chest. Nick places himself in front of Rachel while preparing his gun, just as the door creaks open. Whip keeps his eyes on Nick to tell him what to do while light spreads across the sleeping soldiers.

Whip throws himself and his gun around the door, to surprise whoever is pushing it open. Nothing happens, no weapon is fired, but the soft sound of a young boy with a French accent can be heard. "Are you Americans?"

After a few moments, Whip and a young boy enter the barn together. Rachel watches the boy look around, unphased about what he is walking into.

"You speak English?" Nick asks.

"Yes, a little."

"May we rest here?" Nick looks around at the wounded and tired group.

"Ummm, you kill Hitler?" he asks, wiping his dirty face.

"We fight against Hitler, yes. Can you tell us where we are?" Nick shows him the map.

He shakes his head. "My father."

"He likes Americans?" Whipple asks.

The boy nods. "Americans. Kill Hitler. My father likes you Americans," the boy says with a smile.

"Okay, go get your father." Nick says and the boy runs out of the barn.

Soon, he returns with his father just a few steps behind. Everyone gets concerned when they see a rifle in his hand. "My father say you are welcome here," the boy says quickly. "He say, Hitler's army come in and take whatever they want. He hates Hitler. His brother's wife is Jewish, my uncle. Armies come in. They take my uncle and wife. My cousins hide. But later they come back and take my cousins. My father say he will come with you to kill Hitler and find his brother."

Nick suddenly understands what the rifle is for and puts his hand up quickly. "I'm sorry, we can't take anyone with us. Have the soldiers been back?"

The father looks at the boy, wanting to know every word the

Americans are saying, and the boy translates. Then says, "Not for weeks. The armies don't come anymore."

"Where are we?" Nick points to the map.

The father indicates that they are between Calais and Boulogne-sur-Mer.

"We need to get to the coast without being seen," Nick tells them.

The son directs them with his dirty fingers. "That way."

"Thank you. You've helped us." Nick places his hand on the boy's shoulder. "I'm going to let my soldiers get a little more rest and then we will be out of your way," Nick says. "What's your name?"

"Jonas," He points to himself and then his father, "Leon."

"Jonas, where did you learn to speak English so well?"

"My uncle who was taken studied in America before he marry Anastasia, his wife. My dad say he should have stayed in America. But my uncle came for Anastasia. He taught my brother. He taught me to speak English."

"Well, I'm sorry about your uncle."

"My father say you come in and eat."

"Tell your father thank you. We are grateful for his hospitality, but my soldiers need rest and then we must be on our way," Nick says.

"Okay." The boy and his father speak for a while and then he says, "My father say, thank you. We will win."

"I hope so, kid. I hope so." Nick wipes his tired eyes, then the boy and his father walk away.

They sleep most of the day. The boy and his father stay away until just before dusk when Nick and Whipple get everyone ready to leave. Leon and Jonas stand out on the street waving to every soldier.

Keeping hidden behind foliage, walking through mud and tall weeds, or camouflaging themselves within the branches of large trees is necessary for a group this size. Chuck's crew is tired and afraid, while the soldiers seem unphased, or perhaps the truth is numb, having been through these situations before. Each time they notice small towns, two men run ahead to check it out before the group continues. Nighttime has never felt so comforting and safe, when the darkness wraps around them. It isn't until they hear the deep boom of an explosion, then see the lights in the distance, that they pick up their weapons again.

Nick comes closer to her until she can feel his shoulder against hers. "If it gets any worse, we'll take a different route," he reassures her with calm eyes. She nods as flashes of light spread across the dark countryside. Their group descends a hill keeping the explosions to their right while just ahead, is an open field. "Be careful of the ground. If you see anything unusual, don't take a step until you call me over to check it out. Okay?"

Again, Rachel nods.

The acrid smell of gunpowder floats in the air with hints of sulfur, and the ground shakes with each boom. Rachel's heart is racing and her hands are sticky, while she diligently watches the ground. Soon Daffy, Pacey, and Dell surround her. Pacey, with a cigarette hanging from his mouth, has sweat pouring from his jaw, while Daffy's bloody head is still wrapped in cotton. Suddenly there's an explosion just a hundred yards away, which makes all of them duck out of instinct.

"Get down." Nick whispers, and everyone follows the command.

Minutes pass and they wait, but nothing happens. Finally, they decide to keep moving while only four of them are allowed flashlights. Pacey drops his cigarette, then looks at Rachel. "Get closer for my flashlight." Dell and Daffy do as well.

"So when we get back home I want to come hear you sing," Daffy says quietly as he touches his bruised forehead.

"That's if I have a job when I leave here."

"It'd be a shame if you didn't," Dell says.

"Aho," someone yells.

Just ahead two large German tanks have come into view, traveling along the fields toward them. Everyone drops to their knees keeping out of sight through the tall grass and turning off their flash-lights. For nearly twenty minutes they lay together, just waiting and hoping the tanks will just pass on by.

§ § §

Simone, dressed in her mauve skirt and button-up white blouse, hands the secretary her new notes to write up on their latest plaintiff. "Just add these to the original notes, thank you, Joyce."

"I thought her meeting was last week?" Joyce says as she sets the paper on a pile.

Simone rolls her eyes and lifts an eyebrow, "It was. However, for some reason she continues to remember new things every day."

"Oh my, what a memory," Joyce grins.

"Yes, oh my." Simone smiles then moves on through the office, until she sees the mailman at the door. He doesn't usually come inside. "Good afternoon, Ennio."

"Good afternoon ma'am, I have a certified letter here for you."

"For me?"

"That's right."

Simone signs his paper, then reaches out to take the envelope. Instantly she reads Department of the United States Army, Levi Price, and time stops. "Thank you, Ennio," she says although she's already begun walking away. With shaking fingers, she opens it, her breath getting more shallow. It is a letter from Levi.

Before she can finish it, she sits down from weak knees. Joyce hurries to her side, then John, "Are you okay?" they both say.

"Rachel's plane has gone down." Simone places a hand over her mouth as tears come to her eyes.

"Oh my goodness." Joyce says solemnly.

"He doesn't know if she's okay or not." Suddenly Simone looks up at John, "John, don't tell Sylvia or Minnie. You hear me? Not until we know more."

John's chest rises and falls knowing this won't be easy. "We're going to be late for court." John says finally, after several minutes of silence.

Simone stands up, pulls her jacket on and tucks the letter in her pocket. "She's fine. Let's go."

"How do you know?" Joyce asks.

"I just do. Joyce, we'll be back. Come on John."

§ § §

Everyone's tension falls when the tanks pass without incident. They had avoided a catastrophe at the last minute. Continuing on, they turn on their flashlights once again, until suddenly Daffy cries out in pain.

"What's going on?" Nick calls out from in front.

Daffy, bent over at the waist, cries out in anguish. Rachel is beside him, as is Pacey, yet neither of them can tell what has happened. "Daffy, quiet down!" Nick yells as he runs over. When he's directly in front of him, Daffy has tried to muffle himself using his hands. "What's wrong Daffy?" Nick asks, kneeling in front of him.

"My foot," Daffy pants as tears fall from his eyes.

Nick turns his flashlight onto Daffy's booted feet, and everyone suddenly holds their breath. A piece of long metal, sharpened with a pointy end and twisted in the middle, has impaled Daffy's foot— even piercing through the leather boot. Directly from his laces, it sticks out with blood dripping from it. The pain Daffy is in is beyond what anyone can imagine. Sweat drips down his bandaged head as he struggles to keep quiet.

Nick suddenly gets a worry in his head and starts looking around everyone's feet. "Check around you!" Suddenly the field where they are becomes a show of lights as they check the ground. Nick scours the ground and just beside Rachel's left shoe is another one of the booby traps. "Rachel," he says. He takes her hand and helps her

457

carefully step away, then turns his attention back to Daffy. Several other soldiers yell that they've found more of these buried weapons.

"Whip, hold this." He hands Whipple the flashlight and starts to dig into the dirt around Daffy's boot. Just this alone causes Daffy to cry out.

"Wait Nick, what if it's more than just that," Whipple suggests.

"What do you mean?" Nick asks.

"Here." Whipple points at the metal plate buried in the ground. "What is that? What if this is marking something . . . some sort of explosive?"

Nick stops digging in order to think. Pacey looks at Daffy. "Daffy, can you pull it out?"

"No!" Daffy tries to hush his cries but isn't successful.

Nick drops to his knees on the wet grass, then lays down. Moisture covers the front of his uniform and then washes over his chest as he presses his face flat to the earth in order to see beneath Daffy's boot. "Pull out the book."

Dell digs into his bag, soon revealing a field manual and quickly finds the section for mines. He pulls his small flashlight and reads over the material while Nick waits. "Do you---" Dell stops suddenly.

Suddenly everyone stops, hearing the slight rumble of a nearby vehicle. "Where is that?" Nick asks.

"Over there . . . coming over that hill." Whipple whispers.

Coming through the fog, another troop of Germans is heading toward them in vehicles and on foot.

"Everyone lay down," Nick commands quietly.

Daffy continues to stand as everyone else falls to the ground.

"Daffy, you can get down?" Nick whispers.

Daffy tries desperately to bend over, or kneel down, or even sit, but everything is agonizing. "I can't, Cap'n, I'm sorry." His voice wavers so much that it's hard to understand him under the sound of the German vehicles getting closer.

"Be as still as you can." Everyone plasters themselves to the dirt, while Daffy wraps his head with a green army blanket. The tank and vehicles ramble closer, as Daffy's pain increases so does his terrified breath.

Rachel's panic runs through her gut and down her legs. She doesn't want to be there—she wants to go home. She wants to see Sylvia, Simone, and Minnie. But most importantly, she wants Levi.

Chapter Thirty One

1998

I sit on the bench enjoying the warm weather after having been in the air-conditioned hospital. It always takes me a while to thaw out from visiting my dad. He is doing well and is now able to squeeze our hands. My mom can't be more delighted with the progress even though he still hasn't said anything, but she is sure that it will soon come.

"I'll be passing the story on, Bobby, if you don't get back here." My boss says with zero compassion. Even if my father got better tomorrow, I wouldn't leave. I need to hear the end of the story. After my boss's threatening phone call that morning, my father would usually say, "What in the hell are you doing, son? Get out of here and keep your job."

The pressure of success has hovered over me since I was a boy, and yet something is changing. I can feel it. I've become so invested in Rachel's life that it is now guiding my decisions. I will choose her over my fear, and it feels good.

"Bobby?"

I look up.

"Mandy?" She looks beautiful against the backdrop of blue sky. Her short hair blows ever so gently in the breeze. I stand quickly and hug her. Instantly, I feel the spark from her touch. "What are you doing here?"

"Oh, my grandma has to be admitted."

"I'm sorry about that."

"It's alright. It has to be expected at some point, right? We all can't live forever."

"Yeah. I think we're all afraid of what may come."

"Are you?"

"Yes." I chuckle, which makes her laugh as well.

"I need to warm up after being in that hospital," she says.

"I know what you mean."

"What are you doing out here all by yourself?"

"You really want to know?" I'm not sure I want to tell her. My brain is not something she needs to know about.

"Of course."

"If you're not happy . . ., what do you do?" I stop and breathe. "Look at life, look at my father . . . is it worth being miserable trying to fit a square peg in a round hole?"

"Are you miserable?"

"No!" I say, but then realize that's a lie. "Yeah, I've been miserable for a while."

She looks at me carefully. "Why? Do you know why?"

"I didn't. But now, I think it's because I don't have what I want and in a way, I'm not even working toward it." I swing my neck from side to side, hoping the tension will release. A breeze picks up which fills my nose with Mandy's intoxicating perfume. A ladybug lands on her shoulder, so I reach out and pick it up with my finger. At first she doesn't know what I'm doing, but as I pull my hand back, she smiles at the red and black bug. "That's got to be good luck or something," I say.

"It usually represents prosperity or good luck." Mandy grins, then puts her hand out until the ladybug passes from me to her. "Thank you for sharing your luck and prosperity."

I laugh. "I've been working so hard believing that luck and prosperity has something to do with our money . . . our success."

"What are you believing now?"

"My gramma is telling me a story and I'm starting to understand that success or a name doesn't bring you happiness. Money is fleeting and doesn't always protect you from life."

"If you want to make a lot of money, then do it. Become something," she says. "

I smile. "Easier said than done."

"Is that what you want?"

"I don't know. I just don't want to be afraid that I've missed my opportunities."

"I think, sometimes when we keep our eye on money, we can miss the opportunities. Besides, fear never benefits us. My boyfriend…" she begins and I groan inside. ". . . My boyfriend is a musician. He's now decided that he wants to move to Europe permanently."

There is hope! "Just him?"

"No, he wants me to go with him."

"Do you want to go?"

She is quiet for a while. "No. And it's not that I don't want to move to Europe . . . it's that I don't necessarily want to go with him."

I nearly have to cover my mouth to hide my smile.

"We're taught when we're kids to believe in this perfect relationship that's out there waiting for us. We just need to find it. But I've never once felt that way. And it's not like it hasn't just been the right time, it's never been the right guy. I just know deep in my heart. I think my standards are too high. Does that make sense?" She sits back against the bench as though she is tired from her small speech.

"Yes. Complete sense."

"You feel it too?"

"Yes."

She smiles and my heart races.

Chapter Thirty Two

1942

Rachel buries her face in the wet grass hoping that the Kubel-wagen full of Nazis will pass. Pacey slithers like a snake to her side.

"Nick wants us to get farther away. Rachel, move fast along the ground keeping your elbows at your chest and drag yourself using your knees." She nods and slowly pulls herself as Pacey stays next to her. Together they move inch by inch through the dirt and weeds.

"Captain," Daffy says hurriedly, "you need to go. Maybe they won't see me." Nick is still trying to figure out the best way to free him.

"No. Just give me a few minutes," Nick says sternly.

"Captain, you don't have a few minutes."

"He's right, Captain," Whipple says.

"I can't hurry through this so just hold on," Nick says, ignoring the warnings.

"Captain, we are going to have to take a chance that they won't see him," Whipple says trying to get Nick's stubborn attention. Nick continues to work. "Captain!" Whipple yells this time.

Nick looks up and Whipple tosses his head to the side to point to the road. The Germans have pulled even closer. Finally, Nick scoots back and gets to his knee. He looks up at Whipple with surrender. "Daffy be as still as you can be."

"I'm not afraid of the Germans, Captain," Daffy jokes.

"Daffy don't move. Don't breathe. But if you have to, use your gun. We'll just wait until they pass and then I can get you free," Nick says as he backs away. Daffy turns his eyes away from his captain as a tear rolls down one of his cheeks. It is obvious that the pain is still extreme.

"Captain?" Daffy calls out.

"Yeah?" Nick whispers as the Germans get closer.

"Tell my mom that I love her."

"Daffy, they're gonna pass. Just stay still."

Whipple begins to pull at Nick's arm. "We have to get farther away than this,"

Rachel watches Daffy as the moisture seeps into her clothing from the wet ground and his lips move as if in prayer. She can barely see him in the darkness and hopes that this will play to their benefit. Either way, Daffy's chest rises and falls in fear. War exterminates men without bias, and she wonders how many thousands of prayers have been spoken on these fields in the last few years. Pacey keeps beside her, checking his gun over and over.

The wagon pulls closer as the soldiers laugh and yell, obviously drunk.

Nick hurries to Rachel and drops down in the grass just beside her. "They're going to pass," Nick says under his breath. Rachel looks at him solemnly, so he turns to her. "Don't look. Whatever you do, don't look. Turn around . . . turn around," Nick whispers, hoping his chanting will work.

One small man in the back of the Kubelwagen holds his gun tightly to his chest and surveys the field as they're passing by. Time drags on until suddenly Rachel hears, "Oh shit." She can't help but look up. The man in the back has noticed Daffy standing in the middle of the field and suddenly he starts to yell in German. He jumps from the back, forcing the driver to screech to a halt. The others follow with their guns against their cheeks, everyone yelling at Daffy, so he throws his hands in surrender.

"We can take them," Whipple whispers.

"They outnumber us," Pacey argues.

"So what. They're drunk."

There's no more time to wait and Rachel can see the debate in Nick's eyes. He thinks for a moment with a row of questioning eyes staring at him, waiting for his command while the enemy surrounds Daffy. One of the soldiers pushes at Daffy's back trying to get him to walk.

"I can't. I can't!" Daffy cries out in excruciating pain.

Again, they push him. "Verschieben!" they yell over and over.

"I can't," he screams.

"Verschieben!"

"Look! Look!" Daffy exclaims wildly as sweat drips down his face.

Nick puts a hand on Rachel's shoulder to get her attention. "We have to help him. Stay here."

She nods.

"Let's go," Nick calls out. The Americans pop up from the grass instantly yelling. "Drop your weapons!"

The Germans turn with surprise. Chaos erupts from both sides drawing a line in the middle. Meanwhile Daffy closes his eyes, his lips constantly moving. Both sides come within feet of each other, yet no one fires. The moment one trigger is pulled, there is no turning back and everyone seems to understand this.

Then it happens. The first shot is fired. It hits one of Whipple's men, named Luke. Within seconds, the air is riddled with bullets. Both sides losing men one after the other. Chuck and the crew have continued to hide in the grass beside Rachel.

Daffy, unable to move, yells, "Stop!" His pain is obvious.

Soldiers fall one after the other. Just feet from her, one of Nick's men is hit and lands with a thud on the hard earth. She crawls to him, but can't remember his name as he lay there with his eyes open and blood pooling beneath him. "I can't breathe," he whispers with a strangled voice.

She places her hand on his stomach where the bullet entered, then turns to Chuck. "Give me your shirt!" Chuck is wearing two, but he seems confused at first. "Chuck!"

After a moment, he takes his top shirt off and throws it at Rachel. She quickly presses it hard against the wound, but within moments, it's soaked.

"Where's Dell?" Through the haze of men and dust, she searches for him. "I need to find Dell."

He seizes in pain. "I . . . I . . . I . . ." Each time he tries to speak, the pain stops him. He looks up at her as his back arches and he lets out a cry. Then he stops and takes his last breath.

For several minutes the fighting continues, until suddenly it all stops. When Rachel looks up, Whipple and Nick are quickly alerting all of the men that are left to grab what they can. "We were lucky . . . they were drunk." Whipple says to Daffy.

There's still Daffy. Somehow in the entire scuffle, he only has an ear bleeding. Nick finally looks at everyone. "Stay far away."

Then with determined steps, he hurries toward Daffy as the rest of the group runs to a group of trees several yards away. Daffy looks at Nick with fear in his eyes. "What are ya doing?"

"I'm gonna pull it." Nick lays a hand on his shoulder to give him a second to breathe. Panicked, Daffy closes his eyes and sucks in a big breath.

"Fine. Yeah, let's go."

Nick kneels down, grabs his boot on his heel and toe. "Daffy, keep as quiet as you can." Meanwhile Whipple grabs the dog tags from those they've lost.

Without another second, Nick yanks Daffy's foot and boot from the sharp piece of metal. Daffy cries out, only stifling the last few seconds when his hand covers his mouth. However, everyone, especially Whipple and Nick who are within distance, are relieved that this isn't an explosive. Whipple and Nick quickly help Daffy hurry toward the others.

"What should I do, sir?" Dell asks as he grabs a hold of Daffy to help, when they reach the trees.

"We need to be gone before they come. We don't have time." Nick says. "Daffy?" Nick asks.

"No, I'm good. It feels better now."

"We'll get out of here, then stop to take care of it," Nick suggests. "Come on. Let's get going before the entire German garrison comes over that hill."

§ § §

They come upon an abandoned town. Nearly every structure has been decimated, leaving very little space to walk and the rubble crunches beneath their feet. Daffy is leaving a trail of blood behind him, while Chuck and his crew are still shaking. Nick comes to Rachel's side, "Are you okay?"

She simply nods. The stench of oil, machinery, and death lingers in the air—so much so that she places a hand over her nose. Nick helps her climb the mounds of broken brick. Strangely the main street clock tower is untouched.

Nick eyes roam the streets, which makes everyone guarded. "It just feels too quiet," he says to Whipple. Then he turns to Pacey and points at the clock tower, "Pacey, watch from there and warn us if you see anyone coming."

"Yes, sir!" Pacey hops over the rubble and disappears.

"Meyer, watch from that window," Nick tells the man nearest to him. "Pacey, Garrison, set up a rotation."

468

Chuck has been more than silent, giving her unexpected distance. Only now he comes to her side while Nick directs everyone else. "What do you want, Chuck?"

"I'm sorry, Rachel."

Rachel looks at him with hard eyes.

"I never realized . . ." Both of them are covered in dirt and ash.

"You didn't care, Chuck. It didn't matter to you what happened to us."

"I promise you that isn't true," he says quietly.

"I suppose you believe that." Rachel keeps her eyes on everything else but him.

"Rachel . . ." Nick calls her, giving her reason to leave Chuck with his men. When she comes to his side, the compassion in his eyes, she can feel through her soul. "I found somewhere to hide." Nick explains as they hike over the debris. "It's a bakery with a storage area, a kitchen, and what looks to have been an office, but it's taken a beating." He leads her through what's left of the front door. Flour hand prints line the walls. Rachel shudders as she walks by fingernail marks that are streaked across the doorjamb. Nick touches the indentions. "Someone fought hard."

"It feels wrong to be here," she whispers.

Everyone finds their resting place—some in groups, while others choose to be alone.

"What do you want?" Nick asks coolly.

"A shower . . . a real bed . . ." she answers, but what she really wants to say is Levi.

Nick leads her to a room with stacked crates. "Here. I'll make sure no one bothers you in here."

She lets her body slide down the wall to the hard ground.

"You okay?" Nick stands in the doorway looking calm and strong, neither of which she feels.

"Yes."

"Do you need anything?" he asks.

She rubs her hands together that are stained with dirt and blood. "No."

Nick's eyes drop to the red stains on her dress. "Wait just a minute."

He leaves, but comes back moments later with a bowl of water. "Here."

"Where did you get this?"

Setting the bowl down on the cold cement floor, he kneels down in front of her, then pulls a pair of green fatigues from under his other arm. "Dell found a working well in back and these are Daffy's." Both of them look at the army green clothes. "He is the smallest one here."

She dips the rag in the bowl then squeezes the excess water out. Impatiently, she scrubs her hands, and the water turns an ugly brownish red.

"You have some on your neck and chin." He points.

"It's everywhere," she says. Her hands are shaking, probably from the cold.

He takes the rag from her hand. "Give me a second."

Nick leaves, only to return a short time later with clean water, then he dips the rag. She takes it from his hands and wipes her face clean. The water is bitter cold and it turns red fast. After a moment, Nick reaches out to take the rag, "Would you mind?" he asks softly. She doesn't say anything, so he wipes more blood from her cheek. "You missed this right here." He keeps his voice gentle, and she can't help but appreciate his kindness. No one has been this close to her in a while and she feels her stomach flip. Nick is absolutely handsome and strong, and when he grows concerned, she watches the curve of cheek and the dip of his eyebrow.

"Thank you." she says when he pulls away.

For a moment they sit in silence. "I can't believe we're here," she finally says.

"Yeah." He looks at his dirty boots, then back up at her.

"Is this why your men were so cold when you picked us up?" Rachel asks with a smile. "Somehow you knew this would happen?"

"I didn't know it would, but I knew it could. Besides, Chuck drove everyone crazy, even calling the higher ups to make sure that we didn't say no." He grins at her, with his brown eyes speaking volumes about his stress. "Nah, listen. We just need to stay down, stay quiet, and get to the others."

"You think we can?"

"I know we can." Finally, he gets to his feet but reaches out to place a hand on her shoulder. "Rachel, I'll get you back to Levi, I promise."

"Don't make a promise that you can't keep." She smiles.

"Give me your hand," he says. She lays her now clean, but cold, hand on his. He shakes her hand gently, but doesn't let go right away. "We've shook on it. Now get dressed while I grab you something."

She changes, throwing her bloody clothes to the side. When he comes back in, he laughs.

"Don't laugh," she says as she looks down.

"I've just never seen fatigues look so beautiful before."

"Oh, sure."

"It's true." Nick looks around the room. "You want to be alone? I can leave you alone," Nick says sincerely.

"No. I'd like you to stay," she admits.

"Okay." He nods.

She sits on the ground against the wall and he sits next to her.

"I'm really am sorry this happened, Rachel." A large grin stretches across his face and she looks at him with a furrowed brow.

"What are you grinning about?"

He leans over and shuffles through his bag. Soon he pulls a large picture out that Rachel has seen before.

"Oh no," she groans.

He sets the seductive picture of Rachel wearing a red dress on her lap. "You've helped a lot of men in this war," he teases. "I think it's only fair that since I have saved you numerous times that you sign this for me."

"I can do that. But you have to know, this picture and my signature . . . they're all worth nothing."

"Not to us." He looks her directly in the eye and hands her a pen.

She quickly autographs the photo paper. "Here."

"Thank you." He rolls the picture back up and places it in his bag.

"Thank you, Nick." The tone between them shifts. "Thank you for watching out for me."

"You're welcome. What kind of man would I be if I didn't?"

They are quiet for a moment letting the fatigue settle in. "I'm tired."

"Get some sleep," he tells her.

She rolls a blanket up as a pillow and lays on the tile floor beside him. Then he takes his blanket and throws it over her and him. He wraps his arms around his chest and stays seated as he closes his eyes.

After some time, Rachel wakes to find herself covered in Nick's blanket and his warm body next to hers. Everything hurts from sleeping on the hard floor, plus she shivers from the cold. She gently scoots closer to him to absorb his heat.

"You okay?" he whispers.

"I'm cold."

"You already have my blanket, what more do you want?" Even though she can't see his face because of the dark, she can tell he is grinning. Before she can say anything, he lifts his arm and wraps it around her.

Instantly, his body heat seeps through her clothes. Once again, she closes her eyes and falls asleep.

"Rachel." She wakes to Nick's voice. "Rachel."

She looks up through tired eyes, to find the room speckled with light. Pacey is kneeling in front of Nick with a worried expression.

"Germans," Pacey whispers. "They are just three buildings down. We saw a wagon pull up with three of them and they were met by a

German officer outside of the bank."

Nick jumps up. "They don't know we're here?"

"Doesn't look like it, Cap'n." Pacey throws his rifle over his shoulder.

"Where's Whip?" Nick asks.

"The next room over."

Nick turns to Rachel. "Come on."

Rachel climbs to her feet while holding on to the blanket, then follows Nick and Pacey, keeping just at their heels as they hurry through the dark halls. It takes them only a moment to find Whipple and then wake the other men . . . and Chuck.

"What do we do?" Whipple asks.

Before anyone can answer, something crashes down the hall.

"Turn it off!" Whipple whispers to Dell, and the medic turns the lever of the lantern. Suddenly they are in darkness.

Nick takes Rachel's hand and pulls her close. It is so silent that they are all afraid to breathe and especially when they hear slow and steady footsteps coming closer. Whipple presses himself against the wall just behind the doorway, while Nick does his best to keep Rachel behind him. Whip peeks out, but yanks himself back, sending a message to Nick with his eyes. He lifts his hand in front of his face and raises three fingers. Using signs, he tells Nick there are three men at the end of the hall. The German soldiers' beams from their flashlights swing about the hallway and then everyone listens to their laughter—they have no idea they aren't alone.

Nick holds his gun to his chest then he raises his hand and points to his men that are scattered along the room. They understand he wants them to get closer to the doorway in case these soldiers reach where they are. Whip peers into the hall again.

"They're looking for food." One of Nick's men, who can speak German, whispers.

Something crashes to the ground, echoing into every room and the soldiers laugh again. Then the tapping of their boots gets closer and closer, turning the air thick with tension and fear until Rachel can hear that everyone's breathing has changed. When they are just outside the door, Nick's hand squeezes her harder as he pushes them into the darkest area. Whip is against the wall just beside the doorway, when the unknown soldier comes into view with a bag of flour over his shoulder and his gun readied.

The place, this bakery, is cold in so many ways. Puffs of breath hover for just a moment outside their mouths. It looks to be that the German soldier is staring straight at Nick, Rachel, and the others. However, the darkness is preventing him from seeing clearly and he doesn't have a flashlight like his counterparts. It is all okay, until one of the others comes beside him holding a light. As he swings it inside the room, everyone cowers. With no option, Nick charges forward grabbing a soldier while Whip attacks the other. There's an intense struggle, back and forth, yelling and crying out. Rachel closes her eyes as she hides. The Germans cry out for the others, but no one comes. Before long Nick and Whipple have wrestled them to the ground and blood is running across the floor in every direction. Both soldiers are no longer moving. Whipple has a long slash across his cheek, so Dell pulls out the med kit.

"We can't wait around. Once the Germans realize their men haven't come back, they'll send more." Whipple says as Dell slaps a bandage across Whip's face.

Chapter Thirty Three

To think that, just years before, men and women stood on the beige tile floors waiting for their warm bread to come out of the oven with numbers in their hands and now their numbers are part of a death toll. The smells must have been heavenly and the baker, a man name Achille Claisoux, which Rachel knows because of a gold plaque on the wall, baked some of the most unique and creative recipes in all of France. The plaque said that the Prime Minister himself ordered Achille's cranberry muffins. Rachel pictures the crowds eagerly waving for when their order is ready. Today, under her feet, she notices a small piece of paper with the number 74 written on it. At one time, 74 men and women had waited in this room for their order.

"Are we all here?" Nick asks as they gather by the door.

"Keep that light low," Whipple tells Dell, "We don't want them to see us through the windows." Dell lowers the lantern just a bit more until they can barely see faces.

Pacey, with his rifle over his shoulder, comes to Nick's side. "There is a back way that I took to get here from the tower. Meyer is still up there, but if he can keep a look out, we should be fine going behind the buildings and along the alleyways."

Nick nods. "I need someone to make his way to Meyer to let him know."

"I'll do it," Dell volunteers.

Nick shakes his head. "No, Dell, I'm not sending my only medic."

"I'll do it," Garrison says.

"Okay," Nick agrees.

Garrison rushes away with his rifle held tightly to his chest. Meanwhile Pacey leads the group. A small bit of moonlight comes through torn drapes of the scarce windows, but it isn't enough to keep them from tripping over the rubble on the ground, so, their hands drag along the brick wall for safety. Rachel feels the scratchy texture beneath her fingertips, while Nick travels just behind her and places his hand on her arm every time she stumbles.

They soon step out into the alley that is about fifteen feet wide. This is where several shops connected by one wall used to keep their trash and storage. "Guard up," Pacey warns, so everyone preps their weapons. They continue quietly across the powdered brick with their knees bent and their eyes roaming. Their fingers are plastered to their triggers and their eyes are in a permanent state of awareness. Unexpectedly, the wall beside one of the men explodes. The pop is loud, making Rachel's ears ring. Nick covers her instantly. Everyone dives behind the nearest hiding spot.

"Did anyone see it?" Nick yells. Rachel can feel his heart pounding, or perhaps that's her own.

"No!" Whipple yells back.

Then, another shot rings out and they hear a pained cry.

"Who's hit?" Nick asks. Nobody can see anyone as they are all covered by different things—garbage bins, brick pony walls, old tables with broken pieces.

"It's Allen, sir!" Dell hollers.

Suddenly two shots fire.

"I saw it," Nick breathes out as he checks his gun.

Whipple agrees, "So did I."

Both of them prepare their rifles and wait. They stare at a small window from one of the stores a hundred yards away. Beads of sweat roll down Nick's face as his knuckles turn white holding his weapon.

When the enemy takes two more shots, one of the men cries out and grabs his neck so Dell runs to him. Already, Nick shoots. Then, Whipple sends another. The man's rifle sight explodes and he falls.

"Are there any more?" Whipple asks. When no one answers, Whipple looks at Nick. "Keep your eye out!" Whipple jumps up with his gun pointed and he runs out into harm's way. But nothing happens. No one takes a shot.

"Let's go!" Nick yells. They race down the alley, until more bullets whizz by. Dell cries out when one hits his leg and he drops to the ground. Whipple grabs Dell and helps him to his feet. "Come on!"

Nick turns to Pacey. "Take them out!"

Pacey drops to his knees, closes one eye, begins shooting. One man falls from a window. A shot hits just behind Pacey's head, but he doesn't flinch. "Keep going!" he yells.

The darkness is beginning to lift. Suddenly, Garrison and Meyer burst through one of the doors and they duck with surprise when they see Pacey.

Pacey takes two more shots. Dust and crumbled brick fall to the ground as the last man's body flies back.

Chapter Thirty Four

1942

Exhausted and weak, Nick and Whipple lead everyone across fields squared off like patchwork quilts. A melody of crickets chirping and buzzing flies is nice, except the buzzing gets worse the closer they get to death. Animals have been hit in the crossfire and have turned wretched over the days, yet you would never know by the rich layer of pink that envelops the sky, signaling the dawn of a new day. Rolling hills disappear into flat land, and, as Rachel hikes over one, the land before her is covered in flowers, reminiscent of the chrysanthemums with Simone. Her memory of Simone holding her hand while walking through the flowers is even more beautiful now after all of this time.

They began this journey with so many, but now they are down to eight—three of which are with Chuck. The closer they get to sunrise, the pinker the sky becomes. The soldiers' boots dig into the loose soil and, although it isn't easy to keep their balance, they can't help but watch the vibrant colors. Rachel, however, notices that Nick is looking at her instead.

"You okay?" he asks.

"After seeing all of this? Is that possible?"

They both digest the truth for a moment. "I'm sorry. You shouldn't be here."

"You keep saying that."

"It's the truth. You should be singing somewhere."

"I can sing in this field."

He raises his eyebrow. "Would you?"

"No." She starts walking away and he hurries to her side.

"I've already heard you sing, you know."

"You have?"

"Yes. I went to one of your shows a few months ago. But I also knew you from before. Something Tender was one of my sister's favorite songs."

"Your sister?"

"Okay, one of my favorite songs."

"That's better." She is quiet for a moment. "Are we ever going to get out of this?" It is obvious that he doesn't know how to answer. "I assume that's a no."

"It's not a no."

A gentle breeze moves her hair in front of her face. Without thinking twice, Nick reaches out and moves it away—his fingertips grazing her warm cheek, just as Levi's would. "Come on. Let's catch up." Nick walks a couple steps, then waits for her to follow.

Soon the sun is overhead. They walk all day, and at nearly four o'clock in the afternoon they come upon another decimated town. With night soon approaching, they stop. The men spread across a one-hundred-yard radius making sure to check all corners and behind every crumbled wall.

Nick throws his arm in the air to stop his men when an old lady who is cradling a loaf of bread as though it were a child exits one of the buildings. She doesn't see them until she is across the street, and once she catches sight of them she begins an awkward shuffle through town, then ducks into a small house. The town has clearly been through hell, and the rubble became the grave for many. Nick moves the men forward once more.

"What do you think?" Whipple asks Nick from where he stands atop a large concrete block.

"It's good enough."

"I can see why Hitler has such a following," Whipple says sarcastically.

Across the street, Rachel notices a little dark-haired girl and boy peek their heads out from behind a pitted pillar. She watches their dirty faces and tired eyes. Pacey reaches out his hand with a pack of gum in it. After a bit of hesitancy, the children run forward and take them with dirty fingers.

"Hey, Cap'n!" Pacey calls out. "What do you think the best thing about going home will be?"

Nick looks up with a smile on his face. "Home cooking."

"Ahhh," Pacey says with an open-mouth smile. "You know what I think? I think it's going to be my bed."

Everyone agrees. Even Rachel, who has only seen a few days of the war, knows that she would give anything to sleep in her own bed.

"Nah, I have you all beat," Dell says with a grin. "Her name is Dawn and she's the prettiest thing I have seen in all my life—besides Miss Praline."

Rachel grins.

"She's waiting for me fellas, and the moment I get home . . . her smile will be better than any home cooking or soft bed." Dell looks like a little boy talking about his girl as if she were a shiny trophy.

"You'd better hope she's still there, Dell," Whipple says.

"Oh, she'll be there," Dell says confidently.

"I'm going to go home and be greeted by my daughter." Garrison's eyes are sad even though his smile says otherwise. "I haven't met her yet, but she'll know who I am."

"You have a daughter?" Whipple asks with surprise.

"Born last month." Garrison nods.

"Congrats, man."

"Thank you. What about you, Whip?" Garrison asks.

Whipple is quiet for a moment as his boots kick a flattened tin can. "I think just seeing anything familiar. I can't read a thing that is written anywhere; the buildings look nothing like home and even the sky is different. I'm sick of all of this gray."

"Rachel, what about you?" Dell asks.

"I don't know." She wants to be with Levi. Most importantly, she wants to marry him.

"You know what I want?" Chuck says from behind everyone.

The soldiers don't pay attention. "Nobody cares, Chucky boy," Daffy says with irritation, still limping from his injured foot.

Nick looks at Chuck out of compassion. "What do you want?"

"I want a bathroom," Chuck says with a completely straight face.

This makes the men laugh and for a moment Chuck is a part of the conversation.

Whipple chimes in. "Come on, now. You boys know that it's your mommas you miss the most. Don't be telling me that it's your beds and your girls. Your momma's the best thing about going home. I am sure of that."

Several moments later, they pass an abandoned building, wrecked beyond repair, and, as Rachel peers into a gap between the wreckage, she sees a small family with three young and war-ravaged children. The father pulls his protective arms around them as the strangers pass by and all three children stare at her with terror in their eyes. The smell of smoke, tar, and gunpowder stings her nose, and she wonders how they live within it. She smiles, hoping to calm the children's wounded response. It is obvious the dad is praying that she says nothing, so she stays quiet as the group continues.

"Nick, what are you thinking?" Whipple asks, getting back to something serious.

Nick points to a garage at the end of the street. It has two large doors and both of the men suspect that it can be locked from the inside.

"Looks good to me," Whipple answers. Whip enters first to check things out and when it is all clear, the rest of them enter.

Nick pulls the doors closed behind him, then Whipple helps him place a heavy beam across the arms. A small window at the corner of the room gives them light enough to move around. The men drop to the floor and lay their heads on their backpacks as though the ground is the most comfortable place to be.

Even though Rachel is exhausted, men are snoring around her before she is able to sit down. Nick kneels beside her. "Here, use this," he says handing her his jacket. "Use it under your head. You need to sleep." He then disappears into a small room attached to this large garage.

For an hour Rachel's mind clicks like a metronome, until she finally gets up to search for Nick. He stands in the storage room with a worktable where he has laid out a map that he's studying.

"Do you know where we are?" Her quiet voice surprises him.

He leans against the wall, wraps his arms around his chest, and the concern manifests within the dark circles beneath his eyes. "I think so. We shouldn't be too far from the coast. Why aren't you sleeping?"

"My mind won't let me. You?"

"It's always turning." He moves his fingers in circles at his temples. She walks to him so she can look at his map. All of the routes are lined with pen. He moves beside her, his arm pressing gently against hers.

"It looks like you have it all planned out," she says.

"I have to. I have to get you home, don't I?" He sets his hand on her shoulder, then turns to her with heavy eyes.

"You're worried."

"I am," he answers honestly. When she lets out a long breath, he touches her hand with compassion. "I shouldn't say that to you."

"No," she says quickly and sets closer. "I want you to tell me the truth."

"Okay . . . we're going to die." For a moment his words don't sink in, then when she turns to him and he's smiling, she hits his jacket with a grin. For the first time in a while, they soak up the lightness of the moment. "There seems to be more on your mind."

"How do they recover? How does anyone recover from this?"

Nick nods.

She continues, "Seeing a family out there living in these conditions, and here I am singing. I make my living singing, Nick. I fly from place to place . . . and yet they live here where their home and everything around has been burnt until there's nothing left. How do I---" her voice trails off, and she says nothing more.

"Where do they go from here?" Nick asks the question.

"Yeah."

He steps closer. "I don't know. But, Rachel, what you do is . . . pretty amazing."

"Thank you, Nick. It just doesn't feel that way . . . sometimes. This thing . . . music . . . it's everything to me and sometimes nothing. I've never really had a say in where it took me, or how it took from me. Sometimes it feels as if I've actually done nothing of importance."

"Well, you have." Nick says as he reaches out his hand to touch her shoulder. When they return to the map, his shoulder is touching hers. He shows her several American drop off points, but explains that he doesn't know the best way to get there. "And here," he says, reaching across, "planes would be unable to land close enough." Rachel nods, then looks up at Nick right at the moment he's turning to her. Their faces are but inches from each other. Without warning, he lowers his lips onto hers, but quickly removes them and drops his head with frustration. "I'm sorry. I shouldn't have done that."

"It's okay," Rachel whispers.

"No. I'm sorry. Everything is just so upside down …" He groans and can't finish, then he places his hands over his head with a sigh.

"Really, Nick. It's okay. You just know why I can't."

"I know."

"I have been in love with Levi my entire life."

"I know."

"But it doesn't mean I'm not grateful that it's you who's here with me."

Nick looks away for a moment. "He's a lucky man."

"If it wasn't . . ."

"I know."

They silently look at each other and the magnet pulls at them once again. Suddenly, he breaks it by stepping away. "I'm sorry. I've got to stop doing that." He nearly laughs at himself.

"Yes…yes, you do," she laughs.

"Yeah." He purposely places himself across the small room.

"I'll go," she smiles.

"I think you should."

Just as she's about to leave a loud bang shakes the walls, sending Nick running toward her. Dust pours from the aged wood and broken ceiling, then the bang happens again, this time causing everyone to yell outside. Nick places himself in front of Rachel, but it isn't long before German soldiers rush into the room, yelling at them to get down. Several men with guns between their palms scream and yell, forcing Rachel and Nick onto the dirty ground. Before Nick can do anything, the Germans grab both Nick and Rachel, by the arm and drag them out where the other Americans are on their knees with their hands behind their heads.

One of the main soldiers comes to Whipple hitting him upside the head, asking him questions that he can't understand. "I don't know!" Whipple yells.

Soon Garrison is trying to translate as best as he can. "They're asking who's in charge."

The men look around, but no one says anything for quite some time. It isn't long until the German soldiers get angry and begin hitting many of the men with the butts of their rifles. "Here!" Nick finally says as he stands up keeping his hands in the air.

The Germans yell and scream at him, but Nick hasn't any idea what they need. He continues to look at Garrison, to which Garrison yells, "They're talking too fast! Slow down! I can't understand."

One of the men steps toward Nick, taking the butt of his gun and knocking him to the ground. Again and again, he hits him, until several of Nick's men threaten them. The soldier stops, noticing Rachel on the ground. Nick is barely moving, so the German reaches down and grabs Rachel by the arm, ripping her up to her feet and calling out something in German to the men surrounding. Then he yanks her out of the building and out into the devastated city. More soldiers stand around with cigarettes hanging from their mouths when they notice her clumsily following the soldier. Each one of them points at her suggestively. She stumbles over cement blocks and scratches up her hands when she catches herself, but he yanks her despite the blood on her hands. They make it nearly seventy yards from where Nick and the other men are, then he throws her ahead of a man who seems to be waiting. This man is hard and calloused, appearing to be in charge.

They say something to each other in German, but she doesn't recognize anything until she hears 'Praline'. This makes her close her eyes and take a deep breath no matter how hard this is with her racing heart. She can hear him take a step toward her, and then smells the smoke he blows in her face. She coughs.

"Sing," he says in broken English.

She furrows her brow, noticing that every man standing around is watching and waiting for her to perform. "I can't," she whispers.

"Sing!" He yells this time.

"No!" this erupts from her, but she instantly regrets it. "No, please. I can't."

The men speak to each other, then the officer points in the oppo-site direction. He ushers them away, yanks her arm and throws her behind a tree that has only half of its leaves. Now they are in a dark corner as the sun has fallen, and he looks her over. She's seen these eyes before, many times. Perhaps this is just her curse. "Sing," he says again.

She's paralyzed by this. Nothing in her can give a performance. "I can't," she cries.

He steps toward her, reaches out with a fast hand, and rips her shirt open. Then he grabs her, and she cries out in terror. Nobody will care. They fight on the same side. His hands grope her, finding any way to fight with the material, while she pushes him away as best as she can. Suddenly the building they are beside and the tree that covers them, shakes—forcing him to stop. He doesn't know what has happened, so he waits, looks around, until suddenly, bullets blast from every direction. An onslaught of fire forces every German sol-dier to drop until their chests hit the ground, but the man assaulting her doesn't move. He keeps himself near her and they hide behind the tree. Big, loud explosions keep erupting and the already collaps-ing roof of the building nearby falls some more. The blasts get bigger, making it so loud that Rachel covers her ears and before long, her attacker falls against her. The weight of his body is so heavy that they fall together to the ground. She gasps as she tries to push him off but it's nearly impossible as they've landed between the tree and the building. Heavy gunfire nearly hits her, so she stops fighting to move this man's body and instead curls up tightly beneath him, covering her head. She can hear that the pandemonium has grown when GIs race through the town with guns in their hands, screaming every which way. For several minutes she cowers beneath the dead soldier feeling the air pass from bullets and the walls crumble above. Big chunks of mortar fall on her arm and side, forcing her to cry out.

When it finally stops, she can hear American men running around. "Help!" she cries out. Her voice cuts in and out with the dust cloud in the air, but she calls again, "Help!"

"Sir!" someone yells, then before long, several men lift her attacker's body off of her. She can't believe when she sees very familiar eyes over the dead man's shoulder.

"Rachel?" Levi's voice is everything to her at that moment.

They finally lift the large German leader but she lies there with her clothing ripped and her face covered in blood and dirt. Levi steps on the tree trunk for leverage as he grabs her hand and pulls her up to him. He wraps his arms around her and even in enemy territory, she finally has relief—even if just for a moment. Levi gives just a small bit of space, and he pulls her ripped shirt together with his dirty hands. "Are you okay?" He asks.

She nods, even though she's not quite sure.

"Go get the others, make sure they are all okay." Levi tells the other soldiers who are standing nearby. As they run away, he tries to look her over carefully, but all she wants is to press her head into his chest. "Come on. Let's hurry and get everyone out of here." Levi keeps his arm around her as he leads her back through the obliterated town.

"Nick's in there." Rachel says quickly as they come to the building where he kissed her. Much more of the building has fallen in, leaving parts of the ceiling collapsed, and Rachel gets nervous as they come close.

One of the American soldiers calls out, "Who is in here?"

Soon, they all hear Nick's muffled voice. "We're from Group 4379!"

"Get them out!" Levi commands his men. A large group begins throwing aside remains, digging their way through the rubble, finding men scattered about. Many of them are bleeding from their heads, their hands, and invisible wounds, but they're all grateful to be alive. Whipple sees Rachel with Levi the moment he is pulled out and he notices the blood and dirt all over her. Just as he's about to ask, they hear a loud crash and the rest of the ceiling collapses. After several moments of panic from many of the men, Nick soon drags himself out from under the lumber. He seems to be okay, despite the swelling of his face and blood here and there. Whipple and the other men are grateful to have him okay. When he finally looks up after coughing, he sees Levi.

"Levi?" Nick says with surprise. "How are you here?"

"We've been searching ever since you went down. It's probably best if we don't stay long."

Nick shakes his head when he sees Rachel. "Thank god," is all that he can utter.

1998

My gramma's eyes are looking tired and her skin a bit pale, so I reach out offering her water. "Thank you," she says as she sips it.

"You okay, Gramma?"

She looks up with a smile. "Just old. I'm tired. I've lived a long time and I'm just tired."

"Why do I feel the same way?" I say quietly, but she manages to hear and chuckles.

"Doesn't this story tell you? Life is tiring. If it's not one thing, it's another. That's why we have an expiration date." She laughs. "Imagine if we just had no end, oh heavens. Rachel even had more opportunities than most. Living takes grit and perseverance, but Bobby, I am tired."

"You want me to go?" Bobby asks.

"I have a few more minutes in me."

"Did Rachel ever tell Levi about Nick?" I ask as I look out the window at Mandy who is walking with her grandmother. They disappear around a corner, but I'm smiling from ear to ear as I watch her.

"Do you want me to answer your question, or continue?" Gramma grins, to which I smile.

"Alright, Gramma, continue."

Every day I rush to this place to be near my gramma and listen to Rachel's story and I find myself worried that it will end. If I can be utterly honest, there's a part of me that doesn't want my dad to get better. This sounds awful, I know, but it's not about my dad. Rather, it's the same feeling when you've had a vacation, then return to life. Freedom is hard to leave behind. A day without demands makes you crave it forever. Not only do I care for Rachel, but perhaps there's a part of me that feels free. I don't love what I do, I'm not even sure that I know myself or what I want anymore, and before my father's stroke, I would spend hours every day thinking about this. Yet, I haven't thought about my boss, my past girlfriends, or my 'loser card' in several days. Each morning, I encourage my mother, chat with my siblings at breakfast, make my way to Gramma, remind her why I'm there and who I am, all in the name of some stranger named Rachel. And now, there's Mandy.

In church on Sunday, with my momma on my left, Gramma on the right, and Mrs. Patterson beside them, I prayed for the first time in twenty years—that my gramma wouldn't forget. Meanwhile, everyone else prayed for my father who is currently breathing with the help of machines. What is wrong with me?

"Are you there, honey?" Gramma asks as I fall deeper into thought.

"Can I tell you something Gramma?"

"Of course, anything."

"Somewhere deep down . . . I have a shadow."

"A shadow?"

"That's what I call it because I can't figure out how to fix it, but it just stays near me all the time. It's the thing that tells me I'm nothing. It's the voice that keeps the bar unreachable. And I guess I mention it, because here I am, desperate to learn about a woman who doesn't exist in my generation. The difference between Rachel and the other women I've loved, is that there is no chance she will realize what I am NOT."

I look up terrified of my vulnerability and instantly wanting to take it back. Then it occurs to me that Gramma is safe and won't remember for long. Her eyes are thoughtful though. "It doesn't always feel good to learn lessons. We just have to make sure we're learning the right ones. Which one are you learning today?"

"You're the only one I've ever been able to talk to about my dad."

She nods and smiles as she's done a thousand times, so I continue, "People become martyrs when they get sick or die. Everyone wants to talk about dad as though he was the greatest. Momma speaks about him as though he didn't beat me till I was bruised and broken. She doesn't talk about the man who used to walk around our house like a tyrant when in a bad mood or belittle us again and again."

"Specifically you." Gramma says.

I nearly choke. It's one thing to believe it happened and it's another thing for anyone to validate it. "Yeah. It doesn't matter how much mom wants to forget, I remember. I can't pretend his words didn't tear me to the bone when he used to say, 'You have no idea what you are doing, stupid.' But I couldn't yell at him. He'd raise his eyebrows and say, 'You'll never live up to what I've done'."

Gramma encourages me to continue with just her eyes. "There was one summer when he decided that I was acting up, so he took me camping for a couple of weeks. For fourteen days, I climbed mountains with him. He repeatedly told the story about how he was a fighter. It was just the man he was. By the end of the two weeks, I only hated him more. So now . . ." I refrain from reminding my gramma that her son is sick, " I feel indifferent."

It's true that I've convinced myself, if he doesn't wake up, then I won't have to worry about how I am letting him down. It is only when I see my momma crying over him that I hope for his return— just to make her happy.

"Do you remember the time you sat with a boy across the street because he had been bullied at school?"

I know instantly the story she's broached. "Yeah."

"Then, when he grew up a bit, he sent you a letter that explained how much you saved his life?"

I smile. "Yeah."

Gramma looks at me carefully, "Do you believe you would have the empathy you do without what you've gone through? I'm not sayin it was right and your father never did that in front of me because he knew what I would do." I haven't seen this gramma in quite some time and it makes me suck in a deep breath of love for this woman. "But without judgement on what was wrongfully done to you, I can pick out every beautiful thing that is BOBBY JOHNSON because of and despite what he did. We often think the name, the lights, the success is all that, but what about the boys who are bullied and would not be here without your kindness?"

I lean back in my chair and rub my temple. This is the Gramma Johnson I love.

"Your father saw mine and your grandpa's success and he rode it until it was his. Yet I watched him and warned him for many years to step back and see what he's missing."

"You did?"

"Yes, I did."

"Gramma, I don't want you to disappear again." I figure I may as well say it, despite how it confuses her.

With sad eyes she looks directly into mine, "I don't either."

I reach out and take her hand and we sit there for what seems like an hour, just marinating.

Finally, I bring us back to her story. "If I were Levi, I wouldn't be happy about Nick. He's going after my girl."

"It was an awful situation no matter what. Levi really didn't know everything that happened."

"Nick should never have kissed her."

"Who's to say what people should do in times of war? You could have fifteen minutes left in your life."

"I'm just saying I wouldn't do that. She's another man's girl . .

. a man that he knows and has flown with." I want to beat Nick's ass. Once again there needs to be some way that I can reverse time to 1942.

"Can I tell you Nick was a great man?"

"No!" I nearly yell.

"Bobby, why are you so upset?"

"He kissed her and he shouldn't have. I hope that Levi kicks his teeth in." I sit back in my chair with my arms crossed in front of me like a child on time out.

"Nick was a good man. He did his best for many people." Gramma wipes her eyes, then seems a bit lost. "I could use some coffee."

"Would you like to go with me?"

"No," she says as she looks out the window.

In moments, I am in the cafeteria getting a cup of the same god-awful coffee. Lost in thought, Mandy surprises me with a soft hand on my arm.

"Hi," she says sweetly. "Are you okay?"

"Yeah." I laugh to show her I'm not crazy. "I just have a lot of things on my mind."

"Okay. I saw you standing over here. I thought maybe you might want company."

"Of course," I assure her.

We find comfortable chairs away from everyone else. Mandy runs her hands through her hair as she sits down, and she takes a small sip. Once again, I notice her. She is beautiful. Her hair hangs smoothly down her neck and her black shirt fits her just right. I try to avert my eyes so that I won't stare too long.

"How is your father?" she asks, not knowing that he has been the cause of my near meltdown.

"He still hasn't made much improvement."

"I'm sorry."

"Thank you." I can't stop my feet from moving. I try to press them down and it only makes my hands antsy, so I clasp them together in front of me. I feel like my skin is going to combust and I pull at the collar of my already loose shirt.

"Bobby," she says with her elegant voice.

"Yes? Yeah. Yes. I'm here. I'm sorry. I don't know what's wrong with me."

"Do you want to talk about it?"

I want to tell her about Rachel and Simone, but I can't. "No, I'm alright. What about you? How are you?"

"Oh fine. Grandma's back, but still not feeling great, but I'm okay." She notices my knee bouncing and smiles. "What were you like as a child, Bobby? I can imagine you were pretty wild."

This, I can answer. "A cocky son of a bitch."

"Really?" she laughs.

"Yeah. Really. I thought I could rule the world. I truly believed I would. Probably because I ruled my elementary, jr. high, and high schools, or at least that's how I acted."

"Ruled them?"

"Everyone liked me. I was popular, smart, and charismatic. I knew all the right things to say."

"I can see that."

"Well, my feelings toward my father made me want to be better than him, so when everyone adored me, I convinced myself that I could be." She is silent and when I look at her, I realize she's on to me. "I love my father, I do."

"I'm sure you do."

"I'm just thinking about something my gramma said and trying to believe it."

"If your grandma said it, I'm sure it's something you can believe."

Mandy chuckles which makes me comfortable and secure with her. She continues, "My grandmother always said . . . Maybe you need to just close your eyes, stop trying to pin down the exact location of your destiny, and get out of your own way. Everyone thinks they know what they want and sometimes our true path doesn't look like what we thought. We can't see the bigger picture."

I nod. I know she is right, but I don't want to admit it. Even to beautiful, and well-spoken Mandy. "Does it have to do with how good we are?" I ask.

"If that were the case, then no one in this world would ever succeed." Mandy smiles. "More words of wisdom from my grand-mother," she continues. "I'm sorry. I know that's never what anyone wants to hear."

"No," I breathe out. "You're right."

Mandy reaches over and lays her hand on mine. It feels perfect; and for a moment, I forget about Rachel.

Chapter Thirty Five

1942

Levi and Nick spend some time staring at the map with fur-rowed brows and connecting with the American allies nearby now that they have a radio from Levi's plane. Rachel sits adjacent with her head in her hands, wondering how she let this happen again. Chuck had shown her once who he was, she should have believed him. Her eyes are red, her face is dirty, and she watches as a family appears down the road, covered in dirt and searching for food. What Hitler had done to Europe would take years to rebuild, from the buildings, to roads, but most importantly the generations of humans who lost nearly everything. That's if the war ends the way it should. Fascism came in so subtly that even the most intelligent didn't recognize the drips of hate and now the world wonders: what will happen. Rachel can't take her eyes off of the little girl holding her dad's hand as they climb over the rubble. It seems they are unafraid of the American troops. Before Rachel realizes, a tear escapes down her cheek and she wipes it away. To be worried for herself when this entire town is in shambles and the people taken, seems insanely selfish.

Before she is aware, someone touches her shoulder. When she looks up, Levi reaches out for her hand and quickly leads her behind the nearest building where they are soon alone. Taking her face in his hands, he kisses her for several moments, until her arms wrap around him. Just as his lips let go of hers, he looks at her carefully as if convincing himself that's she still alive. "I didn't know if I'd find you," he whispers.

"I didn't either." She lays her forehead against his neck, just to feel his chest rise and fall against hers. He's warm and comfortable, just as he's always been.

"Are you okay?"

"A little sore, but I'm alright."

He breathes out. "I saw what was left of the plane."

Finally she looks up, recognizing the fear and fatigue in his blue eyes. "But you found me."

"I would never stop until I did." He kisses her again.

"Take me home."

"I think we've found a way out of here. Just stay by me and I'll get you back to Simone." They smile and before long, the group is ready to move.

For hours they quietly push through the countryside. At times, Nick reaches out to help Rachel and she can see the desire in his eyes, despite the fact that Levi is just a short distance away.

The field is gravely uneven beneath their feet, with holes burrowed, and small hills to step over. A commotion builds somewhere behind Rachel, and when she turns, she sees Chuck laying face down in the dirt, after he's tripped over a mound. No one reaches out to help, rather every soldier waits with irritation as he brushes himself off. Levi and Nick both smirk, then look at each other to compare notes.

Finally, just before nightfall, they reach an open field where just under the trees, a plane awaits, covered by the branches until it is camouflaged except for a tip of the propellers.

Everyone climbs on board, grateful that this will all soon be over. After every safety check is done, Levi uses the dirt road nearby to take off. When they reach the pink and orange sky at dusk, without any problems, cheers erupt. Nick and Levi give each other a look. It's done, and she's safe.

When the plane touches down at Bassingbourn airfield, hundreds of people—military, photographers, and news reporters—are waiting for the rescued soldiers and entertainer.

"There's a party out there," Garrison says excitedly.

"It's all for you, Rachel." Dell winks at her.

"Oh God, don't say that." She's grateful to be landing, but a heavy feeling has crept back into her gut. There is a contract telling her that she can't go home.

The plane circles to a stop and Levi comes to her side before the doors open. He takes her hand, then leads her down the stairs as the crowd calls out her name and lights flash. She raises her tired hand in the air, waving hello, but ignores the reporters with microphones. They yell out questions repeatedly, until Chuck hurries toward them and speaks into one.

"It has been a long ordeal and we are tired, but we are so very grateful to the United States military for helping us through one of the scariest situations. Rachel is fine, I assure you, and after some rest, we will be able to talk about what happened! The troops will not have to wait long!"

When they reach the hangar, several superior officers are there, ready to commend Levi for a job well done. Levi quickly points to Nick, "Nick is the one you want to thank. He did it right and I'm grateful."

Nick looks at Rachel; his heart betrays him by the longing in his eyes, so she looks away.

A young nurse comes to her side, "Miss Praline, come with us. We'll check you over and help you get to where you need to go."

With her hand still in Levi's, he nods at her to go. "I've got some things to take care of on this end. I'll come find you."

After the nurses clean her wounds and cover them with fresh bandages, Rachel notices several of Chuck's crew coming into the room with their game faces on. Chuck enters with papers in his hands, "Okay Rachel. We have a conference in the hall set up in a half hour, then you can go rest."

"Why would I do that, Chuck?"

"I promise it won't take long. The higher-ups themselves supported this entire tour, we owe it to them, Rachel."

In only an hour, after they've primped her hair, and done her makeup, several people look her over in Daffy's military pants and shirt. "Let's have her keep them on. It tells them what she's gone through." Walking through the hallway, they reach a banquet hall where a large table is set up for the press junket. Flash bulbs blind her as she ascends the stairs and just as she is to reach the top, there's a large commotion nearby. Coming in the door, with his famous smile and instant charm, is Bob Hope. Rachel holds her breath. As cameras flash wildly, he lifts his hand in the air to wave and then calls her name, "Rachel!"

She waits on the stage in disbelief as Mr. Hope climbs the stairs and, upon reaching her, takes her hand. "I'm sorry to intrude, Miss Praline, but I was here, and I just had to come see you."

"Mr. Hope," Rachel says quietly, "I'm so honored to meet you."

"Oh, well . . . that's a hello if I've ever heard one. But it's me that's honored. Are you okay? Feeling fine, now that you are back?"

"Yes. I'm doing just fine, thank you."

As they speak to each other, everyone waits with bated breath, wondering what the two of them have to say to each other. Chuck inches closer until Rachel pushes an elbow into his ribs and Bob laughs. Chuck backs away when he sees Levi and Nick standing in the doorway with their arms crossed.

"I know that you're probably tired and you have some press right now, but I wanted to let you know that I'd be more than happy to have you aboard my team. I'll take care of you, I really will…" He does his famous look when he is awestruck by a beautiful woman, "Goodness, you are pretty. Anyway, we can talk about it later."

"Are you sure you want my act, Mr. Hope?"

"Please call me Bob, and boy would I…"

"Would you?"

"Would I," he repeats in the same way as before to gather the laugh as if he is in a comedy routine. "Yes, join me and we'll get to as many troops as possible without putting you in harm's way." To this last sentence, he raises an eyebrow of irritation at Chuck, until Chuck clears his throat and looks away.

"I have your word?" she asks.

"You have my heart," Bob says as he places his hand over his chest. Then he walks her to her seat at the long table with microphones. "You shouldn't keep your audience waiting."

Chuck sits beside her, whether she wants it or not. There are several moments while she waits as they prepare the cameras, that allow her time to think. Before Chuck is able to say anything into the microphone, she pulls it away from him and leans into it herself.

"Good evening, everyone, thank you for coming. I just wanted to start this conference by letting everyone know, I have fired Chuck Gerber as my tour manager, and I will be joining Mr. Hope and his company. Any questions?"

The room is like a firestorm. While reporters cry out, Chuck looks at Rachel, dumbfounded. Rachel covers the microphone with her hand. "Chuck, do you want to stay? They might ask questions you don't want to answer."

Speechless and angry, Chuck grumbles as he leaves the stage from the opposite direction from which he came, in order to avoid Levi. Rachel turns back to the crowd. "Now, please… your questions, one at a time."

§ § §

By the time Rachel is escorted to her room, she is so tired she can barely keep her eyes open. The bed feels like a cloud and she wonders if it always was this perfect. Just as she feels herself falling asleep, there is a knock on the door to her hotel room.

"Who is it?" she asks.

"Rachel. It's me." Levi's voice is raspy from fatigue.

Her heart alights and when she opens the door, he has never looked so good in all her life. At the same exact time, his thoughts are similar. Still in his uniform, but with his collar undone, it takes him a moment to step inside, rather he reaches out letting his fingertip touch her nightgown.

"Where have you been?" she asks.

"I went to the bar with Nick and Mr. Hope, your new employer."

"You did?"

"I like what you did up there." He steps into the room and closes the door behind him as he pulls the next button open on his shirt.

"You did?" She takes a few steps back.

"Uh huh." Succinct with his steps, he opens one button at a time, as he comes so close to her, she holds her breath and smiles. Finally, he drops his lips onto hers, gently grabbing her lip with his teeth, then letting his tongue moisten it. He drops in and out for a deep kiss as his hands are busy removing his shirt. Once he has the top shirt off, she takes the bottom of his cotton shirt and pulls it up over his head, throwing it on the end of her bed. For a moment, she stops to recognize the power he has over her, just by the sight of his body. There's something different at play within this moment, no smile, no lightness, but the pressing weight that this could have been lost. When she had been within the rubble, she thought about the feeling of his skin against hers. So as he stands there now, looking down at her, she runs her fingers along the thick curve of his chest muscle, and etches his muscular frame with her fingernail. As he breathes in and out, the squares on his stomach deepen.

He reaches out to the small strap of her nightgown, draws it down her shoulder, until one of her breasts is exposed. Lightly he touches her skin, causing everything to pucker and change. Then when he looks up into her eyes, the idea of losing her makes him breathe in and out again, then close the distance between them. He lifts her chin and drops his lips onto hers. Opening and closing his mouth, he takes no time to breathe, rather he wraps his arms over her shoulders, then weaves his hand into her soft hair. Lifting her into his arms, she can feel his intensity beating through his chest. He lays her onto the bed, but before he crawls over her, he pulls the rest of her clothing off leaving her naked in the darkness. He has to feel his way from her chest, to her naval.

Desperate for him, she grabs him behind the triceps and pulls him up to her. For a moment, he hovers over her, just so he can take in her eyes, her nose, her lips, and the way her long neck arches back.

"Please, Levi," she asks as she wraps her knees around him.

Finally, he obeys her desires and wraps himself around her harder and harder, until she disappears beneath him. She presses herself against him, desperate for his nearness, desperate to never have separation from him again. When she begins to cry out, he presses his thumb to her lips, savoring the sight as her body arches. He holds on, not wishing this to end. Again she rises and falls, then again, and again, as he works to continue. When she reaches down and pulls his hips harder into her, he finally lets go at the same moment she clutches his skin.

He drops over her, breathing heavily with his skin glistening under the moonlight.

"Never in my life have I needed anyone as I need you," he whispers. "I thought you were gone and I couldn't bear it. Rachel, you have to marry me."

"I wondered why I hadn't when I was out there," she says quietly. She brings his hand to her lips, but notices a darkness on his skin.

Pulling the nearby lever on the lamp, a dim light helps her see his red and swollen knuckles. "What's this?"

"It could be anything for a soldier, right?" he says.

"It could be, but it isn't, is it? What did you do to your hand?"

"You should see his face."

"Whose?"

"Chuck's."

"You hit Chuck?"

"He saw us at the bar and started telling me how he would take you to court for breach of contract. If I didn't hit him, Nick or Bob would have done it." He drops himself down, until he can lay his head on her neck and chest. "But I deserved it more than they did."

"Deserved to hit Chuck?"

"Yeah."

"You know, I could use a drink. Why didn't you invite me to the bar?"

"You were doing your press stuff."

"Yes, but now you're relaxed and I'm not."

"Here." He crawls off of her and pulls a flask from his jacket. He then places it against her lips, and she takes a drink. Some of the whiskey drips onto her chest, so he drops his head and runs his tongue along her skin.

"Give me that," she says with a smile. She takes the flask and sips more, letting more liquor wet her lips. When he sees this, he smiles, then grabs her mouth with his. A long and potent kiss makes them alive with excitement.

"You're safe." He pulls away.

"Nick made sure of it."

Levi looks at her, suddenly a bit more sober. "I think Nick likes you."

She only smiles. "I think you're right."

Without another word, he kisses her again.

Chapter Thirty Six

1944

Levi's thumb runs down her cheek as he stares at her just outside the hotel where a military jeep waits for him. "Tell me again that you'll marry me."

"I wish I had already." This makes him smile and he kisses her again. "You'll come back to me?" she asks. He breathes out, squints his eyes at the sun, but doesn't answer. She pulls away, but holds on to his collar and roughly shakes him. "Don't ignore my question. You have to come back to me, Mr. Price."

"That's my plan. I have to make you Mrs. Price."

"Levi, say the words." It is unexpected when she begins to cry. "I have to hear the words."

"I'll come back to you," he says as he wraps her in his arms. As he walks away, he looks back only once, then he is gone.

From stage to stage, she travels with Bob Hope, one of the funniest men on earth. Her fame grows even more after the crash and it becomes harder and harder to find a moment alone, but she enjoys shuffling along with the crew and meeting all the young soldiers. Besides, keeping busy is the only thing that will keep her sane.

§ § §

Simone finally receives a letter from Rachel and as she opens it, tears fill her eyes as she takes in a deep breath.

"Simone, you have a call." John says from the phone in the front hall. "You okay?"

"I'm fine. Rachel really is okay."

John breathes in with a smile, knowing that Minnie will be beyond relieved.

When Simone answers the phone, she doesn't recognize the woman's voice on the other end. "I'm sorry, who is this?" she asks.

"This is Jane Bolin. I'm a judge for---"

"---I know who you are!" Simone accidentally interrupts. Jane, the first black woman to graduate from Yale Law School, and become the first black woman judge in the United States, laughs on the other line. "What can I do for you Ms. Bolin?"

"Nothing, absolutely nothing. I'm calling to tell you that your fame precedes you."

Simone shakes her head and smiles. "Oh Lord. This is . . . I can't tell you what this means to me."

"Well, I heard . . ." Jane begins. They speak for nearly an hour and Simon's smile never goes away. Finally in the last few moments, Jane offers one last piece of advice. "This industry and this society can tell you that you aren't capable, that you aren't brilliant, but YOU have to believe it. And when you do, come find me. Let's work together."

"Thank you, Ms. Bolin. I need you to know what this means to me."

"Of course."

When Simone hangs up and screams, she scares everyone in the office. John runs out again. "What?!"

"Jane Bolin just called me!"

John growls. "You nearly gave me a heart attack."

"A call from Jane Bolin is worthy of a heart attack."

John instantly leaves with a roll of his eyes. Later that evening as the women play poker in the hotel conference room, she tells them about Rachel being okay and of her phone call, despite the fact that many of them don't know who Jane Bolin is. "It was a good day." She says as she lays down a flush, taking the pot. "What Jane's done for women like me is invaluable."

"Simone dear," Helen says as she touches her hand, "You realize that's what we all think of you." Everyone nods.

"You do, huh?" Simone asks them all. "You won't once you hear the last part." She gathers the cards and begins to shuffle. "I'm pregnant." She looks at all of them with a raised eyebrow as the cards mix. "Again."

All of the ladies chime in, some happy and others questioning Simone's life choices. "It wasn't on purpose!" Simone says with hard eyes at Helen. "It wasn't planned. I have my big case next week, where they already treat me like a second-rate citizen and now I have an obvious belly."

When the night is over, as she walks with her purse in hand through the fancy foyer of the large hotel, she stops directly in the middle of the shiny tiled floor. Jane Bolin knows who she is, she's bringing another life into this world, and Rachel is okay. As if Rachel can hear her, she whispers, "Come home soon."

§ § §

One night in July of 1944, Rachel exits the stage to find Bob waiting for her. "Hey Bobby," she says with a smile as she drinks some water. He doesn't smile back. "What's the matter?"

"I have a letter for you."

Rachel looks in his hands. Just the look on his face tells her it isn't good, whatever it is.

"I told them I'd give it to you myself."

"What does it say, Bob?"

"Well, I don't know."

"Can you read it for me?" She looks around her near the stage as the musicians and dancing continue. "I need to sit down. Open it please, Bob."

Bob finds a chair nearby and she weakly falls into the seat as Mr. Hope opens the letter.

"What does it say?"

Rachel isn't prepared for what the letter has to say; nor is Bob prepared to read it. Immediately, before he can even finish it, she falls from her chair to the floor, her body numb and her chest rising and falling too rapidly. Just as she had watched Bernadette pass from this world to the next, and Dick take his last breath, her body knows the ache of this pain too well.

> *Dear Miss Praline,*
>
> *I am so sorry to write this to you as I know the love that you had for Captain Levi Price. On the sixth of June, nineteen hundred and forty-four, Captain Levi Price's plane was shot down over the beaches of Normandy. All twenty men could not be recovered. It is with great sadness that I write this to you. I will forever remember Captain Price as a man that I could trust with my own life. I apologize that I must send this information to you, but I know without a marriage, you would not be notified of these devastating circumstances. All of my condolences to you, Rachel.*
>
> *Sincerely,*
> *Captain William Hill (Whipple)*

Chapter Thirty Seven

1998

I stare at Gramma for so long that she reaches out her hand to me with concern. "Are you okay, Joe?" but I say nothing—not even to correct her. Instead, I look out the window wondering how I can forget this entire story. The disappointment . . . no heartbreak, actual heartbreak is devastating to my spirit. Maybe I should have just gone home?

"After all this, they don't end up together?" I finally say. "Gramma . . . why'd you tell me . . . man, that's . . . I . . . wha . . . I don't know what to say."

"Joe, you of all people know that life rarely works out the way that we think it will."

"It's Bobby, Gramma."

"Oh yes, that's what I meant." She waves her hand in the air as if waving off her embarrassment, then looks back at the clock. "Rachel, didn't know what to do with herself, but in a way, Simone didn't either."

"Simone? Why, Simone?"

"Can I continue?"

The answer doesn't just come to me. Losing Levi is losing my hope that one day it will work out for me. I shake my head and rest my elbows on my knees while holding my temples. Not knowing what happens to her after Levi's death is possibly worse than knowing, I guess.

"Yeah, continue," I practically whisper.

"You sure?"

"No. Continue."

"Rachel didn't know how she got home from England. She was in such a fog with puffy eyes and a broken heart, she did her best, just handing people her tickets, barely eating, and trying desperately to put one foot in front of the other. People everywhere knew who she was, and so it is thought, that strangers helped her in any way possible."

1944 Atlantic City

A kind taxi driver tenderly helps her from the backseat, then pulls her bags from the trunk. In the heat of the summer afternoon, beads of sweat drip down his forehead as he watches the nearly catatonic woman just stand in front of the house.

He comes to stand by her side and clears his throat. "Miss Praline, my daughter just lost her husband. 'Bout seven months ago. I know it doesn't feel it, but it will get better. I'm so sorry, Miss Rachel." This doesn't seem to pierce her trance as her empty eyes stare at the home Levi bought for them. Tears begin to rapidly fall down her face and moisten the ground beneath her feet, but she still says nothing and makes no movement in any direction, so he carries her bags to the porch. Gently, he places a hand on her elbow and begins to pull her forward until she, too, is on the porch.

As the taxi driver stands quietly with Rachel, Simone happens to walk by the window with her iced-tea in her hand and notices them standing ever so still. Just the day before Simone and Sylvia got a call from a Captain Nick telling them what has happened and that she would be home any minute.

"Oh my God, she's home," Simone says.

Without hesitation, she sets down her tea and throws the front door open. For the first time in a week, Rachel is pulled from her daze. Nothing is right, except for her friend standing in the doorway. Rachel falls to the ground weeping and Simone races toward her, wrapping her in her arms.

"It's okay, you can go. Thank you," Simone releases the driver from his duties, and he gives a compassionate nod before driving away. Minnie, John, and Sylvia carry her bags inside, but leave the two alone.

Cars pass, the sun falls, and the mailman lays the mail on the wooden porch instead of in the box, as Simone just waits for signs of life from Rachel. Memories of Jake flash through her mind, but her heart is refusing to beat. If she feels, it will be too much. If she speaks, she will have to acknowledge that she exists.

Finally, when it's dark, Simone helps her to her feet, and she passes Sylvia, Minnie, and John in the house without a word. One creaky stair after the next, Rachel makes her way to their room, where she climbs in bed. But the moment she does, she looks across at his side of the bed and weeps. His scent wafts from the sheets even though it's been forever since he's been home.

Simone closes the door only to let out a large sigh.

"What can we do?" Minnie asks before she and John go home.

Simone shakes her head. "Nothing. Just got to wait it out, is all."

For days, Rachel stays in bed. The women in her life hear her crying, then assume she is sleeping when it is silent. Simone brings her children over as she cooks dinners, and when Simone is at work, Sylvia takes over—but Rachel doesn't emerge from her room.

Finally one day, Simone comes in the front door to see that Rachel has made it to the top step of the stairs. "I wouldn't marry him," Rachel cries.

Simone softly climbs up to the second step and sits down, facing Rachel. "I know."

"I don't know why."

"Yes, you do. But it had nothing to do with him and everything to do with a man who doesn't deserve to be named."

Rachel wipes her face, leaving just red skin. "If I had just said yes."

"It doesn't change anything. It doesn't make your love deeper. You understand that?"

Simone spends every night sitting with Rachel as she falls asleep, then leaves to tend to her family, and returns early before Rachel wakes. Nearly two months pass with no change, until one day as Sylvia and Simone are sitting on the front porch drinking lemonade, Rachel slips out the back door, without them seeing her

With bare feet, she walks alone out into the middle of the field and drops to her knees. For the first time, the sun on her face is wonderful. She stares out into the rolling fields and weeps. At times she doesn't know how she will ever shed one more tear, but then they come, just as they did the day before.

"I don't know that she'll ever come back," Sylvia whispers fearfully as they watch a family stroll by. Without any reply, Simone reaches out and takes Sylvia's hand.

Then slowly, as though looking for an address, a shiny black car pulls into the driveway. Simone and Sylvia look at it with concern as the door opens and a soldier steps out. Neither of them recognize the man in a soldier's uniform standing in front of them. He is tall and handsome. He walks closer and lifts his hand in the air to let them know he is kind. Simone steps to the edge of the porch.

"Can I help you?" Simone asks.

"I hope so. I'm looking for Rachel Anne Praline."

Simone looks him over with her protective glare, "What do

you need?"

He takes another step forward while squinting his eyes from the sun. "I'm Captain Nick Disson. I---"

Simone interrupts, "You're the one who called to let us know that Rachel was coming home?"

"Yes, ma'am." He hesitates for just a moment as he removes his hat and with a small grin he shows his dimples. "I was with Rachel in France after the plane crash. I'm just here to make sure that Rachel is okay."

Sylvia stands. "Would you like to see her?"

Simone scowls at Sylvia, but Sylvia ignores her. Sylvia raises her hand to motion him onto the porch and he hesitantly follows as Simone looks him over with a raised eyebrow.

Sylvia turns to Nick, "Pardon me. Let me go find her."

Sylvia disappears into the hall as Nick waits patiently in the foyer. He tries to ignore Simone's glare, but she's making it difficult by standing severely next to him. "So why are you here?" Simone asks.

Before he can reply, Sylvia comes from upstairs with a worried expression. "She's not there," Sylvia says.

"What?" Simone asks, hurrying to Rachel's bedroom and finding it empty.

For many minutes they scour the house, but it is Nick who steps into the screen room out back and notices Rachel sitting in the middle of the field. Without letting the other women know, he walks through the swinging backdoor toward her.

"Hello," Nick says quietly.

When Rachel turns, her sadness takes his breath away, making him press his palm to his chest, but he waits to see what she might do. It is possible that she won't want to see him.

"Hello," Rachel says in a whisper.

"I'm so sorry, Rachel," he says softly.

Tears flood her eyes, and she weeps with her hands covering her face. Not necessarily knowing what to do, Nick hesitates, but after a moment, realizes there is no other choice but to hold her. Slowly and carefully, he wraps his arms around her, until he feels her melt into them.

Sylvia and Simone, still looking for her, exit the house onto the back porch where they see Nick and Rachel. Sylvia takes Simone's hand when she breathes out. "So that's Nick?"

"I guess so," Simone whispers.

Minnie comes home from work and finds them in the screen room. "What's going on?"

"Shhh," both of the women say quickly.

Minnie notices the stranger and Rachel together on the lawn. "Who is that?"

"That's the man that helped her in Europe. I guess he knows her and Levi."

"Wow," Minnie steps closer, "he certainly is easy on the eyes now, isn't he?"

"Who is?" John says, stepping into the already cramped screen room as he bites into a frosted pastry, his gut getting larger every year.

"The man with Rachel. He's a soldier that knew her and Levi." Minnie explains quickly.

After several minutes, Rachel finally pulls away as she says, "I'm so sorry."

"No, Rachel, I'm sorry. This is the first that I could come. I've just been released from duty." A sudden breeze passes by them, lifting her hair, forcing both of them to look up. The sky has faded into purple and pink with several stars already appearing. "What can I do for you?" he asks.

Behind the backlit sky, Rachel notices how handsome Nick is, with his dimples and dark eyes. As he stands there in his uniform, she finally hears what he has just said. "You're released from duty?"

He grins. "I am. And my first stop was here."

She reaches out to touch his face. "It's good to see you."

Sylvia makes arrangements for Nick to stay in Levi's hotel,

however he spends very little time there. At first, he begins mending what needs fixed around Rachel's house, then Sylvia's. Trying not to bother Rachel, he quietly emerges from his car each morning with his tools in his hand. For several weeks, Rachel stares at him out her window and brings him lemonade when he's done. They don't talk long, but it's consistent enough that Rachel begins to expect him.

One day while Rachel stares out the window, Nick is under her car with oil on his shirt and pants. Sylvia passes by and stops as they both peer out. "What's he doing?"

"I guess I needed an oil change or whatever it is that they do to cars."

"Handy man."

"He certainly is that."

Before Sylvia walks away, she stares at Rachel wondering when she'll notice. "What?" Rachel finally asks.

"Invite that man in for a drink. It doesn't mean you'll get married, but he certainly deserves some kindness." Sylvia runs her hand along Rachel's shoulder as she walks up the stairs—taking a look back with compassion.

Before she goes to him, Rachel pours two glasses of lemonade, then carefully keeps them from spilling as she descends the porch steps. She's waiting there for quite some time before he comes out from under the car.

"Lemonade?" She asks as he looks up at her and squints from the sun.

He reaches out and takes it with a smile. "Thank you, Rachel."

"You're welcome." After they both take a few sips, Rachel breathes out. "Nick, you don't need to do all of this."

He takes a minute to decide how he will respond, then nods. "Yes, I do."

"I'm not asking you to."

"You don't need to," Nick assures her.

A few weeks after this, Nick ends his day sitting on the back porch with Rachel, just before he bids her goodnight. As time goes by, Rachel doesn't say much to anyone. She simply exists one day at a time and Nick knows this. One morning he's there before Rachel wakes, and Sylvia comes out to his side as he paints the cracks on the garage. "Good morning, Mr. Disson."

"It's Nick, if you wouldn't mind."

"Alright, Nick." Sylvia watches him paint carefully for several more minutes. "Can I ask you a question?"

"Of course," Nick answers.

"What is your expectation here?"

Nick stops and looks at Sylvia with genuine eyes. "I have none."

"You would do all of this with no expectation."

"Honestly ma'am, I owe Levi. He asked me when he left to look out for her if something should happen."

Sylvia nods with sudden understanding. "Oh, I see. Does she know this?"

"No. I haven't had the chance to tell her."

Sylvia nods, then pats his arm as she starts to walk away. "Alright, well, I'll be making breakfast."

"Would you like some help?" Nick asks.

Sylvia turns to him with surprise. "You're ready to help me make breakfast? Do you know how to cook?"

Nick smiles. "Well, I had to cook for myself starting from a very young age, so whatever you would like, I can make."

"Well, then. Come on!"

Nick is soon flipping pancakes while bacon sizzles, and Sylvia scrambles the eggs. The radio is playing *You Always Hurt the One You Love* by the Mills Brothers as Rachel descends the stairs with surprise and confusion, so she keeps hidden by the railing. Sylvia laughs at something Nick says, then he shakes the orange juice. Rachel comes out of hiding just in time. Unexpectedly the bottle top flies off spraying Nick and every surface with the sugary orange substance. Rachel laughs out loud for the first time in months. The bright morning sun beams through the windows into the yellow kitchen as Nick watches Rachel forget her sadness, even if just for a minute.

Later, Nick and Rachel sit in the screen room on rockers reading their own books in silence and enjoying the warmth of the day, when Nick notices Rachel with only ice left in her glass. Without a word, he picks it up, walks to the kitchen, and brings out a full cup of tea in just a minute. With a sleight-of-hand, he throws a small flower into her lap before he sits down. Rachel smiles and presses it to her nose.

Sylvia and Simone watch from the garden as they pull some minor weeds. "Now why can he make her smile like that?" Simone says, crossing her arms in front of her.

Minnie walks out, on her way to the bakery, and leans over to see into the screen room where everyone else is staring. "It's the dimples."

Simone gives Minnie an evil glare so Minnie hurries to her 1942 Chevrolet Fleetline. She and John have still not moved out, so she honks to make him hurry. Soon he rushes out with his shirt still unbuttoned.

Just as Minnie and John are leaving, Rachel's smile disappears.

"Are you okay, Rachel?" Nick asks quietly.

Rachel turns to him, "Where's your family, Nick? Don't they miss you?"

"My family is not too far away. I go visit anytime I want."

With careful eyes, Rachel is searching for her answer. "Why are you here?"

He hesitates, then sighs. "I promised him."

"What?" Rachel's eyes begin to burn as tears rush to the edge.

"He knew he was going on a dangerous mission, and he asked me, the night that you had your press conference . . . he requested that if anything should happen to him, that I would watch out for you. He didn't tell me much, but he said that you had been dealt a rough hand in life and he didn't want anything to hurt you. So, I promised him, Rachel. I told him I would watch after you." After a moment, he finally continues, "I would have come regardless."

A tear rolls down her cheek and Nick reaches out to wipe it away. "That is exactly what I would expect of him," she whispers.

Nick continues, "I've found an apartment here. It's not too far away. Rachel, I don't expect anything from you. I'm simply beginning to like it here and I think I might stay for a while. Would you mind if I stayed?"

Rachel shakes her head. "That's fine."

"Yesterday I heard your music. You're all over the radio right now."

"I am?" Rachel asks with surprise.

"Have you thought about singing again?" he asks.

"I have. The woman I've sung for, for years, just called the other day. I'm still thinking about it."

"You should do it. Even if just to get out of the house for a while."

"Maybe," she whispers, then smiles.

§ § §

The year passes quickly and soon, 1945 is upon them. Oppenheimer's bomb is dropped on Hiroshima and Nagasaki and the war finally ends, Navy Flight 19 disappears over the Bermuda Triangle, and Anchors Aweigh and Spellbound are popular movies . . . And Rachel returns to Ada's speakeasy. It starts with one song, then two, then a full set. Before long, this beautiful underground bar and restaurant is bouncing with the sound of her voice. The first night she invites Nick, he walks into the fashionable space with wide eyes and a grin. "This is amazing," he whispers to her.

Together, they make visits to the boardwalk, shop for groceries, and have dinner with Simone's family. Simone still looks at Nick as a stranger, but little by little he's proving to her that he's not there to steal anything he shouldn't.

It's the nights and the mornings that are difficult as Rachel reaches her hand out to the empty space in her bed. This is when the sadness hits her like a hurricane, and she wonders if it will ever go away.

One May morning she lies in bed with the sun shining through her upstairs window, when the sound of her name being called pulls her to her feet. She looks out to find Nick—handsome in the morning light with his sunglasses on and a smile on his face.

"There's good news!" he calls up.

"Oh yeah? What's the good news?"

"Germany surrendered! No more war in Europe!"

"Really?!"

"Yes!"

"Hold on, I'll be right down!" Rachel grabs her thin robe and hurries down the stairs. Sylvia moved back to her house behind Rachel's, and Minnie and John have found their own place since they are expecting their first child in the winter. She rushes through the quiet house and out the back door to run to him. He quickly takes her in his arms and they laugh.

Moments later, after she is dressed, they take a walk around the property. "Reports are coming out of Germany about horrific things." Nick tells her about the camps that are being discovered full of starving men, women, and children. He tells her about the gas chambers and mass graves.

"Sometimes I wondered . . . was it really worth it? But all of it makes you realize there is no black and white."

"There never is." As they near the house once again, Nick takes Rachel's arm. So, she stops and turns to him. "Will you go out with me tonight?"

She hesitates, then looks down at the ground. "Nick, I---"

He quickly interrupts her. "No pressure. It's not a date. I simply want to get you out of the house. We need to celebrate that the war is ending."

"If you say it like that."

That night they dine and dance and she enjoys herself. Nick remains a perfect gentleman; but still, that night, as she lies in bed alone, she cries.

1998

Gramma stops and reaches out to touch my hand. "I have something to tell you, honey."

"What?" I can't help but be skeptical of Nick. "He's using her sadness to get at her. He says that there is nothing, but it's painfully obvious that Nick is in love with her."

"I believe he was," Gramma admits as she rubs her chest heavily and squeezes her eyes as if in pain.

"Are you alright?" I ask.

"Oh, I'm fine," she says quickly.

Although she says the words, her face tells me that she's having pain. "Gramma?" I stand up and come to her side, resting a hand on her shoulder.

"Just some GERD, that's all." She cringes again, still pressing heavily on her chest.

"Are you sure? Gramma?"

After a moment, it seems to subside and she turns to me with hard eyes. "Now you go sit down. I have something to tell you!"

"Alright, tell it," I say with a smile while taking a seat.

"Levi's not dead."

"What?!" I jump to my feet before my butt touches the chair.

Gramma laughs. "Levi was hurt when his plane went down, and he was taken prisoner. It takes him well over a year to get out of Germany or even be in contact with others, but he is alive."

"What!!" I jump around the room like I have just made the winning basket in a game. "Somehow I knew it, Gramma!"

Chapter Thirty Eight

1945

At the end of the war, Germany is left in ruins. There are parts of the country that have been unlivable, untouchable, and frankly, no one quite knew what would be found. Levi, a bit thinner, sits in a German prison camp in dirty clothes, with longer hair, and surrounded by other soldiers as well as Jewish men. His left side is healed after a deep wound from the plane crash.

For many months, he had been healing under the care of a kind German lady named Helene who was more than twenty years older than him, hidden well past the border of Berlin in her country home. Her father, who was always thinking ahead, had built many underground fortresses along his property, as well as hidden rooms behind walls in preparation for war. Helene's father died before World War II, so he was never able to see them used, but she was well equipped to help whomever she could. Levi, and the two other soldiers who had survived their crash, was found by her, wounded. Using her wheelbarrow, she managed to haul them back to her home, where she fed them and nursed them back to health. Levi wasn't healthy for many months and in no shape to take on the German camps that surrounded them on each side.

Many times, Levi and the other soldiers would hide within her walls, as groups of Germans would stop by her house to get water or food. Eventually Levi understood their schedule and they would be hidden before the German soldiers would even arrive. Then, like clockwork, they would appear while Levi and the others kept quiet, sometimes for hours.

Then one day, just a couple of weeks before, several of the soldiers stopped by unannounced. Helene was murdered on the spot with her arms raised to the sky, while the rest of the soldiers were taken to the nearest camp. Here, they starved them, beat them, until one day, a week before, every German soldier disappeared. Not one had been seen again, as the men were locked away in their barracks and left with very little water and no food.

Thoughts of Rachel kept him alive. Remembering how as a child, Rachel was kept alone in a dark basement with no food or water, he would close his eyes and pray that God would bring him home to her. Thinking she'd probably believed that he was dead for nearly a year, his heart ached to let her know that he was, in fact, alive.

Then, out of the silence Levi wakes to the sound of distant talking. He assumes the guards are back and is hopeful that they are there to bring them supplies, until a pounding noise shakes the old wooden door, and he hears an American accent. "Is anybody in there?"

Everyone's eyes grow wide. Levi jumps up and runs to the door. "Hello?" he calls out.

"Hello?" the American man says. "My name is Captain Ailen and we're here to get you out." There is shuffling and commotion outside, until he yells, "Stand back, away from the door."

After so long, Levi can't believe it has finally come. Despite the lack of strength, there is a buzz of excitement and relief from those captured. Running his hands through his hair, he takes in a deep sigh as he waits. Finally, after several locks are broken, the door opens letting light in that hurts their eyes. There has never been a greater sight than the soldiers who stepped inside with clean uniforms and water in their hands.

Levi walks to them with his hand out. "I'm Captain Levi Price. We've been waiting for you."

And the response is beyond what they expect, "Well, boys, the war is over. Let's get you home."

§ § §

Meanwhile, as the days progress, the fall of the Nazi regime is cause for celebration everywhere. Nick and Rachel spend nearly every day together. Her laughter is increasing, but the pain hasn't subsided and she wonders if it ever will. One afternoon, as they sit together drinking tea under the falling sun and orange sky she goes to grab the pitcher, but Nick doesn't let her go far. He carefully cups her elbow, then touches her face with his hand. Slowly, he leans forward and kisses her. She allows him for the first time in over a year. Part of her wished to know whether Nick could ever feel the same as Levi. But it isn't Levi, and she is desperately aware of that fact. Yet still, it feels good. The kiss continues for a while as he runs his hand along her face and down her arm. When he pulls away, he looks at her carefully.

"Are you okay?" he asks quickly.

She smiles, "I'm fine. Thank you."

"Rachel, I know this might be too early, but I want to marry you. You're still mourning and I understand that, but I know that I can take care of you. I can make sure that you get the life you deserve. Would you let me do that? We can go as slow as you would like, but I just want to know that one day, maybe you will be with me?"

Nick is handsome and trustworthy—a man who any woman

would be lucky to have—but the answer to his question doesn't just jump to her lips. It's buried somewhere deep in her belly, and she can feel it churning. It's true that no one else would be better for her and she doesn't wish to let him down. Is she in love? No. She doesn't suppose she is.

When Levi speaks, her world stops. When he touches her, her worries fall away. Levi has known her from the depths of her soul and saved her when she was just a child. He has been in her heart for so many years. His death has left a gaping hole, that may never be filled.

"Can you give me some time?" she asks.

"Of course." Nick states with certainty. From that day forward, Nick stays by her side waiting patiently for her answer to his proposal—never pressing the matter further.

One night, as she waits to walk on stage to sing at Ada's place, Nick is near the bar in conversation with several soldiers in uniform as ladies look him up and down seductively as they pass. When he laughs, people laugh; when he speaks, his charisma steals the attention. As she steps behind the microphone and the band starts, she makes a decision, then and there. Nick is the kind of man that Levi would want for her. She doesn't want to feel broken anymore, and Nick treats her as though she still has a life to live.

After her set, she pushes through the crowd and as she comes near, he notices the look on her face. He leans into her, wrapping his arm around her, always aware of when she needs his love, and asks, "Are you okay?"

"Would you come with me?" she asks.

He looks deep into her eyes and can see that something is on her mind and nods. With his strong body, he pushes them through the crowd and pulls her outside, where suddenly, the noise level drops to near silence.

He lays a hand on her face with concern, "What's going on?"

Rachel hesitates. She waited so long to marry Levi because she was afraid, and she doesn't want to make the same mistake again.

She comes to him, laying her hands gently on his chest. "I'll marry you," she says.

He smiles. "What?"

"I'll marry you."

"Rachel, are you sure?"

"Yes. I know you will take care of me."

He comes close to her and she feels relief as he wraps his arms around her. "I will take care of you, I promise," he whispers in her ear.

In the alleyway, as the steam rises from the streets, she lays her head on Nick's shoulder, and he holds her. For a long while, she stares ahead, and her heart battles the opposing sadness. Nick knows this is hard for her and her decision has not come lightly, yet he loves her so much that he is willing to risk playing second fiddle to the memory of Levi. It is a chance he will have to take.

Later that night, as she sings, Nick can't believe how lucky he is. He has been in love with Rachel Anne Praline ever since first hearing her music on the radio; he had trekked through the French countryside trying to keep her safe; and now they are engaged. Little does he know that as he watches her perform, there is someone else in that room watching Rachel—someone else who wants her. Yet, that someone else doesn't want to see Rachel happy and safe. In fact, he is going to do his best to make sure that she isn't. Unaware of his presence, Rachel and Nick lead him all the way to her house. He carefully watches, hidden in his truck, as Rachel and Nick say goodnight.

1998

Gramma stops and I look up at her. I have been carefully listening as I stare out the window at the New Jersey landscape. She looks around for a moment and I quickly pull myself to the edge of her chair.

"You alright, Gramma?"

"Oh, I'm fine," she says. Her chubby cheeks lift so high that it seems they'll touch her eyelashes. "I just wanted to tell you something."

"Of course." Gently, I lay my hand on hers.

"I love you, honey."

"I love you too, Gramma."

"This has been such a beautiful time getting to share Rachel's story with you. It's helped me. It really has."

I sit down in the chair beside her bed. "No, Gramma, you have no idea how much it has helped me. I've been more alive in the last two weeks listening to a stranger's story than I have been in years."

"Why?" she suddenly asks.

I look away for just a moment. "She's caught my interest more than any other woman I've met in years; and also her life, it's meant something . . . I guess. I guess that's why."

"Well, when she was going through it, she didn't think her life meant anything. It's just the way life is. We don't realize the measure of what we're doing until we can look back. You get me, Bobby?"

"Yeah, Gramma."

"You're still young, Bobby. You'll fall in love . . . you will."

I already had, in my opinion.

"And Bobby," I look up from the urgency of her voice, "Don't let the hate of your father guide your life, do you understand? Don't let hate ever drive your decisions. Make sure you are led from the other side . . . the happiness . . . the joy."

"I got to find it first, Gramma."

"No, you don't. It's there. You just gotta see it, is all."

She is tough and I have known that for years. She doesn't understand that I have done nothing in my career and I have failed at every one of my life goals. She doesn't realize that I am so lonely I have fallen in love with a woman who lived decades before I was ever born.

Gramma closes her eyes for just a moment and although I know she's tired, it concerns me.

"Who is following her?"

Gramma opens her eyes and looks at me. She doesn't say anything so I continue, "Who is following Rachel and Nick? Why would he want Rachel, but not wish her to be happy? It can't be Levi and I need to know that Levi gets to Rachel. She can't marry Nick."

"Why? Nick is a good man."

"It doesn't matter! Even I know that Levi is the man for Rachel. Not Nick." Not me, I want to say.

"Are you believing in love suddenly?"

"I've always believed in love. I've just never known how it worked. Levi can't live just to come back to Rachel married to someone else."

"It happened. Sometimes during the war, that kind of thing happened."

"But not to Rachel."

Gramma smiles. "I told you that her life had moments of bliss and moments of --"

"Tragedy," we both say.

She continues, "Well, I'll let you know tomorrow."

I groan, yet I know that Gramma needs sleep. I nod and kiss her on the cheek. She closes her eyes as I turn off the lights, then I step outside. As I am closing the door, I jump when I hear a soft voice behind me.

"Bobby?"

I turn. Mandy is standing there with her sweater on and her purse in her hands. "Hi," I say with a smile. My heart jumps just a bit and I think about what my gramma said. Perhaps I need to believe in love just a bit more.

"Hi." She smiles, but there is something hesitant about her smile. "I just wanted to say goodbye."

"You what?"

"I'm leaving tomorrow afternoon . . . for Europe."

My heart sinks farther than I expected. In fact, it lands hard against my nervous stomach and my jaw clenches from the pain, so I stuff my hands deep down in my pockets. "You've decided to go with your boyfriend."

"I guess I feel as though there's no other option. I don't want to turn my back on an opportunity, even though it's with him."

I can't believe what the woman in front of me has just said. "It seems like you don't love him?"

She is quiet and I wonder if I have said the wrong thing. Then she breathes in and continues, "Honestly, I don't know that any of us know what love truly is right now or if it even exists anymore."

After a few silent moments, I turn toward the door. "Can I walk you outside?"

"Yes, thank you."

When we get outside there are no cars around, but she leads me to a bike. "That's how you got here?"

"I came right after work. I needed to tell you."

"You came just to tell me?"

"Yeah," she says, but doesn't say much else.

"Can I drive you home?"

"Sure."

After stuffing her bike in the trunk, I turn on the car, but swiftly twist the nob to make sure Rachel's CD can't be heard, so we can talk instead. It only takes about five minutes before we reach a large house. It is a beautiful home out in the countryside, with a second home in the back.

When we step out of the car, I look at her carefully. I have been so involved with Rachel and her story that I suddenly feel I have lost time with Mandy, a real live girl standing in front of me, and now she's leaving.

"Well, I should go," she says quietly. Then suddenly, she stands on her tiptoes and kisses me. It is quick and soft, but it makes my heart tear through my chest—so much so that it is unlike anything I've felt before. I suppose in a way it is unexpected how much my heart pounds and I like the feeling of her lips on mine. "It was so nice getting to know you," she says.

"You too, Mandy." She starts to turn, "Mandy?"

"Yeah?" she looks back at me.

"When do you leave tomorrow?"

"About two. My flight leaves at four."

I nod. "Well, good luck."

She smiles. "Thank you, Bobby."

Then, without another word, I let her walk up the driveway and into the house. I don't know what else to do. I stay for just a minute longer, tempted to walk to the door and knock, yet I don't know what I would do or say.

Finally, I leave, and before long I am in bed, wishing I had done something more. Yet I'm pretty certain, this is just the way my life works. I am destined to be alone.

Chapter Thirty Nine

1998

"Sorry, you can't go in there," one of the nurses says as my Ma and I walk up to Gramma's room.

"What?" I ask feeling my heart rise and fall with a definite crack.

"Something's going on with Mrs. Johnson and the doctor's in with her right now."

I look at Ma who now covers her mouth with her hand. She is panicked and I can tell that losing my father and losing my grandmother all in the same two weeks will kill her. I wrap my arm around her and try to be a kind son, and the thought of losing my gramma rips me up, but I also think about the fact that I will possibly never find out what happened to Rachel. With Dad not fully awake, Gramma in trouble, and Mandy gone by the end of the day, everything seems to be a mess.

"Come on, Ma." I pull her away from the room.

One of the nurses hurries to my side, knowing that I have been there every day with my grandmother and touches my arm. "I will call you when things change."

"Thank you," I nod.

"Take me to your father," my ma says quickly. The last thing I want to do is go see my father, but I am a good enough son that I do as she asks. For a long time, we simply sit in my father's room waiting—for what I'm not sure. In my ma's eyes, she stares at him like he will wake up any moment and she doesn't want to miss it, while I watch the clock. With uncomfortable precision, the clock's hand moves closer and closer to when Mandy will be heading to the airport. As if the nagging tick knows how to irritate me, it reminds me that I may have just made another mistake. I should have done something last night and told her to stay, but instead another woman will never know how I feel.

"What is wrong with you, Bobby?" My Ma's voice yanks me from my trance.

"What?" I ask.

"You keep looking at the clock, you're not saying a word, but I believe your fingers will be rubbed raw by the end of the day." I quickly stop rubbing my hands together.

What do I tell her?

"It's nothing," I finally say.

But of course, she doesn't buy it, so she grabs my hand. "Tell me what's going on with you. You haven't been the same since you came home. You've been spendin' all of your time with Gramma, which is lovely, but not normal . . . and I just can't seem to get your attention. Now I'm your mother and you had best tell me what is going on."

I breathe in and out, hesitant to tell her anything. I'm afraid of sounding crazy.

"Gramma has been telling me a story, that's all. I'm afraid now that I won't get to finish it." Suddenly Ma slaps me upside the head and I turn to her with shock and dismay. "What are you doin'?"

"Your father is in this state and Gramma is in trouble and that's all you are thinking about? How dare you?"

I stand up. Suddenly I'm not only angry with my father, I am angry with my mother. I am reminded of why my dad was able to treat me the way that he did all my life. Her loyalty to him is aggravating. With one look at my ma, I head to the door and out into the hall.

Ma quickly follows. "I'm sorry, honey. I didn't mean it. I'm sorry."

"No Ma, that's what you do. You shame me for having feelings and stand by him regardless of how he ever treated me or any of us." If Rachel taught me one thing, it is that no matter how mistreated you are, you have to somehow keep on living. "Yes, I was thinking about the story that Gramma was telling me. Because this story . . . this one woman gave me more to think about in the last two weeks than the last ten years. She made me want things for myself and she made me realize that I fear my own father. Life is about taking chances and they may not always come out right, but at least I've learned that I need to take them. So, you can hit me upside the head all you want, but I'm upset that I can't finish the story. Possibly more upset than the fact that my father can't speak to me. I guess I should be sad about it, but how can I be when I know that the only thing he will say to me is how I haven't met his expectations? Well, you know what? Rachel has been more alive to me than my father."

My mother's face curls with confusion. "Who's Rachel?" Yet then it seems to occur to her. "Wait, it's Rachel's story that Gramma is telling you? Well, that makes sense."

"Wait, you know about Rachel Anne Praline?"

"How could I not? She is your grandma's best friend. They grew up together and spent most of their lives together. In fact, I worked with Rachel's daughter to get them into the same facility for the last ten years."

My mind is blown. "Rachel's in the home?"

"Sure, she is. Unfortunately, Gramma hasn't remembered that for some time, so we stopped having them get together, but Rachel's family used to come and visit Gramma as well . . . but have stopped over the years. The only one I've seen in recent years is Rachel's granddaughter, Mandy."

My heart skips a beat. What in the hell is happening? Just above my Ma's head is a clock and I buckle when I see that it is already fifteen minutes until two. It will take me at least ten minutes to get to Mandy's home. I've never felt such disappointment in my life.

"But honey, I understand. That's a very interesting story and she lived such an interesting life . . . nearly as interesting as your gramma's."

"Wait, Simone, that's Gramma?" I'm confused, wondering how I missed this. "Gramma was a lawyer in the forties as a black woman?"

"That she was. Mona Johnson or formally known as Simone."

It takes me a moment to compute what I've just been told. "Why didn't I ever know this?"

"Honey, I hate to say it, but you've never been quite known to take interest in other people's business." She raises her eyebrows and I feel that power like a shockwave.

The revelation hurts. "But I should have known that Gramma was a lawyer."

"Yes, you should have. For some reason you always thought that you listened to everything we said, but I couldn't get you to listen to anything you didn't want to. Didn't you ever wonder why Gramma Johnson was invited to the white house?"

I furrow my brows trying to remember. "I just thought it was some women empowerment thing, you know."

"Well, in a way it was, but it was with women who have changed the norms for every woman beyond. Gramma did more for this country, and people of color, than you could ever understand. You're interested in Rachel's story? Be interested in Gramma's story. The only thing is that Gramma Johnson is humble and wished to be just Gramma to all of you. Still doesn't mean you can't ask her about her life."

Everything feels a little off kilter. "Wow," is all I can say.

Ma sucks in her breath. "I'm sorry that I've made you feel as though I care more for your father than I do you. It's not the truth. The truth is that I've seen the way he has treated you and I'm not sure why he's done it. I don't know why he chose you out of all of the kids to belittle except that maybe, just maybe, he saw himself in you. Or, don't tell your sister and brothers, but maybe he saw more potential in that handsome head of yours."

I want to listen to Ma, but I reach out to her shoulder and stop her. "Ma, I promise I want to hear what you have to say, but I gotta go," I say suddenly.

"What?" Momma says with surprise.

"I love you, Ma, but I gotta go." I don't want to give her a reason. So I turn and head out of the hospital. I know that she will now be stuck there, so I call my brother from the lobby phone of the hospital and tell him that he needs to drop what he is doing and pick up Ma. I hang up before he can argue.

I've never driven faster and I make it to Mandy's within minutes, but the gates are closed. I sigh and step outside in the cold air, then place my hands on the gates, pressing my forehead to them.

"I did it again," I whisper.

"Bobby?"

My eyes shoot up and at the top of the driveway is Mandy. She looks at me with concern, but when I see her face, I smile. "You're here!"

"I am."

"I thought you'd be gone."

"I should be."

Then I see a man, not too much older than me, emerge from the house with bags. The gate begins to open, and I run the rest of the way toward her, despite the fact that the man looks at me with consternation.

"Mandy," I say as I reach her.

"What are you doing here, Bobby?" she asks, taking a step closer.

"Can I talk to you for a second?"

Mandy looks up at the man by her side and nods. It doesn't seem that he likes it too much, but with a shrug, he heads back into the house.

"Are you okay?"

"Gramma's not well."

"What?" Mandy puts her hand on her chest with concern.

"Something's wrong with her and they're working on her now."

"I'm so sorry, Bobby."

"Mandy," I can't believe what is going through my head. My heart is racing faster than I can keep up with, yet I have never felt so much confidence in my life. "I think you should stay."

"What?" she asks with surprise.

"Look, I've never been the kind of guy to do this—to take a chance and really be aware of what I want, but that's probably why I have had such disappointment in my life. I haven't gone after things or fought for things, or even been interested in the right things and I know I don't know you all that well, but all of this can't be just coincidence."

"All of what?" she asks with confusion.

"My grandma has spent the last two weeks telling me the story of Rachel Anne Praline. She remembers every word—every moment of Rachel's life, yet she can't remember what happened five minutes ago. And I fell . . . I fell into the story and I didn't even try to catch myself. Rachel was all I could think about and all I could see for the last couple of weeks. I know this sounds crazy because . . . well, it is, but I don't care anymore. I actually fell into something without pulling myself back and she isn't able to finish the story. I don't know what happened to Rachel because there's something wrong with my Gramma." I take a breath and her eyes widen. "I was devastated, until I spoke with my ma. She told me that you are Rachel's granddaughter. This whole time, I've been falling for you, while never knowing that Rachel was your grandmother and never knowing that

Rachel was just down the hall. Then I thought, what if. What if this is one of those moments that the stories all talk about? You know, those moments when life is clearly telling you who you are supposed to be with? I barely know you, but I can't let you leave without letting you know that I think . . . you might be the beginning of my story."

Mandy is silent. Her mouth is slightly open and I can tell that she hasn't any idea what to say. Then finally she grins.

"You've been in love with my grandmother?"

"What?!" Yes. "No! I just found her fascinating."

"She is fascinating." Mandy looks at the house. "This was her home."

I look at it and it takes a moment to sink in. "So, this was her and Levi's home?" I smile.

"So, what do you want? Me, or to know the end of the story?" Mandy chuckles.

I look at her carefully and step closer despite the fact that her boyfriend is probably watching. "You, absolutely, you. And maybe you can tell me the rest. Is that okay?"

"You know last night I hoped that I wasn't too forward when I kissed you but there is something in me that doesn't care. And then when you let me go, I didn't know what to think. I knew who you were from the first time I met you."

"You did?"

"Yeah, every time I came to visit my Grandma, she would always be hanging out with Simone. And your mother has brought Minnie by."

The name startles me. "Minnie?" I say shaking my head. "Minnie's still alive?"

Mandy laughs. "Yeah. I believe your mother takes care of Mrs. Patterson when her family needs it. Isn't she at your house now?"

I laugh. "Wait. Mrs. Patterson is Minnie? She was married to John Ipson? Her last name would be Ipson."

"Mr. Ipson died just after she had their second child. Car

accident, I believe. She then was married to Charles Patterson until he died a couple of years ago."

"Wow." I shake my head.

"Simone used to always talk about you and how amazing you were. I think I had a little crush and then I met you and you were so kind and everything she said you were."

"So, what are you going to do?"

"What do you mean?" I look at all of her things sitting in the trunk of the car and she realizes what I'm thinking. "Oh no, this isn't mine. Last night after you left, I called my boyfriend and I ended it. I couldn't go to Europe with him. This is some stuff for my grandma. I'm just taking it to her."

"And him?" I point to the house where the guy has disappeared.

"Oh that's my brother, Levi."

I laugh out loud. Then before she can change her mind, I place my hand on her face and step close. I drop my head for what will be one of the best kisses of my life.

§ § §

I've been nervous all morning. My gramma has been completely oblivious since feeling better after her minor stint with the doctors. As I wait at the door, I can't get my heart to calm down. Finally, Mandy comes into view pushing a wheelchair down the hallway, with a little old lady who has the bluest eyes I have ever seen. I walk up to Rachel nervously. "Rachel," I say, and she looks up at me with a smile, "It's a pleasure to meet you."

Rachel's smile brightens her entire face, and she nods, "It's a pleasure to meet you as well."

Her words are strong and confident. Mandy comes to my side as we notice Rachel trying to look around the corner into Gramma's room.

"I told her that we are going to try and visit Simone, but that

Simone may not recognize her. She's excited, but I'm afraid she'll be let down."

"All we can do is try," I nod.

Then quietly, as my Gramma is resting, we roll Rachel into the room. For a moment Rachel just stares at Simone with the largest smile on her face, and then slowly tears come to her eyes.

"You okay, Grandma?" Mandy asks quickly.

"She's just so beautiful," Rachel says. Mandy pushes Rachel close to the bed so she can set her hand on Gramma's. After a minute or two, Gramma opens her eyes. For the first time in two years she sets her eyes on Rachel. I think of the two little girls jumping around in the church aisle.

Gramma looks at Rachel for a long time as though she is trying to place her. "It's okay if you don't remember. I won't be upset. It's good to see you, Simone." While weathered with age, Rachel's voice is still rich and kind. Then Rachel, with arthritic fingers that shake, lifts a black and white picture up to Gramma. I glance down at it from over Gramma's shoulder, as Rachel describes it. "You might remember that. The field of chrysanthemums where you and I would run away to. That's you and me."

I set my eyes on the black and white photo, of two little girls, different skin, different heights, and different eyes, hugging each other with matching smiles.

Gramma continues to stare at Rachel then at the photograph, repeatedly. Then slowly, to everyone's surprise, a tear runs down Gramma's cheek. "Rachel?" Gramma asks.

Rachel laughs and claps her hands together. "How are you?"

"Is it you, Rachel?" Gramma sits up and grabs Rachel's hands.

"It's so good to hear your voice." Rachel's chin quivers.

"We're old!" Gramma bellows.

Mandy and I look at each other and laugh.

For a long time, we let the best friends catch up and I breathe out.

"What?" Mandy asks as we sit in the chairs on the other side of the room to give them some privacy.

"I can't believe my grandma is Simone."

"Don't you need to know the end of the story?" Mandy asks me.

"Do you know what happened after the night that Rachel said yes to Nick? I still don't know who was waiting in the truck, watching the two of them. And she hasn't told me anything about Levi coming home."

Mandy begins telling the story.

1945

Rachel sits on her bed in silence, knowing that she has just said yes to marry Nick even though her heart still belongs to Levi. She is not sure why she is now tempted, but something leads her to the papers that Bernadette left for her, Levi had once risked his life to steal them, and Sylvia had once handed them to her and said, "Don't let these define you."

She pulls them out of hiding and begins to read her story. She reads of her mother who searched for months to find her the right home, only to have that burned away. Gently, she runs her finger along her mother's name and suddenly tears fall down her cheeks when she finds a note from Levi.

> *Dear Dick and Sylvia,*
>
> *I leave Rachel with you in the belief that you will give her the greatest care. She is special, more than anyone will know and my heart aches to find her the perfect peace. If anything should happen to either of you, please be sure to contact me. I will forever be at the mercy of Rachel Anne Praline and will give my life to make sure that she is safe and sound.*
>
> *Sincerely,*
> *Levi Price*

Rachel falls to the ground as the papers drop from her hands. She has never read this letter before, and it's as if he's speaking from the dead.

Further in the stack of papers, she finds a picture of her mother, and somewhere along the line, Dick and Sylvia saved her mother's obituary from prison. It reads, "Elizabeth Marie Praline leaves behind one daughter whom she loved more than life itself." The obituary speaks of all the amazing things her mother did in prison, and that she got cancer when she was in her thirties that she passed away from. New information isn't always better. The thought of her mother living in prison and dying so young makes her close her eyes and try to picture what she possibly looked like.

Another clipping in the stack, tells of Bill Manchuron's prison sentence until the year 1951. And lastly, there is the deed to a house.

Rachel looks at it closer. Her mother left her the house since there were no other relatives. Somewhere in New Jersey there is a house that has been empty for more than 37 years.

"What do I do, Bernadette?" Rachel cries out as tears stream down her flushed face and she holds her stomach with painful, stiff hands. "I can't live without him."

As usual, Bernadette doesn't answer back during the hour that she lies on the floor in agony. The pain lingers and she's soon forced to get dressed or else be late to sing at Ada's. After choosing a vibrant green dress, she looks in the mirror. Her eyes are swollen, and her skin is blotchy and red. Even the deep green doesn't help this. The cold air that hits her face as she drives to the speakeasy, helps a bit, but she's grateful Nick has a meeting and won't be there.

Music is already vibrating the walls within Ada's, while the booths and tables are packed with happy people, and the rooms branching off of the main dance floor are filled to the brim with poker players or new romances. Everyone wants to say hello to Rachel as she passes by, so she shakes hands, kisses cheeks, and finally makes it to the stage. The moment she steps up to the microphone, she feels at home. She nods at the band leader, and since they already know the order of her songs, they begin without hesitation. The room is instantly energized by her fast songs, then seduced by her slow ones. There's no greater feeling to her than helping people fall in love.

During Somethin' Tender, the lights are directly on Rachel, making her so hot that sweat beads on her forehead, and she can barely see anyone's faces behind the glare. To her right, at the edge of the dancefloor, she catches an amazing dancer who makes her smile, and just behind her is a group of young men staring at this perfectly shaped, wonderfully smooth woman as she moves to the music. There is nothing better than this. She thinks of the tears she shed earlier, and how this crowd, this smoky smell, and this bouncing club has healed her for just a moment. It isn't until Rachel notices Ada standing behind this group of young men gawking at the dancer that she smiles, but instead of smiling back, Ada seems urgent as though she has something to tell her. Her arms are wrapped tightly around her chest, and she stares at Rachel with trepidation. Rachel moves to the side to get out of the spotlight, but that doesn't work, so she bends over trying to see under it. Ada points to the bar in the back. Rachel tries to cover the light with her hand to see the bar. At first it seems impossible, until a pair of men's shoes move into her line of sight. From these perfectly shined boots, her eyes climb to his ironed slacks, until she notices the metals on the chest of a uniformed soldier. Only when she reaches his neck, does something become familiar. The color of his skin, the shape of his jawline, and his lips. Those lips, she knows them well. Her mouth goes dry and she stops singing.

Levi leans on the bar with a smile and his eyes are as brilliant as she remembers them. If this isn't a dream, he is waiting for her concert to be over. Without thought or care, Rachel runs down the stairs, across the dance floor, and flies into his arms. Everyone around is surprised and it encourages the laughter and cheers.

His arms hold her so tight that she can't breathe, but she's never been so grateful for it. Tears fall down her cheeks onto his uniform. As he releases her just a bit, his hands rise to her face and before a moment becomes too long, he kisses her. They are lost for several moments until Ada rings the bell at the bar and everyone hollers. Levi and Rachel laugh when he won't let her go.

They don't even try to speak in the crowded room, so instead, he leads her by the hand outside to stand under the stars. When they do, he kisses her one more time and she's never experienced something so intoxicating.

"Is it really you?" she asks.

"Yeah," he smiles.

For several moments, they don't speak. They just look at each other. Then, finally, he tells her a quick version of the story. When he's done, she shakes her head. "What do we do?"

"We go home."

That's when he can see it in her eyes. "Rachel?" She doesn't say anything. "Rachel," he says again.

With a cry that breaks his heart, she walks away from him. Instantly he follows her. "I'm so sorry, Rachel."

"You're dead. They told me you were dead."

"I wished the entire time I could tell you."

She finally turns back to him and runs her hands up and down his handsome face. Touching his hair, letting her finger run along his lips, even softly touching the tip of his ear. Levi does the same. Like the crash of a wave, or the sun rising above the mountains, her world is somehow corrected. "I died. Levi, I died when they told me you were gone."

Levi takes her in his strong arms and pulls her close. "I'm sorry, Rachel. I can't imagine what you went through."

Suddenly she laughs, despite the tears. "Me? Levi, what did you go through?"

For a long time, they say nothing, and then he can't help himself.

He kisses her and everything ignites. There is no way they could have forgotten, but there is also no way for them to remember the passion between them. Time stands still.

"What do you want?" she whispers.

"You marry me and have my babies."

"Levi, I . . . a lot of things happened since you were gone. You asked Nick to take care of me and well, he did."

She's quiet and his jaw clenches. "What do you mean?"

"He's just asked me to marry him."

Levi is silent. Then as though he halfway expected this, he nods. "What did you say?"

"I told him that I would, but Levi, he knows that I don't love him like I love you. He knows."

"It's okay," Levi whispers and moves her hair from her eyes. "We'll take care of it. But Rachel. This is the end. I will take care of Nick and then we don't leave each other's side, ever again."

She nods and then kisses him.

§ § §

She watches from the doorway as he removes his uniform in front of the shower. As he pulls his arms from the stiff material, he winces, and she notices a scar running down his side. She reaches out to touch it.

"I was wounded when the plane went down. A woman, to whom I owe my life, stitched me up."

"Are you okay?"

"It's taken me a long time to heal, but I'm nearly one hundred percent."

The steam from the shower fills the room and she runs her palms along his broad chest. "A woman?"

He laughs. "Yeah. A woman named Helene. She was almost sixty."

"Oh." Rachel smiles. Then he undresses the entire way as she stands there with the steam filling the bathroom. His shower isn't long, but once he's done, he lifts her in his arms, carries her to the bed, and for the first time in over a year, they make love. Rachel falls asleep in his arms, where she belongs.

§ § §

They lay there as the morning sun shines through the window, relishing each other. Levi runs his finger down her nose, then kisses her neck, but he can tell that something is on her mind. "You okay?"

"I'm worried about Nick." Levi stays quiet, as she looks up at the ceiling. "He came here when I thought you would never be coming back and didn't push for anything. I feel bad that he's going to be hurt."

"Should I talk to him? I've known him for a long time . . . maybe it's my job?"

"No. He loves me, Levi, and he's a good guy. He deserves to hear it from me."

"When?"

"I'm supposed to meet him today in town." She rolls over onto his chest. "Will you wait for me here?"

"Of course, take my car."

An hour later, she takes the keys and flies into his arms one more time. "I still can't believe you're back." She whispers, then looks up at him. He kisses her with a smile. "I'll be back."

Even though she's worried about Nick, she's never felt so light and joyful. It's been years and she sings a song under her breath as she drives along the outskirts of town. Soon, she notices a truck in her mirror, barreling toward her and her song stops midway through as the confusion and fear sets in. It's only seconds before she sees him to when his truck plows into Levi's car. Her neck whips forward until her head hits the steering wheel, and soon the car is spinning across the street. She holds on for dear life as she cries out for it to stop. When it finally stops, she looks into the mirror as blood drips down her forehead, just in time to see the old rusty truck speed up and hit her again.

§ § §

Back at the house, Simone uses her key to enter. Alone, after convincing Reed to watch the kids, Simone makes her way inside wondering what news Rachel would have to tell her about Nick. With an old saucer in her hands that she borrowed for a dinner party, she clumsily opens the door and steps inside.

"Rachel." She calls out as she sets her purse down, trying to keep a hold of the saucer. No answer comes, so she calls again, but this time louder, "Rachel!"

Just as she's about to enter the kitchen, she hears a deep voice that sends chills up her spine. "Simone."

The saucer falls from her shaking hands, breaking into a million pieces on the ground, as she turns to see Levi standing there alive and well.

"Oh my God," Simone says under her breath.

Levi smiles. Without a second's hesitation, Simone runs to him with her arms open. They hug for several moments, until finally she pulls away and slaps his shoulder. "Where have you been?"

He laughs, but then gives a short explanation. After he's done, the smile has been wiped from Simone's face. "After all this time. Reed is going to lose his mind when I tell him." But then, as if it suddenly comes to her, she gasps. "Where's Rachel?"

Levi nods. "I know about Nick. She's meeting him in town."

Simone shakes her head. "Levi, I was about to kill him the first time he showed up at her door."

Levi grins.

§ § §

Rachel tries to hold the steering wheel as the man in his truck rams her again and again. She cries out. She tries to drive again, but the truck sends her car careening across the dirt road, luckily away from the hill on one side and into a field on the other. This time, she hits her head on the driver's side window and loses consciousness for just a moment. When she wakes, she is disoriented as she peers around with confusion.

Then she sees the man. Out of her side mirror, he's talking to someone in their car on the road, but she's too weak to make herself known. She reaches for the door handle, but it won't budge because he's damaged it from the outside. As blood drips on the white seat, she tries to crawl across the leather to get to the other side. In the meantime, whoever this man is talking to drives away and the old man begins walking to her. Her heart is never allowed to settle.

In just moments, his large body is just outside her door, so she scrambles to lock it, but he is too fast.

"Rachel Anne Praline," he says suggestively. Wait, she thinks to herself. There's something familiar about his voice, so familiar that it nibbles at her nightmares. "Rachel," he says again, but this time it doesn't just nibble, it bites until her fear stops her breath.

Her body goes numb as his voice sends her back in time. His angry growl, his deep and raspy rattle that would smell like nicotine and garlic. Just like when she was a child, the shaking starts in her belly, then moves down each leg and out into her arms. Tears don't hold back but carve deep spaces between each other along her colorless skin.

Bill Manchuron stands outside her window with rage behind his eyes and a scowl. He's aged, but it doesn't change her fear. His hair is salt and pepper, his skin more wrinkled and weathered, but the monster is still there. It suddenly feels like the little girl in the basement never got out and was never saved.

"Get out of the car," Bill Manchuron demands.

She ignores him and holds onto the steering wheel trying to think fast but feeling helpless.

"Get out of the car!" he yells.

So many nights he terrorized her with his fury. For so long this man stole her innocence, forced her to sing, and changed her life forever. He yanks her from the passenger side of the car by her hair, until she falls to the ground in the mud, then pulls her up to her feet and presses her up against it.

He comes up to her until his face is so close that she must turn away and the end of his nose touches her cheek. "I've spent my life in prison because of you," he says quietly. When she doesn't respond, he screams in her face. "Because of you!" She trembles in fear.

There are no options but to cover her face with her hands, ready for the next strike, just as she used to when she was a child.

"Look at me!" He grabs her chin and crushes her skin against her teeth.

§ § §

Twenty minutes before . . .

Nick drives along, until he notices a truck and a car beside each other in the field. It looks to be that the car has been damaged and the man is there to help. Nick pulls to the side of the road, and the man from the truck comes to his window with a grin.

"Good mornin'," the man says with his dirty teeth on display.

"Good morning." Nick lowers his hat with a nod. "Can I help you here? It looks like you all are in trouble."

"No, no . . . " the man says with a grin. "My wife isn't the best driver and she had a bit of trouble. But we'll be fine…"

"Are you sure? That car doesn't look drivable and I can help you get it out of the mud."

"I'm simply goin' to tow it home. You're a bit in the way cause I'm gonna pull my truck around, so go on. Don't worry about us.

We'll be just fine," the older man insists. "She'll be embarrassed if I get too many people involved. So don't you worry. You just go on and we'll be fine."

Nick looks at the man's shirt. It is dirty and appears to be a uniform to a gas station. Just below his sleeve, there is a long tattoo down his arm—a devil's tail and on top of the tail is the name Manchuron.

"Alright."

"Thanks, though." The old man starts walking away.

Despite his concern, Nick drives away but watches the scene in his mirror. Nick rubs his chest as the intuition runs deep.

Chapter Forty

1945

Simone takes in a big breath as Levi hands her some orange juice then sits in the chair beside her. "Nick! Oh, for heaven's sake. Levi, she tried. She tried to fall in love with him because I think she thought it would take away the pain of losing you, but Levi . . . oh heavens, I was worried. I didn't think she would ever come back from losing you."

"Simone, it's okay. I told Nick to watch out for her. I understand."

Just then they hear a car pull into the driveway and peer out the window. "Speaking of the devil," Simone says quietly.

Levi furrows his brow, confused that he would be here, so he stands and walks to the front door. "They're supposed to be meeting in town."

"Hmmm." Simone too sets her orange juice down and follows him to the front door.

As Nick gets out of the car, Levi starts to walk outside, but Simone sets a hand on his shoulder. "Levi, you're dead. You can't just keep frightening people. You're a ghost to us all."

He chuckles. "You're right."

"Let me go first." Simone steps out onto the porch letting the screen door swing behind her.

"Good morning, Simone," Nick says as he jumps out with a smile, believing that he is an engaged man.

"Good morning." Simone's voice is hesitant and subdued. "Weren't you supposed to meet Rachel in the city?"

Nick stops with a look of curiosity. "No, I don't think so."

"That's what she thought, and she's been off for a while to meet you."

Nick turns to see Rachel's car sitting in the driveway. "Her car is there…"

Simone doesn't know how to answer the question. That's when she hears the door open behind her and the look on Nick's face changes. His eyes grow as large as silver dollars and his face turns pasty white.

"Hello, Nick," Levi says.

Nick doesn't say anything for several moments, then looks away, takes in a big breath, and finally finds the nerve to look back. An unconvincing smile spreads across his face. "I didn't expect you."

"Neither did any of us," Simone agrees.

Nick walks to Levi with his hand out and as they shake hands, he presses his palm to Levi's shoulder. "Where have you been?" Nick asks, still in shock.

"It's a long story. But it is one that I should tell you. I suppose my letters telling Rachel that I am still alive and will be arriving shortly never got here. It seems I made it home first. I'm sorry, Nick."

Nick drops his head in surrender. Whether he is devastated and wants to fight for Rachel's affection, or he loves her so much that he is happy for her, really doesn't matter. It is quite possibly a combination of both.

"Welcome back, Levi," Nick says calmly, but after a moment he tilts his head with question. "If Rachel is meeting me in town, what car did she take?"

"Mine," Levi says.

A quizzical look makes Nick look down the road, then back again, as his arms become tense. "What does your car look like?"

"It's a blue and gray Chevrolet."

It's obvious that he doesn't like this bit of information, as his hands rub the back of his neck red. "Is the license plate LH 12W?"

Levi is surprised. "It is."

Nick looks at Simone, then Levi, then starts backing up to his car. "I think you two should come with me."

"What's going on?" Levi asks.

"Something that doesn't feel right." Nick says quickly. "Come on."

They pile into his car and soon Nick sends gravel flying as he peels out of the driveway.

"What's going on Nick?" Levi asks.

"I passed a blue and gray Chevrolet on the side of the road, and it just didn't feel right, you know?"

"You think it was Rachel?"

"No, I know it is Rachel. I stopped and there was a man that told me everything was fine and that I should pass, but it didn't feel right . . . so I memorized the license." he says getting quieter as he speaks, yet Levi pays attention to Nick's white knuckles.

Simone sits up in the back seat. "Why would he tell you everything is alright?"

"I don't know. I just…" he hits the steering wheel with his hand, "I just didn't feel right about him. I should have stopped."

"Where?" Levi is trying desperately to see ahead, but he sees nothing on the side of the road.

"Past this hill," Nick says.

"Get going, Nick," Simone warns him.

§ § §

It's hard to believe she is here again. His cheeks are just as red as they used to be when he was angry, only this time, they are surrounded by deep wrinkles and, if possible, harder eyes than before. Many nights she cried herself to sleep waiting until he opened her door because she didn't want to be near him. Today, he leaves no space between them. It seems a nightmare, as she bites her tongue when he won't let go of her face. It doesn't matter how much life has been lived between their years together and now, her body still freezes while her heart plays a heavy beat against her ribs. Her vision grows white, as she struggles to breathe in order to protect herself. Levi had said he made sure Bill was still within the walls of his penitentiary, but Levi had been gone for over a year.

"Do you know what happens in prison?" he says, as he yanks her away from her car and toward his truck. "They treat you like a dog. They don't care if you're cold, if you're hungry, or if you're beaten. They don't care." When they reach his truck, he throws the door open. "Get in."

As a child, she jumped when he said jump, she sang when he said sing. Yet today, his truck is the last place she wishes to be. If she gets in, no one will know where she's gone. So instead of doing as he says, she pulls away from him and runs. Through the mud as it splashes on her clothes and even her face, she cries out, knowing that he's only feet away. He chases her but is not as fast as he used to be. It isn't until she slips and falls to her knees that he's able to grab her ankle and pull her until she slides across the muck. There's a difference in his stature, with his back curved slightly, yet he is still large and capable.

With a swift kick, her foot connects with his stomach, and it knocks the wind out of him, making him wheeze and take a couple of steps back. This doesn't stop him. He wraps his arms around her and despite her flailing arms, she's just too small next to him. Before long, he sends a heavy fist flying, connecting it with her jaw. Instantly everything blurs and she gets sick to her stomach while guarding her face with her arms cupped tightly. While everything is spinning, he manages to drag her to his truck, lifts her inside, then pushes her in to the passenger seat. He stiffly runs around to the other side then jumps into the driver's seat. Every muscle on her body shakes as she pulls on the passenger door handle, but it is locked and wrapped with a leather strap so that it won't turn. The vehicle's tires spray dirt as he shifts into drive. Soon, they head down the road.

§ § §

Nick presses faster and, as they round a corner, Levi's disabled car comes into view.

"Is that it?" Nick asks.

"Yeah. That's my car." Levi's heart sinks.

"I don't see anybody," Simone cries out. The door stands wide open, and it sits alone in a large field.

"What did you see?" Levi asks Nick as they screech to a halt beside it and they all jump out.

"The car had clearly run off the road, but he was adamant that it was his wife, and he would take care of it. I never saw Rachel."

"What man?" Levi asks.

"I don't know. He was tall and big . . . and wearing a uniform for a gas station or something like that . . . and he had a tattoo. A devil's tail and on top of that it said Manchuron."

Levi has been checking everything on his car, but when he hears the name, he stops. Simone and Levi's eyes meet as his jaw clenches. "Manchuron?"

"Yeah."

"Look!" Simone points to the muddy tire prints that disappear down the road.

None of them wait, instead they jump back into Nick's Chevy. Nick revs the engine and the tires spin out. It isn't until they reach the road that they finally gain real traction.

"Is something going on that I should know about?" Nick says as they race down the road.

"We know Manchuron . . . and you need to hurry." Levi says over the roar of the engine.

"How much trouble is she in?" Nick asks.

Levi can't answer. What she went through with this man, only to now be taken by him again. Levi can feel the rage clawing its way out, so without warning, he hits the top of Nick's truck with a fist, and yells, "Ahhh!"

Simone sits up beside Nick. "That much," she says.

Suddenly as they round a corner, they see the old and broken truck just ahead. It can't outrun them, and Nick easily gains on the old man. Heading into a busier part of town, there's a mini mart and several stores side by side, with people all around. Simone closes her eyes at how fast they are going and prays as her fingers grip the leather behind Levi's head. Levi places a hand on hers in comfort.

Then, before they can stop him, Nick clips the man's bumper.

Bill Manchuron peers in his rear view mirror while Nick presses the gas and hits him again. Simone cries out.

The truck begins to lose traction and crashes into a nearby tree just in front of the mini-mart. People from all around yell and scream. Some hurry toward it, while others run away. Nick slams on the break, but Levi is out before the car stops.

Bill yanks Rachel from the crushed vehicle.

For a moment, Levi is taken back to the years he was just an obstinate teenager who somehow had to protect her. He remembers the broken little girl with the bruises on her arms and the fear in her eyes when he found out. The look in Bill's eyes is still crazy—still dangerous. Possibly even more now.

§ § §

Rachel opens her bloodstained eyelids, to see Nick, Levi, and Simone standing not too far away. The old man has his gun, then points it at the crowd, "Stay back!" he yells.

The look in Levi's eyes is different now. Bill isn't someone to be afraid of like he used to be. In just moments, Levi rushes the man until they crash against the truck and Rachel falls to the ground. Levi rips the rifle from Bill's hands and throws it to Nick. Then he punches the old man, while he tries to fight back. There is no comparison. Anger drives his strength and before long Bill falls to his knees. Simone sees an officer hurrying toward them, pulling his gun from his holster.

She calls out. "I'm a lawyer with the D.A.! He's a criminal, officer."

The officer yells, "Back away!" to Levi, so he does as his chest rises and falls with a mixture of anger and adrenaline. His hands are bloody and he wants to keep going, but knows it's best if he doesn't.

"This man tried to take my wife!" Levi yells.

"Thirty years in prison," Bill says with spit dripping from his broken teeth and sweat from his withered skin.

"You deserved life," Levi shouts.

"She ruined my life," Bill whispers.

The officer, not knowing what has just happened, places Levi in handcuffs, while Simone tries to explain. Then he pulls Bill to his feet and cuffs him.

"I told you what happened!" Simone yells as she hurries to Rachel.

"I'll figure it out, lady," the cop yells back.

Finally, after two more officers show up, one looks at Levi and smiles. His name is Howard Burns and Levi recognizes him immediately. "You're David Price's son, aren't you?"

Levi looks at Howard with a nod.

"Good man. Good lawyer." Then Howard turns to Simone. "You are also . . . a good lawyer." Simone smiles, never needing his approval but appreciating it, nonetheless. "Can you meet us down at the station? I'll take him straight there."

When they take the handcuffs off of Levi, he races toward Rachel, grabbing her in his arms. "Are you okay?" She nods, but melts into him getting dirt and blood on his shirt. "I'm sorry," Levi whispers. "He'll never touch you again."

Chapter Forty One

Months later, as they stand in a courtroom, Simone is at Rachel's side and Levi and Nick are behind them. Simone stands before the judge and her perfect words and indestructible charisma tell the courtroom everything they need to hear.

"Your Honor, we come before you today, in this beautiful courtroom, under these dire circumstances in order to make sure that justice be served on this occasion so that any exploitation of women which follows may seek the same ruling and judgement in their own cases. We tell you the truth that we are here, not just to seek penalty against Bill Manchuron, but upon any man from this day forth who preys upon children and women alike. My client remembers the day she was found in the basement of Mr. Manchuron's home; malnourished, sexually assaulted, and abused—both physically and emotionally. Taken at the age of six and forced to sing for money, this man proved his evil far beyond what we can measure in any moral court. It is our children who suffer from the hands of cruelty so fierce that time does not heal, nor allow one to forget. For twenty-seven years, he served a sentence for his wrongdoings, continually getting more time added within prison due to his misbehavior and obvious immorality. However, despite these things, he was released and within two months found his victim again in order to right what he felt was wrong, in his depraved mind. Within our system, there are men who receive longer sentences for much less, but it is the "Bill Manchurons" of this world who, I believe, are without remorse and unable to be rehabilitated. We ask that this court and your Honor will make sure that Bill Manchuron never has the ability to harm another. We ask that you set a precedent here, for all men with the same evil intentions, that this court will rise to the occasion, seeking the most aggressive penalties for the gravest of crimes—those against our women and children."

The jury and the court room are silent as Simone addresses each and every one of them in turn. "We cannot continue to put away men for far less simply because of . . ." she turns to the back of the room, noticing that Officer Hannah has made his way into the courtroom, having heard about and remembering Rachel very well. ". . . socio-economics, race, and creed. Rather, we must align the crime with the correct sentencing and give peace to those who fear what Mrs. Price had to go through."

Just after closing statements, and being convicted by the jury, the judge comes back with his sentencing. "Mr. Manchuron, do not think for one second that your thirty years in prison remotely pays the price for the irreparable damage you have caused throughout your life. I am going to see to it that you never see the light of day. You are sentenced to life in prison without parole."

§ § §

Just after court, Nick and Rachel stand outside of Levi's hotel as Nick holds his bags in his hands. "I might still love you for a long time, Rachel."

"I'm so sorry, Nick."

"Don't be sorry. It was meant to be. Besides, we all know you were meant to be with Levi."

"Come back through here someday?"

"Maybe." Nick says with a grin. He sets his bags down and hugs Rachel for one last time. "Take care of yourself, Rachel. I love you even though you can't say it back." When he lets go, he kisses her on the cheek, hesitates for just a moment while looking her over, then takes in a big breath. Soon, he jumps into his car and drives away.

Nick does go on to live a happy life. It takes him a long time to get over Rachel, but when he does, he travels across Europe searching for what he is truly meant to do and, somewhere in Ireland, he runs into a sweet waitress with dark hair and a bar-owning father. For the rest of his life, he remains contentedly happy as he takes over the family business and fathers many children.

Chapter Forty Two

1998

Mandy stops telling the story.

I look up at her, a bit in disbelief that the story has ended.

"Grandpa Levi died just a few years ago. I think my grandma is simply waiting to be with him again," Mandy explains as we watch Simone and Rachel together across the room. "It's hard for me to believe you've never heard this. Your grandmother and grandfather, Simone and Reed, were amazing."

"Yeah. They were always more interested in what I was doing than telling me what they'd done." For several moments I stay quiet. Something occurs to me as I hold Mandy's hand. "Mandy?"

"Yeah?" She asks.

"There's something I need to do."

"Right now?"

"Yeah. But I'll be back."

"Okay. Are you okay?"

"Yeah. Better than ever. Just need to make sure someone knows that."

"Well, we'll be here."

Before I leave, I take another long look at Rachel and Simone. They are so happy to be together. You might think that seeing Rachel as an old woman would change my interest in the story, but it doesn't. Now, my grandma is part of the puzzle—now I want to hear gramma's whole story. I chuckle and take one last look at Mandy before I head out.

In a few minutes I am at the hospital taking the elevator to my father's room. Everyone scurries about the place, completely oblivious to me as I walk through. At my father's room, I push the door open slowly so as to not make any noise, in case my ma is there. Luckily it is as empty as I was hoping.

I pull up the leather chair to sit down beside his bed. It doesn't matter that he can't hear me, I am still afraid, and it shows as I bounce my heel. My breath is revved, making the room unbearably hot until my shirt is covered in sweat.

"I'm still afraid of you," I say with aggravation. Then I look at him—his feeble body lying so still—and I remind myself that he can't hurt me. Even today, his words can't sting me. "How do I start, Dad?" The blood rushes to my face. "I've hated you. I've hated you for a long time. Yet, here I am. For the last two weeks, I have spent my days listening to a story about a woman that wasn't even from my time. You know why? Because I would have done anything other than sit here . . . with you." I rub my face with my palms. "Why couldn't you have been kind? Just for one day . . . why couldn't you have told me that I had done well? Instead, nothing I ever did was right to you. Nothing I ever did made sense. In your eyes, you always did better than me. You always made more money and had more women…" I can feel the heat rising through my body, so I stand and put some distance between us. "I don't care anymore, Dad. I don't care what you think of me. I'm quitting my job. And I'm going to go after a girl that I barely know, because when I look in her eyes, she understands me. Times have changed for me, dad. I believe in something that you always told me was a waste of my time." I lean over my father, "Destiny. Maybe this is my plan. Maybe this is what is meant to be. I'm just a regular guy. So, go to hell if you want to tell me otherwise. Go to hell if you want to bring me down. It's not going to happen anymore. I'm not going to second guess myself because of you. I thought I should let you know."

Suddenly, I see his eyelids flutter and I hold my breath. Then slowly his eyes open and for the first time, my father is awake. He doesn't speak, not that I'm sure he can, due to the stroke, but his eyes are staring straight into mine. I take a step away, but that's when he reaches out to me with a few fingers from underneath the hospital sheet. At first, I do nothing, just letting his fingers reach. However, it's his eyes that change my mind. Deep within them is fear and possibly sadness. I take a step forward, but keep my hands at my sides, until his fingertips brush mine. Just my forefinger alone, he lifts it slightly and he's able to wrap his around mine. A tear rolls down his temple and that's when my heart shifts. I sit down and raise my hand higher. As best as he can, he takes my fingers in his palm and weakly squeezes it. My throat tightens up, as another tear falls down his face.

I can tell, he heard everything I said. At first it looks like he's just moving his lips, but after a while it becomes more apparent that he's trying to say something. The hospital bars are cold as I lean over to hear him better. It sounds like just gasps of air at first, but then, he tries harder, and again harder, until finally his lips are able to get out, "I'm proud." It's the first thing he says and my eyes tear up. Then he tries again, this time saying, "I'm sorry."

I nod, wipe my face, and smile. "We are going to start fresh, Dad . . . okay? You got that? No more hateful remarks. You're going to tell me how proud you are of me and you're going to support me . . . whoever I become. You understand?"

He nods.

I sit on the edge of his bed. "And here's the thing, I'm going to tell you how proud I am of everything you've accomplished. I'm going to pay attention to our family, to our history, to what made us who we are. Grandma and grandpa built something here and you followed. I will too. It just may not look the same."

Another tear falls down Dad's temple and then he weakly pulls my hand to his lips.

§ § §

Mandy continues to tell me the rest of Rachel's story. I find out that it wasn't long after Levi saved Rachel from Bill one last time that they finally got married. Both of them knew that there was no longer any time to waste. They had been torn apart too many times to allow it ever again. So, with Simone, Sylvia, and Minnie in attendance, Levi and Rachel get married at the courthouse. Months later, they find out that they are having their first baby.

Singing stays in Rachel's life on and off. She and Simone fight for women's rights during the fifties and march with Martin Luther King, Jr. in the sixties. I laugh when Mandy shows me pictures of my Gramma and Martin Luther King, Jr. laughing with each other. Mandy mentions that it is the Reverend himself who helped my gramma's career reach new heights.

"I clearly had no control of where I went," Rachel says from her wheelchair one day when my gramma was having a bad day. "I put one foot in front of the other and trusted that all would fall into place if I just stepped out of my own way. The world will let you down at times, but love never will."

Rachel and Levi lived in the same house on the outskirts of New Jersey for years where their favorite thing to do was play with their children and sit in the sun while drinking iced tea. Levi tries to hold Rachel back from her adventures, but finds after a while, that he can't change the way things are meant to be. Instead, he laughs and knows that he is there to protect her the best way that he can.

One afternoon, I hear commotion down the hall and run to my gramma's room. Rachel has tears in her eyes as Gramma is struggling to breathe. Mandy is at work, so I hurry to Rachel's side and start to move her away. "No!" she cries. She reaches out and takes my gramma's hand as I race out to the halls and call the nurses. An hour later, I watch as Rachel sings to Gramma Johnson as she takes her last breath in this world. Rachel refused to leave her side for several more hours.

On June 9th of 1999, at the age of ninety-three, Gramma Johnson leaves this world to be with her husband, Reed, who remained by her side as she challenged the world, redefining a black woman's place in law. Four months later, at the age of ninety-one, as Mandy and I sit by her side, Rachel follows Gramma Johnson to heaven, leaving a legacy in music.

As for me, I quit my job and marry Mandy. Rachel left her home to Mandy in her will, so we move in. Every day I fall more in love, first with my wife, and then, with our three little girls who come after. As for my father, he helps me fix things at my home. We talk and laugh and as we step out onto my driveway, he pats me on the back and says, "I'm so proud of you."

I place my hand on his shoulder and smile. "I love you, Dad."

As I look back on it all now, I realize I should have believed all along. I didn't need to do anything special. Success is subjective and should never be graded on an uneven scale. I am simply alive and that is enough. Once I figured this out, that's when things started making sense. Rachel and Gramma Johnson showed me that. They spoke life back into me.

On August 23rd 2002, I sit before an audience reading the last few lines from my bestselling novel called Rachel and Simone. "Now some say that there is no God and that is fine, except this makes it hard to understand life's magic. As Bernadette always told Rachel,

'When the Almighty intervenes, there are some things that just cannot be explained.' Their friendship, Simone and Rachel agreed, was more than magic, it was Divine."

The End.